Broken Blood

Broken Blood

Book 5 in the Dirty Blood series

By
Heather Hildenbrand

Broken Blood © 2015 Heather Hildenbrand
Book 5 in the Dirty Blood series

This is a work of fiction. Names, characters, places and incidents are either the product of the author's imagination or are use fictitiously. Any resemblance to actual persons, living or dead, events, business establishments or locales is entirely coincidental.
No part of this sample may be reproduced, scanned or distributed in any printed or electronic form without permission. All rights reserved. Please respect the hard work of the author.

Cover design by Robin Ludwig Design Inc.
Editing by Kristina at Red Road Editing

Interior formatting by

www.emtippettsbookdesigns.com

A special thanks to Natalie Thomason for her brilliant contributing line. I'm so lucky to have readers and fans like you!

16 March

I saw her today in the window of a flower shop downtown. Tara. It almost gave me a heart attack—I mistook her for Elizabeth. She looks so much like her mother but there's a stubborn glint her mother doesn't have. She's a fighter.

The visions are more frequent. I'll have to approach her soon. Elizabeth will be angry but I don't see another way. In order to survive what's to come, she'll need to understand what and who she really is.

Steppe is already aware of her and so she is in danger even now. Her journey is not an easy one. I can't yet see the outcome. The future—her future—is liquid. She may or may not find her way. If she does, it will be the best thing that ever happened to her—to us. If she doesn't, it will kill her. It will kill us all.

I wish I had more time.

—*Vera Gallagher*, an entry from her personal journals

Chapter One

The echo of the boom rang in my ears. Not loud by anyone's standards. At least, not anyone who hadn't been confined to sixteen days of straight silence. The grunts of Gordon's goons as they'd handed me my ass that first day for refusing a meal—that didn't count as sound. My own cries and screams and name-calling as I'd pounded bruised and bloody fists against my cell walls and the perpetually locked door—that didn't count either. But this. This was bona fide noise.

Another boom. This one louder than the first.

The wall behind my head shook with a subtle vibration. A thin sheen of dust rained down on my head along with a few chunks of concrete. I sat up and shook the dust out of my face and eyes. And listened.

Far away—or maybe nearby, I couldn't tell with the concrete walls and immovable door that separated me from them—voices shouted. A faint siren went off, drowning out everything else with its high-pitched whine. What the heck?

I should've cared on a deeper level than simply having my sleep disturbed. I did. I tried to. It was the first disturbance I'd experienced in the two weeks since Gordon Steppe and his men had trapped me and my friends in a warehouse and taken us hostage. Or, well, taken *me* hostage. I had no idea what'd happened to the rest of them. George, Logan, Victoria, Wes, Uncle Astor, innocent Emma. I'd like to think they'd gotten away, but I knew better. Gordon, leader of the world's population of Hunters—a race of super humans created to protect the world from rogue Werewolves—had filled that warehouse with the one thing he knew would stop my Werewolf-hybrid friends: a rare and potent metal called Unbinilium. Basically, a hybrid's kryptonite.

I still remembered the sickly green color George and Wes had turned when the metal's properties reached them. They'd looked miserable. Completely incapable of defending themselves. And that's when Gordon and his goon squad had shown up. I don't know where the boys were taken but I knew they were here somewhere. They had to be. I didn't believe for one second those cops had been human. No way was Gordon going to let Wesley St. John be handed over to civilians. Their rivalry was way too strong. Gordon would want Wes close.

Or that's what I was afraid of, anyway.

Then again, after two solid weeks of solitary confinement, without a clue as to what Gordon Steppe wanted with me, I was beginning to wonder. Maybe I didn't know what I was talking about. Maybe I was wrong about everything. Maybe he was done with me, done with all of us. Maybe he was just leaving me here to rot.

He did have all the caged hybrids an evil dictator bent on torture could want…

Another boom shook the walls. This time, the vibration knocked a large square of plaster loose from the corner. It fell in a pile near the small sink across the tiny room. I debated whether to get up and inspect the damage. I could see well enough. The lights were always on in here, making it impossible to tell what time of day or night it really was. But the drugs from dinner were still circulating and I couldn't be sure my legs would work properly even if I tried.

For lack of anything better to do, I swung my legs over the edge of the bed. They were pale under the bright fluorescents. Vitamin D would be nice right about now. UV rays—natural lighting—wouldn't be so bad either. My toes touched the cold, dust-laden floor, and I pulled them back with a sharp breath.

From somewhere down the hall, a deep voice full of bass cut through the high whine of the siren. My entire body stilled—and jumped and danced and yelled and froze.

"Alex?"

My voice cracked, no more than a whisper. Out of practice. I cleared

Broken Blood

my throat and tried again.

"Alex?" I called.

I knew better than to think I'd be heard over the alarm. I stood and half-ran, half-hobbled to the concrete door. I hit it with open palms, willing it to be enough, and called out again. "Alex? Can you hear me? It's Tara! I'm in here!"

I pressed my ear to the cold surface, straining to hear something meaningful over the song of the alarm.

Shots fired in staccato sequence. One, two, three, four. An automatic weapon being fired. I jerked back and winced, pressing my teeth together to keep from calling out so I could hear what came next. But nothing else sounded over the screaming of the alarm. A moment later, that went quiet too. My breaths were either magically quiet or I'd forgotten to take them.

I ordered my lungs to work and swiped my hand down my itchy cheeks. They came away wet. I stared at the moisture like I'd never seen tears before. Is this what it felt like to go crazy? Your entire body feeling like a foreign object in your possession? Like I'd left my luggage alone with strangers and come back to find all sorts of extras thrown in; I had no idea what was me and what was a product of my environment.

And, most importantly, I had no idea what'd just happened out there. Had Alex really been there or was I so far gone, I didn't know what was real? I hoped, for his sake after hearing the shots fired, it was more the second. I didn't want to think about what it meant that whoever had been firing had already stopped.

Up in the corner, a buzzing whine sounded. I looked up as the tiny black camera shifted, tracking me and settling on a direct shot of my face as I stared, wide-eyed, at the little red dot behind the lens.

They were watching me, I realized with a fleeting sense of discomfort. They'd been doing it so long, I could barely care. I didn't even both covering my torso with my arms to hide the fact that my undergarments had been taken and never returned upon arrival. Relieving a girl of her bra, the vulnerability and sense of exposure it caused, was its own kind of torture, but I cared less today than I had yesterday. And the day before that ... and the day before that.

My reality was becoming more and more normal.

I shuffled back to the thin cot and pulled the blanket over my head.

The only way I knew the drugs had worn off was the smell. I hadn't showered in—Okay, I couldn't think about it without my stomach rolling sideways. I knew they drugged me to keep me compliant. Or at least lethargic and weak. But I was grateful for it in moments like this, moments during which my hyper-aware senses couldn't help but point out the drawbacks of long-term confinement. You know, the little things that no one ever mentioned. Things like personal hygiene. I would seriously kill innocent people for a toothbrush right now.

And a shower? Entire villages. The odor coming from my body right now—Trust me, the ends would totally justify the means.

I had a suspicion my bodily functions and hygienic standards would be way easier if I shifted. But I'd been trying to do so every day for two weeks. I hadn't been able to shift into a wolf since day three. Maybe Unbinilium affected me after all. There wasn't a whole lot of exposed metal to be seen inside my cell, but I had a feeling it was here somewhere.

Astor De'Luca, my mad-scientist great-uncle, had said I was immune. A gift of sorts from my dad before his early death at the hands of his deranged brother back when I was a baby. Leo and Gordon Steppe would've been great friends, except for the whole race divide.

My dad had been super smart about inter-species breeding. I was a product of a Werewolf dad and a Hunter mom. Something definitely frowned upon in both societies. He'd known about Unbinilium being a Werewolf's most dangerous weakness so he'd secretly injected me with some sort of blood protectant when I was a baby, ultimately blocking the adverse effects of the metal. Being stabbed or shot with it was a different story.

I wasn't immortal. Just tough.

Apparently, prolonged exposure did have its consequences. I'd never had reason to test it before, but after almost three weeks of sitting inside a cell lined with the stuff—it was weird, but sometimes I thought I could almost smell it—I could no longer shift to my wolf form. Any time I tried, I felt vaguely nauseous. It didn't stop me from attempting it every so often, but it made me worry what would happen if I stayed here much longer.

Something shuffled outside my door.

The lock disengaged and I sat up straighter as the concrete slid aside. I expected breakfast. Scrambled eggs a la morphine. Maybe I'd change up my silent routine for questions about that voice I'd heard. But it wasn't the usual guard with no personality and no ability to carry

Broken Blood

intelligent conversation and a gun at the same time. Instead, Gordon Steppe himself stood at the threshold.

At the sight of my captor's face, sixteen days of captivity melted away. In an instant, I was Tara Godfrey, Hunter-Werewolf hybrid. Alert, muscles-bunched, ready to go for the throat the moment I saw an opening. Even without claws and fur, I'd rip his jugular out. But Gordon was obviously ready for all that. He took a step inside, pointed a shiny, silver gun at my neck, and fired.

Chapter Two

Tranquilizer hangovers sucked. I bet not many people knew that kind of thing firsthand. So, yeah. It should be known, the headache and muscle stiffness caused by sleeping-poison-infused bullets were so much worse than anything alcohol could ever hope to do. On top of that, someone else breathed nearby, letting me know I wasn't alone. I wasn't ready to tackle that problem yet. Not with my temples throbbing hard enough to make my un-brushed teeth rattle in my gums.

I waited until I couldn't convince myself I was asleep any longer. The mouth breather nearby shifted and papers rustled. It sounded too loud in my sensitive ears. I groaned, and then regretted my attempt at using my voice box. It hurt. Everything freaking hurt.

"Tara." Gordon Steppe's voice was the absolute last noise I wanted filling the silence right now. I pried my eyes open with a scowl in place. I'd rather take another bullet than listen to him talk. But since nothing was going my way, Steppe's weapon was currently holstered.

"Steppe," I returned, although my sad croak spoke volumes for who held the power in our exchange. It didn't help that I was also flat on my back. I struggled to push up onto my elbows, blinking away the dizziness as I rose. A pin prick of pain emanated from my neck and I laid my palm against it gently.

Steppe waited until I was sitting upright. I blinked up at him and finally noticed the breather I'd heard before. A man with sandy-blond hair was seated in a rolling chair and bent over an empty cot beside me, his cheek resting on his folded arms. His glasses were tilted crookedly against his wrist as he slept, a clipboard tucked underneath his chin where he'd set it on the mattress. Gordon ignored him so I decided to make that my plan too. For now.

"How long was I out?" I asked.

"Six minutes."

I blinked at him. "Seriously?" Wow. Talk about a power nap...

Steppe smirked. "I can tranq you again if you like."

"Uh, thanks, no." One was plenty. This headache wasn't going anywhere. At least, until my next drug-laced meal. Part of me was already looking forward to that. But another part, the part too terrified to appreciate it, recognized the weight of this moment. I was no longer being ignored. Something had changed.

He cocked his head sideways, illuminating the heavy shadow of light-brown stubble running along his jaw. Underneath his eyes were puffy bags. They weren't darkened and I wondered briefly if he'd used something to cover the up. I shook my head at that. The last thing I cared about was whether Gordon Steppe wore makeup.

At least I wasn't the only one disheveled, although his dress slacks and button-down shirt weren't quite as worn as my stained jeans and wrinkled tee. "What do you want?" I asked warily.

"Right to the point. No chit chat? Nothing? Not even after all of that alone time?"

"Fine. Where are my friends?" I asked.

"They're not here."

"Liar," I muttered.

"What was that?"

I glared. "My mom always told me, 'If you don't have anything nice to say, don't say anything at all.'"

Gordon clucked his tongue. "Not entirely true. The trick is to smile while you say it. People will let you insult them over and over if they think you're on their side."

I scowled. "Said the crooked politician."

"I need your help." His swift topic change threw me off. Or maybe it was that he'd failed to take the bait and engage me on the insult. Steppe wasn't a patient guy. Nor was he forgiving. I'd seen him pissed off. I'd heard it firsthand. He always struck below the belt when he could. But not now. And it made me more wary than any jab or offensive barb he could've thrown.

And I was out of practice at hiding it. I couldn't deny the fear that ate at me as he watched with that smug expression. He enjoyed my pain, physical, mental, or otherwise. That, more than anything, made me nervous. I couldn't bring myself to engage him in a battle—not even one where the weapons were words.

"Help with what?" I asked instead.

"Your pack of hybrids," he answered as if it should've been obvious.

"What do you want with them?" A ball of panic shot from my stomach to my chest. I hadn't seen or heard from Chris or the others in weeks. Even before Gordon had nabbed me and the others, they'd been taken. The bond I'd shared with them had suddenly vanished, leaving me helpless to find them.

The only reason we'd been in that warehouse in the first place two weeks ago was to get them back. Victoria's tracking senses had led us to a room full of cages, each holding a member of my pack. All of them had been detained partly by the confines of the cage and partly because the bars themselves were coated in Unbinilium. And my pack was more susceptible than most when it came to the rare metal.

I wasn't sure exactly why that was, but I had a theory. Unlike me and Wes, this pack of hybrids hadn't been born this way. They'd been born Hunters and through a convoluted and highly unethical experimentation process led by Miles, my delusional and sociopathic—and thankfully, now dead—cousin, they'd been infected with Werewolf blood and had eventually become a mixture of both. Only, the experimental serum had been missing something vitally important to the change-over process and many of them died before the change could take effect.

The missing factor? My blood.

A fact I'd discovered only when I'd given a bag full to my friend George after he'd become infected with the serum during that final showdown with my cousin, Miles. I'd been terrified it wouldn't work and I'd lose him like we'd lost so many others once Miles injected them. But a bag of Tara Godfrey blood was just what the doctor ordered.

In no time, George was well again, back from the brink of death. He was strong and fast and, most of all, happy. He was, quite possibly, the most content Werewolf I'd ever met. And then my blood had really

Broken Blood

kicked in and we'd bonded.

As in, thoughts shared, emotions passed between us, completely aware of the other's thoughts: bonded. It had scared the crap out of me. And then it put a huge damper on my love life. I might've figured it all out from there, found a way to balance and learn to live with it, but then Olivia had come along. Mother to Miles. Ex-lover to Leo, my also crazy, also dead, uncle. My dad's side of the family tree was a little nutso.

Olivia had wielded a blood bond strong enough to lead an entire pack of hybrids against me. Then through a showdown and defeat, I'd cured the entire dying pack through injections of my blood, and thus inherited the bond.

Fifty shades of voices, my best friend Cambria called it. My head had never felt so full of thoughts. Eat your heart out, Albert Einstein. So, I was more surprised than anyone at how much I'd hated the void left behind when the bond vanished. I couldn't remember the last time I'd heard another thought inside my head besides my own. I missed it. The emptiness made life seem less urgent. Like everything happened through slow-motion.

Nearby, the sleeping man shifted and snorted before settling again. I raised a brow but Gordon wasn't in the explaining mood. He barely glanced over before returning to the topic at hand.

"I know all about your bond with them," Gordon said. "It's a handy tool. And, to be frank, a mysterious one. I've spent months working with the best researchers trying to understand it, to develop it."

"Develop it?" I repeated, a nervous swirl in my stomach. "For what?"

"To take it for myself, of course."

He paused. I had a feeling he wanted some sort of response, maybe to gauge my reaction to his admission. If he was expecting surprise, he was mistaken. A need for power was nothing new for the enemies I'd faced. A smug smile tugged at my lips at the thought of his failure. Clearly I was Plan B. And since we were having this conversation at all, Plan A hadn't worked out.

Given all of that, I decided on sarcasm. "How's that working out for you?"

"Getting closer," he said quietly, his eyes gleamed where they burned into mine. "I had it working for a moment there but then George's remaining connection to you severed what little hold I could gain."

"Wait, you tried bonding … with me?" I crossed my arms. "I think I'd know if you were in my head."

His smile tilted into something ominous. "Precisely. You know I'm right, because you've already heard me."

I stared back at him, utterly confused as he went on.

"In fact, I even warned you before you came to the warehouse that night. Look around you. This building you're being kept inside, it's not a deep, dark hiding place somewhere off the grid. We're right where no one expects us. Right in plain sight."

I didn't need to follow the sweep of his arms to see that he was right. I was sitting in an infirmary of sorts, but it was large and state of the art with its lab equipment and high-tech machines lining the counters across the room.

"Where are we?" I asked, suspicious I already knew.

"We're in DC. In CHAS headquarters. Well, the lab and offices underneath but still. There's a public entrance. We're easily accessible. I tried to tell you."

My eyes narrowed as I tried to understand what he could mean—and then the memory returned and his words wormed their way into a place of horrific understanding. But Gordon didn't wait for me to process it; he enjoyed the shock far too much. He leaned in, his smile electric as he added, "The best place to hide is in place sight."

I let out a cry but it sounded like a muffled choking.

"Shall I get you some water?" Gordon asked.

I glared at him. "That was your voice in my … All that time I thought I could hear—" I broke off, unwilling to share it out loud. Especially with him. My cheeks burned—with anger and humiliation. I thought I'd bonded with Alex. And it had been Gordon.

A wolf in sheep's clothing, I'd heard just before he'd grabbed me. He'd been telling me it was him, warning me of the trap all along. And I hadn't understood.

"Relax. Your attachment to George kept shoving me out. I didn't get much. It was sort of a one-way radio. I've been working for weeks to get it back but I can't quite seem to achieve it, not alone at least. Which is why I need to try it again, this time with your participation."

I snorted. "I would think your researchers would have filled you in on the obvious by now. First rule of bonding: you have to be a wolf."

"Lucky for me, carrying the gene and taking the animal's true form are two different things. These days, I can have one without the other. In fact, I already do."

"Are you trying to tell me you're a Werewolf?" I asked, disbelief coating my words.

"I'm telling you I carry the necessary DNA structure that allows me the mental capacity to handle something like a bond."

I shook my head, struggling to keep up. "How?" I asked.

But he didn't answer. He leaned away, hands stuffed into his pockets, his voice as matter-of-fact as if he were lecturing to a classroom of eager students. "The wolf gene must be present in order for the bond to happen. On both sides. But my cells are considered weak compared to yours, for instance. I'll need a strong host to connect with—and to show me the ropes." His grin reminded me of a crocodile's.

My stomach flipped and I was sincerely glad it was already empty. "You can't just take it or shove your way in. And if you think I'll just hand my mind over, you're wrong," I began.

"No, it has to be freely given. Olivia explained all of that."

"Olivia? You're working … with her?" The pounding in my temples intensified. Maybe I'd been in here too long. I didn't understand a single thing about my world any more.

"Working is a strong word. She pushed a little hard and we've had to offer her a respite. See for yourself," he said, pulling back the curtain separating my bed from the next.

In the adjacent bed, wrapped securely in a pile of blankets and sheets, eyes closed, breathing even, Olivia slept.

Wires protruded from the edges of the linens, trailing up to the screens and machines parked beside her, silently reporting her vitals. Her face was barely visible under the sheet, but even from here I could see the dark circles ringing her sockets like bull's eye bruises. Her hand was curled around the blanket, clutching it tightly as if, even asleep, a chill seeped in. She'd lost weight so that her already slender fingers were thin and bony. Frail.

She was clearly unwell. And being used for something other than justice or judicial trials for her crimes—which is what the rest of the Hunter world assumed would happen once she'd been caught all those weeks ago. Olivia had, along with her deceased son—my cousin Miles—made and almost killed an entire pack of hybrid Hunter-Werewolves. Why wasn't she in prison? And conscious?

"What did you do to her?" I asked.

"Me? Nothing," Gordon said. But his voice was deceivingly light with the lie. "Not for lack of trying, though."

Olivia rolled over and muttered unintelligible words. Her eyes never opened but her shoulders thrashed violently several times—hard enough to wake a normal person—and I knew she was in a deeper sleep than just a good night's rest. Along with the monitor wires, an IV line attached to a clear bag of fluid disappeared underneath the blankets. Whatever Gordon was doing to her was taking a serious toll. Possibly something was being fed to her—like my own dinnertime cocktails.

Olivia shifted again and the blanket shifted. Her arm fell loosely open against her side, revealing track marks left by multiple needles along her forearm. The scars left a nasty trail from just above her wrist all the way up to the crook in her elbow where I spotted the IV line taped in place. For a moment, I wondered if Gordon was simply keeping her under like he'd done with me. Maybe the tracks on her arm were evidence the IV had been moved several times to accommodate a blown vein or some discomfort. But then I noticed her sallow complexion and stark-blue veins, and I knew.

Blood. Gordon was taking her blood.

"You said she's working with you?" I asked, still too muddled from the tranquilizer to read between the lines of whatever this was.

"Yes, until she collapsed two days ago." His features hardened. "Not that it's done any good. I still don't have the bond."

I stared at Olivia with a growing sense of dread. Solitary confinement, drugs, heartache—all of it paled in comparison to what Gordon had done to Olivia. There was something other about her lying there unaware of reality. Something horrific in the way I could sense her brokenness even without her eyes open. I pictured myself lying there: unconscious, sick, mentally absent. And I shivered at the thought of putting up a fight—only to end up like her in the end.

"If I give it to you—my blood, the bond—what are you going to do with it?" I asked quietly. I suspected I already knew the answer, but I didn't trust my intuition any longer.

"To do what you won't," he said with a shrug, as if the reason were so obvious. When I didn't reply, he went on, "To rid us of the monsters."

"The monsters are among us," I mumbled.

"What?" His tone changed to something with a sharper edge.

Broken Blood

I shook free of the memory tugging at me. "Something my Aunt Vera said before she ... never mind. What do you want from me?"

Steppe's smile was sugar and acid and reminded me of Lindsey Lohan from *Mean Girls*. In a suit. Possibly wearing the same amount of concealer. "I want your blood. And your mind. And I want you to give both willingly."

Revulsion rocked through me and I shut my eyes against the wave. "And if I say no?"

"That would be unwise."

"If I say no?" I repeated through clenched teeth, summoning determination I didn't feel.

Steppe's smile remained intact as he explained, "The rest of your pack dies. One by one. But not until I make sure your bond is strong enough to feel every splice into their flesh and every drop of blood as they bleed out on my dirty floor."

He'd said "the rest" as if he'd already done it to several. But I hadn't felt anything during my weeks alone.

"You wouldn't." I crossed my arms, fully aware that, by calling his bluff, I might've just sealed the fate of an undeserving pack member. I stuck my chin out, refusing to back down but knowing I lacked the strength to see it through.

Steppe's chin jutted to match mine and he bent down so we were eye to eye. "I already have," he said.

My mouth opened but no sound came. He'd killed them? When? Which ones? My pulse raced while I struggled to accept it.

Steppe's nose wrinkled and I knew he'd finally caught a whiff of my skin, my breath. He was close enough to reach out and touch. I could see the pulse jumping steadily against the vein in his throat. Suddenly, I wished it would stop. Not pause, but completely halt in its attempt to shove this man's life force through his body. I wanted to end him here and now. And walk out while the rest of this place crumbled behind me.

The warped disgust that showed on my face was apparently taken for concession. Steppe pulled back and straightened, a satisfied set to his shoulders. "You need to detox before the transfer can take place. And we need to run some tests. My men will take you to your new quarters while the doctor prepares." He walked to the sleeping man still hunched over the cot beside mine and shoved him.

The man slipped over the edge of the bed, barley catching himself before he tumbled out of his rolling chair. The clipboard went flying, sliding along until it hit the wall and stopped. "Sandefur, get up," Steppe said.

Sandefur? I stared as the sandy-haired man righted his glasses and shoved to his feet. His eyes were wide as he took in the sight of me and then looked back at Steppe, his hands shaking.

"Sir," he said.

"Take her to the prepared room for monitoring and healing," Steppe said. "And then come find me to go over the numbers on the recording we sent."

"Yes, sir," Mr. Sandefur mumbled. He bent over to retrieve his clipboard and smoothed his hair.

Gordon turned to me. "I'll see you in a few days."

My argument never made it to my lips before Gordon walked out.

It's official, I thought. *I'm screwed.*

"Let's go." Mr. Sandefur's tone sounded much more confident now that Steppe was gone. He waited with a tight frown while I climbed to my feet.

"You're Logan's dad," I said. He grunted. "I'm Tara, I know your son."

"I know exactly who you are," he snapped.

"Then you know I'm not a bad person or that—"

"Please shut up," he said, sounding desperate rather than rude.

"Why are you helping him?" I pressed. "Logan is in danger because of your vote."

His expression flashed from irritated to painfully defensive. "I don't have to explain my choices to a kid. Now, move."

He stalked off, and I followed him slowly, taking in everything as we passed through the lab to the exit. Counters full of equipment and, closer to the door, a wall lined with metal cages like I'd seen in that warehouse.

My knees wobbled, but when I looked, they were empty. On the opposite wall was a row of bed with white fitted sheets. They were all empty and unused. I wondered why he had so many of them—and thought again about the voice I'd heard yelling after the explosion. The gunshots. Was Alex here? Wes? Where were the others? Had they used any of these beds before me?

We passed through a set of automatic doors into a concrete hallway and two armed guards fell in behind us. I had no idea what Steppe meant by "new quarters" but I was banking that it had to be better than my living quarters up until now. Especially since, as far as he knew, I'd just told him what he wanted to hear. I was holding out for something with running water. I didn't see any other option, what with the guns currently pointed at my back. When Mr. Sandefur turned right, I went willingly.

A familiar face loomed up ahead and I hesitated. He'd been the only one I'd recognized during my mealtime visits. Not that the familiarity had been a comfort. He'd remained as mean as ever through all of our interactions, limited as they were.

"Faster," Mr. Lexington snapped, waiting for us with a glower. "We don't want her out here in the open for longer than necessary." He began walking just ahead of Mr. Sandefur, leading the way down the chilly hall.

My head pounded anew as I forced my feet one in front of the other and left the clinic behind. I wished briefly for a meal laced with morphine, anything to knock this headache out, but as we rounded the next corner, the desire vanished. I wanted my wits. No matter how much discomfort it caused.

During my weeks inside my concrete cell, I'd concocted all sorts of images of what the rest of my prison might look like. I'd expected stone walls carved from caves, dirty floors, no windows. Basically, some version of a CHAS hideout placed deeply off the map, filed away under some nefarious-yet-vague corporation.

This was not that.

This was exactly what Gordon had said. Shiny linoleum underfoot. Well-lit tiled ceilings. On either side, nondescript doors all locked tight against nosy employees without proper clearance. I imagined that farther down, around the bend, probably industrial-strength walls gave way to public waiting areas. A reception desk with a side entrance for deliveries. Maybe even a conference room to hold Steppe's board meetings when he couldn't make it uptown during rush hour. The whole thing looked completely corporate America—all except for the giant gaping hole where a wall should've been across the hall from my new room.

I stopped and stared at the rubble before me. Vaguely, like a smokescreen over a dream, I remembered the boom I'd heard before.

"What happened?"

One of the goons at my elbow needled me forward. "Arma-freaking-geddon happened," he muttered.

"Who did it?" I asked, too afraid to hope.

The other guard smirked. "You," he said.

I had no idea what that meant, but he didn't offer anything more. Mr. Lexington muttered an oath laced with threats if the guards didn't shut their mouths so I left it alone. Instead, I forced my feet to shuffle forward in the direction the man prodded.

The room was clean but almost as sparse as the last. There was nothing but a sink and toilet on the far wall. As a bonus, an old plastic lawn chair sat tucked up against a scarred desk with only a single sheet of paper and pen. A twin bed—nothing more than a mattress and box spring had been shoved into the corner. That was it. Nothing sharp. No mirror. Probably a good thing.

I took a step inside. The cheap, cold tile on the floor made the thin blanket and lumpy mattress look like a haven. At least until the door swung shut behind me. Then it was more a prison than a getaway.

As the lock turned over, I wondered what could've happened that would cause an entire wall and doorway to collapse right across the hall from me. The answer was the same one I'd thought of when I'd asked myself what would happen if Gordon Steppe and I blood bonded: nothing good.

Chapter Three

The next morning, I'd just finished pulling the thin layer of cotton over my head when Mr. Lexington poked his head inside my room. I flipped my freshly washed hair and raised my brow.

"You have a visitor," he said.

I'd barely opened my mouth to ask who when he stepped back and pulled the door wide, allowing passage for someone to slip around him into the room.

I dropped the comb and stared, my stomach a swirling mess of trepidation and dread and that tiny drop of hope that made up human nature even in the face of impending doom. But as I looked closer, I realized he was unharmed, unmarked, and unafraid. Seeing him now, clearly not a prisoner—clearly one of them—made that thread of hope as useless to me as the SPF in the moisturizer they'd provided.

"Alex," I breathed.

"Hello, Tara," he said.

Like a villainous miracle, Lexington left and closed the door behind us, sealing us in. Alone. Just Alex and me.

A thousand words passed between us in a single fleeting stare. Alex looked away first, scuffing his toe and making a big deal out of inspecting my room. "It's not bad," he said finally. I wasn't sure who he was trying so hard to convince.

I looked down at the comb I'd dropped at my feet and wished like hell its teeth were of the flesh-eating variety instead.

"You're one of them," I said, and the eerie calm I felt at hearing myself speak the words scared me more than realizing their truth.

"No, I—" Alex took a step forward, hand out, maybe to stop me from thinking all the things I was already thinking. But he halted midway and stood still. The whining of the camera as it turned to track his movement sounded loud in the silence.

Alex glanced up but then looked away again before he could complete the movement. His hands fell to his sides. He looked so guilty I wanted to scream.

A thousand words remembered—all of them lies.

"That day in the park, I told you my plan. I told you everything. The bond, my pack. Did you set me up?" I asked, somehow still calm.

This time, Alex's gaze flicked all the way to the small black box mounted in the corner of the room near the doorway. I could see the message written in his expression when he stared back at me. We were being watched. He was being careful with his words. But all I could think about was his betrayal.

How deep did it run? How far back did it go?

"Have you always been...?" I couldn't finish. It wasn't even about the cameras. "Never mind. Why are you here?"

Alex sighed, and with it went every layer of brick he'd used to wall off his emotions. His shoulders sagged, his knees almost buckled, and his eyes filled with tears. I stepped back, thrown off by his drastic reaction.

"I wasn't always," he whispered so low I almost missed the words. "Please believe me. Or at least hear me. I'll tell you everything."

I steeled myself against the sight of his watery eyes and crossed my arms. Warrior Alex was a force to be reckoned with, but emotional Alex scared the crap out of me. I had no idea how to read him. "Are you sure that's a good idea?" I challenged, my voice full volume just to spite him. "Telling me everything, I mean."

"I don't care." His shoulders drooped a little more and he sank into the chair in front of the scarred desk. "I think that's why he let me come. He's hoping for it."

"Why?" I didn't have to ask who. We both already knew that.

"Because he hopes it'll hurt you."

I didn't answer. He was probably right and I refused to give him the satisfaction of hearing it.

"He came to me right after graduation. I was in Kane's group and I wasn't happy. I wanted more responsibility. I wanted to lead."

"I remember you telling me something about that," I said.

He nodded. "I told everyone else I took some time off to visit family and get my head screwed on straight, but I didn't."

"You came here," I said.

He hesitated for a split second and then said, "Yes. He told me I would be doing my country and my species a great service. I would help rid the world of the confused, the abominations, the unaligned and evil. He told me I would be a hero."

"I bet you ate it up," I said.

He flashed me a glare and, for a split second, I was pinned with guilt for goading him. This was Alex. He wanted to do the right thing, whatever "right" meant to him in that moment. And he was loyal. How was I doubting that?

But then his story caught up with me and I blinked back into the reality of my cell. My imprisonment, most likely thanks to the boy sitting in front of me. And the guilt evaporated.

"I did a few small recon jobs for him and then he got wind of your tangle with Olivia. And the Lexingtons. He came to me and made sure I …intervened."

"You removed the bond between George and I," I remembered.

"Steppe had been experimenting with Unbinilium and his cocktail needed a guinea pig. He decided to test it on you."

"The metal rod you hit George with," I said.

He nodded. "It suppressed the bond without harming George physically. It worked, but it was only temporary. He sent his scientists back to work."

"And Kane and the others?" I asked, going back over every moment of that day, angrier and angrier as I went.

"As far as I knew, Kane had no idea," Alex said. His eyes found mine and pleaded silently for something I couldn't quite understand. "It really was supposed to be an extraction only. I suspect Kane had his own set of orders."

I cocked my head. "You expect me to believe that?" I asked. "You betrayed me and everyone I love and you want me to believe you stopped just short of ordering people to try and kill me?"

He leaned forward, his body language searching for some sign of forgiveness, but I didn't move. "I'm sorry, Tara. I would never hurt you. Please know that."

I didn't say anything.

Alex leaned another inch and his voice dropped to a whisper. "He's disbanded almost the entire board. He's passed new laws, blamed the violence on you. He's been watching you for ... well, longer than you've known him. It's always been Steppe, Tara. He's the bad guy."

"What are you talking about?"

"Every single problem you've had, right down to your first shift in the alley that night, he's behind it all. He wants your power. In his head and his hands. He's manipulated you and the others into doing exactly what he wants. Everything has been about controlling you. Everyone. Leo, Miles, all of it."

I stared at him as uncomprehending as if he'd just told me the Earth was flat. So much disbelief and denial—I shook with anger.

How had I ever felt anything for Alex? Looking at him now, I couldn't believe I'd kissed him. Or fought beside him. Or trusted him with anything. He was clearly unworthy of any of those things and I'd handed him all of it without a thought.

"I must've been such an easy mark," I said.

"That's not what—"

"No," I said, cutting him off. "You're lying. He sent you in here to mess with my head. To break me. But it won't work."

There was more intensity in his expression than I'd ever seen. Even more than the day he first kissed me—right after saving my life. I wavered but held fast as he said, "Whether you want to believe me or not, it's true. If you don't accept it soon, he will break you, Tara. He wants your blood, broken or not, and he'll do anything to get it."

Chapter Four

Days passed. The only person I saw other than a guard bringing my meals was Mr. Sandefur—twice he came to take three large vials of my blood. When he stopped coming, I broke off a tooth from the comb and went back to a habit I'd developed when I'd first arrived of recording days with scratches on the wall.

I began to wonder if I'd dreamt Alex's visit. And then I began to convince myself I had. It was easier than accepting his betrayal. So, I pretended. And I slept.

And when I slept, I dreamed.

Fog licked at the walls of my mind. Sleep thinned into a loose thread, dangling me somewhere between awake and dreaming. Behind closed lids, hills sheeted in white snow stretched out farther than I could see inside the landscape of my own mind. A few yards away, a figure flickered, undulating, white form against white backdrop until it began to take shape. A woman, long hair blonde enough to disappear against the background. I couldn't recognize her through the haze of my own confusion—and I was just aware enough to feel a nagging sense of nerves at what the picture might morph into should I reach for it.

Dreams and reality were equally scary in my new world. But I'd never been very good at caution. I walked toward the figure.

Slowly, as if drawing a twig through molasses, I raised my hand

and reached for the woman in white. My fingers brushed her shoulder and both felt brittle against the softness of the ether surrounding us. As if understanding my unasked question, she shook her head without turning.

Who was this woman in white? I needed to know—and I had nothing to lose.

I reached again for her shoulder but this time she yanked away, floating just out of reach. I took a step, but no matter how close I got, she always darted an inch or two farther. I ground my teeth and gathered my energy. Then I bent at the knees and lunged, arms out.

She flitted away as the vision began to fade.

I woke to the shape of the figure still at the forefront of my mind and the face of a man hovering above me.

"Wake up."

I jumped—more from the sudden sight of him than the sound of his voice—and scrambled backward into the corner of my new room. Cell. Whatever.

Mr. Lexington stood over me, glowering. I studied him, chest heaving with angry breaths, while tracing the scent as he left. His hair had thinned and he'd lost weight. His shoulders weren't nearly as broad and confident as when I'd first met him. The again, he'd been a hybrid Werewolf-Hunter that day. What the heck was he now?

Pissed at me, for one. And the feeling was mutual.

"What do you want?" I asked.

He straightened but didn't back away. I saw the gleam in his eyes from underneath his brows as he stared down at me, and I knew he enjoyed making me nervous. I sniffed the air.

As always, when he came around, something smelled … off. I had no idea what it was, but I think it had something to do with Steppe. He'd done something to "cure" Mr. Lexington from his Werewolf abilities before he'd taken me prisoner. I didn't know what but I also didn't trust it. And I hated how the strange smell called what was left of my own wolf to the surface. I'd yet to find a way to pull it all the way out and embrace it, but I wanted to. So, so badly.

And I wanted to use it to put Mr. Lexington in his place. Before he could put me in mine. Normally, I'd understand his side. I'd killed his wife, after all. But that had been self-defense after they'd both aligned themselves with Gordon Steppe and tried to kill me. Betraying their own daughter in the process.

I could still see the hurt in Victoria's eyes as she'd watched them dismiss her in favor of following Steppe's orders and attacking me in that warehouse. How they'd ignored her, left her behind, and cast her off—over and over again. And despite mine and Victoria's rocky friendship—okay, that was probably an understatement considering the exploding dog food in my locker—I still felt a ping in my chest when I saw how little she mattered to the two people who were supposed to love her most.

"Get up," Mr. Lexington said, still unmoving. "I'm to bring you to the clinic. You'll start your trials today."

"Trials for what?" I asked, perking up at the idea of finally leaving this room.

Mr. Lexington scowled. Apparently, I'd asked a stupid question. Or, more likely, he considered me a nuisance simply because I still breathed. "For the bond," he snapped. "Put these on." He threw a pile of fabric at me. I put my hand up and blocked it before it could hit me in the face. It fell into my lap instead.

"You know, I keep wondering what your daughter would say if she could see you now," I said.

"Don't talk about my daughter," he snapped, his face reddening. "You've involved her enough."

I bristled at that but let it go. "Fine, let's talk about your wolf," I said. "Where is it? How did Gordon get rid of it?"

"He cured me." His smile turned sharp. "Just like he'll cure you if you choose it."

My stomach tightened at the thought. "You're wrong," I said, swallowing hard and hoping like hell I spoke truth. "A Werewolf exists in you as a second spirit. You can't cure a spirit. You can only—"

"Only what?" he pressed. I bit my lip, unwilling to finish. "Kill it?" When I still didn't answer, he leaned down close enough that his warm breath washed over me and I wrinkled my nose. "I was willing to do whatever necessary to reclaim my birthright. Just like I'm willing to do whatever necessary to avenge your crimes. It's why I'm here. Don't forget that." His voice was overly loud and I shrank back against the excessive volume, but there was no ferocity in his expression, not like when the irritation had flickered first in his eyes and then in his words. These lines were delivered with a hollow expression. Practiced. Almost rehearsed. Still, I couldn't help but respond. If for no other reason than to keep him talking.

"My crimes, as you call them, are wanting peace and equality for all creatures," I shot back. My face heated as my temper flared. I felt angry and helpless and resigned to knowing I would never change his mind. But I couldn't sit back and let them pass judgment so unfairly either.

"Exactly," he said as if I'd just admitted my guilt. "You've decided to play God, handing out sentences and passing judgment where you see fit. Just like him," he muttered, his voice dropping from stage volume to a near-whisper as he said the last part.

"Steppe? I'm nothing like him," I said.

He offered a nefarious smile that didn't quite reach his eyes. "The video footage of your method of leadership would suggest otherwise." Then he straightened and gestured to the clothes in my lap. "I'll be back in five minutes. Be ready."

He turned on his heel and left.

Video footage? What had I missed?

I got dressed quickly. No part of me wanted to be halfway exposed when Mr. Lexington returned. The clothes he'd provided were made of thin cotton and I shivered even as I tied the drawstring around my waist to hold the pants up over my angled hips. Turned out being held prisoner was an excellent weight-loss plan.

Mr. Lexington returned a moment later, the strange smell wafting in with him as he pushed open the door and poked his head inside. "Let's go," he said.

"What did you mean by video footage?" I asked, planting my feet.

His expression tightened—but not before his eyes flicked up to the mounted camera in the corner. "You'll come willingly or I'll force you. Choice is yours."

It was a standoff.

In the end, my curiosity won out and I blinked, muttering under my breath. Without bothering to ask, Mr. Lexington turned and led the way.

The rubble across the hall had been mostly cleared away. There was still a giant depression in the wall where someone had attempted a hole and hadn't quite gotten it right, but it baffled me. Why would someone set an explosion from the inside? Wouldn't it make more sense to break in rather than break out?

Unless this was done by someone else Gordon was holding…

Broken Blood

I followed Mr. Lexington, watchful of the twists and turns we took back to the clinic. I strained to expand my senses as we walked, searching for some sign of my friends. Of another cell or evidence of more prisoners, but there was nothing.

No extraneous sounds on the first hall. All of the doors we passed were closed and the rooms on the other side were dark. Nothing was labeled. We passed no one. With the nondescript décor and plain white-tiled floor, we could've been in any generic office building under the sun. Nothing clued me in as to where I was being kept. If Steppe hadn't told me we were underneath the main floor of CHAS headquarters in DC, I would never have known.

Up ahead, Mr. Lexington stopped at the door with frosted glass and waved his ID badge over the card reader. The light changed from red to green with a beep and the doors slid wide. Inside, I eyed the shiny metal cages once again. Like the last time I'd been here, they were empty, but this time, I spotted clear traces of past occupants. Swatches of fur in various colors littered the floors. One had a large blood stain near the cage door. I shivered and turned away before I could see anything more.

I caught the scent of wolf as I passed. My nose wrinkled and I shut my eyes, hoping I wouldn't recognize anyone specific from my lost pack. Mr. Lexington snickered when he caught me watching the empty cages.

"That one put up a serious fight," he said. "But in the end, she was cured."

I hated the way he said the word. Like it was a rebirth and death all at once. "Screw you," I said and he laughed.

Like before, empty cots lined the opposite wall with curtains separating the spaces. I focused on how empty they were, how devoid of victims, until I'd left the cages behind. Near the center of the room, I spotted an open door that led into an office carved out of the atrium of the space. Inside, a desk strewn with files and loose papers sat against the wall. Random tools littered the desk and the counter behind it. A pair of reading glasses winked back at me from the reflection of the desk lamp. There was a strange familiarity to the scent lingering but I shoved it away. All of my recognition brought pain.

At the end of the rows of cots, in the back of the room, monitors beeped out a soft rhythm where they sat hooked to Olivia. Mr. Lexington herded me over to her bedside and I scooted as close as I could bear until he stopped shoving at me. Her skin was paler than my last visit, almost translucent underneath the glaring lights. The beeping of the machines was a steady thing, but slow. Too slow. Her chest barely rose and fell with each breath.

I tried to remember all of the life, the evil and bitterness, with which she'd hunted me all those months ago. But there wasn't a trace of it left on her. And the beeping of her vitals reminded me instead of another person I'd stood and watched as they fought for life instead of death. Someone else I was responsible for bringing down.

Alex.

Technically, he was also responsible for bringing me down, I thought—and then kicked the idea away. I couldn't go there just now. Not after everything. I needed to be strong; I could mourn his betrayal when I was free. I needed to be tough. I could do it. I'd learned it from him.

Alex always been tough on me. Since he was first assigned as my trainer at Wood Point Academy, he'd never cut me any slack. He'd also never let up on his complete faith and belief in my goodness. My capability. My strength. And I'd forfeited all of those the moment I'd hurt him.

I'd bitten him by accident in the middle of battle. I hadn't known it was him. My wolf, distracted by my newly formed bond with my pack, had sensed a threat and simply reacted. And he'd almost died from the poison I'd injected into his bloodstream when my teeth had broken his skin. For months, I'd blamed myself. And for even longer, Hunters—CHAS—had done the same. They'd launched an investigation that included formal inquiries and interviews with everyone I knew. I'd been asked to come in for questioning when I'd realized Gordon's plans for me didn't include a fair trial or anything to do with a fair justice system.

Did Alex mean that my biting him had all been part of Steppe's master plan? But how could Steppe have known I'd do that? I hadn't even known. It was merely a reflex to my wolf feeling threatened. But Steppe had always been one move ahead of us.

To prove it, he'd gone so far as to frame Wes for a murder Steppe had committed himself. My memory flashed back to that last moment in the warehouse, right before I'd been knocked out. Wes sick and helpless against the chemicals in the room conspiring against him. Police pouring into the space and heading straight for him, cuffs at the ready. His arms wrenched at a painful angle behind him. The uniformed officers leading him out, guns pointed even after they'd restrained him.

But it wasn't on Steppe.

All of that was on me. My ego, my callous disregard for everything and everyone in my smug certainty that I couldn't be harmed. I was immune. Nothing could touch me. Like a ghostly reminder, the stab wound where Mrs. Lexington had pierced my side panged with a pricking pain. It had healed nicely thanks to whatever Steppe had been slipping me in my drugged-up dinners, but it still ached. Sometimes, I suspected the pain came more from guilty penance than physical wounding.

Maybe Gordon was right about ridding us of monsters. Maybe I was one of them.

"There's our patient."

Gordon's voice startled me out of my self-loathing. I blinked and looked up, mouth already set to wage psychological battle against my captor. But no words came. I stared—past Gordon and straight ahead to his companion. He was the last person I'd expected to see here. My stomach dropped.

For the first time since Gordon had told me his plan, I realized the possibility of its success. And my heart broke all over again at my failures.

"Uncle Astor? What are you doing here?" I asked.

From underneath a mop of bushy graying eyebrows, Astor peered down at me between the gap of his brow hairs and a pair of wire-rimmed glasses. He looked absolutely the same as the first time I saw him, although his bathrobe had been replaced by a lab coat and his ratty bunny slippers had been replaced with newer versions sporting floppier ears. My dad's brother was the smartest man I'd ever met—and the strangest.

"Killing spirits left and right. It's a sad, sad story I have to tell," he said with a despondent shake of his head. And the timbre in his voice was proof that, despite his response, he was completely lucid. Which made me sad for him. I'd much rather he went through this a little unaware of the horror.

Gordon ignored him. "He'll be conducting a round of blood trials on you and running labs while we figure out the best way to approach our bonding."

My skin crawled at the last two words. I couldn't imagine Gordon invading my mind—so I hadn't yet allowed the thought to sink in. But it nudged at me now and I shuddered at the thought.

Gordon's mouth tipped upward at my reaction and my skin buzzed with the ache to shift. I grabbed at it, the feeling of my wolf—or what was left of it—and snarled, but there wasn't enough. My wolf slipped away.

"What's the matter?" Gordon asked. "Trying to be something you're not again?"

"Just imagining how it'll feel to rip your throat out," I threw back.

"Oh," Astor muttered to himself.

Once again, Gordon ignored him in favor of baiting me. "Funny, I'd heard it was next to impossible to injure someone bonded with you. Worse than dying, they say."

I snarled—the closest I'd come to being a wolf in weeks. "Paws, hands, a friend willing to do me a favor—the weapon isn't important. And I can stand the pain. The question is, can you?"

"Can you can you can you can you?" Astor echoed in a breathy voice.

Neither of us answered him.

"Where are my friends?" I asked.

"I told you before, they're not here," he said.

"And I told you, I don't believe you."

"Believe what you must. I don't have them."

Gordon's stare was like a brick wall. But even if I couldn't see them, I refused to believe there weren't chinks. A weak spot. And I was determined to find it. I held his gaze until he finally nodded at Mr. Lexington. "Keep an eye on this one," Gordon said, pointing at Astor. "Make sure he sticks to the plan."

Mr. Lexington agreed and Gordon walked out.

"Come. This way," Astor said, leading the way to a fresh cot a few beds away from Olivia's space. His words were high-pitched and clipped, a sign my exchange with Gordon had left him rattled. Guilt tugged at me, stabbing into the wound left behind by Victoria's mother. Another tick mark against my ability to protect my loved ones.

Astor gestured to the bed and I sat while he rooted through drawers and laid out his supplies. Needle, vials, alcohol swabs, bandages—all of the same things I'd used on myself when I'd drawn all that blood for the hybrid pack. It made my eyes water just remembering. My knowledge about how to save them had come directly from Astor himself. None of those people would have lived if not for him. And now, was he the one helping Gordon kill them?

"Astor, why are you here?" I whispered. "Why are you letting him use you?"

Mr. Lexington either hadn't heard or didn't care based on his disinterest. He was scrolling his phone and I wondered just how many guards must be posted out of sight for him to seem so unconcerned.

Astor barely looked up from his careful arrangement of the tray in front of him. "I am here. You are here. I am here." He shrugged, a jerky twisted sort of gesture, and I sighed.

"Did he hurt you?" I asked, searching him for some sign of injury even as I asked the question. His movements were sure and his coloring good. He looked fed and healthy enough but I knew not all wounds showed on the outside. Astor's pain at Steppe's hands had always been emotional. But he shook his head.

"No hurting. Not me. Not you. Not yet. Except." He looked up at me sharply. "You will hurt. Less if it's me but you will still hurt. And I'm sorry. Tell Jeremiah I'm sorry."

"Astor, Jeremiah—my father's dead," I said.

"Oh. Right." His gaze fell and I felt strangely guilty for saying it out loud, even if the statement had been true for almost as long as I'd been alive. This wasn't new information. Whatever Astor had been through in being forced to work here had regressed him. Or affected him psychologically. He'd always been prone to weird bouts of forgetfulness or odd distraction, but this was worse. This was more ... complete.

"Where is Mr. Sandefur?" I asked, hoping to redirect us both to more solid ground with something easy.

But a shadow passed over Astor's features. He mumbled something and kept working. I glanced at Mr. Lexington but he was staring hard at Astor now. An uneasiness filled my gut.

"On an errand," Mr. Lexington said finally.

I sighed in strange relief. Errand. For Steppe, probably. Of course he couldn't be here all the time. And why did I care? He was the enemy. Maybe I was going crazy under the pressure of all the trauma; maybe I got that trait from my uncle.

Mr. Lexington went back to his phone. Astor went back to his methodical arranging and I watched in concern as he picked up the same vial three times, moving it left and right and left again before nodding in satisfaction over its placement on the tray. When he'd finished that, he caught his tongue between his teeth as he slowly removed labels from a printed sheet and stuck them to the vials. I caught sight of my printed name and lettered codes I didn't understand as he smoothed them into place on the rounded plastic casing.

Finally, he turned and pulled at my arm, laying it with my forearm and elbow exposed in my lap. "Like this. Time for blood," he almost sang. "The hybrid queen's blood."

He started to turn away but I grabbed his wrist and laid my hand over his lightly. He went still, but he didn't meet my eyes. "Astor, why are you here, doing this for him? What is he threatening you with?" I asked quietly. Desperation leaked in. Not for myself but for what Steppe would do with him once he'd served his purpose.

But there was no fear or worry in his answer. He met my eyes, blinked once, and said simply, "You."

The tone was so clear, so directly honest, I forgot the rest of my questions and released my hold on his wrist. Before I knew it, he'd stuck me. We both watched as my blood poured into the first empty vial.

Astor filled five tubes before he withdrew the needle. "Hold pressure here," he instructed, replacing his fingers with two of my own pressed over the prick point. I applied pressure while he readied a bandage and smoothed it into place.

"All better." He beamed.

I smiled back, a soft encouragement, and glanced over Astor's shoulder. Mr. Lexington still scrolled through his phone in the corner, eyes down, posture relaxed. But I knew better. He might not be watching us, but he knew our movements. Anything rash and he wouldn't hesitate to retaliate. He was probably hoping for it. Either way, I probably didn't have much longer to talk before I was herded back.

"Astor, what's wrong with Olivia?" I asked. "Why won't she wake up?"

Astor shoved his glasses up his nose and glanced down the rows of beds toward the far end of the room. "She is not strong," he said with a frown before going back to his cleanup.

"Strong for what?" I pressed. "Did you take her blood too?"

"I took it, and I gave it. But they did not accept."

"You gave it? Did you give her Gordon's blood?" I asked, trying to keep the alarm out of my voice.

But Astor shook his head. "No. I gave her theirs. And hers to them. Some chose it and it worked for a moment. But then ... the darkness came. And the ones who chose the wolf got sick."

His explanation was so fragmented but at the mention of the darkness, a chill swept over me. I remembered Nick and Janie, how they'd inched closer and closer to some cliff's edge I couldn't reach. No matter how hard I tried to pull them back, in the end, they had thrown themselves over. And I couldn't save them before I was forced to stop them in order to save myself and the others. The bond wasn't always a pleasant connection. Losing a bond was a pain Gordon only thought he could imagine. And I'd bluffed back. It wasn't something I ever wanted to feel again.

But something else Astor said was nagging at me. "What do you mean the ones who chose the wolf? How was it a choice? What was the alternative?" I asked.

"They chose their other half," Astor said.

I looked at Mr. Lexington. "They were made into Hunters again."

Astor pressed his mouth together and huffed a breath through his nose. "They were whatever they were. Not all were strong enough. But they chose."

"I'm surprised Gordon let them," I muttered.

"It can't be forced or it's not real," Astor said.

"Aren't people angry over all the ones who ... aren't strong enough?" I asked, my voice dipping low. "I mean, Steppe is killing them."

Astor looked up and blinked at me, his face inches from mine. "He's telling them it's on you."

"Are you almost done?" Mr. Lexington called, pushing off from the wall and walking over.

Astor and I exchanged a final look and something passed between us. For a second, I saw awareness behind the confusion and disjointed coercion. Painfully, torturously aware. But then it was gone and he was a confused scientist again, capable of world domination only as it related to beakers and Bunsen burners.

"For now," Astor sang out. He gathered the blood he'd taken from me and turned for the office, but a sound from the far end of the room stopped him.

A moan, low and unintelligible, sounded from the other side of the half-drawn curtain. Before anyone could investigate, the curtain was ripped aside on its metal rungs. Astor dropped the tubes of blood back onto the tray and stumbled back. His legs hit the bed where I sat and he sank next to me, both of staring in shock at Olivia. Even Mr. Lexington was surprised into stillness.

"You," she said, her voice hoarse. Blood dripped from her hand where she'd ripped the IV out in order to travel this far. Her dark hair was stringy and unkempt, hanging dully around her pale face and matching the darkened sockets of her eyes. The veins in her arms and throat stood out in stark contrast to her translucent skin. Her chin jutted at a hard angle and her collarbone created deep pockets of skin around her throat. She looked like a zombie come to eat my brains.

For a fleeting moment, I considered letting her have them.

"You are his new prize," she said and the words were a croak of despair. Was she actually jealous Steppe had chosen me as his next victim?

"Trust me, I'm completely open to being superseded. You can have him back anytime you're ready," I said.

Her eyes narrowed and her back hunched. I wondered how she had the strength to stand barefoot on the cold tile this long. "He promised me. He said I could sit at his right hand. I could be his…"

"His lapdog? His patsy? His weapon?" I asked. "Because any of those fill in that blank perfectly."

Olivia lurched forward. A strangled sound escaped her throat and I suspected she meant for a yell but got more of a whisper. She didn't need volume. Her eyes gave away her intent. Maybe it was her fragility or maybe I'd underestimated the sheer will of her hatred for me, but when she landed on top of me, we both went down.

Her hands were ice cold as they slid around my throat and squeezed. I cried out before the sound was strangled into a hiss. Behind Olivia, Mr. Lexington reached down and yanked on her arms but she held on. Like a pit bull with a locked jaw, she screamed obscenities and squeezed against my windpipe. My eyes went blurry and then glazed over with unshed tears. I clawed at her and gave my wolf everything I had, demanding, pleading for it to come.

But nothing happened. My stab wound ached and I squeezed my eyes shut against it all.

A second later, Olivia's hands released me, her nails scratching my skin as she was dragged off my body, bare legs kicking against the air as Mr. Lexington struggled to get her under control.

"Oh my oh my oh my," Astor said where he still hovered beside the bed.

I stared at Olivia, my throat burning, the skin on my neck smarting from her scratches. My shoulders rose and fell with labored breaths. Olivia looked ready to drop but her eyes still burned just as brightly as before.

She opened her mouth to say something. but I pushed to my feet and cut her off. "I am your enemy, yes, but he is not your friend. He's a liar. He would use you to kill and then when he's done with you, he'll kill you. And you're a fool if you think otherwise."

"I am the future," she said, each of the words strewn out into twice the syllables. Her chest heaved by the time she was done. She raised a hand, to say more—about what she thought I was, no doubt, but instead she coughed.

It wracked her shoulders and buckled her knees. Mr. Lexington caught her as she collapsed. He swung her roughly into his arms, looking none too pleased at having to carry her, and walked her back to bed. She craned her neck so that her eyes met mine and held as she was ushered back into her corner. Behind them, Astor followed, already readying a new IV with a syringe full of clear liquids standing by.

I shuddered. "If you're right, the future is bleak," I muttered as they went.

Chapter Five

Unbinilium coated everything: the floor, the doors, the windows, the world. Every single speck of something inside my mind was made of it.

Like the dreams before, this one was foggy. Diluted. But unlike the others, faces showed themselves. Grandma dashing into the warehouse all those weeks ago, a semi-automatic slung over her shoulder. A pistol in her hand. Her "Number One Grandma" sweatshirt dirt-smudged and wrinkled where it hung over her pedal pushers.

"Grandma!" I rushed toward her but she floated off, always just out of reach without ever seeming to move. Maybe she didn't. Maybe it was the fog. Or me.

"I miss you so much," I called out. I knew better than to think this were real but I couldn't pretend everything was okay, either. "Please tell me you made it out of the warehouse that night. And the others; are they all safe?"

She smiled a glittering, dangerous sort of smile at me through the window of her Hummer and then sped off into the fog. Nothing made a sound while I waited for the next face. I didn't bother looking for it, that strategy never worked here. I had to wait for it to find me.

Cord was next, but she was distorted. I was too surprised to see her face showing up in my dreams to notice the differences at first. But

Broken Blood

when I failed to react to the scars slashed down her face, they broke open and morphed into fresh cuts. Blood rose to the surface of her otherwise flawless skin and dripped off her jaw and chin, where it disappeared into the fog below.

"Cord, oh my God. Did I do this to you somehow? Is this my fault too?" I asked.

She scowled her usual perfect scowl at me and was gone.

The next face wasn't so easy to resist. He walked slowly out of the fog, looking every single inch like the boy I'd met in that alleyway those months ago. God, months. I'd missed the end of summer and half of fall sitting inside this prison. Sadness over the time lost slipped inside my chest and settled in the outer reaches of my already broken heart.

But despite the passage of time, he looked same as ever. Brown-bronzed hair shoved back from his forehead, worn leather jacket draped over broad shoulders and a proud chest.

"Wes," I whispered. My mate.

He turned and went still at the sight of me, and I realized he hadn't seen me before I'd spoken. Not like the others who'd come expecting this meeting. He looked surprised and just as confused as I was. I moved forward, slowly at first, but when the fog parted and he didn't move, I went faster.

"Tara," he said.

And every tension-filled cavity inside my body emptied and refilled with the love that brimmed over at the sight of him.

"You're all right," he said and then I ran.

My feet made no noise against whatever floor the fog hovered over. When I'd almost reached him, he spread his arms wide and I leaped, hands outstretched. I felt myself lift high and then drop low and I held my breath in anticipation of the feeling of being caught and held by Wes.

Just before I reached him, he vanished. In his place, a pack of wolves appeared. Yellow eyes, mangy fur, and frothing jaws—all of them growling and gnashing their teeth at me. I fell toward them, arms out in protest now, a scream building in my throat.

The one above me opened his jaw just as I fell toward his face. My heart seized and my muscles tensed for impact.

And then I woke.

The scar on my rib ached so hard I peeled off the covers and lifted my pajama shirt to double check for fresh blood. But the skin was unbroken, only marred and pulled tight where it stretched to close the hole that Mrs. Lexington left behind. I exhaled.

The dream was vividly real. And I was inching toward convinced on how alike Astor and I might be after all. My brain felt looser against its hinges every day.

As the fear faded, snapshots of the dream flash through my mind. Just the faces. Grandma, Cord, Wes, the open-jawed wolf. None of them were real, but something about it wasn't exactly fiction either.

I spent the next few hours wide awake, lying on my side.

In the morning, the lock turned and the door opened. Mr. Lexington stepped inside. Behind him, another figure hovered in the hall between a set of armed guards.

I shot to my feet. "Chris!"

His face was crisscrossed with the scars of old wounds overlapping fresh cuts and swollen bruises. But it was Chris, my second in command. Some forgotten spark of connection flashed in my mind, remnants of our bond stirring at the sight of him. His face brightened into relief and then shut down just as quickly into disappointment.

"Tara, you're okay," he said, but he didn't sound nearly happy enough.

My heart sank at the sight of him so beat up. I knew exactly how he felt even without a mental link. Yes, we were okay. But for how long?

"Shut up," I heard from out in the hall and Chris was nudged sideways. A third guard stepped into view, glaring. Something about his features, the upturned slits of his eyes, felt familiar, but I couldn't place it. Especially when my attention was being drawn to the shiny gun he had wedged into Chris's ribs. "Both of you stop talking."

"Get dressed in this," Mr. Lexington said, tossing clothes at me.

I held them up, curious. "Not my usual uniform," I said, eyeing the black leggings and matching pullover hoodie. He dropped a pair of black lace-up boots at my feet. They landed with a thud.

"You're welcome," Mr. Lexington said and strode out. "You have two minutes," he called over his shoulder before slamming the door. I caught the sound of lowered voices in the hall but no words came through.

I hurried to get dressed, anticipation and worry equal parts in my twisting insides. After five days full of blood draws and medical exams and little more, the uniform had changed. So had the cast. Chris was here.

Today was different.

"Where are the others?" I whispered to Chris as we walked down the hall a few minutes later.

A gun poked me in the back. "Shut up," said the guard.

"Are they alive?" I whispered, ignoring the painful jab.

Chris glanced sideways at me, his mouth set in a hard line. A horizontal scab along his cheekbone caught the light, making it look wet all over again with the crimson blood still staining the edges. "Some," he said simply.

The other guard brought his gun down against Chris's shoulder. "We said shut it. We won't tell you again." His voice was a dare. He wanted Chris to step out of line. He wanted to hurt him. I glanced back and saw the man's irises glowing yellow before I was nudged roughly and forced to turn around.

We were herded to the clinic in a path quickly becoming familiar to me. Chris grunted with each step and his hand clenched tightly against the railing. I didn't ask any more questions. At the frosted doorway, two more guards were stationed on either side. Both armed. Both had eyes that gleamed yellow.

The door slid aside and Gordon greeted us, all smiles. "Right on time," he said warmly, as if he'd invited us to a party instead of ... whatever this was.

Chris didn't respond, his gaze darting everywhere but Gordon. I suspected this wasn't their first encounter and my chest ached at what Gordon must've done to him to warrant such deference. I clenched my hands into fists, hating how weak the motion felt without a wolf's strength behind it.

"Let's get started," Gordon said.

The first thing I recognized on the other side of the threshold was Astor. In the center of the room, he waited at a long table, his fingers held together in a way that allowed him to tap the ends together. It might've looked like hungry anticipation of a mad scientist to anyone else, but I knew his nervous tics when I saw them. He was terrified.

The second was the cages. Unlike my last two visits, they were now occupied. I scanned them, my lungs closing as I inspected the inhabitants. After the first few, I looked away in relief. I didn't recognize any of the furry faces that stared back at me. Not unless you counted my recent nightmares.

Every single metal cage contained a pair of gleaming yellow eyes exactly like the ones I'd seen in my dream. Jaws open, hungry for my flesh and blood. Unable to shake those images, I couldn't bring myself to inspect any more of the faces. Beside me, Chris was a rigid wall of shoulders and bruised arms. He didn't look inside the cages either.

"Tara?"

A deep voice, marred by exhaustion and whatever other injuries, pulled at my memory, and I stopped to peer inside the cage beside me. A brown wolf blinked back. A small patch of fur near his ear was missing, along with another along bare patch his shoulder.

"Rafe?" I asked in disbelief.

"I thought they'd ... I've been worried for you," he said in a scratchy voice whose gloominess reminded me of Eeyore. The patches of missing fur stirred memories of the past. Back when I'd had to fight for him. Back when I'd been his alpha, his pack leader. He'd looked mangy from his fur being burned ever since then, but this was more. He was scrawny with hunger and the distinct smell of animal clung to him. His eyes were wild. I wondered how long it'd been since he'd been human.

I reached out to touch him through the bars, but the metal coating was like an electric current, sapping my strength the closer I got. I pulled away and let my hand fall to my side.

"What happened to you?" I asked, struggling to keep my voice from breaking on the last part. My fault. All of it.

"I made my choice," he said. "I'm who I was meant to be."

Through my confusion, I tried for a smile, but it fell flat. "And the others?" I asked.

"We all made our choice," he said as if I should be comforted in that. Maybe I would be if I knew what the heck he was talking about. *Made their choice?*

Someone pushed me from behind and I stumbled onward. "Keep moving," the guard said roughly.

Up ahead, Chris had already been herded into one of the chairs set up on either side of Astor's table. His wrists and ankles had been secured with straps attached to the chair's frame, though he didn't look as if he'd struggled. I met his eyes, unable to keep the fear out of mine.

"No," I said, planting my feet.

The guard tried nudging me but I remained where I was. "No," I said again.

No one else argued. I wondered what Gordon was waiting on. He'd have no trouble forcing me, I was sure. But I couldn't tear my gaze away from Chris long enough to find out.

Chris stared up at me, eyes pleading. "He's going to give it back, Tara. We can be bonded again."

"He's using us," I told him.

"Not if we use him first," Chris said.

I hesitated and then took a single step forward, but Gordon stepped in front of me. "Oh, this chair isn't for you," he said. Your place is there, along the wall with the guards. The viewing area." He motioned for someone behind me to come forward. "This chair is for our other participant."

"What?" Chris asked, but Gordon ignored him.

Someone bumped me as they passed by and I was jostled sideways before I caught my balance. I saw her just as Gordon finished explaining, "My second in command. Olivia."

She lowered herself to the chair across the table from Chris, aiming a triumphant smile at Gordon and then me. She didn't look much better than she had a few days ago. Her color had returned only to the extent that she didn't look like a bottle of glue. Someone had exchanged her hospital gown for a sweater and long pants. But otherwise, she was death warmed over.

Her IV remained firmly in place, attached to a bag of fluids on wheels and a metal pole that she held beside her chair. Her hair had been swept up to reveal her sunken eyes and hollowed cheeks. "You look like death," I told her.

"You look like your mother," she shot back primly.

I gave her the finger. It wasn't much, but it wouldn't get me shot.

Gordon laughed. "You two are entertaining, at least. Astor, you can begin whenever you're ready."

"This isn't what we discussed," Chris said, finally beginning to fight against the restraints. But it was too late.

I stared at Gordon. "You're going to bond them?" I asked. "Now? They're too weak."

Over Astor's left shoulder, one of the caged wolves yelped and pawed at the bars. Beside it, another joined in. Gordon looked at them and they abruptly died off. Then he looked back at me, brow raised.

"They seem in favor."

I stared in growing dread at the wolves, at Olivia, the entire scene. "Go ahead," Gordon said, the picture of calm. Before I could think of anything to say, Astor rounded the table and stuck Olivia in the arm.

She sucked in a breath and her head dropped back to lean against the chair before lolling sideways. Gordon took a tiny step forward, arms crossed, before going still and watching her instead. Chris stared at the woman he'd once called master with a look of horror.

Astor finished the injection and then moved to Chris without bothering to check on his first patient. He didn't look over before grabbing the next syringe and inserting it into Chris's waiting vein. Chris flexed his fist, his arms straining against their restraints.

I curled my fingers in and pressed my nails into my palms.

No one spoke while we waited. Even the caged wolves were eerily silent.

Astor withdrew the syringe and tossed it aside before picking up another and going back for round two. First Olivia. Then Chris. By the time he was finished with the second dose, Olivia's eyes had opened. Her color was already returning and she was breathing deeply, taking turns working the joints at her wrists and ankles in circular stretches.

"How are you feeling?" Gordon asked, taking another step forward. Excitement, not concern, I realized.

"Better," Olivia said, sitting straighter now. She cracked her knuckles and I didn't need to be told the bond had worked. At least to some extent. She'd walked in half-dead and already she looked revived.

Across the table, Chris was silent, his face pale. His hands sat limply on the arm rests, no more of the flexing fists he'd made as the blood entered his body. He stared straight ahead with a blank look, his mouth hanging listlessly open, and my stomach dropped. Whatever was happening in his mind wasn't bringing him to life. He was shutting down.

Behind him, the two wolves from before whimpered softly and lay down.

"You're hurting him," I said, struggling to go to Chris, but the guards had clearly anticipated this. They grabbed and held me before I could take a single step. I fought against them and several howls lit the air. I thought I picked out Rafe among them.

"Quiet!" Gordon's voice boomed with power—not that of an alpha.

Broken Blood

More like a tormenter. Most fell silent. A few turned to whines and yelps before they too died off. It was only me. And I was helpless.

Gordon strode over to me, his chest puffed up in assumed victory. "I told you if you didn't agree to help me, I'd kill them all. One by one. Tell me." He cocked his head. "Do you feel anything as he slips away? Is there anything left of your connection now?"

My eyes filled with tears, but I refused to answer him. I refused to give him the satisfaction. Gordon's lips quirked—the ghost of a smile—and he walked away.

Chris sank lower in his chair until he was leaning against it for full support to keep him upright. Olivia pushed to her feet and went to Chris, standing over him with purpose. She took several deep breaths while Gordon hovered nearby, watching, waiting. Chris didn't make a sound as his lids grew heavy and his head lolled against his chest.

I felt the tears slipping down my cheeks, leaving hot tracks of my own pain and failure as they dripped off my chin. Somewhere along the way I stopped struggling against my guards and went still.

Olivia took a final deep breath and Chris slumped sideways, the only sign of his consciousness the occasional blink of his eyes. She whirled to face Gordon, a smile lighting her pale features. "We did it," she said.

"Of course we did," Gordon told her. "But what's wrong with him?"

Olivia shrugged. "I needed his strength for myself."

"And what about him?" Gordon chastised. "He was already weak."

Olivia shrugged again. "You shouldn't have pushed him so hard to make his choice." Her lip curled on the last word, as if she found it funny.

Behind them, the caged wolves yelped and scratched. Inside my mind, the memory of the fog was almost a real thing. It coiled and built. It licked up the walls and snaked into the far corners and I wanted so badly to summon that yellow-eyed pack from my dreams to swallow up this entire horrible moment.

"No," I whispered over and over again. "No."

Steppe motioned at two of the guards. With little more than a nod, they set their weapons aside and unstrapped Chris, carrying him to a gurney nearby and laying him flat. My guards were either pre-occupied or no longer under orders to contain me. I broke free and rushed to where Chris lay, half-awake and clearly hurting. The bond pulled at me, like a weakened magnet, and I bent toward him.

"Chris, hang on," I said, grabbing his hand in both of mine. It was cold and limp, his eyes unfocused even as they found mine. A surge of pain wound from his hand to mine and I welcomed the faint link.

"Tara..." His words were slurred as if he'd been drugged. I glared at Olivia. She was feeding him this. Somehow. And taking his strength. What little he had to offer. I wanted to claw her eyes out.

"Tara," Chris said again, a whisper so faint I had to bend down to hear the words. "He's offering a choice but it's not. It's a lie. You have to stop him," Chris said.

"I can't even free myself," I whispered back. "How can I stop him?"

"Don't let him bond with you." His words ended in a coughing fit. His head came up off the table as he struggled for breath. Gordon said something, and I was shoved backward out of the way by the guards. Astor was nudged into my place and ordered to help. He muttered nonsensical words under his breath while he worked but he did as ordered.

I was shoved too far back to see Chris any longer but I knew it wasn't good when Olivia's smile suddenly slipped and she pressed her fingertips to her temples.

"What is it?" Gordon asked.

"My head ... it's...No," Olivia yelled and then moaned, her knees buckling. Gordon caught her and dragged her back to an open chair, depositing her in a heap. She grimaced but didn't try to get up. She bit her lip but cries escaped her throat even through her closed lips.

"What is happening?" Gordon asked again, but Olivia was obviously in too much pain to answer. The guards hovering around Chris shifted to also encompass Olivia and I caught sight of Chris. His eyes were closed, his chest not moving. Astor's flurry of movement abruptly went still.

"I just lost him," Astor said matter-of-factly.

Olivia slumped over in her chair, unconscious.

"What the hell is going on?" Steppe roared. "You told me you fixed this!"

The guards scurried to herd me and Astor to the sidelines while working to revive an unresponsive Olivia. Everything in my mind felt stretched. Slow. Too obvious to the point of irritating. I glared at Steppe and roared back, "She's feeling his death, you idiot. I warned you about this."

Steppe's shoulders stiffened. "Take her to her room. Sedate her," he told the guards, his back to me. The guard still holding his gun tucked his weapon into the waistline of his pants and scooped Olivia into his arms. Her head and arms hung limp as he carried her to the door. Astor moved to follow, but Steppe stopped him. "You stay. I need you here."

Astor's eyes widened but he didn't argue. Apparently satisfied, Steppe rounded on me, eyes blazing. "Your turn," he said.

"My turn for what?"

"Astor, get the samples."

"But ... you just saw what happened. The new variation isn't ready. She'll get into your thoughts just as easily as you'll get hers—"

"Dammit. I don't care about that," Gordon yelled. "I want it done. We're running out of time. The public needs to see her as the villain. Forget it. Take fresh samples. Do the exchange now."

Astor scurried to a cabinet at the back of the room, his slippers sliding over the tile floor.

Steppe nodded to someone behind him and seconds later, hands closed around my arms. I kicked out but the guard was faster. I was herded to the chair Chris had vacated. Beside me, his body lay cold and lifeless on the table. I looked away before I caught sight of his face.

"Get him out of here," Gordon snapped.

Out of the corner of my eye, I watched a guard collect Chris in his arms and carry him out. I couldn't watch. A sob rose up but I bit down on my cheek to hold it in. The metallic tang of blood filled my mouth and a sniffle escaped before I could silence it.

"Don't cry for him. He made his choice. You're making yours."

I whirled and stared across the table at Steppe. "This is not my choice," I said through clenched teeth.

"You can refuse this anytime. It has to be given freely, remember?"

"Fine. I refuse. Take me back to my room."

The remaining guards eyed Steppe.

"You heard the girl. Escort her back," he told them. I pushed to my feet. They moved to approach me and Steppe added, "Just keep in mind what you're giving up." He flicked his wrist toward where Astor gathered syringes and cotton swabs at the back of the room. "An uncle who loves you enough to risk his life in order to be the one to treat you. Who would kill, in fact, if it meant saving his niece. A pack, or what's left of them, of hybrids that will probably end up like your second in command being buried out back. Olivia's not nearly as good at this as you."

I lowered myself back to my chair. The guards stepped back again but I ignored them, my confused expression sweeping both Steppe and Astor. "What do you mean … kill?"

Gordon's enjoyment sent off warning bells and I stared at him, my breath caught. "Mr. Sandefur had decided to take matters into his own hands," he said off-handedly, as if I'd asked for the forecast. He stared at his nails as he spoke and anger burned hot and neat in my veins at his cavalier attitude.

"What matters?" I asked.

"Precisely? You. Much has happened while you've been hiding inside those four walls of your little room, Miss Godfrey. The world has seen a different side of you and," he paused to click his tongue, "I'm afraid it doesn't paint a very nice picture."

"What are you talking about? How can the world have any picture of me when I'm stuck in here?"

"Just because you can't see them doesn't mean they can't see you. You've been busy. Usurping me at every turn according to the various videos released. I offer everyone here a choice and those who choose wrong." He gestured to the metal cages. "Let's just say the public assumption is that you are the reason they never return to their families."

"But I've been in … I've barely left my room. Why would…?" The cameras, I remembered. Alex, even Mr. Lexington had been hyper-aware of them. Choosing their words so carefully. Always only saying what was necessary. Or what Steppe approved of. "The explosion," I said.

"Yes, destroying an official building is a capital crime," Gordon said. "I'd say the safest place for you now is by my side. Making me an ally is maybe the only thing left that will save your public image."

I glared at him, but when I caught sight of Astor, my temper waned. He was shaking, his hands stuffed in his lab coat pockets, the entire jacket shivering in his fear. He'd killed Mr. Sandefur to protect me?

I sighed, terrified I would be unable to return the favor, but finally determined to try. "I'm listening," I said in a flat voice.

"Smart choice," Steppe said and I hated the smugness in his words.

"But I don't understand. What is this choice everyone keeps talking about? Is it blackmail, like with me?" I asked.

"Not at all. Every hybrid I find is given the option to either take the cure and become a Hunter again or have their Hunter side stripped and remain a Werewolf."

"What's the catch?"

"The current law states all hybrids shall be taken into custody in order that they may be killed. Once here, I'm allowing them mercy, to first make a choice that might save them."

I leaned forward in my chair, half a step from overturning the table and attacking him, wolf or not. "But that's entrapment. You're letting them choose Werewolf and then executing them. You call it a choice but if they don't choose Hunter, they're dead."

Is that what Rafe had meant when he said he'd made his choice? Is that why I couldn't find the rest of my pack?

"Don't be ridiculous. No one is executing anyone."

I stared back at him. "Bonding then." It wasn't a question, but Gordon dipped his chin once in a nod and I finally realized his end game. "You're using them to experiment on your new bonding technique while the public dubs you a hero for offering to cure the ones that want it. But that's not possible. There is no cure," I added.

"You've been gone for some time. There are many impossible things happening in our world that would surprise you." I wasn't fooled by his casual tone.

"Like what?"

"Hmm, let's see. Like the fact that your mother has already found a new daughter to replace you."

"You're lying."

"Am I? The court papers have already been filed for a proper adoption. Oh, and the fact that your grandmother was voted out of CHAS. It seems your family no longer has a foothold in Hunter affairs."

I scowled, unwilling to admit his words bothered me.

"Or, my favorite," he went on. "Your mutt boyfriend being arrested for murder. Of a Hunter girl, as a matter of fact. Capital punishment in both worlds." He clucked his tongue in mock concern and I went numb.

The fog returned. Licking and poking and filling all the empty space in my mind. Cord's face with the scars and the blood running in rivulets down her perfect cheeks. Staining her shirt. Her hair. And I was covered in it. Because it was on my hands.

"Fine. I'll do it," I said. I could practically feel Gordon's triumph, but I ignored it, promising myself it was the smartest—if not only—

option I had left.

Within seconds, Astor appeared beside me with a needle perched against my skin. His eyes offered their condolences. "I'm sorry," he whispered.

"This is the part where I hurt, isn't it?" I whispered back.

He sighed and pushed the needle point through my skin. "It is. I'm sorry. It is."

I winced as Gordon's blood filled my veins.

Chapter Six

Being held prisoner in that cell had sucked. Being stuck inside my own mind with a man whose dark thoughts had become so twisted he thought killing innocent people was the highest form of justice—that was so much worse.

The images pressed in around me; awake, asleep, it didn't matter. The moment I let my guard down, they flooded in.

"She can't be allowed to get away with this," Mr. Sandefur said in my memory—only it wasn't my memory. His voice was full of anguish as he stood before another man.

"You know Steppe is twisting this, right?" The second man stepped forward, out of the shadows cast by the closed blinds in the small office and I gasped. Professor Hugo, one of my teachers from Wood Point, stood before Logan's dad. His face flashed with fierce determination I'd only ever seen him aim at me—in the form of distaste. "He's manipulating you, man. You're one of the last loyal to him and he'll do anything to keep it that way."

"You saw the video," Mr. Sandefur said. "Tara was there. She has turned my son against me. She ordered him to fight us and he did it. What will she do next? I don't have anyone left to lose." His voice broke and he hid his face in his hands.

Professor Hugo reached out, but the door opened and they both jerked back. Uncle Astor stood in the small slant of light showing through from the hall. He was breathing heavily and his eyes blazed as he pinned Mr. Sandefur with a look.

"She is not to be touched," Astor said. "She is family."

Mr. Sandefur shoved Professor Hugo out of the way. "She turned my family against me," he roared. "Logan won't speak to me. He refuses to see me."

"That," Professor Hugo said, "is your own doing. You voted with Steppe. Your boy saw it as a betrayal. You will leave that girl alone. Don't make an enemy of us too."

"Don't tell me what to do," Mr. Sandefur roared. He whirled and the gleaming weapon was drawn so fast, I almost missed where it slid into Professor Hugo's ribs. Soft and easy, with the quietest of sounds. The metal must've been razor sharp.

Professor Hugo's eyes widened and he went limp, falling in a crumbled heap only after Mr. Sandefur pulled the knife free and shoved his friend aside. Mr. Sandefur hesitated. His hands trembled as he turned to face Astor.

But Astor was gone.

The memory shifted into another scene, almost like a fast-forward on a recording. Mr. Sandefur standing outside the door to my room. His shoulders were hunched and his expression was one of contrasting sadness to the wild anger he'd worn a moment ago. His cheeks, his skin, his jaw—all of it sagged under the weight of the guilt he carried. His steps were slow but full of purpose. He paused and retrieved his ID card, holding it ready to swipe over the automatic reader that controlled the lock.

Abruptly, his hand went rigid and his arm fell heavily against him. He hit the wall, leaning hard, and slid to the floor. I heard myself cry out but it felt foreign, like someone else picking up the noise through a wall. I was so solidly wrapped in the memory it felt as if I were there.

When Astor looked up from where he stood over Mr. Sandefur, it seemed as if our eyes met. We stared back at each other for a long moment before he looked away—down at the stake buried in Mr. Sandefur's back. "No one must hurt her. That was our deal," Astor said in a wispy voice.

"I never said I'd be the one to protect her." The deep bass rumbled from my chest—only it wasn't my chest. Disoriented, the memory abruptly faded and I tumbled back into the reality of my room.

Night fell and I struggled to hold back any more memories. I'd seen enough already. Steppe had been there and done nothing to stop it. I didn't want to feel or think or know anything else he had to offer.

But keeping Steppe out of my head space wasn't easy. And it zapped my strength. Now I understood what had killed Chris. It wasn't Olivia taking his health. It was the fight to keep her out of his head. Within minutes of the blood transfusion, I'd felt the darkness that signaled Steppe's arrival into my awareness. The black cloud that made up Steppe's mental capacity was so much worse than Nick or Janie or any of my pack before this. It was smarter for one, cunning even, and it had purpose: me.

It wanted the alpha spot and I'd be damned if I gave it up. From the second the blood bond had taken effect, we'd been battling—and I wasn't about to concede.

Astor came to check on me once and managed to slip me some more drugs. The pills kept me sedated enough that my thoughts were inaccessible through the night. But now, I was awake, and Gordon Steppe was pressing into my awareness like water through a thin sheet.

He wanted to merge. My head hurt and my chest pounded with the effort of keeping him at bay. I lay down, pulling my knees to my chest, and curled into a tight ball. It probably wasn't an effective way conserve my strength to huddle this way, but I pretended it did some good.

Across the room, the lock turned over with a click and the door opened. I rolled over, expecting Astor again, but it was Mr. Lexington instead. He was shaved and dressed in a gray suit and, for once, his strange scent didn't knock me over upon arrival. Something was different. I sniffed. He smelled like fresh air that could only have come from his being outside this place.

I sat up when he came close. He offered me the mug in his hand. "Drink this," he said.

"What is it?" I asked as I reached for it, but he didn't bother to answer.

I stared into the murky white liquid inside the little cup. It looked like watered-down milk, but I knew better. Nothing they'd done to me or asked of me was as pleasant as that. I'd been poked and prodded, smacked and shoved. But the worst was the bond trying to shove its way from my veins to my brain. I'd choose physical assault over this type of warfare any day.

Mr. Lexington sneered while I hesitated and I didn't need a bond to tell me that he was clearly hoping I'd refuse the drink so he could do whatever necessary to forcibly convince me. No way could I stand up to that *and* block out the bond trying to shove its way in. And he knew it.

I hesitated a little longer but, in the end, I took the shot.

The liquid was cold and sickly sweet in my mouth. It felt fuzzy—almost like champagne bubbles in my stomach. Warmth spread from my belly to my chest and then it dissipated and I felt like me again.

Mr. Lexington took the empty cup and gestured for me to follow. "Come on. Mr. Steppe wants a word," he said.

"I'm not dressed," I said, gesturing to the sweatpants and long-sleeved tee I was still wearing from last night.

"Luckily it's not a formal event," he said. "Come on."

I followed him out the door and fell into step behind him with two armed guards behind me. Not that I planned to try anything. My entire focus was on keeping Gordon out and myself conscious. There wasn't anything left for an escape attempt. I barely noticed the state of my surroundings as we made our way back to the clinic.

Astor greeted us just inside the door. He wrung his hands when he spotted me. "Goodness gracious. You're here."

"What's going on?" I asked.

"Nothing. You're here," he repeated. His left brow twitched twice as often as he blinked.

"Yes," I said slowly. "And so is Steppe and … Olivia," I said by way of greeting as I spotted the group assembled.

Steppe and a healthy-looking Olivia stood at the center of the room, halfway between the empty rows of cots and the metal cages. Behind them, along the wall, stood a row of guards. All armed. All with matching expressions of blind obedience. And Steppe thought my pack was a bunch of lap dogs.

"Tara, how are you feeling?" Gordon asked. Something stabbed at the edges of my thoughts, a silent inquiry to go along with the question, and I scowled.

"You tell me," I said, wandering closer to where they stood.

A table had been set up with various medical supplies strewn about. Several tubes of blood, now empty, lay discarded between torn packets of alcohol swabs and bandages. I gave each of them a once-over and spotted a bandage peeking out from underneath Olivia's sleeve.

My eyes narrowed. "What am I doing here?" I asked.

"Proving yourself," Steppe said.

"And either killing or saving your pathetic uncle in the process," Olivia added, earning a warning glare from Steppe.

My pulse sped and I glanced to where Astor stood huddled in the corner near the door. Guards stood nearby, awaiting orders.

"What do you want from me?" I asked, wary now.

"You need to stop fighting the inevitable and let me in," Steppe said. He leaned toward Olivia but I could still hear every word as he said, "She's stronger than her pack mate. Still fighting this losing battle and shoving me out."

Olivia folded her arms, obscuring the bandage. Her color was lovely and that fact alone made my jaw ache for her flesh. "Not for long. She'll choose. Just like the rest of them."

"So you say. We'll see," Steppe said. He straightened and raised his chin at one of the guards. "Bring her out."

A door opened. I hadn't noticed it before, wedged between a gap in the cages on my left, but now three armed guards stepped through. Their weapons were drawn and the moment they entered the room, they turned and pointed guns at the doorway.

A moment later, a girl stepped through. Her head was down, both cheeks swollen and red. Her exposed arms were bruised and she walked with a limp. For a second, I couldn't believe my eyes. But the piece of Steppe that sat in the bleachers of my subconscious applauded and I knew I wasn't seeing things.

She stopped just inside the room, eyes aimed at the floor.

I gasped. "Victoria?" I asked.

Slowly, she raised her eyes to mine. Her eyes widened, then filled with moisture. It was the only reaction she gave at seeing me. And then, just as quickly, she ducked her head again and stared at the tiled floor. If she saw her father across the room, she gave no indication. No sarcastic remarks, no witty comebacks. It broke my heart—and made me determined to fight Steppe to the very end for doing this to her.

I growled and took a step, ready to launch myself at the man to blame for this, but the guards swiveled and re-aimed their weapons at me. "Hold it there," Steppe said and I stopped.

"Right reaction. Wrong target," he said.

"What does that even mean? Why did you do this to her?" I demanded. Before he could answer, I turned to Victoria. "Which one of them did this to you?"

She didn't respond.

"She's not going to answer you," Olivia said.

I rounded on her. "You will, though. I can promise you that," I said.

"So quick to point fingers, cast blame." Steppe nodded at one of the guards over my head and for a second, I thought they were being ordered to grab me. I braced myself for it but instead, they moved away and grabbed hold of Mr. Lexington.

"What the hell?" he demanded, twisting in an effort to break free, but they held fast. "What are you doing?" he yelled.

Steppe barely flicked a glance in his direction before his gaze fixed on me. "This is the part where you make that choice you wanted so badly," he told me.

"I'm not giving up my wolf," I said.

"I wouldn't dream of asking. This is a different kind of choice but a choice nonetheless." His gaze slid left to a mute Victoria and then right to a still struggling and now furious Mr. Lexington. "The choice is your friend or her father. You must kill one of them. The other gets to live."

"No way. Absolutely not," I said. "You want me to carry out your orders, distract myself so you can slip in and take the alpha role. Not happening."

"You know, I may not have full access yet, but I've made some interesting discoveries just spending some time at the outskirts," Steppe said. "You miss your pack. Their voices. The mental company. You enjoyed the bond."

I didn't answer. I couldn't. He wasn't wrong, but I knew where this was going and it wasn't even close to the same thing. And internally, it was taking everything I had to keep him blocked while trying to figure out how to end this standoff. I was not, under any circumstances, going to kill Victoria Lexington.

The irony of it wasn't lost on me. Once upon a time, I would've actually entertained the idea of taking her out. But now, after everything we'd been through, I'd do anything to protect her. And unfortunately, that included refraining from killing her God-awful dad while she was forced to watch.

"You could have that camaraderie again, you know," Steppe said, smiling as he stirred the mental pot.

My reasoning became muddled. Hazy. And I glared back at him. "Get out of my head," I said.

"Make your choice," he said.

"Neither."

"Then you've sealed both their fate. And the fate of your uncle. It's a shame. I would've thought you had enough blood on your hands by now. Olivia."

She nodded at the two guards still hovering beside Victoria and then at the two near Astor. They took a step back, dropped their weapons, and planted their feet. The air around them shivered and then popped and fabric exploded, raining down in a pile beside them. One by one, they shifted, dropping to all fours as they became mangy, nearly emaciated Werewolves.

They locked onto their targets, two aimed at Victoria and two at Astor. With slow steps, they approached, jaws open, growling and snarling.

"Stop this!" I yelled.

"Only you can do that," Steppe said.

I jerked toward the sound of snapping teeth; the last two guards had shifted and were advancing on Mr. Lexington. He backed away and fell onto an empty cot, scrambling back toward the wall it butted against. It wouldn't do a bit of good. They were all going to die; none of them had the strength or skill to stop it.

I screamed at my wolf but it only shrank farther away from my grasp. Steppe's slimy mental fingers grasped for a firmer grip and I screamed again, struggling for control that was quickly slipping away.

"Stop! I'll choose!"

Olivia flicked her chin and the wolves paused. I looked at the one closest to me. It had a mangy coat of dull brown, scarred and matted in places. It smelled different than any of the hybrids I'd ever bonded with and I realized, not for the first time, these were different. Not Olivia's original creations. Not from Miles.

Something about them was familiar. The subtle slanting of their eyes, the scrawny, sinewy build of their muscles. But I couldn't quite place it and there wasn't time. Whatever it was, they were obviously bonded with Olivia now. Some failed experiment on Steppe's part, made into his very own disposable army.

Inside the walls of my mind, a voice whispered promises of information in exchange for my surrender. *Screw you, Gordon Steppe. I'm shutting you out.*

Gordon blinked.

"Your choice," he prompted, irritation pulling the corners of his mouth down. "Which one will you kill?"

I hesitated, not sure whether to hate myself or Steppe for whatever happened next. The silence stretched and my stomach twisted with dread and indecision.

I looked at Victoria, thinking of our friendship, such as it was. The way we'd been at odds during our term at Wood Point and then our slow progression toward something resembling friendship since she and Logan had become a couple. Even in her worst moments of cruelty, I understood her. She was the way she was for a reason. Namely, the man standing across the room.

Mr. Lexington. I looked at him, contemplating. But he wasn't watching me. He was staring at his daughter, his expression pained. Concern was etched into the space between his brows. And even though they looked nothing alike, for some reason, Mr. Lexington's worry made me think of Astor the day he'd transfused my blood with George's, creating that first bond. He hadn't wanted to do it; he knew better than anyone how complex it was to bond with someone. But George would have died without it. There was no changing my mind.

I thought about after that, how I'd fought the bond's pull—and George—and managed to shut him out. At least for a while. That's what I was doing now, with Steppe, but I already knew from experience it was only a matter of time before I had to let Steppe in or let it kill me.

And while I waited, I had to kill someone else.

This moment was such a freaking mess.

"Your choice," Steppe repeated, louder now. Olivia huffed in impatience. "Do it now. Or your time is up," he added.

"I choose Mr. Lexington," I said. Behind me, Mr. Lexington slumped—in relief? "But you have to call off your dogs," I added.

Steppe's eyes lit up. "Done." He nodded at Olivia, who snapped her fingers at her new pack. They stepped back and filed toward the door.

"Her too," I said, nodding at Olivia.

"No way," she said.

I crossed my arms. "She goes or I don't choose." Olivia opened her mouth to say something, but I cut her off. "And we both know you want my willpower broken bad enough. This is a small concession."

"Fine. Olivia, wait outside," Steppe said.

"Gordon, I don't think—" she began.

"I don't care what you think. We both know how important this is. Just do it," he snapped.

She threw a death stare his way but he didn't even bother to acknowledge her. Fuming, she stalked out. The guards all followed and the door shut behind them.

"And then there were five," Steppe said, flashing a slippery smile. "You're up."

I took a deep breath and walked over to Mr. Lexington.

"I'm sorry," I said.

He cleared his throat. "Don't be," he said in a small voice. "You let my daughter live."

"It wasn't for you," I said.

"Doesn't matter. Tell her I love her."

My brow quirked. "She's right there. Tell her yourself."

He shook his head. "Some words are so overdue, they're worthless. Just get on with it."

I searched his face for proof that he meant that. Did he actually want me to hurry up and kill him? I shook my head and refocused, blocking out the man standing in front of me waiting to die. Or his daughter watching across the room. And my terrified uncle still hovering in the corner. At least, I thought he was.

I glanced over, but Astor wasn't there. What the—

"I'm waiting," Steppe said.

No more time.

I turned to face Mr. Lexington again and tried to look like I was about to deliver a fatal blow. Was he not even going to fight back? He eyed me with a dubious expression. Neither one of us believed what I was about to do.

Against the walls of my mind, the darkness leaned in. Very deliberately, I squared my shoulders—and lowered my defenses.

Instantly, the teetering grip on the edges of my mind became a stronghold. The dark tentacles surged in and latched on, suction cups of greed against the stores of my will.

I could feel its triumph. Its eagerness to explore the reaches of my knowledge, my memories. But more importantly, I felt its distraction. This was it. There wouldn't be another chance.

With a final fleeting glance at Mr. Lexington, I turned on my heel and leaped.

Chapter Seven

Steppe's desire for access to my thoughts was more consuming than I'd imagined. His distraction was total. I launched myself across the room and slammed into him, taking both of us down in a grappling heap before he ever saw me coming.

My advantage ended there.

Get off me!

His was the order of an alpha and my body responded in kind. In my haste to get to him, I'd left myself wide open. He was in. And I wasn't entirely in charge.

Whatever was left of my subdued wolf reared at the order and I doubled back, snagging the edges of Gordon's clothing as he rolled away. I hooked a finger into his belt loop and yanked. I threw myself at him, clawing and punching and hoping like hell I'd do enough damage before Olivia returned to have gained some leverage.

Steppe's insistence in my mind was like a steel plate against my will. I struggled to break through, but I couldn't quite get there. Instead, we wrestled and rolled in a sort of stalemate grappling match.

Behind me, the door opened, and I bit back a yell as I realized Olivia must have returned. My chance had slipped away. And now, I really would be forced to kill Mr. Lexington.

At the sound of a gunshot, my panic paused, and I whirled. Two more shots followed in quick succession. Someone cried out, the words drowned out by the sound of a fourth shot, and then the yelp of a wolf before it died off.

Steppe shoved me off him and we both sat up, searching for the source of the sound. Beside the open door, Astor stood gripping a gun in two shaking hands. Three guards-turned-wolves lay on the floor at his feet. Their edges shook as their bodies settled into one form or another, a final shift as death claimed them.

In front of Astor, Olivia stood, expression wary, hands out.

"Careful, old man," she said in a breathy voice. It cracked on the last word and I knew she must be feeling the loss of the three Werewolves. Suddenly, she hunched over, bending at the knees and stumbling back a few steps in an effort to stay on her feet.

Her last two wolves hovered behind her, waiting for orders.

"Don't speak to me, devil," Astor spat at her. I couldn't tell if he was waving the gun for effect or just overcome with the trembling that stemmed from his buckling elbows.

Beside me, Steppe pushed to his feet. I could already sense his intention and reacted purely on reflex. I grabbed his ankle and wrapped my hands around it, sliding across the floor as he took a step.

"Let me go," he yelled, shaking his ankle in an attempt to break my hold. But I tightened my grip and shoved at the force in my mind echoing his words. The bass of his internal voice hurt my head.

"Gordon," Olivia said, her voice pained.

I tightened my grip on Steppe with a smug sort of relief.

"You'll let us leave now," Astor said, arms shaking. I could see the fear and indecision in his eyes. And I remembered that look from the memory I'd borrowed from Steppe, the night he'd killed Mr. Sandefur. I wasn't sure how much longer he would hold that gun in place.

Let us go, I sent through the bond.

At the edges of his presence, the darkness screamed at me, echoing from temple to temple as Gordon fought against my attempt to dominate.

Steppe didn't answer, but he didn't need to; his silence said it all. Olivia cried out and moved toward Astor in stumbling steps, but Mr. Lexington shot over, inserting himself between them. The remaining wolf growled, but it didn't attempt to intervene. Its yellow eyes were unfocused and glassy. I wondered how much of Olivia's pain it felt—and I hoped it was enough to distract it.

Broken Blood

As if he'd read my thoughts and agreed, Gordon sighed heavily. "This isn't over," he said simply.

A hand appeared above me, dirty and bruised. I followed its arm and found Victoria standing over me. I let go of Steppe's ankle and let her help me up.

She smiled at me. "We should go. I'm sick of the wet dog smell all over this place," she said quietly.

I laughed. It came out a little wild. I wasn't sure if it was my own loose hinges after being here so long or Steppe's contribution to my behaviors. But I didn't care. I swung my elbow backward, landing it square in his ribs for good measure. He doubled over, coughing and gasping.

"We're going. Don't wait up," I said and looked at Lexington. "Do you have the keys to the cages?"

"They're on the wall. There," Mr. Lexington said, nodding at a board filled with keys just inside the door.

"Victoria, help me with them," I said.

One by one, Victoria and I matched keys to cages and opened the doors. Mr. Lexington deposited Olivia inside the first one. She screamed from the moment the door shut on her and the lock clicked.

"You won't be able to hide forever," she yelled, her eyes bloodshot, her face red with anger. "We will find you. You think you've won but you've only delayed the inevitable."

I ignored her and returned to where Steppe stood. "You're up," I said.

Instead of answering out loud, the voice in my mind went into overdrive. *You can't do this, you can't do this, you can't do this,* it whispered over and over again, an unrelenting alpha chant. The darkness slammed against the tender spots of my consciousness. Memories. Promises. Affections. All of them were ripped into, faces blotted out, hearts left bleeding.

You cannot leave me when you and I are the same, the voice taunted. *Don't forget, according to the world waiting for you out there, you have just as much blood on your hands as I do.*

"Stop it," I said, but he continued his assault and I faltered under the weight of it. My mother's face floated to the center of my mind, smiling and cheering. An old cheer competition. She clapped and beamed, full of pride. Until her expression morphed into accusation and betrayal and she screamed at me about letting her down. Letting everyone down.

A snatched conversation floated through my mind via Steppe's recollection. "We would only proceed with the adoption if you want it," my mother was saying. And then it was gone and I was left hollow and confused until the next image swooped it.

And Wes. His face turned away from me, smiling softly at someone I couldn't see. And the darkness whispered to me that he'd already moved on. Already found someone else to love. I reached out for the table's edge to steady myself and almost missed. The darkness laughed.

"Tara?" Victoria asked, taking my elbow. "Are you all right?"

"I'm good," I managed.

I pressed my lips together, grinding my teeth, and bit down on the pain. With all of my strength, I shoved back against the lies licking their way into my heart. Steppe grimaced and I knew I'd made headway. I shoved again, this time facing him, but I couldn't shove him all the way out. Not now that I'd let him in.

Inch by inch, I chased him into a space where I could find myself again and pushed off from the table. With Victoria's help, I stumbled to Astor and laid a hand on his shoulder. He handed me the gun. "Thanks," I told him.

He patted my head and his eyes took on that vacant look that I knew so well. "Anything for a niece," he sang, already checked out. "Now where are my slippers?"

"You're wearing them," I said.

"Oh. Right."

He wandered off and I used the gun to herd the last wolf to the waiting metal cage. He whimpered, hesitating at the open door, his cries growing louder. I faltered, wondering if I was doing the right thing in forcing him in with Steppe and Olivia, but then he rounded on me and our eyes met. And my memory mixed with Steppe's own knowledge bank, newly accessible, and I realized where I knew these wolves from.

"You," I said, bending closer and breathing the word. "I remember. In the woods last spring. I left school looking for Miles and you found me ... you attacked me. I thought you belonged to Miles, that you worked for him."

The memory came flooding back and I sucked in a breath as it filled into the gaps left by Steppe's knowledge of that day. The wolf glared at me in stubborn silence, his contempt written as clearly as the darkness he'd long since embraced. I waved the gun in his face and shoved him into the cage.

"You've made your choice," I told him. "And it wasn't me. The metal hurts, doesn't it?"

He growled but I turned away, disgusted. I'd have to take some time later to think this through but for now—

"Olivia is right, you know. You're only delaying the inevitable. I'm sure I don't have to explain this to you … out loud," Gordon said.

He sat hunched over in the squat cage but somehow, even with his legs pulled up to his chest, his socks poking out from where his pants rode up, he managed to look completely at ease with his current predicament. Worse, he didn't look worried—and that rattled me. Something I knew he'd already gleaned the moment the smile spread across his face. "The world thinks you're the villain," he said.

"The world knows better than to believe you." I shoved him back against my mental walls but there was no chasing him out. Not entirely.

He tilted his head knowingly. "Do they?"

I walked over to his cage and stood before him. "Your days as the leader of CHAS, the voice of Hunters, are numbered. I will remove you."

"Sounds threatening. Just like the world already expects thanks to the videos I've been releasing regularly of all your exploits." His smile stayed in place, lazy and infuriating as ever. "And when you've usurped my authority, then what? You'll rule? Please. Even I can see what that will look like to your constituents. A power play, and not a very good one. You might be able to overthrow me—"

"Usurp, usurp," Astor began.

Mr. Lexington growled at him and he fell abruptly quiet.

"But our laws are steeped in tradition," Steppe pointed out calmly. "Hundreds of years old. And the law states the director's seat is generational. A family business."

"You don't have family," I pointed out.

A strange sensation washed over the bond and Steppe's expression flickered with something. It was gone too fast to name and he said, "Quite. In the event of my death, the new director is selected from the board. A board your family no longer serves on. A board that consists only of myself and Mr. Lexington here come to think of it. Tell me, will you nominate Mr. Lexington here? Use him as your puppet after condemning me for the same?"

He pressed on before I could think of an answer. "You and I are the same, Tara. The sooner you realize that, the sooner we can get on with the business of cleaning up the gutters of our world. Eliminate those that would threaten our exposure and survival to the humans."

"Please. You're not here to save anyone but yourself," I said.

"I won't deny that my motives will solidify my leadership and remove any threat to my position." He cocked his head. "But then, isn't that what you're doing as well?"

I didn't answer.

"I know you think you were born to bring the worlds together," he said. "They told you to make a choice. They called it destiny." He snorted. "In the end, we're the same. We both want to sit on the throne." He leaned forward, his face almost touching the bars. "The difference is," he whispered, "I already do."

His words were punctuated with a mental jab that forced me to take a step backward before I caught myself. My thoughts twisted and squeezed until some of the things he said began to make sense.

I shook my head to clear it and, when that didn't work, I slammed my palm against my temple.

"Tara," Victoria said in alarm. She stared back at me with wide, glassy eyes and a neck that swiveled this way and that in jerky movements. Seeing her still so shaken was enough to bring me back—and to help me make my decision. I couldn't trust myself with Gordon in my head—not even if he was locked in a cage. He was right...

"Unlock his cage," I said.

"Tara, no," Victoria said and tears sprang to her eyes.

I took her hand, and when she tried to pull away I held on. "He's in my head, Vic. He's reading every thought I have. If we leave him here, he'll get free. And I can't ever hope to stop him if that happens. We have to bring him with us."

She took a deep breath and, with a tortured expression, nodded. "Does that mean we're bringing my dad?" she whispered.

I hesitated, wondering which answer she was hoping for, but her expression was unreadable. "Yes," I said.

She opened her mouth, shut it again, and then said, "Don't trust the two of them together."

Mr. Lexington winced at her words, but he recovered quickly.

Broken Blood

Victoria didn't look his way and I squeezed her hand. "I know," I said.

I turned to Astor. "Can you find some medical supplies for Victoria?" I asked him. "Gather whatever we might for a few days."

He looked up from where he'd been running his hands over the clean sheets of the cots and nodded. "Sure, sure. Where do we go next?" he asked, cocking his head.

Victoria and Mr. Lexington hovered close by. I could feel their eyes on me, asking the same question. I looked at them both, the weariness of my internal war taking its toll. I couldn't leave them behind. Not even Mr. Lexington. It was too dangerous. Besides, I'd rather have him close, to keep an eye on him. And I was certain Grandma wouldn't mind a word with him either. They'd served on CHAS for a number of years together.

I looked back at Astor and smiled tiredly at him and then Victoria. "Home," I said softly. "We're going home."

Chapter Eight

Victoria stared into the woods lining the far end of the rest stop with pursed lips. Her blonde hair was matted and hung limply in a ponytail, her bruised arms hidden by the jacket we'd found thanks to Mr. Lexington on the way out. She'd crossed her arms in a selfie hug, her fingers tucked underneath her elbows against the chilly October air. Even from my vantage point, I could see the pain she was in. Not all of it physical.

I glanced up and down the otherwise empty lot and made my way to where she stood. I planted my feet, folded my own arms against the cold, and waited.

After a few minutes, my breath started to puff in front of me and I watched as it gathered into a small cloud and then dissipated. Over and over, I watched the process. Even when the cold seeped through my layers and I shivered in my hoodie and sweats, I watched it. And stood. And waited.

The trees in the distance were a mixture of bare oaks and regal pines. A thin layer of frost covered the ground in the graying evening light. I'd always considered a wintery Virginia landscape to be barren and lonely, but seeing it now, I knew I'd been wrong. It wasn't lonely. Just waiting. Dormant. Like my time in that cell. I breathed it in, along with the scent of a sharper cold to come once night fell, and hugged my arms to myself in gratitude.

After so many weeks in a cold, concrete room, I planned to never take the outdoors for granted again. That included all of Mother Nature, no matter her temperature.

"Logan knew you'd get out," Victoria said, jarring me.

"What? When did you speak to him?" I asked.

"I didn't. I overheard Mr. Sandefur ... he tried calling Logan all the time. Even when he was supposed to be forcing me to find them all, he'd..." Her nose twitched, but she made no sound as a single tear streaked down her cheek.

I waited.

"Edie got him out. In the warehouse. Steppe—my father—knocked you out after my mom fell. And the police started grabbing us all. Edie showed up and there was a split second where I could see it all so clearly." She licked her dry lips and stared away from me, some memory replaying while she spoke. "I was closer but I couldn't—I couldn't let them have him. So, I ran. I shoved Logan at her and I ran."

"You saved Logan," I said.

"But not the others. The police took Wes. And George. I don't know what happened to Emma. I can only assume your grandma got her out. And then Astor showed up and I wondered if anyone had really gotten away. They wouldn't tell me anything."

"Not even your dad?"

"I never saw him until today," she said and the hurt in her voice was impossible not to feel. "I only knew they were all free because Gordon made me track them."

I didn't know what to say to that. She'd known more than I did, but at what cost? I looked at the purple bruise blooming along her jaw. Neither of us spoke for a long moment.

"He only kept me alive so my dad would obey him," she added softly. Her voice didn't so much break the silence as lace itself through it. I glanced over, but she was still staring straight ahead at the tree trunks and naked branches that dotted the landscape before melding into deep shadows.

I'd already assumed the reality of her words and now, I didn't know what to say. In the silence, the only sound was the engines as they raced past on the highway at our backs.

"I don't want to go home," she said when I didn't answer.

In this, we agreed. Lexington Manor. Home. It was the last place I wanted to go, but we didn't have a choice. According to Victoria, everywhere else was being watched. Including the studio apartment Wes had rented. We'd nearly passed by there on our way out of the city, according to Victoria. The only thing holding me back from deserting them all in search of it was Victoria's refusal to tell me the address. And Steppe, waiting in the van.

My chest panged with irrational disagreement at what we were doing even as I saw the logic in it. "Do you believe your dad?" I asked. "About the others being watched, I mean."

Small lines pulled at the corners of Victoria's eyes. Her profile looked ten years older than her driver's license. She reminded me of Cord, months ago, when Olivia had captured and tortured her. She'd almost died. And in the midst of her pain and agony, she'd never complained. Never cried out. Somehow, it'd only made her stronger. Wiser. Victoria's face looked that way now.

"Yes." She let out a heavy sigh. "I've seen enough of the footage Steppe has put out there about you and well, all of us. Beside, after everything he's done, my dad's ... trying to make amends to me, I think. He saved me in there. Did everything Steppe told him so that I would live."

"But you said everyone scattered after I was taken. Grandma and my mom and Jack and Fee ... they ran. How did he find them all?" I pressed.

Victoria's gaze cut to mine, and in it was a vacancy that only came from complete loss. I knew because I'd been there. "He used me," she said, the vacancy bleeding into apology. "I tracked them for him. I'm sorry."

I blinked at her. Some Hunters were born with special gifts. Kind of like my Aunt Vera—although hers had killed her in the end. She had been able to draw magical wards that acted like invisible bars shutting a place out or in for safety against enemies. She'd also seen visions of possible futures, a gift that had led to my alternating commitment and rebellion to this leadership role everyone always seemed to throw at me in a crisis.

Victoria's gift was tracking. All she needed was a personal item belonging to whomever it was you wanted to find and she could sense them to the ends of the earth.

Broken Blood

"All of them?" I asked in disbelief. Her lack of answer or change in expression told me all I needed to know. And if that weren't enough, there were the raised welts along her neck and the cuts still healing across her cheeks.

She went back to staring out over the trees behind the brick buildings that held restrooms. "He sent teams ... to watch them. Or attack. I don't know," she said in a strangled voice. And I understood the bruises and cuts she wore. She'd fought back, but in the end, that hadn't mattered. The damage was done. At her hands.

I couldn't tell her it was okay. I couldn't tell her don't worry. She wouldn't have accepted it if I had. I knew what guilt looked like. And I thought of Alex. Had he been on those teams? Watching and reporting back to Steppe every move my loved ones made while I'd been away?

Victoria didn't speak again. Without another word, I turned and made my way back to the van where the others waited. Anger simmered, unfair but undeniable, in the corner of my heart. I couldn't bring myself to unleash it on her.

I couldn't yell or scream or accuse her of anything. I'd killed her mother.

Did this make us even?

Never. You will never be even. Or like her. Or like any of them.

Gordon's voice in my mind was like salt in my wounds. Not the average table-salt variety. The Himalayan sea salt kind, large and course and rubbing. Thanks to our handy new connection, he knew exactly when and where to hit me.

I slammed the van door open and climbed inside—all the way to the back until we were nose to nose. He sat in the corner, wrists and ankles bound. Instead of replying to his dig, I rubbed at the edges of the tape covering his mouth, making sure it was secure.

It was.

In a clean, swift motion, I yanked it free. Gordon cried out and shut his eyes, mumbling. I ignored him while I cut a fresh piece of tape and secured it over his mouth. He glared at me and I smiled.

When I'd finished, I flopped into the other corner and stared at the paneling where a window would've been if this weren't a creeper van. A few minutes later, Victoria returned and we were moving again. Mr. Lexington merged back onto the highway in silence. In the passenger seat, even Astor was quiet. He had been since we left, but I was too wrapped up in my own distress to check on him. The gun I'd taken from him was tucked into my bag under the seat. At least he wouldn't have to hurt anyone else.

Victoria sat behind her dad on the bench seat, eyes forward, shoulders stiff. She still hadn't eaten anything even after our fast food run before exiting the city. But I couldn't quite care just now. She'd led the enemy to everyone's doorstep. And now that we were free, we were still running.

My chin quivered and I bit down on my tongue in an effort to stop the tears that threatened. Every mile that put me farther from DC was a fresh heart break. I'd suggested calling but no one had a working number for Wes or Derek or Jack. My mother and Grandma were being watched, Victoria had insisted.

"The only reason we got out without a fight was because his teams are all deployed," Mr. Lexington had insisted. "They're out watching the rest of your friends. But when he doesn't check in, his absence will alert them," he'd warned. "We have to leave now. We'll stop and contact your family when you're safe."

He'd had a point, as much as I'd hated to admit it. Now, I felt Gordon's eyes on me, his mental voice whispering from the edges of my mind where I'd shoved him. Reveling. He was enjoying my misery.

My heart ached for Wes. Or Chris. Or George. Anyone else whose mind rooting around in my own didn't feel so awful or so much like losing.

But they were gone. And all I had was—

Me. You have me now. And I am much more capable and powerful than any of your pack ever was.

Despite the quicksand coating my determination, I glared at him. My strength waned and the voice in my head grew louder, closer.

You and I are one mind now. And one intention.

Along with the words came a picture. My eyes cut up to Mr. Lexington in the driver's seat. Hands draped over the wheel, eyes forward as he navigated us through the sea of red parking lights that made up rush hour traffic on the interstate.

"I'm not going to hurt him," I said quietly. I refused to speak through the bond right now, to acknowledge our connection in that way.

Again, the mental voice didn't so much speak as deliver an image. And desire. I couldn't tell how much of it belonged to Steppe and how much of it was mine.

Fury rose up, blooming hot and heavy in my chest. And I realized why Gordon was suggesting it in the first place. My compliance would solidify the bond—and his role as alpha. My ability to refuse was overshadowed by the fact that part of me wanted to attack Lexington even without being ordered. I could still remember him attacking me in the warehouse, fighting to injure me or worse.

I bit my lip and forced my own willpower to the surface. My wolf, buried deep, stirred. *I don't take orders,* I growled. *I give them. I am alpha.*

There is no alpha. If you'd let your resistance down, you would see that there is no alpha. No master. Only us, together; one force.

I have no intention of letting down my walls, I snapped. *Save yourself some time and get out of my head!*

Oh, but your mind is such an interesting place.

I tried to ignore what memories of mine he'd already sifted through and searched instead for a worthy comeback. A believable threat that I could actually make good on. A way to defeat him against the invasion I was experiencing. But there was nothing.

Instead, a snapshot of a memory forced itself to the surface. Mr. Lexington standing as a wolf on a lonely desert road. Me in a car with George beside me, fast approaching the wolf blocking our way. George and I barely missing a collision as the wheel jerked sideways. My desire for retribution.

He underestimates you…

Hatred clung to the words, and I realized how badly I want to attack him. Or how badly Steppe wanted me to. I couldn't quite pinpoint the difference. Anger pulsed through me. I'd already been furious when I got in the car, I realized. And he was using it.

Horror crept in like a silken cloud, misting at the edges of my mind and holding there, a wet curtain of dread. This wasn't a physical force I could combat. It wasn't even mind games. It was me against me. Because I really wanted to give in and do what he'd suggested.

I tried to push him out, but I was too long out of practice at shoving away an unwanted lurker. Through the darkness and cruel thoughts, Steppe's laughter rang in my mind. My muscles tightened and my hands curled into fists. I glared over at him, my skin humming in readiness.

Instead of attacking the target I was being fed, I launched myself at

Steppe. He went down underneath my weight with a grunt that escaped mostly through his nose. Victoria yelled something but I didn't bother listening to the words as I slammed my fist into Steppe's unguarded gut. He grunted again and curled up on the floor of the van, trying to protect himself without the benefit of arms and hands. The van lurched as Mr. Lexington slammed on the brakes and veered onto the shoulder.

My wolf howled on the inside. On the outside, I heard myself yelling without ever making a conscious decision to produce sound. My fists pummeled—his face, his throat, his ribs. And my jaw ached to elongate into something with canines. I wasn't a human. I was a wolf trapped in a human's body.

I was the alpha. Dammit.

I crouched over Steppe full of rage as I thought about how he'd stolen my wolf. I still didn't know how. And I wanted nothing so much as my beast in this moment. Somewhere in the midst of my yearning, the thirst for his blood on my hands waned. My need for violence was overshadowed by a sudden sense of awareness. And pain.

I felt it inside me as a dull ache that pricked sharp with every draw of breath. I'd hurt him. And I was hurting me.

This isn't right.

I barely had time to register my own internal voice of conscience before reality crashed in around me. Victoria's hands grabbed my shoulders and then upper arms as she pulled me off of Steppe. I let her, chest heaving with my efforts, and stumbled backward onto my ass. My shoulders bumped Victoria's legs and I rested there, catching my breath.

Huddled in the corner, Steppe wheezed through his nose. Blood and snot ran from his nostrils, down the tape covering his mouth. His eyes were wide in surprise and pain. His chest rose as it filled with air and then fell heavily as he sank farther back against the corner and away from me.

"What happened?" Victoria asked.

There was no judgment in her voice and I knew, at least when it came to Steppe, she wouldn't condemn me for a single punch. I picked myself up and sat on the edge of the bench seat, turning my back on Steppe. I needed distance. But my mind wasn't something I could run from.

Victoria slid onto the seat, and I felt her eyes running the length of me. I didn't know what she was looking for, but I wasn't capable of giving anything of value. Not when I was barely hanging onto myself as it was.

Then just give in and let go. It'll make you stronger. Clearer. And you need that if you're going to lead.

The anger was a dull ache now, mixing with my homesickness and my despair. Muddling the fury I felt at Victoria for her forced betrayal. For the disdain I felt for Olivia and Lexington and even Alex. Every negative emotion melded into one and it made me sick. My stomach rolled with nausea. I needed out of this van. I needed Wes.

One thing my most recent failure had taught me was that I needed help and support. Someone on my side. My friends and family. A team. Not the one I was currently stuck with. Two Lexingtons, an enemy, and a mad scientist were not enough support for the mental war I waged. And maybe that team could think thoughts of victory for me since I wasn't capable. I was lucky just to hold up and not give in against the whispered offerings of sharing world domination. How would I ever defeat an enemy that knew my every thought even as it entered my own mind?

Chapter Nine

The phone rang three times before someone picked up. Enough time for me to lose patience and begin pacing. I was more focused on finishing the conversation so I could hang up and dial the next person than to even hear her voice. I was only calling her first because if she ever found out I didn't, she'd skin my wolf hide.

"Hello?" I heard after what felt like forever.

"Grandma?" I said. The wind seemed to rip the word from my throat as I offered it.

"Tara? Oh my God, Tara, is that you?" Before I could answer, there was muffled movement and then I heard, "Elizabeth, get over here. It's your daughter."

My mother's voice in the background sent waves of relief through me. I hadn't even realized the stress of worry until it unraveled at hearing them bickering in whispers over who got to hold the phone. Some things never changed.

"Tara?" my mother shrieked.

"It's me," I assured them. "I'm okay."

"Where are you?" Grandma demanded. "We've been searching high and low."

"I'm with Mr. Lexington and Steppe. In a van—"

"Tell us exactly where," Grandma said. "We'll be there faster than you can say tough titties."

"Does he know you're calling us?" my mother demanded.

"Just stop for a second," I said and they fell silent. "Yes, he knows I'm calling." I threw a glance back at the van in the darkened lot behind me where I knew Steppe waited, still tied and gagged. Which was mostly for everyone else's benefit since I could still hear him loud and clear in my mind. Ragging on me for being "that girl who called her mommy when she got into trouble." I ignored him and concentrated on filling them in.

"There was an … incident. Astor helped. It's kind of a long story. The important thing is that I'm free," I told them.

"What kind of incident?" my mother asked, worry coating the words until they were barely recognizable out of her mouth.

"I'll explain when I see you, I promise. I'm with Mr. Lexington. He's helping me. And I have Victoria and Astor and—"

"Don't trust Lexington," Grandma warned.

"He's working against us," my mother added.

"Guys!" I let out an exasperated sigh. Two months of captivity, of not speaking to them, of them probably wondering if I was dead, and this was their idea of a reunion. "I can't stay on the phone long. Mr. Lexington says we have to keep moving. It's not safe. We're going to meet up at his house so get in the car and drive. I'll meet you there as soon as you can make—"

"Lexington Manor?" Grandma snapped. "No. You can't go there, Tara. He's right, it's not safe."

"Why not?" I shot a look behind me at where Victoria was pacing. She had a phone to her ear as well. Gordon's actually. I couldn't make out the words but I knew she'd try Logan first. I hoped she reached him. I hoped he was okay. That they all were—

"Tara, this world is a lot different than you remember," my mom said gently. "We'll explain everything when we see you. But don't go to Lexington Manor."

"Where can we go?" I asked. "There isn't anywhere else safe. Mr. Lexington said all of our houses are being watched."

"They are," Grandma said. Her tone was grim and I wondered just how far I'd have to go in order to preserve Steppe's life once the others found us.

"What about…?" my mom asked in a muffled voice. There was

rustling on their end of the line while they whispered and probably tried covering the phone. Impatience got the better of me and I paced and huffed.

"I don't have all night," I said.

Even as I said it, my eyes scanned the trees for danger. I had no idea exactly who or what we were up against. None of them had been very specific in describing the danger, only to say that it was lurking everywhere. To always be on guard. And Lexington had insisted that we had exactly ten minutes at this rest stop to call everyone we could.

"Go to Flaherty's," Grandma said in a voice that brooked no argument.

"*Professor* Flaherty?" I asked. "My teacher from Wood Point?"

"That's the one. We'll meet you there," she said.

"But … how do you know…? I don't know where she lives."

"Astor's with you, right?" Grandma asked.

"Yes," I said.

"He can show you the way. We'll see you there…" She paused, calculating, and then added, "In the morning."

"Tara, be careful," my mom said.

"I will. You too," I said.

"We love you," they said in unison and I smiled.

"Love you too."

I'd barely hung up before punching the numbers that dialed my next call. Instead of pacing, I bounced. I didn't even know if this number still worked. Victoria had said he moved to DC to look for me after the police let him go. Maybe he'd changed numbers.

One ring. Two.

Victoria sniffled and I looked over in time to see a tear escape before she brushed it aside. Our eyes met but there was no time to read what had caused her tears before the voice on the other end of my phone snatched my attention.

"What?"

My knees threatened to buckle. Despite the less-than-warm greeting, the sound of that one word was like honey over warm bread.

"What?" he said again, this time warily. In the background, I heard glasses clinking, voices humming in vague conversation. Country music. But none of it really registered. It was only him. Just there, through the phone, so close.

Broken Blood

I licked my lips, my throat suddenly dry. "Wes?" I managed, my voice cracking. I tried again. "It's me."

The line went quiet for so long I checked to be sure the call hadn't dropped.

"Tara," he said. The sound of my name on his lips was like falling in love all over again.

"It's me," I said, warmth rushing up from my toes and flowing out into all the points on my body.

"Holy Christ. Where are you? How are you? Is this real?"

I laughed through tears that were already raining down my cheeks. "It's real," I assured him. "I'm somewhere west of the metro area. Near the mountains, I think. I'm free."

"You're free," he repeated and now that the anger was gone, his shock sounded laced with something not quite steady. Something a little slower than usual. "You got away from Steppe?"

"Yes, I…" I trailed off, my thoughts racing full speed ahead as I tried to pick carefully what to share and what to save. His face, God, I wanted to see his face. Did he have day-old stubble? Was he wearing after-shave? Cologne? His leather jacket that smelled like his car and—

"Whoa, slow down," he said, "Not so fast."

My thoughts skidded to a halt and my brows drew together. "I didn't say anything," I said. There was a too-long pause and then he smacked his lips together on an appreciative exhale. In the background, ice cubed clinked.

"Where are you?" I asked, finally picking up the background noise and piecing it together with his slow reactions.

He sighed. "I'm in a bar."

"What are you doing in a bar?" I snapped out before I could rein in my temper—or understand it. He was supposed to be looking for me, searching to the ends of the earth. Had he given up that easily and decided to drown himself in a bottle instead?

Something Steppe had said whispered through my mind, about Wes giving up on ever finding me and moving on, and I realized this wasn't my own anger or suspicion. This was being planted. I exhaled and forced it away; Steppe was not taking this moment from me.

"Turning on the mute button," he said and then hastily, "But now that I know I need the volume, consider me exiting."

"Whatever," I said, brushing it aside before I could dwell long enough for Steppe's anger to take hold. "I'm with Victoria and Astor. We're headed to Flaherty's, my professor from Wood Point. Grandma says we'll be safe to meet up there. Can you meet us?"

I decided not to mention Steppe. Or Victoria's dad. Not yet. Better to wait until we were face to face. Wes responded with a growl-wrapped curse and I winced, pulling the phone away from my ear and looking at it in surprise. For the second time, I felt like we were having entirely different conversations.

The wind whipped by in a particularly sharp gust. Goose bumps broke out over my arms and neck, shocking me with the intensity of their discomfort as I shivered. It'd been so long since I'd felt that sort of…

Wes let out a string of fast curses and in the background, glass shattered. Someone yelled something about paying for it. The line was jostled.

"Is everything okay?" I asked.

"No, everything is not— Tara, get out of there."

Behind me, Victoria's voice rose in a yell that cut off, and I turned, half-curious as to what was going on between her and Logan. But Victoria wasn't on the phone. I let out a growl of my own when I saw what had startled her.

In the darkness of the empty lot, orange beams played light and shadow off each other in a slanted graph. At the edges, I caught slippery movement before it slid away. The goose bumps on my arms rose as I spotted the object of her horror.

"Tara, there's someone there with you," Wes said. "Get out."

I had a fleeting moment to wonder how he'd known before the shadow emerged and spoke. "Put the phone down, sweetheart."

The wolf was enormous. Dark fur, powerful muscles that bunched when he shifted his paws, and teeth that glittered in the light of the street lamp. Two more like him crept from the shadows behind Victoria, but she never wavered from her wide-eyed stare at their leader. Her face was pale, stark white broken only by the brilliant purple bruise along her jaw and the harsh red marks slashing down her cheeks and throat. She was almost scarier than they were—if not for the fear in her eyes and the way her hands trembled at her sides.

I stared back at the wolf. He stood less than three feet from her, his jaw hanging open, flashing his ample canines to intimidate her—and me.

It was working.

"Tara?" Wes called through the phone that now hung suspended a foot away from my ear where my arms had flung out in a defensive position.

"I'm here," I said. The wolf's ears twitched.

"Everything's jumbled, I can't hear you," Wes said, his voice distant, like being filtered through a funnel. My inner wolf whined, willing Wes to sense the danger and come. But wherever he was now, it was too far to help us.

This one was all me.

"This is between us. Let her go," I told the wolf.

"Gladly. We're not here for her," the wolf growled. He took a step away from Victoria—toward me. My relief was short lived. Behind him, two more wolves moved in. I threw a desperate glance behind me and then backed away in a slanted retreat, trying to draw them away. I couldn't let them surround us.

I took another several steps sideways, away from the van where the others waited.

"Tara, talk to me," Wes yelled. "Tell me where you are." I ignored him but left the call connected. The wolf's eyes flickered to the phone.

"Tara?" one of the other wolves repeated from where he stood near Victoria. "Tara Godfrey?"

"Yes. What do you want?" I asked.

His head tilted and he shot a look at his friend. "We found her," he growled.

Victoria blinked as they drew closer, coming out of her frozen shock, and let out a small whimper. Inside my head, Steppe's presence was open curiosity. The only hint of concern seemed to be whether I would tell them he was here with us.

What a guy.

"Two minutes," Wes said, the words muffled by movement. I sighed. Wherever he thought I was, there was no way he could know for sure. Or get here. Or—

The wolf snorted. "He'll never make it in time."

"What do you want?" I repeated, my voice rising with desperation.

"We didn't want anything but to be left in peace," he shot back. "Look what we got instead. New laws that made us outcasts, fugitives.

We are criminals simply by the fact that we exist. What do I want? For being convicted before I was ever guilty, I want justice."

"None of that is my fault," I said.

"Don't even think about denying it. I know who you are. I've heard all about your war with CHAS. I've seen the footage of your destruction. It's your fault, your act of treason to your own kind that drove them to change the laws in the first place."

I had no idea where he was getting his information, but the look he wore made it clear he believed his own theory. Utterly. "Killing me won't change the law," I said.

"No, I'm not naïve enough to think anything will. I'm not here to change things," he said, creeping closer on silent paws.

Victoria backed away, but it only drew the other two wolves toward her. I took a step back, hoping to lead them toward me instead. But they didn't stray from their target. I bit my lip. Through the phone, I heard a car door slam and an engine rev. I couldn't allow myself to hope. There was no more time.

The black wolf opened its massive jaw and leaped for my throat.

I dropped the phone and sidestepped his angry teeth, closing my fists around a handful of fur as we both went down. Behind me, I heard Victoria yell over the sound of screeching tires and squealing brakes. Headlights cast a bright beam of light over me and the wolf, illuminating a patch of grass where the concrete ended and the picnic area began. I angled toward it as we fell. If I was going to be knocked over, that was the best place to hit the ground.

I managed only a glance of a rusty red fender before the momentum of my fall sent me rolling. I hung on and prayed I'd be at the far end of the wolf's open mouth when we righted ourselves again.

We both landed on our hip, side by side, limbs tangled. The wolf growled and twisted, intent on pinning me down. I knew if that happened, there'd be no getting up again. The wolf's jaw snapped and I scuttled backward, just far enough to avoid the teeth. The air between us echoed with a loud snapping sound as his jaw closed on empty air instead of my forearm.

There wasn't time to feel relieved before he twisted and arched out to bite at me again. I shoved him away, barely holding him back by the handful of neck fur I held. But then his weight shifted and I felt my shoulder rolling awkwardly. I tried pushing against his momentum, but my piddly hundred and ten pounds were no match for his mass. I rolled onto my back and his paws came down painfully in the fleshy space just below my shoulders. I cried out and fell still, pinned.

The wolf stared down at me with zero remorse in his wild eyes. There was no hesitation, only methodical purpose. He wasn't drawing it out. He wasn't hurrying. It wasn't about me. It was about justice. A fact I knew made arguing pointless.

I strained internally, willing, begging my wolf to take over. I could feel it rising, slowly, as if through mud. But it wasn't fast enough—or capable enough—to give me the form I needed in order to stop the inevitable. The wolf let out a low sound from deep in its throat, a growl turned howl, and it leaned in.

I gave up and shut my eyes and waited.

Hot breath washed over me and my muscles tensed in anticipation. I waited for the agony of sharp teeth cutting into my flesh—but it never came. A second later, the weight pinning me suddenly vanished. I heard a grunt and then a set of scuffling growls.

I opened my eyes and blinked at the empty space where the wolf had crouched a moment ago. In its place, a hand appeared.

I followed its arm up and my mouth fell open. "Cambria?" I said.

She stood over me, a flash of teeth gleaming in the glare from a new set of headlights. "In the flesh," she said. "And I come bearing gifts." She pointed to where Derek, fully Werewolf, was locked in a head-over-tail wrestling match with the wolf that had just tried to eat me.

"Derek," I said, my shoulders sagging now that the danger was being taken on by someone capable. "But how did you know I was here?" I asked, squinting up at Cambria again.

"GPS Barbie called Logan," she explained, nodding to where Logan and Victoria were locked in an embrace so tight, they looked like a two-headed paper doll. "You want some help up or are you going to hang out down there for the duration?"

I grinned at Cambria, took her offered hand, and let her pull me to my feet. The moment my body was upright, I threw my arms around her and squeezed tight. There was a suspended moment of indecision and then Cambria's arms wrapped around me, awkwardly patting, before morphing into a full-on death grip.

When we finally stepped back, her eyes brimmed with tears. "Are you crying?" I asked, unable to keep the disbelief out of my voice.

Cambria sniffled. "Shut up. I thought you were…"

She didn't finish and I smiled crookedly. Until this moment, I hadn't appreciated how glad I was that I could answer, "Well, I'm not."

"Good. Because I've come to realize Logan is pretty sucky at a lot of BFF things, and you couldn't have come back at a better time. My hair color is fading and I can't choose the next one. Logan doesn't know the difference between fuchsia and firebrick."

"It's red, okay. God." Logan let go of Victoria and walked over, holding his arms up in existential frustration. "Of all the things you could say, are you seriously bringing this up right now? After all the time they've been missing … We just got them back and this is what you want to say?"

"My priorities are straight," she protested. "I hugged her first."

Logan rolled his eyes and threw his arms around me. The brim of his tattered baseball cap poked at my forehead. I tucked my face lower and breathed in the familiarity of dryer sheets and dusty books that Logan always smelled like—and blinked back a new round of tears.

"I am so glad you're all right," he said into my hair. I nodded, at a loss for words, and hugged him back. "Both of you," he added, pulling away to draw Victoria into his arms again. She looked back at him, her eyes big and round, her expression completely breakable. A tear escaped and slid down my cheek.

"Oh, hell," Cambria said and threw her arms around all three of us in a group hug. I smiled through my sniffles until we all broke apart.

Out of the shadows, Derek appeared, his yellow wolf eyes shining as he looked at me. He stood close enough to brush Cambria's arm and she automatically lowered her hand to his furry shoulder in a familiar gesture. "You are a sight for sore eyes," he said and the way his jaw drew back to reveal his teeth looked like a really scary smile.

I bent down and threw my arms around his neck. "So are you," I said.

"Whoa there," Cambria said. "You can hug him for real later, when he has some clothes on."

I straightened and shook my head at her. "Cam, he's a wolf."

"I know. He's completely naked."

I snorted and hugged her again. "I missed you so freaking much," I said.

"Ditto."

Broken Blood

So adorable, the two of you. Can we go now?

I stiffened, the smile fading abruptly from my lips.

"What is it?" Cambria asked. Beside her, the hair on Derek's neck stood up as he sniffed the air. Before I could answer, their eyes lit on something behind me. I turned, half terrified of another wolf, but it wasn't an enemy.

Or at least, not anymore.

Mr. Lexington approached warily, his steps small and measured. His shoes scuffed uncertainly over the asphalt. Beside me, Derek's legs bent into a crouch. I could feel him readying to spring at the new enemy.

"No!" I jumped between them and held up my hands. "He's with us," I explained. Victoria, her hand firmly in Logan's, led them both to stand in front of her father.

"He helped us escape," she said.

"But didn't he also help get you captured?" Derek demanded.

"Yes, but—it's a long story," I said.

"A story we don't have time for now. We need to go," Mr. Lexington called from around Victoria's shoulder. I nodded.

"He's right. We're headed to—"

"Professor Flaherty's," Cambria finished for me. "Your mom called."

"We can caravan but we have to go," Mr. Lexington said in a wavering voice that belied his anxiety. I caught him staring into the shadows where the two Werewolves that had attacked Victoria now lay, courtesy of Logan and Cambria judging by the metal stakes protruding.

"He's right," Derek said slowly, obviously wary of Mr. Lexington's allegiance. "There will be more like these. They travel in packs, especially the ones bent on this kind of revenge." He moved away, toward the red sedan they'd arrived in, still parked and running at the curb where he'd left it. He ducked inside and returned with a mouthful of clothes before disappearing behind a cropping of trees.

"You want to ride with us?" Cambria asked me. "We can fill you in and catch up on everything."

I hesitated, debating my options, and then sighed. "I think it's better if Victoria rides with you guys. You only really have room for one more anyway. I'll see you there," I said.

Cambria looked disappointed but nodded. "Okay, that works," she said.

Logan gave me a grateful smile and led Victoria toward their waiting car. She caught my eye and held it for a moment before giving me a tiny nod. I gave her one back, grateful she wouldn't say anything about Steppe until I was ready. Derek returned, human and clothed, and slid into the driver's seat of his waiting car. I waved and followed Mr. Lexington to the van, the glow of the street lights falling away as I went.

That was a close one. If not for your friends coming along, I'd hate to think what would've happened. Strange how the whole world thinks you're the one who caused their problems.

I remembered what Grandma and my mom had said about the world being different. And the video footage everyone kept bringing up, evidence of my supposed crimes.

Not strange, I said. *Or surprising. Of course you'd paint me to be the bad guy. You're becoming more and more predictable, really. It's almost boring.*

A smirk formed, painting itself along the walls of my mind until it stretched from left to right. I ignored it and climbed inside the van, opting for the empty bench seat and strapping myself in.

I gave a fleeting once-over to Steppe, who still sat in the far corner, and then faced forward. Astor was in the front seat munching on sunflower seeds.

"Everything all right?" he asked, unconcerned and thankfully unaware.

Clearly, he hadn't been filled in on what'd just gone on at the other end of the lot. "Everything's fine," I assured him as Mr. Lexington slid in and shut the door. "Derek, Cambria, and Logan caught up. They're going to follow."

"That's your young scientist friend, yes?" Astor asked, spitting a few seeds out the open window as we eased forward.

"Yes," I told him.

Astor grunted. "I like him all right. More than that baseball player, anyway."

"George plays football," I corrected.

"Well. I forgive him," he said before upturning the bag and sliding the last mouthful of seeds onto his tongue. I decided to leave that one alone.

"Crap, the phone," I said, sitting forward and patting my empty pockets. "It fell out of my hands before and…" I sat back and caught Mr. Lexington's eyes in the rearview. "Sorry," I finished.

82

Broken Blood

"Here," he said, holding out something squared off and black.

"Another phone?" I asked, taking it and turning it over in my palm, already preparing to redial Wes. My heart hammered at the thought of simply hearing his voice. And worry—for what he might've done once the call dropped. How worried he'd sounded when I'd stopped responding. And after he'd been drinking…

"It's Steppe's. The one Victoria had," Lexington explained, but I was only half-listening. I already had the first five numbers dialed as he added, "She said you should use it to call your friend, George."

"No, I was going to wait. I don't want to put him in danger," I said, my finger hovering over the "send" button.

In my mind, I heard, *No getting away from danger for that one.*

I swiveled to Steppe, my cheeks heating. Anger and fear for my friend were a dual mixture in my veins. "What did you do?" I demanded.

He shrugged at me across the darkened interior, wide-eyed, and mumbled something around the tape covering his mouth.

His voice in my mind was a big fat blank.

I faced forward and fumbled with the phone, canceling the call to Wes and dialing George. As it rang, I prayed George was all right. That Wes hadn't done anything crazy. And I thought of how they were all going to react when I showed up to Flaherty's with public enemy number one on my arm.

They were all going to hit the fan when they saw him. Grandma, Mom, Wes, George. I wondered idly how many of them I'd have to fight off as they all rushed to kill him. I wondered how badly it would hurt me if I decided not to stop them.

Chapter Ten

I woke just in time to feel the sensation of being driven forward against my straining seat belt—and snapping back sharply when the brakes and momentum all caught up. Behind me, Gordon snapped out of his dozing.

"What's going on?" I asked, rubbing at the spot on my chest where the belt had cut in.

In front of me, Mr. Lexington was busy offering calming words to Astor, who wasn't hearing any of it. He gripped his bright-green Slurpee cup in tight fingers, his eyes wide and everywhere at once.

"They're coming, they're coming, the British are coming," Astor chanted. He sat bent forward leaning toward the window and his rounded side mirror. I moved to see what had his attention and, in the darkness, caught sight of a pair of bright white headlights close on our tail. Too close.

"Who is it?" I asked, the last traces of sleep evaporating as I remembered the large black wolf as he'd stood over me with his jaw open.

"I don't know," Mr. Lexington said, his eyes darting from the curvy state route we were following to the rearview and back. "But they've managed to move in between us and your Werewolf friend. Whoever it is has been honking and riding our tail. I even exited the interstate in favor of back roads, but I can't shake them." He sounded grim as he darted glances into his rearview before returning his attention to the road ahead. The van lurched forward quickly and then continued until our speed leveled out again.

I checked the road ahead, but it was all clear. "Did you just brake check him?" I asked.

His eyes flicked over my face in the rearview and I shook my head. "Not the best idea. You should let Derek handle it."

"He's not doing anything," Mr. Lexington said in a strained voice. "They've dropped back. It's like they're letting whoever this is take a go at us."

I was thrown left as we took a sharp curve slightly too fast. Up ahead, the road straightened. The moment we were out of the shoulderless loop, the headlights swerved out as the car pulled into the lane next to us.

It accelerated until its passenger window was level with my view from Mr. Lexington's. Without the blinding glare of the headlights obscuring my view, the make and model of the car became visible and my breath caught.

"Stop the car!" I didn't wait for compliance before I unbuckled my seat belt and scooted for the sliding door. "Stop the car now," I repeated.

"What?" Mr. Lexington shot me a confused look and another wary one at the car mirroring us, but I felt him slowing.

"Hurry up," I said, breathless, heart pounding. My fingertips tingled, my toes went numb. The van couldn't stop fast enough.

Vaguely, I felt Steppe's mental probing—he was just as mystified as Lexington about the newcomer. But I wasn't giving anything up. Mostly because my thoughts had become paralyzed with the urgency to close the distance.

"Do you know who it is?" Mr. Lexington asked.

"They're coming, they're coming, the British are coming," Astor sang again.

Mr. Lexington navigated to the shoulder. I laughed out loud as our tires hit gravel, knowing full well I probably looked and sounded like a lunatic right now.

"Yes," I said, throwing the sliding door open even as we continued to roll. I jumped out at the same time the tires finally came to a stop and tore into a run.

The other car had already come to a stop in front of us, herding us onto the shoulder so that we stayed tucked behind it. An unnecessary precaution. I spotted the logo and lettering that I'd already recognized but read it anyway: Aston Martin. Volante.

The door opened and a head appeared, hair ruffling as the wind caught it, then a neck, shoulders, torso—until finally, he stood erect. I'd forgotten how tall he was. I stopped and stared; it was like seeing for the first time. He looked worried, as usual, and almost untouchably handsome; his arms were empty only a second before I careened into his broad chest and buried my nose in the folds of his leather jacket.

My hands clutched fistfuls of clothing and whatever parts of him I could grab onto. "Wes," I said on an exhale that released every lonely, terrifying moment I'd endured for eight weeks. When I inhaled the scent of him—leather, soap, and wild animal—it brought security and safety and more love than I'd ever thought possible stacked inside a single scent.

He started to pull back. I held tight in protest, but he only pulled my face to his in a warm kiss. His lips were smooth and lingering on mine and my knees buckled underneath the overwhelming sensation of being held, being kissed by this wolf I'd loved for so long. Missed for so long. I clung tighter, locking my arms around his neck, hand to elbow, so that neither of us could escape. The kiss turned hungry, searching and crushing every square centimeter of mouth and lip and tongue and flesh it managed to find with eyes closed and bodies pressed. His hands ran over my shoulders, down my arms, and I knew he was just as desperate as I was for this moment.

Somewhere behind me, car doors clicked open and slammed shut. Voices hummed with muted questions while others mumbled explanations around us. Footsteps shuffled closer, gathering around us to wait. Ignoring them all, Wes and I stood locked in a tangle of clinging arms and searching fingertips, lips and torsos pressed tight.

I never, ever wanted it to stop.

Ugh, I'd almost forgotten what teenage hormones felt like.

The interruption and the wry flavor of the voice in my head drove a ripple of shock through me. My hands and mouth stilled and Wes jerked away, rounded eyes regarding me with wary concern.

"What was that?" he demanded.

"You ... how did you hear...?" My confusion was drowned out underneath the noise inside my head. Mental chuckling coupled with the most annoying and embarrassing clichés to ever grace a Life &

Health classroom circled my brain, a tornado of words overlapping into nonsensical barbs.

I do hope someone's talked to you about the birds and the bees. Being safe? Wearing a raincoat? Oh, wait—I see you haven't taken it that far. I felt him sifting through memories, turning them over one by one until he chuckled, adding, *Not for lack of trying, eh?*

"Oh my God. Eww," I said, stepping away to press my hands against the sides of my head. "Get out!"

"Tara?" Wes hovered, following me wherever I sidestepped. "Who is that? Who's in there?" he demanded.

My hands dropped away and I stared up at him, momentarily dismissing Gordon's mental baiting. No one behind us said a word but I knew they were there, just as confused. All at once, I realized the number of listening ears and watching eyes bearing witness to my secret as it unraveled.

"How do you know someone's in my head?" I asked. "And how did you find me?"

Wes looked up at the sky and, for a moment, I was lost, but then I followed the direction of his gaze and realized what we were staring at. I looked back at him again, unsure whether to be relieved or more apprehensive. "It's a full moon," I said quietly.

"It is." He stepped closer, his hand cupping my cheek. I leaned into it, relishing the way his calloused palm scraped lightly over my skin. "I heard your thoughts, searched for some clue as to scenery," he explained. "When I realized it was a rest stop along the interstate, I only needed to hone in on which direction." His gaze roamed my face, drinking me in as I hung on his breathy words.

"And how did you figure it out?"

"Once I found you, there was no way I was losing you again. Your thoughts have always been so clear, so loud for me." My cheek warmed where he touched and I leaned in, forgetting all over again the conflict or danger or anything that wasn't his mouth or arms on my body.

I heard Gordon's thought as it ran like a whisper through my head: *Ugh. Is this necessary? You probably should've just killed me.*

"Who is it, Tara?" Wes asked again, halting my advances and holding me away. My kiss dried up and my mouth open and closed.

I met his eyes, cringing as I answered on a defeated sigh, "Gordon Steppe. We're bonded."

The collective gasp seemed to suck all of the remaining joy from the reunion.

"Did you just say Gordon freaking Steppe is in your head?" Cambria shrieked loud enough to echo in the empty night air.

"That son of a ..." Derek muttered.

Logan said something quietly to Victoria, but she simply shook her head without a word. Everyone turned back to me. When I didn't offer anything else, they all rounded on Astor. He'd gotten out of the van and was sipping loudly on his empty Slurpee cup where he stood next to Mr. Lexington.

"Someone needs to start talking," Derek said through closed teeth. He glared at Mr. Lexington. "You," he said.

Mr. Lexington hesitated, but I didn't give him a chance to talk. There was still one more bomb to deliver. Instead, I said, "And because of that, I couldn't leave him behind." The group fell silent. At the end of the gravel driveway we were parked in front of, a porch light came on. A dog began to bark. In the quiet of their shock, I said, "He's in the van."

Wes narrowed his eyes. His hand on mine tightened. I could feel his gaze searching, poking through my thoughts, probably, in his impatience for an explanation. Nothing I could do would stop him. I looked back at him, my expression open and honest. Whatever it was he wanted to know, he could have it.

"What the actual hell," Cambria said, her chunky black boot grinding into the pebbled asphalt.

Astor made a noise and I thought he was maybe scared of Cambria rather than the situation. Derek offered a quiet curse. Logan agreed. The Lexingtons were the only quiet ones in the bunch.

I didn't look at a single one of them. Instead, I held the gaze of the boy I loved. This was the part where he always went a little crazy with worry and the need to control and fix it all. And when he realized he couldn't, then the anger would be next. Not at me, at the situation, but still. Right now, I was the situation. And I knew him well enough to understand he only used it to shield himself from the fear of losing his loved ones.

I braced myself for all of that, but it never came.

Wes never made a sound as he regarded me, his head cocked sideways. I realized too late he'd probably just heard every one of my mental predictions. Which wasn't going to improve his reaction. But his hand never left mine. His jaw twitched once and warm breath escaped his nose into the cold air in a small puff. Then he relaxed and pulled me to his chest, smoothing my hair.

"It's okay," he said finally.

Calmly.

Gently.

Full of confidence, empty of worry or anxiety.

And I wondered who the heck this Wes was and what he'd done with mine.

The dog's barking grew louder. Another light came on at the farmhouse down the lane.

"We need to get moving," Mr. Lexington said.

Always the herder.

Wes pulled back and nodded at him. "You're helping us," Wes said. It wasn't a question. If anything, it was a warning.

Mr. Lexington lifted his chin. "I'm committed to protecting my daughter, no matter what," he said.

Wes looked at Victoria and his hand tightened in mine. "He hurt you," he said to her.

She lifted her chin, much like her dad had done. "He hurt you too," she said, managing to sound compassionate and haughty at the same time. She was recovering. I might've smiled if her words hadn't frozen Wes.

"Steppe is in the van?" Derek echoed, finally catching up. "That van?" he asked, pointing. He didn't wait for my answer before striding to the van and yanking the door open.

My throat closed. I opened my mouth to call out and stop him but no sound came. I wasn't sure whether I was scared he would hurt Steppe—or scared he wouldn't.

"Tara's bonded to him, Derek," Wes warned, reading my thoughts.

Derek disappeared inside the van. The barking, a background annoyance until now, suddenly reached full volume as the dog escaped whatever restraint had been holding it and it raced toward us at the edge of the road. Even in the darkness, I could see it wasn't a puppy.

I reached a hand out, caught between the threat of Derek and the threat of the dog, my words of warning becoming tongue-twisted in my mouth. But Cambria turned just as the dog leaped at her calf and slammed her fist into the mutt's nose. It went down with a yelp and then turned away, whining as it retreated.

I stared at her.

She shrugged. "Despite what you people think, I am not a dog person," she said.

Mr. Lexington rolled his eyes. "We need to go," he said again, this time more urgently.

Derek reappeared from the depths of the van, dragging Steppe by the back of his collar. Steppe's foot caught on something just inside the van door, so instead of following Derek out on his feet, he landed on his stomach with a grunt, half in, half out of the vehicle. Derek heaved and Steppe tumbled onto the pavement.

Derek wasted no time landing a hard kick to Steppe's gut. "That's for taking my friends prisoner," he said.

I felt the pain like a sucker punch but held it in, steeling my muscles and my face. At the second kick, I gripped Wes tighter in silent support. None of the others moved to stop him.

Astor threw a nervous glance my way. He was the only one here who knew even this was agony for me and I intended to keep it that way. If nothing else, I didn't want Steppe knowing how harm to one caused harm to both. I wanted to keep as much as possible from his awareness. It might be the only advantage we had when the time came.

Wes suddenly swiveled to stare at me and I sighed. *Stupid full moon.* His eyes narrowed in response and his mouth tightened.

Several yards away, Derek kicked Steppe again. "And that's for making my other friends sick from the Unbinilium," he said.

This time, the pain almost doubled me over. Wes pulled at our joined hands, stepping forward, and I knew he was about to intervene. I tugged on his hand to get his attention, looked right at him, and thought, *Don't.*

Derek planted a final kick, his mouth grim, his forearm muscles working as his hands fisted at his sides. "And that," he said, wiping the back of his hand across his face, "is for getting my friend arrested and almost convicted of a murder you committed."

This time, my physical reaction had nothing to do with the pain radiating from Steppe's gut to the very ends of his hair. I watched in grim satisfaction as Steppe gasped and rolled sideways to escape Derek's wrath.

With a hollow click, across the field, a door opened at the farm house and the darkened silhouette of a man in a cowboy hat walked out onto the porch. The dog disappeared inside and, a second later, the man stepped out. Even from here, I could see the outline of a rifle clutched in his hand.

"Like I said before," Mr. Lexington said.

"Time to go," Logan said, already pulling Victoria toward the waiting car. Astor scrambled for his seat in the van and Cambria took Derek's hand, gently pulling him away as well. Derek took a step back, met my eyes, and I saw the apology written there.

"You good?" he asked me.

I nodded. "I'm good," I assured him. I slid a glance toward the farmer. "Can you put him back now?"

Derek bent down and heaved Steppe up over his shoulder like a sack of potatoes. He walked him back to the van and tossed him inside. Steppe landed with a relieved grunt that was nothing after the rib-cracking kicks from before. I sighed.

"Come on," Wes said, leading me toward the Aston Martin.

I hesitated, but Mr. Lexington was already seated in the van. His window rolled down and he called out, "Go. We'll follow you."

I nodded and followed Wes to the car. In the distance, I heard the distinct click of a rifle being cocked and broke into a run. Wes and I dove into the car, he shoved it into gear, and we sped off. Gravel kicked up behind us and I held my breath, my eyes locked on the side mirror. My lips moved in silent prayer.

A second later, two sets of headlights appeared through the dust and I relaxed against the soft leather of the seat. Wes reached over and wrapped his hands around mine. "He didn't fire," Wes said after another moment. "Everyone's fine."

I exhaled.

The cold leather of the seats seeped into the back of my thighs. Wes reached over and switched on the seat warmers. "Better?"

"Yes, thanks," I said.

Silence fell and I realized Wes was reading me. "There's a lot to catch up on," I warned. "Not all of it is pleasant."

"None of it is pleasant," he said, voice grim. His left hand tightened where it gripped the steering wheel.

"What happened to you?" I asked, my voice breaking on the last word. It was as if weeks' worth of worry had been bottled and the container poured over my head in this moment. I couldn't contain a single drop of my panic any longer. Tears brimmed along the edges of my lids, but I didn't care if they fell. Not when Wes stared back at me through them, so completely and beautifully in one piece.

"We can talk about it later," Wes said gently, glancing over. He lifted his hand to swipe away a tear, but I shook my head and grabbed his hand, wrapping both of mine around it.

"No. I want to talk about it now. You get to know everything you want just from pulling it all from my head. I need to know what happened to you too," I said.

His chest rose and fell with a heavy sigh and I knew he was weighing how much it would upset me. "It'll upset me more if you don't tell me," I said quietly. His smile was soft and slick, disappearing even before I fully saw it.

"All right," he said finally.

"You were arrested," I said. It wasn't a question, but he nodded.

"They took me into custody that night. Dumped me in a community cell and didn't come back for almost twenty hours. I think they thought I was drunk."

"Because of the way you acted from the Unbinilium," I guessed, remembering the way he'd swayed and become so out of it.

"When they finally brought me in for questioning, it was obviously only a formality. They had photos, doctored surveillance footage, everything needed to put me away and throw away the key for killing that girl, Mal," he said. Hot fury lit his irises. His hand tightened on the wheel again.

"I'm sorry. She didn't deserve that … Neither did you." Mal had tried warning us of Steppe's intentions to bring down The Cause—and everyone in it. Her only crime had been speaking the truth. And Steppe had killed her and framed Wes.

I took a mental stab at Steppe but Wes called me back. "I know what you're thinking. Leave him alone," he said. "Soon, we'll be there and everyone will descend, wanting to know what happened to you. Until then, I want you and me in this car. No one else."

He was right, but it wasn't easy putting aside my anger and refocusing. "How did you get away?" I asked to distract myself from all the things I wanted done to Steppe the moment we were able to undo this mental connection.

"I waited it out for a few days, hoping Edie or someone would figure out another way but …" He hesitated. "Steppe used civilian police because he knew it would be harder for anyone to help me. And he knew … If I used my gifts, anything supernatural, well, that's another strike against me in our world. Using my gifts on humans is against the law." He shot me a glance and then added, "I didn't hurt anyone. I removed their memory of the crime so that they'd have to let me go."

"Why is that so bad?" I asked. "You didn't deserve to be framed in the first place."

"Because, Tara. If the crime doesn't exist then the guilty party can never be brought to justice."

"Oh." I stared out the windshield at the winding road, watching as it was eaten up by our tires. I'd forgotten how quiet this car was, how smooth. I glanced at the dashboard and saw that we were going much faster than it felt. "You did the right thing," I said. "I don't know what I'd do if you weren't here."

"I would've lost my mind being trapped in a cell while you were … I had no idea where you were or if you alive and it was killing me." The raw pain in his expression was enough to make my chest ache. "I looked for you every day from the moment I walked out of that station."

"You rented an apartment in the city," I said.

He glanced sideways at me, a strange look on his face. "How do you know that?"

"I … Victoria told me," I said, my brows wrinkling. "Why?"

"Nothing," he muttered, his attention snapping back to the road.

I caught a faint blush creeping into his cheeks before the GPS on the dashboard beeped. "Take this right," I said, pointing.

We slowed and made the turn, and I watched as the others followed, falling in behind us again. "I can't believe we found each other," I said quietly, relief and desperation melting into an adrenaline rush that left me dizzy.

Wes squeezed my hand. "It's all right now," he said quietly. "We're together. And we're safe."

I smiled over at him, but even with my mouth tipped up, the expression felt sad on my face. "I was so worried you wouldn't find me," I said.

He squeezed my hand. "I'll always find you, Tara. Always."

My smile tipped up a little higher at the edges and I squeezed back, warm fuzzies settling in the depths of my fear-stained gut. I had no idea how we were going to figure things out, but I knew we'd find a way. We'd found each other. We were together. We were safe. And, right now, that was all that mattered.

Chapter Eleven

"Tara? Time to wake up."

"Hmm?" I muttered, disoriented as I woke. I blinked, the shadowy interior of the car jarring me until everything came flooding back: the rest stop, Derek and the others, Wes tracking us down. I looked over and he gave me a small smile of reassurance.

"We're close. Maybe twenty minutes," he said.

I stirred, sitting higher in my seat and wiping the corner of my mouth with my sweatshirt. Outside, the friendly glow of street lights lined the four-lane road. An elementary school, deserted and shiny with its bright white trim, sprawled opposite a public park.

"Suburbia," I said, adjusting myself in my chair. "Feels weird."

"The whole world feels pretty weird these days," Wes said.

Guitar strains leaked softly from the radio and the warmth seeped in from all directions. Wes reached over and flicked the seat warmer off. I glanced up at the low-hanging moon and my mouth curved. "Thanks," I said.

"For you, anything," he returned with an almost-smile of his own.

"Did you get anything interesting while I was asleep?" I asked, pointing to my temple.

"Tara …" And just like that, the lightness vanished and the fading horror returned. "I'm so sorry," he whispered and the tears that filled his eyes shocked me.

"For what?" I asked.

"I should've found you. I should've known. Your mother and Edie, they went to that building several times but they didn't know … Laws be damned, I should've gone there myself."

I laid my hand on his. "You couldn't have known. Steppe made sure of it. None of this is your fault."

"I saw your … confinement. In your memories. You were so alone." His jaw tightened. "And I saw all of the blood draws, the sedatives, the mind games. He's going to pay."

"That was nothing compared to—" I stopped but he looked over at me, full of understanding.

"Not knowing if you were all right," he finished. "That was the hardest for me too." He hesitated, but I stayed silent, knowing that for every detail he'd already shared, there was so much more he hadn't told me. When he spoke again, the words were slow and soft and I knew he was reliving it all as he called it up. "I knew he wouldn't take you far. I don't know how but I just knew. Ego, maybe. Anyway, I was sure it was DC or somewhere near it, so I rented that place. Besides that, Frederick Falls wasn't safe anymore." He shot me a worried glance but I let it pass. I wanted to hear this more. "Coming home to an empty house. Searching for you every day. Not knowing where to look. Every lead a dead end. That was far worse than any physical pain."

He glanced over and the emotion reflected back at me was more intense than anything he'd shared yet. Raw and broken and desperate—and I knew it was a glimpse of everything he'd felt during our weeks apart. "Steppe knew I was looking. I realize now he used Victoria to track me and have me followed, watched. He sent men one night when I'd had a few too many. Drowning out the reality … Anyway, I didn't see it coming. One of them slipped me something so I couldn't shift and they took me home, tied me up. They told me if I kept looking for you, they'd kill you."

"What was it?" I asked, leaning toward him. "What did they give you?"

"No idea," he said and then added, "But it wore off in time. We'll figure out how to get your wolf back."

I sighed, still frustrated over that one. At least Wes could read my frustration, share in it. "Victoria said you weren't the only one," I said.

Broken Blood

"He followed everyone. Had everyone watched."

He nodded. "Your mom and your grandma. Jack and Fee. Derek. All of us. He threatened to hurt you if we kept searching. Edie wouldn't stop, though. She hired people to do it instead." His pained expressed lightened, took on one of awe. "That woman is far more resourceful than any of us know."

"So, they're all scattered because they're running from Steppe's people?" I asked.

"Not people," he said grimly and I remembered the mangy wolves doubling as guards. "But it's not just them. The Werewolf packs, a lot of them our old allies, they're angry. They blame us. Me and Jack, mostly. They started coming after us. And Fee … well, you know how she worries over him since he was shot. They decided to disappear for a while."

I did know. All too well. And more than knowing it, I felt responsible for it. "And The Cause? Are you still in charge?"

"Nothing left to be in charge of," he said with a sad snort. "The allies are finished with us. They all want blood. Retribution for what they see as our betrayal. They want Steppe and until they get to him, they want us."

"I know about the videos Steppe released. They make me look like the villain instead of him," I said. "How do we stop them from coming after us? How do we show them it's not our fault, it's his?"

"They won't stop unless we can get Steppe out of power and change things back. Maybe not even then. They're scared and angry, not a good combination."

His voice was hoarse by the end and we both fell silent. My fingertips grew cold as I pictured the reality of what he was saying. Werewolves everywhere out for blood—our blood. Steppe sending those men to Wes's place. Being forced to give up. To let it go and just move on. Is this what Steppe meant when he'd tried to make me believe Wes had moved on? Because Steppe had forced him to give up the search?

An image rose, unbidden in my mind, of Wes bloodied and battered on a hardwood floor I didn't recognize. Steppe's twisted tone coated it and I knew it was sent by him, a nastygram to remind me exactly how much it had taken for Wes to be convinced to stop searching for me. Wes growled and glared at me—or through me. His furious gaze all but burned a hole in the center of my forehead.

"Leave her alone," Wes yelled.

Steppe skittered away.

Hot anger rose in me and spilled over into whatever corner Steppe had slipped into. I shoved at him until I was sure he was no longer eavesdropping. It felt unfair to Wes, to the vulnerability he wore like an open book as he looked back at me.

"He won't get away with this," I promised Wes.

Wes hung his head, shaking it slowly. "He already has," he said.

I opened my mouth to argue, but he beat me to it. "His bond with you assures his safety. No one's going to hurt him or let anything happen to him as long as it means you'll feel it too. Especially me. In fact, I'm suddenly his biggest protector." His laugh was sharp and humorless. "He probably wanted this all along."

"What do you mean?" I asked, the idea a sharp sting of possibility. One I'd failed to see before now. Alex's words rang in my ears, but I dismissed it before Wes could read it in my thoughts. Alex was the last person I wanted clogging up the shared emotional head space in this car. "You think Steppe wanted me to escape? To bring him with us?"

"It's not hard for me to imagine," Wes said dryly. "He is right where he's always wanted to be. In the thick of our group, physically and mentally. Where it's easiest to tear us apart."

As Wes followed the GPS directions, I lost myself in my own speculation. It was entirely possible this had been Steppe's intention all along. But there was no going back now. Nothing could convince me to return to that basement, not even to put him back in that cage beside Olivia.

"Tara? Are you all right?"

I blinked and realized I'd zoned out on the memory of that cold room. "Sorry, just ... remembering," I said finally.

"I know," he said in a strained voice.

"I just don't understand why," I said, frustrated that I might've played right into the man's hands. "Why does he hate us so much? Why does he want to destroy us from the inside out? Why is he so consumed with that? What did we ever do to him?"

Wes stared out over the road and exhaled with sagging shoulders as we slowed. "I don't know," he said quietly. "But we're going to figure it out. And we're going to stop him."

We came to a stop at a lonely red light and Wes turned to me, his expression insistent. "I know I've had my moments, Tara. Overprotective, controlling, always worrying and trying to push you behind me when danger comes around. But losing you like that … it made me realize my way won't work. We can't operate where one follows and one leads. We're in this together, side by side. You and me, we're a team. You're my mate, Tara, from the first moment I saw you. There was never any question in my mind that you and I were going to make it. And we are, I promise."

"We are a team," I whispered, my breath filling the empty space between our mouths and drawing us closer. I looked up at where his unruly hair fell to the edge of his forehead, down to his wide eyes and parted mouth. The sight of him, so changed, offering himself this way, moved me. I thought fleetingly, once again, of how different this Wes was from the one I left behind, but then I focused on his words, on the way they filled the empty spaces left by our separation. I placed my hand on his cheek, running my palm over the shadowed stubble along his chin. "You are my mate," I echoed. "We're going to do this together."

He let go of my hands, slid his arm around my shoulders, and pulled me close, planting a kiss on my temple. I turned and offered my lips instead, tingling to the tips of my toes when he took the bait. Gordon's voice piped up about teenaged hormones threatening his lunch but I ignored him and gave myself over to the kind of white noise that only ever happened with a really great kiss.

Chapter Twelve

Professor Flaherty's house was nestled smack dab in crowded suburbia. I read the number on the mailbox to be sure and stared up at a sage-green two-story with white shutters, a manicured lawn, and a yard that overlapped both of her neighbors. It was picture perfect, unassuming, and the last thing I expected for someone like her. It was also not a very convenient safe house for a caravan full of fugitives.

By the time we pulled up just before dawn, exhaustion had left me with a headache and droopy eyes. I was tired; mentally, physically, and whatever other way a person can be depleted.

Wes parked at the curb, leaving room for Mr. Lexington to pull the van into the empty driveway, and cut the lights. Derek pulled in behind us and cut his lights as well. I didn't see anyone out and about this early, but just in case, we sat in silence and scanned the empty street for movement before getting out.

When he was satisfied, Wes turned to me. His hand had barely left mine since we got in, but now he pulled it free to sweep the hair back from my face. His brows were pinched in concern.

"Are you sure it's safe?" I asked.

"Are you sure she's home?"

I sighed. "No to both," I said.

I grabbed the door handle but Wes stopped me. "You should wait here. I'll go up and see."

"She doesn't know you like she knows me," I protested.

Wes hesitated and then added, "I'll take Astor."

I let go of the handle. "Fine. But you have five minutes before I come in after you."

A smile ghosted across his features, reminding me of the old Wes. He leaned in and planted a smacking kiss on my lips. "God, I've missed you saying stuff like that. I'll be back in three," he said and got out.

My lips tingled from the kiss, and I smiled back as I watched him coax Astor from the van and lead him to the front door. Wes knocked and positioned himself at the opening with Astor tucked beside him. A moment later, the door opened. It was only a sliver and no light shone through to illuminate the face. I squinted, trying to make out what was happening, but the shadows swallowed them up. I gave the key half a turn, rolled my window down, and strained to hear, but my wolf still wasn't cooperating. Not even with heightening my senses.

I ached with longing for my animal.

Without sound, I could only watch and try to interpret. They spoke for another moment and then the door opened wider and I caught sight of red hair spilling down past a feminine but strong set of shoulders. Astor bounced up and down where he stood and then leaned in as the two of them hugged.

I exhaled.

Wes turned and motioned at me to join them. I was halfway out of the car when someone pushed Professor Flaherty aside and flew out the door headed for me.

"Tara!" A curtain of brown hair flew behind her as she ran toward me. She wore a bathrobe over flannel pajamas and a wide smile. Her relief was a force all its own. A tangible thing that engulfed us both the moment she threw her arms around me.

"Mom," I said, burying my face in her hair and inhaling what could only be lemon-scented furniture polish. Some things never changed.

Another familiar voice behind my mother called out and I raised my head in time to see Grandma join us. She threw her arms around us both, crowding in and squeezing us tight in a group hug. "Thank God," Grandma muttered and my chest swelled at the sound of her relief and being held in an embrace that included them both.

I hadn't realized just how much both of them mattered to me until I'd been taken from them. Standing in front of them now, I wasn't sure how to say it out loud. The sound of car doors being pushed shut reminded me it wasn't exactly the time or place anyway, and I reluctantly pulled away.

My mother wiped her eyes and smiled at me. Grandma did the same but without the tears. "Are you okay?" my mother asked, looking me over.

"I'm fine," I assured them. "Just tired."

They both nodded. "Let's get you and everyone else inside," Grandma said.

"You can rest. There will be plenty of time to talk later," Mom added. "Come on."

I followed them as far as the front door where the group of us bottle-necked trying to get inside. Up ahead, Professor Flaherty greeted everyone and directed them to bedrooms, refrigerators, or bathrooms as needs dictated.

"Tara," Professor Flaherty said, surprising me with a warm hug. "It's good to see you. I'm so glad you're all right."

"Good to see you too," I returned, returning the hug halfway between awkward and friendly.

When she released me, I stepped back quickly. Behind me, I realized someone held back. "Mr. Lexington, you should come inside," I said.

He threw a look at the van, his set of keys dangling in his hand, but didn't move. "And what about our … guest?" he asked.

Wes squeezed my arm and slid past me. "I'll handle him."

"Guest?" Grandma echoed, brows wrinkling.

I glanced at Wes and then back to Grandma, avoiding the curious stares from my mother and Professor Flaherty. I had no idea how they were going to take this, but there was no going back now. He and I were a package deal.

The exhaustion made it all that much harder to ease into. I took a deep breath and decided to rip the bandage off quickly. "Gordon Steppe is in the van," I explained.

"What?" Grandma and Mom shrieked in unison.

Professor Flaherty was silent. At my admission, she regarded me with sharp eyes and a neutral expression.

"What in the Sam Hill is that man doing in your van, Lexington?" Grandma demanded. Suddenly it was his fault? I shook my head as the others returned from where they'd already wandered inside. Cambria and Derek hovered near the front, all of them watching the show without a word. Everyone knew better than to interrupt Grandma.

"It was my decision," I said and all eyes swiveled back to me again.

Of all things, my stomach growled. Dizziness swept over me. I did not have the energy for this.

"Steppe used Tara to experiment with blood bonding in order to manipulate the hybrids that chose their Werewolf side and now, she's bonded with him," Wes explained. I smiled tightly at him, grateful for his help. "It's not ideal, having him here, but it does ensure he can't use their connection to come after and hurt Tara again. Or anyone else for that matter. Now, Tara's exhausted from trying to push him out so she needs rest more than any of us. Professor Flaherty, can you show us a room for Tara to sleep?"

Grandma frowned, my mother blinked, and Professor Flaherty nodded. Thank goodness for Wes. "Certainly," Professor Flaherty said. "This way."

"I'll come back for Steppe in a moment. Let's get you settled," Wes said to me, ignoring the rest of them.

I followed Professor Flaherty inside with Wes behind me, his hand on my back, guiding me along. Behind me in the doorway, I heard my mother and Grandma talking in quiet voices.

"Do you think we should tell her now or wait?" my mom whispered.

"Let's wait," Grandma said, sounding exhausted herself. "It'll only stir her up and Wes is right. She's going to need her strength against that man."

I knew I should probably care they were hiding something from me, but right now I only wanted that bed the professor was promising. With that in mind, I followed Professor Flaherty straight upstairs without a backward glance.

The railing was sanded smooth underneath my fingertips, and the hallway upstairs smelled like pine. Carpet sank underneath my feet and I imagined it would be even cushier with bare feet.

"You can have this room here. It's already made up for you," Professor Flaherty said. "I didn't realize you were bringing so many or I'd have readied the other rooms," she added.

"I didn't realize it either," I said, following her inside the first door at the top of the stairs. The low lamp burning just inside the doorway sent a cozy orange glow over a full mattress covered in a Chevron-patterned quilt. The pine scent and wood-stained furniture was a strange contrast to the modern façade of the house's exterior, but I decided to go with it.

I turned and found Professor Flaherty staring at me. "I'm sorry," I blurted before she could leave. Or yell at me. Or whatever that look preceded.

"For what?" she asked.

"For dropping in with all of these people and for putting you in danger and for..." My face fell as I realized the real reason for my apology. "For Astor."

"I'm not angry with you, Tara, for any of those things," she said.

"Well, you should be. He's your closest friend. Like family. And I put him in danger."

"He put himself in danger. And he's your family too. I know he'd do it all again if it meant protecting you so don't apologize for a choice that wasn't even yours to make in the first place. Or prevent." She smiled wryly. "You know Astor. He would've done it with or without your permission."

Something loosened inside me and a weight lifted. "Thanks," I said. "I thought something was wrong. You haven't said much," I said.

"Just confused, I guess," she said. "You said you and Steppe are blood bonded, right?"

"Yes," I said. "Why?"

She tilted her head, staring at me as if searching for something. And coming up empty. "Nothing," she said after a pause. "I just thought you'd be able to see..."

She trailed off and shook her head, as if to clear it. From downstairs, something crashed. "Anyway, I'll let you rest. Spare pajamas are in the top drawer and I left a toothbrush in the bathroom. I better get downstairs."

She disappeared before I could protest. Wes, who had been hovering near the door, came over and pulled me against him. His arms held tight and he tucked my head underneath his chin. "You all right?" he asked.

"I am now," I said. "What do you think she meant?"

"Who knows ... Can we figure it out when you've had sleep?"

"Yes." I stood in the circle of his arms until he reluctantly pulled away. He turned down the covers and gestured to the space he'd created between layers of clean sheets. It was the best invitation I'd had all day.

"I'm going to find something to change into first," I said, going instead to the dresser.

"I'm going to bring Steppe in, find a place to keep him and set up a schedule for someone to be watching him at all times, and then I'll be back to check on you," he said.

I nodded. He kissed me on the forehead, his mouth lingering half a second longer than necessary before he slipped out.

I changed into an oversized T-shirt and pair of pajama pants I found. For a split second, as I brushed my teeth, I considered removing the pants but the thought of Wes slipping in beside me scared me more than it thrilled me. I just didn't have the energy to be sexy tonight. And with Steppe in my head and my mother down the hall, I couldn't if I wanted to. So I rinsed my mouth out and kept the pants on.

I slid in between the cool sheets and sighed, every muscle in my body going gloriously limp in the process. My eyes shut and I was pretty sure they wouldn't open again even if I wanted them to. I breathed deeply in and out and felt my body relax another few inches.

Besides Wes, this bed was the best thing I'd pressed my body to in weeks.

Downstairs, a door slammed hard enough to shake the walls of my bedroom. Outside my window, someone shouted and below me, footsteps pounded, hurrying. Another door slammed.

I sat up, this time listening to the echo left behind by the door and the perpetual hum of voices as they rose and fell. My pulse raced. Had we already been found?

I waited, listening for another clue to help gauge the danger. More shouting, this time from inside the house. Raised voices all yelling something different, overlapping, drowning each other out.

In my head, the bond, which I'd managed to dial back to an annoying whisper, sprang to full volume. *This is not what you promised me when you kept me out of that cage, my dear.* And when I didn't answer, a second later Steppe's voice came again. *You may want to have a look at what your Dirty Blooded friend is up to. Not sure his agenda quite lines up with yours.*

Underneath the sarcastic calmness he exuded, there was the hint of fear. I threw the covers back and hurried out of the room and down the stairs.

At the bottom, I almost ran into Victoria. She stood with her back to me, her attention focused on the living room.

"What's going on?" I asked, breathless from the adrenaline.

Victoria mumbled something I didn't catch and gestured to the crowd gathered in the living room. Cambria and Mr. Lexington stood near the back of the group but they, too, were spectators. In front of them, I caught sight of Grandma and Wes ducking in and out of the center of things but I couldn't see enough to understand what was happening.

"He is not happy about Steppe," Victoria said and I realized she was repeating her answer from before.

"Who?" I pressed, but she only pointed toward the others.

Voices rose and the crowd was shoved backward. Cambria stumbled and almost fell but Mr. Lexington grabbed her elbow to steady her as they both backed away from the surge. I ran into it, Gordon's voice in my mind growing louder, more adamant that I step in.

"Tara, wait," Cambria warned, but I ignored her and shouldered my way through. I slipped past Professor Flaherty and then Grandma and Derek and out the other side—right between a cowering Gordon Steppe and a growling Werewolf.

"Tara, stop," Wes called in a much quieter voice. I knew that tone; it meant whatever was happening was not good.

I looked from Steppe, who already had a scratch across his forearm and cheek, to the wolf facing him. I blinked at it as familiarity washed over me. Even still, it had been so long that it took me a moment to place him.

"George?" I asked, tilting my head as I took in the slightly off-center ears and the familiar streaks of blond in his fur.

His recognition and relief were both short-lived as his temper took over. Now I understood Wes and Grandma and the rest when they'd cautioned me to stay away. George was wholly committed to his vengeance and there wasn't anything more dangerous than a Werewolf consumed with rage.

"Get out of my way," George growled as he pushed past me to stand over Steppe.

"Stop, you can't hurt him," I said, reaching for George to pull him back.

But George jerked away and snapped his teeth at Steppe. "Don't try to talk me out of it like the others," George said. "Screw mercy and forgiveness and strategy or whatever you're going to say. He deserves this. We deserve justice."

Before I could argue, he lunged at Steppe.

"No!" I yelled. I managed, only barely, to yank on Steppe's shoulder and pull him away in time for us both to get clear. Another hand darted in and shoved Steppe sideways. This time, George's teeth narrowly missed Steppe's midsection. He got a mouthful of carpet instead.

Someone yelled, but George ignored it and straightened; I could already see his intention to attack again. Panic rose at the thought of Steppe being killed. The pain it would cause me—but also, the regret I knew George would feel after, when he finally calmed down. I knew better than he did what it felt like to take a life. I couldn't let him live with that. Not even for someone like Steppe.

Something wild rose and sliced its way into my veins. My ribs and muscles pulled to a taut line, squeezing tighter and tighter until all at once, something popped. My pants tore first and then, as my torso expanded and elongated, my shirt ripped free.

Unlike the first time I'd done this, there wasn't enough pain to dampen the experience. The relief of shifting—finally—filled me like a tall glass of water on a hot day. By the time my four paws hit the ground, I was overcome. I had missed my wolf. And now I knew it had missed me.

"George." I opened my mouth, calling his name, and closed it again as my jaw locked onto his shoulder.

With a mouthful of his fur caught between my teeth, I yanked.

George yelped and spun—and stalled when he saw my wolf. I stepped between him and Steppe, although the others had pulled him far enough back that he was surrounded by another layer of bodies now, some human, some wolves.

George's eyes narrowed as he regained his composure. "Let me have this, Tara. You can't tell me you don't agree with me," he said. The words were garbled by his wolf jaw and more than that, his wild anger.

"I don't want to take it from you," I said. "But he and I are bonded."

"What?" His wolf eyes went wide and he stepped back. "You're … When?"

"A couple of days ago."

"I didn't know. I'm sorry." He stepped back and hung his head.

I grunted at him and felt my panic dial back some as the threat of the fight disappeared. Now, the bond came rushing in from all sides. This.

Oh God, this was what had been holding it at bay—and I hadn't even known.

My wolf let out a whine and I buckled underneath the weight of the voices and pictures and thoughts being poured into my mind. Dark rooms and secret deals. Politics—smiles and lies. Whispered orders, murder. And long before all of that, a boy. Young and happy save for the rooted hate for all things four-legged and furry. Innocent and ingrained from generations of ignorant racism for a cause he believed was truly noble. A girl who felt the same. And love. Once, there was love. And a baby girl.

"Oh God," I heard myself moan, followed closely by the sharp voices of my friends as a pair of hands and bodies swarmed closer. A blanket landed over me and it stung my raw skin. I hadn't even realized I'd shifted back.

You can't see this. I won't allow it.

Gordon's voice started as a whispered plea amid the physical pain from left over from George's claws. I felt both like a pain of my own. When I didn't comply, he yelled it.

Get out! These memories are mine, not yours.

Hands slid underneath me, wrapping the blanket around me like a cocoon. Still, the images hit me like a barrage of enemy fire. I barely knew whether my eyes were open or closed. What was real and what was being remembered?

How had I not seen any of this before now?

My wolf strained against the confines of the blanket as the hands scooped me up and carried me away. Now that she was loose again, she didn't want to be shoved aside. But the bond was full and tossing me around like a rag doll against the tide of his thoughts.

It was nothing like what I'd ever felt before from the any of the others.

Steppe had power. And knowledge. And more than that, pain. And laced through it all was his own conviction—commitment to his beliefs. The problem was that he'd managed to convince himself that killing Werewolves was a worthy and noble cause. It was hate disguised as duty. And it made me want to vomit.

As proof, my stomach swirled and flipped as the hands carrying me jostled their way through the crowd.

"Get him out of here. And George, find some clothes and stop running around on four legs," Wes called as he pushed his way through the crowded room. He adjusted me at the bottom of the stairs and I could feel him looking down. I kept my eyes shut tight against the brimming flow of emotion.

"I keep trying to feel her but our connection is gone," I heard George say to the others. I felt the sadness in his words even without the benefit of an emotional bond. The pang hit me dully in the center of the onslaught of Steppe's ranting, and tears filled my eyes.

Wes pulled me close, kissing my forehead. "You're going to be okay," he said. "Your wolf will take care of you. And so will I."

I tried nodding or responding, but there was nothing. Only silence. My head swung sideways as he turned to carry me to bed and a face swam into view. Familiar blonde hair, soft skin, and angry eyes stared back at me, the chaos of the room a perfect backdrop to the tunneled clarity through which I saw her.

The bond shifted and my view of her became double-paned. Two realities. Past and present. Then and now. Lies and truths. All of them attached to secrets. All of them his greatest failure, her greatest fear.

"Cord," I said softly. I had no idea whether I'd managed the word aloud. And she didn't react to my greeting.

Then, Wes swung me up the staircase and back to bed. I didn't open my eyes or mouth again that night.

Chapter Thirteen

I woke hot and flushed in the stuffy bedroom. Warming sunlight streamed through the window, hurting my eyes and sending them blinking as I struggled to take in my surroundings. For a panicked moment, I couldn't remember where I was or how I'd come to be in bed in a room that smelled like pine, decorated like a log cabin. Blankets and limbs were wrapped in each other, creating a hot cocoon. I needed to breathe. I tossed the cover aside, revealing an arm that was not my own wrapped firmly around my hips.

I followed it to its owner and remembered. The night's events came flooding back, starting with my escape from Gordon's lair—had that really only been twenty-four hours ago? I checked the bedside clock and sure enough, I'd only been asleep a few hours. It was barely lunchtime. In the cheerful sunlight and quiet bedroom, yesterday seemed so distant.

I relaxed and snuggled back in against a still-sleeping Wes. His arm tightened around me, pulling me closer, and I let him, forcing my brain—and my lungs—to calm down.

But the longer I lay there, the more awake I became.

My escape the previous day had been the easy part. The rest of it had been nearly overwhelming to my senses. The attack from those wolves at the highway rest stop. Derek roughing up Steppe at the side of the road while I stood by, feeling the pain. George's attack on Steppe.

Broken Blood

I needed to see George and the others. Make sure everyone was calm after the events of last night. I didn't have to poke very far to know Steppe was hurting. Both from the scratches left by George's claws and from my trespass across the stretch of his mind. Cord. No, I couldn't think about that now.

I lay back and stared at the ceiling, disbelief still coating everything else.

I'd been so focused on keeping him at bay, pushing him out of my thoughts and memories, that I hadn't realized I'd failed to push my way into his. But the moment I'd shifted, I no longer had a choice. My wolf made everything stronger, including, and especially, a blood bond.

There was no way to unknow what I'd learned. And no one was going to like it when I told them, either. I shifted underneath the heavy blankets, debating the possibility of escaping Wes and this room without waking him.

The moment I slid away and sat up, Wes cracked an eye. "Going somewhere?" he asked in a voice that let me know he'd been awake long before this moment.

I sighed. "I need to talk to Steppe."

"Not a chance." He slid his hand around my hip and pulled me back down to the mattress, sitting up on his elbow and planting a kiss on my cheek. "We're actually in an alternate universe right now where only you and me and this room exist. There's nothing out there for you," he said, planting kisses between words. "Only this, here. With me."

I smiled and gave in, turning my head to meet our lips. My hands slid up and around his neck in a movement so familiar, so heartbreakingly absent from my life these last weeks, tears welled and escaped before I could catch them.

Wes broke the kiss and dusted my cheeks with his fingertips. "What's this?" he asked softly. "There's no crying allowed in this alternate dimension."

I tried for a smile but it felt small and sad. "You're different," I said, and behind his eyes, worry and fear flashed and were gone.

"How so?" he asked but he leaned away, his expression serious as he abandoned the jokes.

"You're not so intense with the need to control," I said slowly, choosing my words carefully. Something about his show of nerves put me on edge, like I might offend him by pointing out his pain. "Usually, you'd be a mess by now with everything going on and worrying about me."

A shadow passed over his features as the fear flickered in and out again. "I'm still a mess worrying about you, but … I'm trying to make you feel better. You've been through a lot and I don't want you to be scared because you see my worry. And I don't want to fight about it," he added quietly. "Like we usually do."

"Wes, it's okay to let your feelings show. I'm not going to break."

Or maybe I already was. But I couldn't say that.

"I know that. But I can't do anything else for you." His grip on me tightened as he spoke and frustration leaked into his words. "I wasn't there. I couldn't stop … everything that happened to you. I couldn't protect you then. And now, with Gordon in your head, I can't protect you from that either. So if I can distract you, give you happiness or a smile or whatever for just five minutes, that's what I'll do. Because that's something. And sitting on the sidelines doing nothing, *that* will make me feel like a mess."

"In that case, distract away," I said.

He grinned and leaned in, his eyes on my mouth in a way that made me shiver. I raised my chin, eager for more kisses, when the bedroom door opened.

"Aren't you supposed to be on babysitting duty?" My mother glared at Wes.

Wes jumped to his feet, clearly guilty, and shoved his hands in his pockets. "My shift ended an hour ago," he said without quite meeting her eyes.

Thank God he had his jeans on.

"In that case, we could use some extra hands for breakfast duty," my mom said.

Wes glanced at the clock. "It's closer to lunch," he said, and then when my mom's expression darkened, he added, "Ma'am."

She only glared.

Wes grabbed his discarded shirt from the floor beside the bed and yanked it on. "I'm on it," he mumbled.

He glanced down at me and then slipped past my mom without another word. I pressed my lips together to keep from laughing at how he could go from alpha Werewolf to intimidated schoolboy so quickly.

My mom had that affect.

Broken Blood

"That wasn't nice," I said when he was gone.

She leveled her stern expression at me and I shrank back. Okay, now I knew why Wes had broken so easily. "You might not be under my roof but you are still my daughter. And I am still your mother."

"I turned eighteen a couple of months ago," I pointed out.

My mother's expression softened. "I know. I'm sorry we never really did much to celebrate that."

"It's fine. Cambria took me out, remember?"

"A night at the pool hall isn't what I would've ..." She trailed off into a sigh and I tried not to think about where we stood back then. My mother and I had been in a rough place ever since I'd learned what I was. "We'll make up for it this year," she added and I wondered if she meant more than just a missed birthday party.

She sat on the edge of the bed and smoothed my hair back. "That was quite a show last night. How are you feeling?"

"Better," I said. And then, because I wanted her prediction of making up for it to come true, I asked, "How are you feeling?"

She blinked. "Me? I'm fine, why?"

"Mom, your only daughter was held captive for weeks. You saw me shift into a wolf last night right before your eyes and then shift back, stark naked, in a room full of people. And you just found me in bed with my boyfriend, half-clothed. If anyone should be having a breakdown here it's you."

She smiled wryly. "Well, when you put it that way ... There's got to be a dirty oven around here somewhere."

Her smile faded quickly and the moment turned heavy. "I wanted to talk to you alone because ... I ... there's something..."

"Spit it out, Mom," I said, my voice teasingly light compared to the ball of knots twisting away in my stomach. My mother was high-anxiety and high-stress, usually in the form of too much cleaning products and a lack of sense of humor—but this was strange even for her.

"It's not that easy," she said, her gaze darting every which way but at me. She twisted the edge of the bedsheet between her fingers and licked her lips. When her eyes finally found mine, there was only one thing reflected back at me. A thing I understood well by now: secrets.

"Mom, tell me," I repeated firmly.

She opened her mouth, ready to spill ... something, and the door opened again. She shut her mouth and we turned toward the intruder.

"Fee!" I said, jumping up and running to her, arms open, irritation already evaporating. There would be time to talk later. Not like my mom hadn't kept things before.

"Hello, Tara." Fee smiled and opened her arms, folding me into a warm hug. I inhaled the scent of her—the same scent her entire house had carried back in Frederick Falls—and my chest ached with the memories that came with it. I'd woken up in that house more than once after a fight and Fee had always been right there, her ability to heal saving my life from Werewolf bites and scratches—and even once, my mother's anger at finding out I'd lied. But I refused to let my reminiscing dampen the moment.

I smiled back at Fee and stepped aside so my mom could lean over and hug Fee too. When had my mom adjusted this way to Werewolves being back in our lives?

"When did you get here?" I asked. "Is Jack here? Did you have any problems?"

"One question at a time," she said, laughing. Her blonde hair shook lightly where it hung in pretty waves over her shoulders. I remembered the first time I'd seen her. Wavy hair spilling down her back, petite, pretty frame. Her entire aura had been gentle and nurturing on a day where everything else had been uncertain and terrifying. Seeing her had taken away my fear. And I'd had plenty to be afraid of that day. Just like today, in fact.

"First," she continued, holding up a finger, "Let's get you feeling better. I heard you've had some problems shifting lately. And you've been running on fumes, exhausted, from what it sounds."

I hung my head, guilty as charged. "Those are probably the least of what I've got going on," I mumbled.

Fee took my hand, squeezed. "Then let's talk about it and get you well. Elizabeth, would you mind gathering some ingredients for my tea?" she asked.

"Sure, tell me what you need," my mom said.

Fee rattled off a few things I'd never heard of and a few things I had. Somewhere between lavender and chamomile I was pretty sure I heard her ask for Hawkweed and something called Holy Basil. I decided I'd rather not know.

"I'll get them together and have them brought up," my mom said. She planted a kiss on my forehead, whispering, "We'll talk later," and slipped out.

Fee wasted no time guiding me back to bed and beginning an official exam. Pulse, temperature, blood pressure, reflexes. Questions.

"And this bond with Steppe? Is it manageable, I mean, like the others?" she asked when I'd told her everything I could about my confinement and the experiments done. Something about the clinical way Fee approached my answers made it easier to relive. I took a deep breath, thinking it over before answering that last one.

"It's different than the others," I said slowly, doing my best to understand it before attempting to describe it to someone else.

"Go on," she said.

"He's darker. Smarter. And pushy. He won't back off and let my thoughts be mine. He wants them all. The others were polite ... at least as much as possible given the situation. They would back off when they neared something private but not Steppe. He's ... intrusive." I said.

"And you're exhausted trying to push him out," she concluded.

"Yes. Until last night when I shifted, I'd concentrated only on keeping him at the edges. But my wolf opened things the other way, I guess, and now I'm in his head too." I smiled tightly. "He doesn't like it very much."

As proof, Gordon mentally scowled and I sucker punched him.

"Good for you. See what you can find out," Fee said, patting my hand.

I mumbled that I would and fell silent, fighting my temptation to spill what I'd already gleaned. My discovery was huge, but more than the truth itself, the secret belonged to someone I couldn't afford to betray or make an enemy out of. Not when enlisting her help could be the wild card we needed to take Steppe down once and for all.

"I will," I promised instead.

"I'm told last night was your first shift since whatever Gordon did to suppress your wolf during those weeks you were held. How are you feeling?"

"Twitchy," I admitted. "My wolf didn't want to be shoved back inside so quickly."

"I know the feeling. Or, opposite, in fact," she said. "Jack and I spent much of the last few weeks as wolves. It was safer and easier to hide that way."

My expression clouded. "I'm glad you're both safe."

"Me too," she said. We fell silent and I knew we were both thinking about what lay ahead and how not everyone involved would come through as safely as we had so far.

Fee took a deep breath and said, "In the meantime, I'm going to check on that tea and I want you to relax and rest. There's a meeting after breakfast to discuss our next steps. I'll send Wes up to get you."

She rose and stood over me, a stern expression already in place. I knew she expected me to argue and want to come down now, but I just nodded and let her tuck me in tighter before she left.

There was plenty I could do from right here.

Steppe, I thought. *We need to talk.*

Do we? I'm surprised, was the almost instant reply.

Something about his smug confidence rubbed at me wrong. *Why is that?*

I would've thought you'd be far more eager to talk to—Oh, never mind. I see.

His voice abruptly shut off and pulled back, almost like he waited in the stands. I shoved at him, demanding to know what he saw but just before I could shove my way in and find the answer for myself, someone knocked.

"Come in," I said, distracted by my mental tug of war.

I expected Fee or my mother or even Wes, bringing my herbal medicine, but it wasn't any of them standing there holding a tray containing a teacup and steaming kettle.

Every nerve ending from my hair to my big toe stood up. If there'd been anything in my stomach, it would've threatened a reappearance. I could only stare, drinking him in with a thirst I hadn't known I possessed—and frankly, wished would dry up already.

"Alex," I said, my tone sticking somewhere between anger and affection.

"Tara." My name said it all. Worry, fear, regret. Relief. I sighed even as he said it and felt the anger give way to the rest. Despite everything, I was glad to see him.

"Come in," I said simply.

The uncertainty in his expression dissolved and the lines around his mouth and eyes relaxed. His muscles went from bunched to reactive as he crossed the room and drew me into his arms. Not exactly what I'd meant, but I was too shocked to protest.

Broken Blood

I braced myself as emotions rushed in and out again. For a brief moment, my arms hung limply beside me but then, despite my better judgment, I slowly reached up and wrapped them around his shoulders—and did my best to pretend everything was this simple between us.

I held on, both arms locked, hands to elbows, and shut my eyes against the onslaught of the feels. He did the same, neither of us saying a word, neither of us letting go. His fingers curled around my hips, every tip a point of relief that infuriated me just for feeling it.

In the back of my mind, I felt Steppe watching. Reading it all. Sifting through my thoughts like the aftermath of a bomb's blast. But I couldn't care enough to block him out. There were too many other things to think.

"I've been worried ever since…" He trailed off, his lips moving against my hair, his hands finally releasing their pressurized grip from the small of back. Vaguely, I felt the surprise that came with the realization that the strongest thing I felt when I looked at him was comfort and relief instead of the fury I'd felt last time. "I'm so sorry," he added quietly, reading my expression.

In my thoughts, Gordon smirked and I caught fleeting pictures of Alex's narrow escape that day. He'd told me too much. Gordon had tried to punish him for it.

"You're okay," I said, halfway between a question and a statement.

Alex's brow rose. "More okay than you, I'd imagine."

"You told me too much," I said. "Gordon only wanted you to ruin my trust. He didn't want me to know how far back it went for him."

Alex cocked his head at me, but the surprise was small. "You're reading all that through the bond," he said.

I stared at him, my mind still stuck on the events of that day Alex had come to see me. "He outed you," I said. "You're off the strike team."

"I had it coming," he said. "I also have a warrant out. Did you get to that part yet?" he asked wryly.

A small part of me wanted to snap back something about just rewards and betrayal, but I kept my lips pressed tightly shut.

"I know what you think of me," he said quietly. "I'm the last person you wanted to see, I know. But that's why I came. I can only hope I'll regain your trust someday." His lips quirked in a hopeful smile. "The hug was a good sign."

"The hug was …" I had no idea how to finish that one. I shook my head. "You're right. I don't trust you, not completely. And that's your own fault. But I have had some time to think about it, not to mention seeing it from Steppe's point of view. I understand why you did it and I know that you were ultimately trying to protect me. I see how he used that to manipulate you."

Alex's eyes lit up. "Does that mean you forgive me?"

"I'm working on it," I qualified.

His smile widened. I needed to change the subject. Alex Channing was such a gray area of my life.

"Do the others know you're here?" I asked.

"Well … they know I'm in the house, yes. This particular room at this particular moment, not so much."

I thought of Wes and what he'd say when he found out. Gordon grinned in my head. "When did you get here?" I asked.

"Last night," he said. "Edie decided it would be better to wait until today to see you." The whispered questions between her and my mother all made sense now.

"Better for you or for me?" I asked. Alex shrugged and something else hit me. "So you were here to see me … shift?"

"And your streaking exit," he said, clearly trying to contain his laughter.

I groaned. "And out of morbid curiosity, which one do you think I should be more embarrassed about?"

He grinned. "I can promise I will never, no matter what happens between us, ever complain about seeing you naked."

I thought about punching him. Surprisingly, the voice in my head agreed, which is the only thing that kept me from following through.

"What's wrong?" Alex asked, the smile disappearing as he took in my expression. "Are you okay?"

"I'm fine. It's just a little loud."

"Do you—I mean, can you hear him? Like, right now?" he asked.

"Yeah. He's here, I guess you could say."

His expression darkened and I knew the ferocity was meant for Steppe. "Anything good?"

I hesitated, the light moment instantly gone. I opened my mouth and closed it again, suddenly uncertain as I thought of a hundred other moments just like this one that we'd shared—and how, despite them all, Alex had betrayed me. "I'd rather not share," I said quietly.

"Right. Earning the trust," he mumbled. He rose awkwardly, his hands shoved into his pockets. "I'll just … see you downstairs."

I watched him go, his shoulders stiff and straight, as my mind drifted back to the secret I'd learned "Alex," I called and he turned back. "Can I ask you something?"

"Anything. Always."

"Do you ever think about your dad and the kind of person he was? The kind of person he tried to make you be and who you are now without him?"

Alex stared at me as if searching underneath my words for whatever was making me ask, but finally he answered. "All the time," he said. "At first it used to make me feel like crap. It's one of the reasons it took me so long to accept you being…" He trailed off and his cheeks flushed.

"My being a Werewolf," I supplied.

"Yeah," he said a little guiltily. "I had this idea in my head that I was supposed to make him proud. End of story. Rejecting that picture, going against his beliefs was the hardest thing I've ever done."

"I thought training me was the hardest thing you've ever done," I teased, but it fell flat because we both knew he'd just admitted once again to being so torn, he'd actually carried out orders against me.

"Right. Second hardest," he said.

"Would you still have made this decision if he were alive?" I asked.

"I don't know," he admitted. "But thank God I did. I can't imagine my life without you, Tara."

"I didn't—"

"I know. I meant that strictly platonic," he said.

I arched a brow. "Okay, not strictly. Loosely," he corrected. When I still didn't answer, he said, "Metaphorically?"

A small laugh escaped. "Don't worry. Metaphorically," I said, "I'm not going anywhere." There was nothing metaphoric or figurative about the look he gave me when I said it.

After he left, I replayed it over in my mind, the conversation overlapping with Steppe's memories of all the times he'd played on Alex's emotions, on his feelings for his dad and for me. Alex had come so far, become such a stronger person since we'd met. I knew a lot of that was because of meeting me, being forced to see the world from another viewpoint. For the first time, I was able to identify the root of Alex's feelings. That he'd mistaken his desire to live, to be a different person for feelings for me. I knew he still couldn't see the difference. He probably still thought he was in love with me.

    I thought about the way he'd smiled at me when I told him I'd forgiven him, the relief in his eyes at seeing me here, unharmed and out of that prison. He'd looked radiant with relief when I'd assured him I wouldn't go anywhere. I hoped, for his sake, he knew I'd only meant that as a promise between friends. And I wondered if I'd just made some sort of promise that, in the end, I wouldn't—or couldn't—keep.

Chapter Fourteen

In the streaming light from the window, the faces of my friends and family seemed to shine with an otherworldly determination. The living room was filled to the brim with the people I cared about. Each of them reflected a fierceness that I couldn't quite muster as the conversation flitted from suggestions of violence to espionage.

I stayed mostly quiet, unwilling to admit I didn't share their zeal. Maybe it was Steppe's voice in my head pointing out the flaws to every suggestion they made or maybe it was my conversation with Alex and how I still felt like I was straddling both worlds. A decision I'd yet to make about whose side I was really on. I couldn't shake the feeling that no matter how much time had passed, no matter how much progress had been made since I'd joined this group of warriors, we were still at a stalemate. Werewolves hated Hunters. Hunters hated Werewolves.

Only one thing currently united them, thanks to Steppe's doctored video footage: they all hated me.

I wasn't sure how—or even if—it would ever end.

Beside me, Wes rose and ran a hand through his tousled hair in a cursory gesture. His cheeks were flushed as he paced in the small space between the edge of the couch where I sat and the bookshelf lining the wall behind him. Even the air around him seemed to pulse with anxious energy. This was the Wes I knew, the one that required action in the face of a crisis.

"I don't understand why we're still discussing this. It's not even a question. We have to remove their bond," Wes said, frustration and impatience equal parts in his tone and body language.

"There's no way to do that—" Logan began, but Wes cut him off.

"There is a way. Steppe managed it and now Tara's free from that entire pack, thank God. Imagine what it would've felt like having to experience their deaths, one by one. This bond is only going to hurt her. We have to sever it before it does."

I winced but kept silent. He didn't need to know the pain I'd felt over losing Chris. I caught Cambria looking at me and smoothed my expression, but her frown remained.

"Wes is right. Steppe obviously figured out a way to do it," my mother said warily. I knew she and Wes agreed in this, at least. Removing my bond. Protecting me. This was always their first and last priority. "But not without help," she added with a pointed look at my uncle.

Astor fidgeted in his chair, his slippers peeking out from the too-long flannel pajamas he wore. A few glances flickered to Astor and then back at me before everyone's attention settled on him.

In my head, Steppe was grumpy, but he was quiet. His mental energy was focused on cataloguing Professor Flaherty's collection of hand-blown glass she kept in her basement. It made me suspicious, and I tried to remember everything I'd overheard while in Steppe's custody.

"Astor, how did Steppe remove the bond?" Professor Flaherty asked. He looked from face to face with a handful of nervous glances. Professor Flaherty laid her hand on his shoulder. "Take your time."

When his eyes landed on mine, his expression softened and cleared. He was himself—at least for now. I exhaled and watched him do the same before he spoke. "He didn't remove it, exactly," Astor said.

"Then how did—?" Wes began, but now it was Logan who cut him off.

"Let him talk," Logan snapped.

Wes glared but said nothing.

"More like he redirected it," Astor said. "After researching the two cortices of the cerebral cortex, we found that the area buried in the sulci controlling conscious thought streams could be redirected by an emotional or sympathetic—"

"In English, man," George cut in, earning a disapproving look from Astor. Beside George, Emma tugged on his arm and gave him a disapproving look and he scowled.

"We re-bonded the hybrid pack to Olivia by making them feel sorry for her."

A beat of silence passed. Everyone stared at Astor until, one by one, they shared glances with each other. It was a roomful of silent communications.

"Was there a blood transfusion involved?" Fee asked.

"Of course. But the bond wasn't complete until the emotional connection was made," Astor explained. "Just like with George and Tara that first time or with Gordon last night. They had to let go and let each other in."

"Why didn't Steppe do it himself?" Wes asked. "Surely he would want to bond with them himself so he could control them."

"We tried," Astor said with a frown that turned to a twitch. "Our attempts were unsuccessful."

"Why?" Wes pressed.

"Because there was no emotion to connect to," I said.

In my mind, Gordon cursed.

Everyone shifted to me. "But you and Gordon are…" Logan pointed out, trailing off as if he'd realized too late he'd hit a sore spot.

"I feed his darkness," I said dully.

"No, you keep it at bay," Emma said. I looked at her in surprise. For one, that she'd spoken at all in such a large group, and for two, the knowing look she shared with George and the way their expressions both softened as they looked back at me, hands clasped.

"It's true," George said. "With the pack before and with…"

"Janie," Emma finished.

"And Nick," George added. "You kept them sane for so long simply by balancing out the darkness that was in them. Even we could see that and we'd already fought ours back. You held us all together, Tara."

I could only stare at them in muted gratitude as a single tear slipped down my cheek.

"You think that's what she's able to do with Steppe," my mother said and the conversation turned back to a scientific speculation of my mental capability to handle more than the average hybrid. Even Grandma, Jack, and Fee weighed in that it seemed to be an anomaly of my own Dirty Blood and maybe my dad's stabilizing cocktail that had made me immune to the weaknesses most Werewolves faced.

None of them seemed to notice my reaction. I swiped hurriedly at the tear and hardened my face into something business-like. If I was able to bond more easily to Steppe, it was stripping my emotional strength faster than PMS during the flu.

I caught Cambria looking at me again. When she saw me watching, her attention flickered away to something behind me. A second later, Wes returned to perch on the arm of the couch beside me. His hand came down on my shoulder and rubbed circles along my neck and back.

"...bonding her with Olivia," my mother was saying when my attention drifted back. "That's almost worse than being bonded with Steppe."

"Is it?" Grandma said. "Olivia's weak-minded, malleable. Maybe our girl could use that to—"

"I'm not bonding with Olivia," I said. Everyone fell quiet and I gathered my strength, ignoring the way Grandma's mouth opened in preparation to return fire. I pressed on, suddenly overcome with irritation at my own lack of contribution up until now. I was not letting Steppe hold me down.

I stood up, my hands fisted. "With any luck, Olivia is still locked in that cage we left her in. A team should head out, today if possible, and retrieve her, put her somewhere more secure until we can figure out what to do with her. In the meantime, we need to move on from this idea about removing or redirecting the bond. Steppe is in my head but I'm in his just as much."

My eyes flickered to Derek and then, beside him, Cord. She sat with arms folded and a set line to her mouth. All business. My pulse quickened.

"I plan to use that," I went on. "In the meantime, we need to come up with a plan for reversing the law and fixing things between our races. This has been our goal all along. We can't get distracted now."

"Tara's right. If we don't do something soon, it might be too late," Derek said. "They're already after Tara. Next up, they'll go after each other."

"We need a leadership," Grandma agreed. "If we can remove Steppe from power, we can change the laws." She cocked her head at me. "Although, getting him to rescind the changes would be easier considering CHAS protocol. I don't suppose there's any chance of that happening?"

I scowled at the images Steppe was throwing at me. Images of his signature on the documents decreeing the dissolution of the treaty with The Cause. A raid he'd ordered on Jack and Fee's house. I pressed my lips together and sighed. "No, not at this time."

"We could spend some time with him," Derek said quietly. He nodded at Wes beside me. "Between Wes and myself, we would eventually get through to him."

"That would hurt Tara," Wes reminded him. "No one's having a go at Steppe," he said to the rest of the group. His glare challenged anyone to argue. No one did.

"So, replacing him," Cambria said. "What would that take?"

"More than we can do," Grandma said sadly. "CHAS leadership can only be changed one of two ways. First, the person stepping down would appoint their position to their next of kin."

"So, family," Cambria said. "Does Steppe have any?"

"None still living," Grandma said.

My stomach fluttered at that, but I said nothing. Not yet. Not like this. In my mind, Steppe threatened and cursed but I ignored him. When that didn't work, I watched while he took his temper out on his current guard, Jack.

Jack took it in stride, ignoring Steppe in favor of exploring Professor Flaherty's sea glass collection. It only made Steppe angrier—which only made Jack smile.

"His lack of family makes this that much harder," Grandma went on. "According to our laws, which date back as far as The Draven was written, the only other way to replace leadership is to hold a vote among the other members of the board."

"Why is that so hard?" Cambria asked. "Let's just get everyone together. I'm sure we can sway them enough to swing it in our favor."

One by one, everyone turned to look at Logan. My chest felt weighted and I blinked back tears for the second time in as many minutes. My emotions were strung so tight between the bond and my friends … Everything we'd lost.

Not just Logan's dad and the vote he'd represented. I thought of Victoria's mother. Bailey. My father. Even Miles and Leo. The past was littered with the victims of bigotry.

"It's fine," Logan said in a hoarse voice. Beside him, Victoria reached over and took his had in hers. Logan stared down at it and then back up at Astor. But Astor was looking down at his buttons and mumbling to himself.

"Astor," Logan called. Finally, he looked up and their eyes met. "It's okay. I understand." Logan's words were strained but heartfelt. Astor nodded, sucking his bottom lip into his mouth so his chin lifted, and looked away. Logan cleared his throat.

"With Mr. Sandefur and Hugo gone and me fired, there's not enough of a board left," Grandma explained.

I looked at Wes, whose features had hardened into an impenetrable shell. He didn't look surprised, though. Most of them didn't. In fact, almost everyone had lost their determination from earlier. Now, they all looked resigned.

"Don't forget about the video," Derek said.

"There's footage of that?" I asked, horrified.

The ensuing silence made me more nervous that the idea of the video itself. I'd seen the way it happened, but I'd also seen the events leading up to it.

"It was released on the secure channel for Hunters by CHAS," Wes explained quietly. "It shows Astor attacking Mr. Sandefur." His hand hadn't stopped its circular pattern on my back, but I could no longer feel it. Everything felt numb. These videos they kept talking about, the ones painting us as the bad guys—I finally understood the seriousness of the effect they must be having.

"That was the night our allies stopped being our allies," Fee added.

At the mention of allies, Jack's gaze flicked over to Mr. Lexington, who stood stiffly behind his daughter. Neither of them had said a word during our meeting. Victoria's hand sat limply in Logan's, a faraway look fastened to her pale features. She somehow seemed to look right at and straight through whoever was speaking at the time.

"Are there no packs still open to peace talks?" Grandma asked quietly.

"None that we found," Fee said in a sad voice. Jack put his arm around her and something inside me pulled tight, cracking along the edges.

No one spoke for a long moment. I could practically feel the discouragement in the room and it flipped a switch inside me.

I looked across the room to the far wall, straight at Alex. "I need you to take Mr. Lexington and Victoria and go get Olivia from that cage we left her in. You can take the van and bring her back here."

Alex pushed off from where he'd been listening from the back of the room and folded his arms. "Now?" he asked.

Victoria made a noise of protest but Logan patted her hand. "I'll go with them," he said before she could argue.

"Yes, now," I told Alex. "Victoria can track her in case she isn't where we left her." I looked at Mr. Lexington. "Can you bring back any of the medical supplies Astor would need to form a blood bond?"

He nodded. "Not a problem. We can be there and back by this time tomorrow."

"Good. Professor Flaherty, we need a place to keep both Steppe and Victoria and we'll need them close by so we can guard them both at once instead of adding to our shift schedule."

"The basement can be divided. I have an old chalkboard and some other wood we can use to partition the space," she said a little uncertain. "It'll take some time to construct it."

"Derek, can you help with that? Maybe ask Jack?" I asked.

"Sure," Derek said.

"Grandma, we need a shift schedule for guarding the prisoners."

She winked at me, never missing a beat. "On it," she said.

"Tara, this is—" my mom began, but I cut her off.

"Mom, Fee, I could really use an extra pair of eyes or two on The Draven. We need to study the laws to see if there's a loophole in reversing anything Steppe has done," I said.

My mother's eyes widened at me and her jaw hung slack as she regarded me from behind Astor's chair.

"Mom," I pressed when she didn't answer. "Can you do this for me or not?"

"I ... yes," she said finally and promptly closed her jaw.

I glanced down and found Astor grinning at me. He caught my eye and winked just as Grandma had. My mouth twitched. It felt good to be in control again, ready to fight, to plan, to take action.

"I'm sorry, this all sounds great, but someone's got to say it." Across the room, Cord pushed to her feet. "We're ignoring the bigger problem here. Sooner or later, probably sooner if I had to guess, these ex-allied packs are going to find out where we're hiding and they're going to do the same thing they've been trying to do for weeks. We're sitting ducks here, just waiting to be picked off. We should be coming up with a plan for counter-offense or something, not figuring out how to extricate Olivia and a bunch of syringes."

"Olivia controls some of those packs," I said. "If we can control her, we can stop them."

Cord's eyes narrowed. "Who died and left you in charge anyway?" she snapped.

I took a step forward, angry and determined—and finally ready to fight. Not my problem the only people here to fight with happened to be my own army. Wes grabbed my hand, not so much holding me back as expressing his support. I could all but feel him ready to blast Cord. But I wasn't the first to respond. Neither was he.

"No one died, Cord," Victoria said in an even voice. "Not for this."

It was the first thing she'd said all day and at her words, everyone stared. Including me. "Tara's always been the leader. It just took her a while to step up."

I stared at Victoria, unblinking, as her words registered. With me, with Cord and the others—and with Steppe. Even he didn't argue with it, and I realized as I looked around, I'd been right; they *were* my army. Always had been. They were just waiting for me to take the helm. If their reaction didn't convince me, Steppe's did. He seemed to agree with her, albeit begrudgingly, and I realized he'd always seen me this way. It was the reason he'd felt threatened enough to come after me even after he'd dismantled The Cause and ruined their progress.

I stepped forward, my jaw tight and my shoulders squared. *Here I am*, I thought. And the memory of Vera's predictions and visions wove through me like a twirling ribbon of truth. This moment, standing in the center of their circle, taking my place, felt more real than anything I'd been through these past few weeks. Or maybe it felt real because of everything I'd been through. I wasn't sure.

All I knew was I was ready.

Chapter Fifteen

I waited while everyone filed out, my knee bouncing along at the speed of my apprehension. Of course Cord had challenged me. Of course we weren't friends, despite everything that had happened. The one time I needed her to trust me—

"Holy crap, did you feel the heat from her laser beam eyeballs?" Cambria hissed when the room had emptied. Only Wes and Astor were left, but I couldn't hear their hushed conversation from my perch on the couch.

"Cam, please don't remind me," I said, rubbing my temples in a circular motion that wasn't doing much for the tension headache I had.

"Sorry. I thought she would've chilled out since she'd been Tara-free for a few weeks. Looks like not," she said.

"Where has she been, anyway?" I asked, suddenly curious.

"Wes said she spent a couple of weeks with the family of that girl Steppe had killed. Mal ... I guess Cord knew the girl's parents and wanted to pay her respects." Cambria's phone rang and she paused long enough to check the screen and frown as she ignored the call.

"Who was that?" I asked, instantly suspicious. Cambria never missed out on the chance to talk if she could help it.

"No one," she said.

"Liar," I said.

"Dictator," she shot back with a smirk.

"I am not a dictator. This will be a democracy. And none of that has a thing to do with whose call you're ignoring."

"I know. I meant that's who is calling. The dictator," she said. Her shoulders sagged. "Otherwise known as … my mother."

"Your mom is calling you?" I hissed, lowering my voice to secret-status volume. Cambria had a rocky history with her mom, in that her mom had treated her like a mutant for having the gift of compulsion (when it actually worked) and shipped her off to Wood Point Academy to be rid of "the problem," as she'd called it.

Added to that, Cambria's mom was considered a social outcast in the Hunter world due to her being Werewolf friendly. (I theorized she was just friendly in general when she'd been drinking.) There'd been an incident that had led to her arrest by CHAS, and, thankfully, her release. But even once she'd been free, the two of them hadn't spoken much.

I had to wonder what had prompted the communication now.

"What does she want?" I asked.

Cambria shrugged. "No idea. She calls. I don't answer. It's our thing."

"Cambria, with everything going on, you should think about talking to her. The world's not safe for any of our kind. She might be in trouble."

Cambria scowled. "You think I haven't thought of that?" she demanded in the same whisper-hiss. The kind that meant she didn't want to share this information with anyone else just yet. "But I'm in trouble too. My whole life is trouble. The last thing I want is to drag her into it all."

I couldn't think of a good enough argument against her logic, not when I understood all too well the danger we were all in right now.

"Do you think Cord was right?" I asked, "About the ex-allied looking for us? To attack?"

Cord's brow went up. "Do you even have to ask? You saw what happened at that rest stop before Derek showed up. They want your blood, Tara. And they want your head on a platter."

"I guess I was hoping it wasn't as bad as she made it seem."

Cambria laid her hand over mine in a rare gesture. "It's worse," she admitted.

Our eyes met. Hers were haunted with experiences I'd yet to hear about. A part of me wasn't sure I wanted to. Not now. Not when I'd just found the strength to step up. I couldn't let guilt and regret and whatever else cloud me. Steppe would love that. He was gunning for it. And, according to visions of those no longer with us, I still had a decision to make.

"They're wrong. The enemy is Steppe, not me. Not us," I said, frustrated all over again.

"I know that. But you're bonded with him now," she pointed out. "Which means you'll have to protect him like you'd protect yourself. Cord has a valid point."

I scowled and it came out like a growl that had Cambria patting my hand in sympathy. "I hate it when she's right, too, believe me," she said.

"It's not that," I said.

"What is it?" she asked.

I looked away, toward where Wes and Astor still huddled in deep conversation. Astor's brows were knitted into one hairy caterpillar above his eyes. Wes was bent forward in earnest as he talked, his shoulders hunched. As much as I was curious what they suddenly had to talk about, I knew I needed to find Cord.

"Nothing," I told Cambria, rising. "Or maybe everything. I'll let you know."

***

I found Cord in the kitchen with Logan and Victoria. Their conversation, already low, halted when I walked in. Despite being a leader five minutes ago, my cheeks heated and my chest tightened. It was middle school lunch room all over again, and I realized, no matter how old you get or how many enemies you fight, there will always be a sting when you walk into a roomful of people talking about you behind your back.

"Time to go already?" Victoria asked, breaking the awkward silence.

"They're loading up now," I said. "You better get going."

"Thanks." She pulled Logan along with her and I heard the front door open and shut. Cord hovered only a second longer. When she moved to exit, I stopped her.

"We need to talk," I said, hoping the words were delivered with a neutral tone. Regardless, she glared, arms crossed.

"So talk."

My eyes flickered to the open—and publicly accessible—doorway behind her. "Somewhere more private."

Her glare sharpened. "Based on the squatter in your head, I'm guessing it's never going to be private," she shot back.

"Considering he is the topic of our discussion, I'm going to give you one more chance to take me up on my offer," I said quietly. "Let's take a walk."

Cord's arms fell to her sides. A look of alarm washed over her defenses and she gestured at the doorway. "After you."

No one stopped us as we made our way through the house and out the back door. Cambria watched us, but she didn't say a word. I felt eyes on us from the window as we wandered farther out into the yard.

We got as far as the fence and stopped. There was a gate that led to whatever lay behind the subdivision, but I wasn't ready to be quite that alone. This conversation was going to go one of two ways. And, knowing Cord, it wasn't the easy one.

"What do you want?" she asked, rounding on me, her back to the fence and her arms crossed. Everything about her stance was defensive even before I'd said a word. Between that and Steppe yelling at me to *shut up or else*, I almost turned around and walked back inside.

But nothing he threatened was going to change my mind.

I sighed. "I want the truth, Cord. Your story," I said.

As predicted, her eyes narrowed and her mouth twisted. "My story is none of your business," she said.

"CHAS is my business," I said. "It's more than relevant. Why didn't you say something?"

"What would I say, exactly?" she challenged. "No one would trust me if I told them the truth. They'd look at me just like you are now. Wondering if I were a double agent or what I was going to report back."

"I'm not—No one who knows you would ever think that," I said. "But you can help us now if you come forward. They'll understand why you didn't before but doing it now could mean reversing—"

"You have no idea what it would mean. Not for me. You're only concerned with you. Your cause. Your mission. As usual, you're only thinking about yourself." She snorted and threw up her hands. "I don't have to stand here and listen to this. I don't owe you anything."

She started to walk away but I stepped in front of her, blocking her and breathless with the fear I'd only made things worse. "You're right.

Broken Blood

You don't owe me. I owe you," I said. "When Olivia took you ... what she did because of her hatred for me ... I still owe you for that. Whatever happened in your past that made you lie, whatever you're forced to dig up and relive, I'd owe you for that too. And I'll never forget it, but this is bigger than us. Bigger than your dislike for me or your fear of him." Images flashed through Steppe's mind and I caught a blurred rendition of them before I deliberately forced my attention away. I didn't want to see it that way. Knowing this was enough. I refused to betray Cord's trust by digging any further.

Although, what I saw was enough to make me understand her hesitation. "Don't be scared, Cord," I added. "I won't let him hurt you."

For a split second, her walls came down and I saw the pleading and fear that lived behind her carefully constructed façade. But then just as quickly, the gate came crashing shut and she closed herself off again.

"Screw you, Godfrey. I'm not scared and I don't appreciate your demands that I offer up my past on a platter for your dissection." Her hands shook at her sides and her eyes were wide—not with anger. There was something else.

Even Steppe was quietly deciphering it while she ranted and raved at me. I sank back on my heels as Cord continued, her finger poking its way into my shoulder as she spoke. "I will not be made into a political maneuver now any more than I let myself become one five years ago. I am not going back there. Ever. So don't ask me again."

Desperation.

Steppe named it at the same moment I did. And just as quickly as her vulnerability faded, Steppe's thoughts rose to the surface, confirming what I already suspected.

"This is why you challenged me inside," I said, realization finally dawning. "You knew I would say something. That I would ask you this."

"The moment I heard about the bond, I knew you'd figure it out," she said, her voice ragged. "I don't ... I'm sorry, but I can't do this," she said, her voice breaking into a whisper before she cut off and pressed her lips together in a tight line.

This time, when Cord moved around me, I let her go. I watched her, feeling Steppe's own retreat into the recesses, and thinking about what he'd felt when she'd denied him just now.

Disappointment.

Some small part of him had wanted her to claim him. Some small part had wanted to claim her back.

But if Cord was anything like her dad—and unfortunately, when it came to stubbornness, she clearly was—there was no changing her mind. Without his daughter's public acceptance of her rightful place as leader of CHAS, Gordon Steppe might never be removed.

Chapter Sixteen

Two things bothered me about being woken by a ringing phone. First, I didn't have a phone, not since Steppe had confiscated mine back in DC. And second, Wes took one look at the screen and answered in a slick voice that sounded like death-by-civility. "Hello?"

The second I heard the caller's voice drift through the speaker, I shot up.

"Hang on, she's right here. In bed. Next to me," Wes said in a smug voice. "It's Alex, for you," he added, handing me the phone almost lazily.

The moment I took it, he sank back to the pillows and rolled over. I was way too tired to decipher whether he was mad at being woken or satisfied Alex knew we'd been in bed together. I decided to save that puzzle for later.

"Alex?" I said. "Is everything okay?"

"Everything's fine. We're fine," he said and the emphasis he put on "we're" made my pulse jump.

"What happened?" I asked, sitting up straighter.

Wes rolled back over and eyed me.

"My guess is some sort of ambush," Alex said. In the background, something crashed and shattered. "It must've happened shortly before we arrived because Victoria's tracking still put Olivia here but…"

I gripped the phone tighter. "But what?" I prompted.

"Olivia's gone," he said finally. Another crash followed by muted voices.

"Gone where? What is that noise?" I asked.

"Sorry, the place is pretty trashed. We're trying to be careful but most of the medical supplies are shot," he said. "I don't know where she went, but Victoria's working on it. We found some discarded clothing Olivia wore so she'll use that to try and get a new reading."

My eyes slid to Wes. Judging by his strained expression, he could hear every word. Just in case, I put it on speaker and held it out between us. "Do you think it was one of the angry packs?" I asked.

"Most likely. There are several dead hybrids. Looks like the only one they took alive was Olivia herself. And there are scratch marks along the walls and doors. They didn't come in with opposable thumbs."

Wes rolled his eyes.

"I'm going to check in with V and see what she finds out but I wanted you to know," Alex said.

"Okay, fine, yeah," I said, distracted by the eavesdropping and interjections going on in my head.

"Everything okay there?" Alex asked, a heavy note of concern in his voice.

I stared straight ahead without really seeing anything inside the room. I was too busy manhandling Steppe in my thoughts. "We're fine," I said.

"Good. I'll call you back when I know more," Alex said.

I almost told him to call another number, but that would mean explaining why. I looked over at Wes. "Sounds good," I said instead and disconnected.

I handed Wes the phone and we lay together side by side in the dark room, staring up at the ceiling, each quiet in our thoughts.

"You awake?" he asked a moment later.

"Yes. You?"

He sighed and instead of answering, he said, "Without Olivia, we can't undo Steppe's new laws."

I let that settle around us, chewing my lip.

"There is another option," I said finally.

But Wes went on, either ignoring or misunderstanding my words. "Forming a new board would take months and months. I don't think any of us has that long before these angry pack leaders find out where we are." Wes snorted. "Figures their first real act of cooperation would be to kill us—the ones who tried bringing them all together in the first place."

"They're not going to kill us," I said. "And I didn't mean forming a new board. At least, not that way."

"What do you mean?" he asked, propping himself on his elbow and looking down at me. Distracted, I reached up and smoothed away the hair that fell over his brows.

"You let it grow out," I said softly.

"You said you liked it longer."

Heavy silence settled, charging the air. It had been a long time since the pull between us had allowed for a moment like this. If eyes could dance, we were doing the tango. By the time he gave in and brought his mouth down over mine, my lips were aching for it. My hands slid over his back, up his broad shoulders, and locked around his neck. His hands roamed my body from hips to shoulders and back down over my chest. It was a frenzy of mouths and tangled legs and pressed parts—and still, I ached for more.

"Wes," I said, breathless.

He tugged at the hem of my shirt at the same time my fingers fumbled with the buttons on his jeans. I felt the button slide free and managed to yank the zipper down as Wes went still above me.

"What is it?" I asked as he drew back. His brows were wrinkled, but whatever question rested behind his hooded lids, I didn't recognize it.

"You don't ... I mean, do you remember us ... Never mind," he said. But instead of resuming, he sat up and ran a hand through his hair.

"Do I remember us what?" I asked, propping myself up beside him with my elbows and straightening my shirt. I felt silly or rejected or ... I wasn't sure what.

"Nothing, it's nothing," he said.

I sat up straight. "Wes, tell me."

He opened his mouth as if to respond and then quickly shut it again. He blew out a heavy breath and then asked, "Can Steppe hear what I'm saying right now?"

"I don't know, sort of. It's more a feeling or impression of my thoughts as I respond to what you're saying than—"

"Forget it," he said quickly.

Alarm ran through me. "You're acting weird. Just tell me what' going on."

"I can't."

"Why not?"

"You made me promise not to tell. Not if meant Steppe finding out."

"When the heck did I promise that?" I demanded.

"Right before you made me remove the memory of the conversation," he said.

I started to argue, to spew out a string of demands in response to the hot irritation rising from my stomach to my chest—but something about the severity of his words, the desperate way he watched me, made me think better of it.

"You make it sound like we had a conversation during my confinement," I said slowly. I remembered my strange dreams, the nonsensical images, the foggy picture of him walking toward me in an empty space. No way he knew about that ... right?

His expression was impassive. "Don't make me answer that."

I considered his words—and the sly interest Steppe was showing to my thought stream just now. "All right. Not today," I said finally.

A blush colored his cheeks as he exhaled. "Thank you," he said, clearly relieved, and I almost broke down and demanded answers right there. Since when did Wesley St. John blush?

"You were about to tell me your idea," he said, so successfully changing the subject that I decided to let it go. For now. "About how to handle Steppe with Olivia gone?"

"Right," I said, "About that. So, the easiest or quickest way to fix this is if Steppe were to have some family surface. A relative he could pass his seat to, right?"

"Right." Wes frowned. "But he has no family. Edie already checked and if there were a record, we would know—"

"Not if that family didn't want to be found," I said.

Wes stared back at me. I watched as he considered it, the wheels turning as he worked it out. "You make a valid point. I wouldn't want to be recognized as Steppe's family either. Doesn't change facts. Edie has more contacts than anyone and if she says he has no family, then it's probably true."

"What if this person slipped under the radar? On purpose? Because they didn't want to be found no matter what," I said.

Wes narrowed his eyes to slits that almost glowed white in the shadowy room. "Then I'd say you lucked out," he said. "Who did you find?"

I hesitated. Part of me hated to think about how I was betraying her trust, but like I'd told her already, this was bigger than her. "Cord," I said finally.

A split second passed where Wes simply blinked—and then he burst out laughing.

I folded my arms over my chest and waited. I knew that laugh. It was the same condescending, I-know-everything laugh he'd used the day he'd found out I'd been using a plunger handle as a concealed weapon. It had pissed me off then and it pissed me off now.

"Okay, seriously, this is a little out there, even for you," he said when the laughter had subsided.

"What is that supposed to mean?"

"Nothing," he said, talking quickly now, "I mean that sometimes you come up with ... ideas that are ... not quite..." He trailed off as he took in my souring expression and cleared his throat. "How do you know? Or think you know?"

I tapped my fingertip to my temple and his forehead wrinkled. "Huh?" There was a beat of silence and then his eyes widened in the darkness and he sat up. "Ohhh," he breathed. "Holy…" His jaw dropped. "Have you talked to her about it?"

"Sort of," I said.

I told him about our conversation in the backyard and he sighed. "That sounds like Cord," he said. "I can't believe this. She never said a word. She obviously didn't want anyone to know, ever, or she would've told us. What are you going to do now?"

"I don't know. I can't force her to step up and take the position," I said, and in my mind, Steppe felt smug. "But with both sides out for blood, I don't know what other choice we have."

"Are you going to tell the others?" he asked.

"I don't know."

"Bullying her into it won't work," he warned.

"Believe me, I know. The only other possibility is to make her trust me." Wes gave me a look and I rolled my eyes. "I know," I said. "Also impossible."

His skepticism melted into a smile and he leaned in, planting a quick kiss on my mouth. "I've learned nothing is impossible," he said.

"Especially for you."

Someone knocked. I looked at the clock, but Wes jumped clear of the bed and into the attached bathroom in one swift motion.

"Yeah?" I called out warily.

The door opened a crack, a single beam of light streaming in from the hallway. "Is it safe?" Cambria called through the opening.

Wes reappeared from the bathroom. "As it'll ever be," he called out before I could answer. The door opened just as he leaned over and scooped his discarded tee off the floor. I reached over and clicked on the lamp.

"Liar," Cambria said when she spotted him. And then to me, "Does your mother know he's sleeping in here again?"

Before I could answer, the door opened again and George appeared with Emma hovering behind him. At the sight of Wes pulling his shirt on and Cambria making herself comfortable beside me on the bed, George grinned and pulled Emma into the room with him.

"Shut the door," Cambria called and Emma pushed on it with her heel.

"Now that the party's here," Cambria said, crossing her legs, "You can finish the joke."

"What joke?" George asked.

"There's no joke," I said, exchanging a glance with Wes.

"Oh, there was definitely a joke," Cambria said. "I could hear Wes clear down the hall."

The door opened as she said it and Derek walked in, adding, "Your mom's a joke."

Cambria's brow shot up. "Who are you talking to?"

"Wes, of course," he said, sitting beside her at the foot of the mattress.

"Dude. My mom's dead," Wes pointed out.

"Oh, right, sorry," Derek said, ducking his head. "Tara's then."

Wes snorted and I gave him a look. "You're not going to defend my mother?" I demanded in mock indignation.

He shrugged. "Have you met your mom? Pretty sure she can fight her own battles."

Cambria made a strange noise and George asked, "Did you just laugh snort?"

"Okay, why are you all in my room in the middle of the night?" I interrupted.

George, Emma, and Derek all turned to Cambria—who turned to me with a guilty expression.

"What happened?" I demanded. "And this better not be like the time you set the kitchen on fire with bread dough and cooking wine," I said. "Because I am not lying for you again."

"It's nothing like that," she assured me.

"Then what?" I asked.

"What did Alex say?" she asked.

"He said—" I looked from her to the others, taking in their collective expression of *busted*. "Wait, how did you know he called?"

"We were up late and…" Cambria trailed off, not meeting my eyes.

"Why were you up late?" Wes asked—at least I wasn't the only one in the dark here.

"Something happened. We … didn't want to bother you," George said, his nervous gaze cutting up to where Wes stood beside me.

"You better tell them," Derek muttered.

"There was an attempted attack by a pack of Werewolves," Cambria said.

"What? When?" I demanded.

"Was anyone hurt?" Wes asked at the same time.

"No one was hurt. They didn't breach the house. Edie," George said to me, "apparently travels with an arsenal in that Hummer."

"Where's the Hummer?" I asked, confused as I thought of the empty driveway we'd seen upon arrival.

"In the garage," Derek said.

"Anyway," George went on. "Edie unloaded enough weaponry to arm a small country. She and the others formed a perimeter along the back fence. Derek and I took care of the ones coming in from the front." He put up a hand to stop the argument I was about to unleash. "From the safety of the dining room windows," he added. "Edie gave us crossbows. We never even shifted."

I looked from him to Emma, who tried for a reassuring smile. I felt too bad not to return it and the gesture softened me.

"Why didn't you come get us?" Wes asked, not quite as forgiving.

"We didn't want Tara caught up," Derek said, but he looked guilty again.

"Your mom said you needed rest," Cambria added and I could almost hear the words in my mother's voice in my head as she said them.

"I need to be informed," I said through gritted teeth.

"Next time, come get us," Wes said.

"But we handled it," Derek began. Wes silenced him with a look. "You got it, bro," he muttered.

"Do you think they'll come back tonight or wait?" I asked.

"At this point, we're assuming the worst," Derek said, rising. "We need to make a patrol schedule. Cord took first shift. I told her Wes and I would relieve her. We need to make regular rounds of the woods in back."

"What about the street view out front?" Wes asked.

"Edie's using a contact to hook into the security cameras installed by the homeowner's association. It should give us a clear street view," Derek said.

After everything I'd learned about Grandma, this barely surprised me.

Wes leaned in and kissed my cheek on his way out the door. "I'm going to check in with Cord. I'll find you in a bit."

I grabbed his arm before he could leave. "Can you put me on the next rotation with her?" I asked.

He frowned. "Tara, you shouldn't be—"

"Wes. I'm not asking," I said. After a moment, he nodded.

"All right," he said quietly. Another kiss and then he handed me his phone. "In case Alex calls back. I'll find you later."

I stared after him, trying to read the meaning of the phone hand off. I hadn't come any closer by the time the door shut behind him and Derek.

"He seems ... adjusted," Cambria said.

I turned back, about to give her a look for bringing it up in front of George and Emma. But then I realized they knew just as much as her—if not more. They'd been inside my head up until a few weeks ago, after all.

"He's different," I said and I wondered if I meant Alex or Wes.

"We all are," George said quietly, a shadow crossing his features. Emma squeezed his hand and Cambria looked away to stare out the window at the moonlit forest.

"What happened while I was gone?" I asked. "I get the feeling it was more than just running from Steppe's goons and a trumped-up YouTube channel. No one will tell me anything straight."

George and Emma said nothing.

Broken Blood

"They're just trying to protect you," Cambria said.

"I think I've proven I can handle it," I pointed out. "Besides, if you don't tell me, I'm forced to go on what Steppe wants me to see. Which isn't pretty."

"None of it's pretty," Cambria agreed.

"So, tell me," I pressed. "All of you keep alluding to bad things and you sit here like it's no big deal that we're being attacked right now. I don't get it. What am I missing?"

Cambria exchanged a look with George who nodded. "There's a reason we don't seem more surprised or riled up," Cambria said. "This isn't a new thing for us."

"So, there were a few attempts at violence?" I pressed. "What? They're angry. Taking it out on us."

"Not exactly," she said.

"Then what?"

Cambria took a deep breath and George said, "I'm surprised Steppe didn't show you this, to use it as some sort of psychological torture B.S."

"The law we keep referring to, the one you think is about killing Werewolves on sight," Cambria said. "That's not it."

I frowned, mentally going back over what I knew. "What is it then?"

"Same death penalty. Different target," Cambria said. "He's put out a blanket call for extermination. Anything hybrid and anything it talks to. He's even offered a reward."

"What sort of reward?" I asked.

"For the hybrids that come forward on their own, they get to choose. If they choose to become a Hunter again, he turns them back. And if they don't ..." Cambria drew her pointer finger across her neck.

"He's not killing them," I said, everything Steppe had said at the clinic now falling into place. All of the jumbled images, the cages—empty then full then empty again. "He's bonding them. Using them as his personal army." I told them about the twisted version of hybrids that had doubled as my guards.

"Ugh, gross," Cambria said.

"But she can't shift?" Emma said. "Olivia, I mean."

"We have no proof they can't shift anymore," George said.

"They can't," I assured them, thinking of the strange smell on Lexington. Another leaked thought from Steppe clicked into place.

"How do you know?" George asked.

"Unbinilium. Steppe had Astor develop some sort of... immunization, I guess. They're not so much cured from being a wolf as it is suppressed. It's still in there, just unable to reach the surface."

"Is that what he did to you?" George asked. "Suppressed it?"

"Yeah, I thought you were immune?" Cambria said.

"Immune does not mean immortal," I said, remembering with a pang the last time those words were said to me before I was captured.

"So, that's why it's a permanent thing for them and only temporary for you?" George asked.

"Yes." I smiled. "And seeing you cured me. Thanks for that."

"I'll go rabid dog on Gordon Steppe any day, especially if it helps you. Just say the word."

I scowled at him and he laughed. "Seriously, though, I'm glad you're okay but..."

"But what?"

"Cord had a point the other night," he said. The hesitation in his voice made me wonder if there'd been a vote about who would be the one to actually say those words to me. Judging by the exchanged glances between the three of them now, I had a feeling George must've drawn the short straw.

"About what exactly?" I asked, careful to keep my voice even.

"These attacks aren't going to stop," he said. "They know where we are now."

I remembered what Wes had said earlier about Werewolves and Hunters finally banding together in order to come after us. "I know," I said quietly, looking back and forth between my friends' faces.

"You guys are right," I said. "We can't expect to stay here and be safe for much longer. But there are too many of us to move without being spotted. And there's not really anywhere else for us to go."

"We could go to Wood Point," Cambria said. "The wards there are stronger at least."

"I don't think it's fair to put everyone there in danger for us," I said.

"We can't go back to Frederick Falls," George said. "They're all over the place back there."

"And we can't involve anyone else," Emma added. "Any hybrid and anyone they contact," she reminded us.

"Emma's right. We can't put new people in danger," I said.

Broken Blood

I bit my lip, running through options like a mental grocery list. One by one, as I thought of each possibility, I crossed it off. There wasn't a single place I could think of that would keep an entire pack—or packs—out while still managing to seal us in. With Vera gone, our ability to construct wards that powerful was pretty much nonexistent.

"I could call my mom," Cambria said finally.

"How will that help?" I asked.

She hesitated and I realized there was more to the thing with her mom than she'd let on earlier. "She might have a friend who can help," she said.

"What kind of friend?" I asked warily.

She forced her eyes to mine. "I spoke with her after you and I talked. She's seeing someone. I think he can help."

"Cam, we can't involve anyone new," George began, but I waved him off, eyes narrowed. Something about the way she was staring at me…

"Who is it?" I asked.

Cambria rolled her eyes, crossed herself Catholic-style, and said, "A Werewolf from Frederick Falls. You met him once, I think. His name is Benny."

Chapter Seventeen

I stared at Cambria. I couldn't have been more confused by her words if she'd said them in Russian.

"Your mom is dating … Benny?" I asked.

"That's what I said. Why? He's crazy, right? You told me that story of the night—"

"He's a Werewolf," I said.

"Her type," she agreed grimly. "Gah. Why can't I have a normal mom like yours?" she asked, eyes cast to the ceiling.

"Uh, have you met my mom? Not normal," I said.

She sighed and stood. "I guess we'll be able to make an accurate comparison soon enough."

"What do you mean? You didn't tell them to come here, did you?" I asked. But something told me I already knew the answer.

"Your mom said I should," she said, her voice rising in defense.

"My mom? Since when is she calling the shots?" I demanded. "This is bad, Cam. It's not safe. There are packs of Werewolves watching the house."

"Apparently Benny has *contacts*. Whatever that means," she muttered.

"Cam, this is bad. Dangerously bad. I can't believe you talked to my mom about it before me—"

Broken Blood

A phone rang, the sound of it startling me until I remembered Wes leaving his here. I picked it up and, when I saw the name on the screen, abandoned my argument with Cambria.

"Alex, what'd you find out?" I snapped. In the background, a car door slammed and then another one rolled shut. An engine roared to life.

"Victoria's picking up something really strange," Alex said. "We're coming home."

"Why? What did she find out?" I asked. Beside me, Cambria leaned in close.

"According to Victoria, Olivia is there. At the house with you," he said.

"What?" Cambria and I said together.

"I know, it doesn't make sense. We're on our way, just ... tell the others to be careful." Alex said something too low for me to hear and the engine in the background roared again.

"What?" I asked.

"I'll be there soon," he said and the line disconnected.

Cambria and I shared a look and then we both jumped up and ran for the stairs. George and Emma were on our heels. Three steps into the hall, something crashed below. Someone yelled—Derek maybe? The front door opened and slammed shut.

From the basement, Steppe's anxiety spiked and adrenaline poured into my veins. My pulse sped as I soaked in his fear as he peered out of the high window in the basement wall to the yard beyond. Images of wolves locked in combat—some familiar, some strangers—poured in.

And another face, startlingly familiar but not necessarily a comfort. Steppe recognized him first as an ally and I felt his relief—followed quickly by shock and dismay.

I ran faster.

At the bottom, I rounded the staircase in a hard left toward the loudest of the crashes and Cambria followed. In the living room, I found chaos.

Both windows were broken, the glass shattered in piles and strewn across the wood floor and in piles along the windowsills. Grandma stood alongside one of them, a crossbow in hand. My mother stood alongside the other. She didn't see me as she quickly slid into position, aimed her weapon, and fired off a metal arrow into the backyard.

"They're after him," Grandma said without looking over as she fired off another shot.

"After who?" Cambria asked, but Grandma was too distracted to answer.

From my angled view, I caught sight of a russet wolf streaking by. A second later, a round of human shouts came from the yard and Cambria and I ducked aside just as an array of arrows hurtled toward us from outside. I landed with a thud on my stomach and rolled behind the couch.

Arrows being shot *into* the house? As Alex would say, how did anyone outside have opposable thumbs? Cord—but stakes were here weapon of choice. And her aim wasn't bad enough to have her shooting into the living room. Professor Flaherty, maybe? I didn't see her anywhere.

"Tara," Cambria whispered, her eyes widening as she spotted something over my shoulder.

A growling sound came from behind me and I rolled again, catching sight of the ebony Werewolf as it leaped at me. I shifted, my sweatpants and tee ripping away, but there was no time to right myself before my opponent was on me.

I had no idea who he was or what pack he'd come from. He gnashed his teeth and craned his neck trying to lock his jaw around my throat and I scrambled back, sliding and clawing out of his reach until I could find my opening.

Cord had said this would happen. She had warned us to be ready and my damn political agenda hadn't allowed me to—

Steppe had created this reality, not me.

I growled and fought back. The dark wolf's teeth caught me in the shoulder and tore through fur into flesh. I yelped, my wolf's elation at being freed instantly dampened as the pain ripped through me. Steppe crumpled, his thoughts dulling as the pain washed over him too. Someone stood over him—on two legs, not four.

I fell back, distracted by trying to identify his attacker, and knew the mistake I'd made even as my weight gave and the wolf landed on me, jaw open. I snarled but braced myself for the second bite. The one that would undoubtedly put me down.

Suddenly the wolf's weight gave and it collapsed on top of me, jaw still open. His eyes turned bright yellow and then the life faded from them. Footsteps approached—human feet—and then a hand appeared, first knocking the Werewolf aside and then offering its assistance to help me.

I jumped to my feet on my own, careful to keep my distance as

Broken Blood

I took in the familiar dark hair and ragged scar carved into hollowed cheekbones. The face of Steppe's ally from a moment ago, the one he'd realized too late hadn't been here to help him escape after all.

"Professor Kane," I said, glancing side to side. "What are you doing here?"

"I came to—well, I can explain that later," he said as another yelp rent the air.

My head snapped sideways, searching for the source. Across the room, Mom and Grandma still stood alongside the windows. Cambria had joined them and they took turns providing cover fire for the larger battle raging in the backyard.

But none of them had yelled. The sound came again from deeper inside the house. And buried inside my mind. I glanced behind me, toward the kitchen and the basement door on the far wall beside the pantry, and my blood ran cold.

"Steppe," I said warily. "It's him they want."

Kane's eyes widened in surprise, but he recovered quickly. "Which way?"

"Basement. Come on." I leaped, navigating the hallway in one step, and stopped inside the kitchen. The door to the basement hung open. From below—and through the bond—Steppe screamed again.

I tried catching sight of his assailant in my mind's eye but the lighting was bad and Steppe's panic covered everything else. Instead, I waited for Kane to catch up and ran for the steps that led to the basement below.

Steppe lay in a heap at the bottom, unmoving. The single bulb had been shattered so the only light was a filtered shadow from the high window behind the stairs. Someone in a skip cap leaned over him, a human with slight shoulders and a slender wrist. My wolf eyes took in the pointed knife clutched in tight fingers and panic shot into the back of my throat, coating my tongue.

Behind me, Kane ploughed down the wooden steps, his boots thundering as he came, and Steppe's assailant looked up. The light reflected off the whites of a pair of sharp brown eyes and I sucked in a shocked breath. Steppe's panic suddenly made sense. So did Alex's phone call.

I kept moving, but I wasn't fast enough. From behind her mask, Olivia smiled at me, a gleaming set of teeth in a dark, damp space, before she looked down at Steppe and drove the knife into his stomach.

I bounded down the remaining steps and, with slicing pain burning through my gut, I leaped.

My teeth closed over Olivia's wrist and I felt her flesh tear as my momentum and the sympathy pains in my gut carried me up and over my intended target. Olivia screamed and crumpled to the floor beside Steppe. I slammed into the bookshelf beyond them both, momentarily stunned by the impact and the stabbing pain.

I looked down at my own midsection in a daze, half expecting to see blood pooling there, but my light-brown fur was unmarred. Kane reached the bottom of the stairs and our eyes met in the low light. He looked from me to Steppe with a strange confusion and then bent low to snatch the knife from a slowly recovering Olivia.

She snatched it away and glared up at him.

"It's over—" he began.

Olivia screamed and plunged the knife into Kane's boot. It stuck through the top of his foot and then his yell replaced hers. He stumbled back and Olivia stretched and crawled for the stairs. In my mind, Steppe's pain only intensified, but he roused enough to grab at her ankle.

With a wince, I forced myself to my feet and crawled over him to reach her. My teeth found her ankle and I bit down—hard.

Olivia screamed, the sound shaking the glass in the tiny dirt-coated window and echoing off the cement walls. She collapsed a second time but I didn't stop. I couldn't. What had started as a defensive tactic quickly became something else. Steppe's fury ripped through me, painting a layer of hate over everything else. I bit harder and tore sideways, satisfied only when I felt the muscles rip free and tendons loosen and tear.

Olivia's blood coated my tongue, erasing the taste of my own panic and pain. My wolf—driven by Steppe's goading whispers—wanted more. Needed more. Hurting Steppe was hurting me. She knew it. I had a feeling it was why she'd done it. Unlike when Steppe had tried coaxing me to attack Lexington, this time I gave in.

I crawled over Olivia's body and lifted a shaking paw, raking my claws down the length of her arms. Her body arched and fell, but otherwise, she didn't react. Her eyes were closed and her breathing too even. After all of the medical alterations Steppe had made, she wasn't immune to my venom. But even know that, my wolf wouldn't stop.

I raised my paw again and Kane yanked me back. "She's down," he said gruffly, winded and pained. "Let her be."

I whirled, growling at him and showing my teeth. Beyond Kane, Steppe still wasn't moving. In the back of my mind, I knew whatever malice I couldn't shake was coming from him, but I didn't care. Olivia had hurt me. More than once. And she'd hurt the people I loved. My wolf wanted justice. Steppe wanted retribution. Semantics. I leaned toward her, ignoring Kane's warning.

"Tara, stop." Another Werewolf ploughed into me, knocking me back. I landed on my side and stared up at a big blur of russet fur and dark, round eyes staring down at me in concern.

"Are you all right?" Wes asked. A small stain of blood marred the tip of his ear but otherwise, he was intact.

"I'm fine. It was Olivia," I said, still unsure what "it" referred to. Had she found her own army?

"I know. She brought a pack with her," Wes said. He looked from Steppe, a large stain of blood seeping into his shirt over his belly, and back to me. "Are you hurt?"

"No," I said.

Behind Wes, Kane rose to his feet next to Olivia, his scar pulled taut at the corners of his grim lips. He'd removed the knife from his boot and, aside from the small hole in the material, didn't show any evidence of injury. "She's dead," he said in a flat voice.

Something inside me uncoiled. Guilt poked at the edges; I knew I should be ashamed for my relief at her death, but I couldn't quite get there. Not yet.

"Dammit," Wes said and moved away from me to pace in the small area between dusty shelves. Kane moved to Steppe next and I watched with disinterest as he checked Steppe's vitals.

At the top of the stairs, the door swung wide, smacking the wall behind it. Cord stood at the top, chest heaving with exertion. A bloody stake hung from her hand as she blinked down at us. I saw her irises dilating as she tried to focus in the grainy light. For a split second, hope rose, as I spotted the concerned dip of her brow.

"Is she alive?" Cord called—and my hope sank. Anger took its place.

"She's dead," I snapped, rising to my feet to face her. "You're welcome."

"Welcome?" she repeated. "Tara?"

I answered with a snarl. Nearby, Steppe began to come to. I could feel him struggling for the surface of the abyss that kept pulling him under. Kane steadied Steppe's shoulders and raised him to a sitting position.

I looked back to the top of the stairs where Cord still stood. "Your dad's fine, by the way," I added. "In case you were wondering."

Steppe, barely conscious of the conversation, sprang to frozen awareness in my thoughts. Wes whirled to stare at me and Kane's jaw dropped. At the top of the stairs, Cord glared at me. Her hand tightened around the stake.

Behind her, somewhere in the house, someone called out. It sounded like my mom. We both ignored her, opting instead for a tense stare down across the space. Light spilled in around Cord, illuminating the edges of her blonde hair and the fierceness in her warrior stance. Her cheeks flamed red, in anger at my comments. I didn't care.

Olivia was dead. I didn't care about that either. Except—

"I wasn't wondering, actually," Cord said. "Since he's not my dad."

"Say what you want. You're being selfish," I snapped.

"Tara, now's not the time," Wes began.

"It's the perfect time, actually," I argued, my gaze locked on Cord. "Olivia's dead. We've just been attacked and we've no place left to hide so there will be more where that came from. Cord's the only one here that can stop it and she's choosing to walk away. I'd say it's the perfect time."

Cord's mouth tightened. She shifted her weight, and for a moment, I thought she was going to walk down here and give me the fight I wanted. But in the end, she turned on her heel, her hair swishing out behind her, and disappeared.

"Are you saying Cord is Steppe's—?" Kane began.

"What are you doing here?" I demanded. My words were barely more than a growl. Steppe was angry. I was livid. All of it boiled and brewed into the biggest storm of temper I'd felt since—

Since the first time I'd shifted and saved Wes from that pack of hybrids.

I thought about the black wolf upstairs and how much he reminded me of the one I'd locked up with Olivia back at Steppe's lab. She'd brought her army, all right. And they'd never liked me.

It hadn't been an ambush; it had been a rescue mission. Pure and simple.

"I came here on behalf of Principal Whitfield," Kane said.

"Why did he send you here?" I asked, struggling to refocus as my temper stirred and swirled my disjointed thoughts.

Kane's mouth tightened, pulling on the nasty scar. A few weeks ago, I would've been intimidated by that, but now I couldn't get past the anger. "Because, hybrid war or not, fugitive or not, life goes on, Tara. Your friends are missing from school. Clearly, they've chosen you over higher education, but it's not their choice to make."

"Cambria?" I asked, anger and confusion muddling his words.

"And Victoria. And Logan. They need to return or face disciplinary action."

"But…" I looked at Wes, but he said nothing. "They didn't choose me," I said. "They're in danger. If they go back there—"

"They'll be protected," he finished. "They'd be safer at Wood Point. So would you for that matter." His words were gentle but more a slap in the face than a comfort since we both knew I couldn't return as long as I was a fugitive—or a Dirty Blood. His compassion only fed my anger.

"We both know I'm not welcome there," I said.

"You'll need to fix your legal problems first," he admitted and glanced at Steppe before stepping over him and heading for the stairs.

"Where are you going?" I asked.

He turned back, his scar nothing more than a jagged rivet across his cheek in the shadows. "To speak with Edie. And to get some help cleaning up down here."

I stared after him, my temper leaking away with every breath and blink. Wes stood by, watching me. I felt his eyes but I didn't turn. In the absence of the anger, I saw the truth. Kane was right. My friends were better off at school. Maybe Cambria had been right to listen to my mom and keep me out of the fighting.

I couldn't lead, not when I broke confidences and exploited trust in the face of danger or obstacles. Not when Steppe controlled me this way.

Steppe, chest heaving and shirt soaked in blood, eyed me as I padded past him toward the stairs. He looked terrible, but I knew from the bond that he wasn't in danger of anything worse than a piercing flesh wound. Nothing Fee couldn't fix.

"Tara?" Wes called behind me. "Where are you going?"

I stepped over Olivia. Our last hope.

"I'll send Jack and Fee down for him. I need some air," I said. "Don't follow."

If he wanted to protest, he didn't show it. I could practically hear the words forming on his tongue. "Be careful," he called after me.

I didn't answer.

Chapter Eighteen

I ran fast and far—until my lungs burned and my paws ached and my wolf wanted to disappear. Several miles from the house, in the depths of thick woods, I crept into an abandoned hunting cabin and snatched a pair of sweats and a hoodie and shifted back to two legs. Back outside, I ran again, this time in loose-fitting hiking boots and oversized socks. My chest heaved and my lungs ached but I pushed on.

The sun had arched from the eastern horizon to just above the tips of the trees to my left by the time I stopped to rest. Inside my head, Steppe's voice echoed off the otherwise empty space, coating it with accusations and guilt-laden reasoning. But there was nothing left for him to accuse or convict me for. I'd done it all myself already.

There was nothing left of my temper. Only quiet understanding that I'd been foolish yesterday to assume I could lead. Victoria's words echoed back at me like a bad dream.

I had *not* always been a leader.

I'd always been a dictator. There was a huge difference. Immune did not make me immortal. And in charge did not make me elected.

It didn't matter anyway. Olivia was dead. Cord refused to step up. By the time we dismantled Steppe's seat of power or his cruel new laws, every hybrid would be dead, including me and my friends. The attacks were never going to stop. In fact, I suspected Kane's arrival to retrieve my Hunter friends stemmed from his own theory—one that Wes shared and who knew how many others. Pretty soon, it might not only be the angry ex-allied Werewolf packs attacking us. It might be Hunters too.

I paused to drink from a stream that ran down the hill I'd come over. The sounds of the Shenandoah forest in winter were muted. Crunching leaves, wind rustling through nearly naked branches, the distant call of a crow.

It felt lonely.

Almost as lonely as I had been in that cell. I wondered if I'd ever really forget or recover from those weeks he'd held me in solitary. Or if I'd ever be free of his smug voice in my mind, holding that time over my head like a last victory.

I won. I always win.

If I'd had anything left to give, I would've summoned up actual hate. But I couldn't quite find it in me to feel anything quite that hard.

We were losing, I thought dully. *Fast.*

Behind me, leaves crunched in a staggered but quick rhythm and I whirled. Even without my wolf's heightened senses I knew it wasn't a squirrel. Those were footsteps. I held my breath, scanning the naked trees that blotted out the shiny daylight that filtered down to the forest floor.

The sound grew louder as the intruder got closer. Whoever it was, they weren't even trying to be stealthy. By the time I spotted him zigzagging along the trail at a jog, my panic was a heavy taste in my mouth.

"There you are," he said, slowing to a stop.

"Alex," I breathed. I rested my palm on the nearest tree trunk for support. "What the heck are you doing out here?"

"Running a marathon, apparently," he said, propping his hands on his knees as he worked to catch his breath. "Since when do you run farther than the nearest snack machine?"

I rolled my eyes. "Since I screwed everything up."

He straightened to his full height and his eyes sparkled. "So, just a normal day, then. Here I thought it was something serious."

"Not in the mood, Channing," I said. I used his last name, like we always had when he'd been my trainer and only barely my friend. Instead of all this ... whatever we were.

But Alex ignored my attempt to keep him at arm's length. He

stepped closer, invading my personal space and my thoughts before I could prepare. "What are you in the mood for?" he asked quietly.

I opened my mouth, but no sound came. My racing pulse suddenly had nothing to do with cardio. "Running," I said, stepping back and shaking my head to clear it.

Alex grinned. "I knew I'd convert you eventually."

I glared and started walking instead. Alex didn't move.

"If you insist on staying, you can walk with me," I threw over my shoulder.

Alex appeared at my side and fell into step without another word.

The trail was easy to follow here, winding but wide enough for two. The silence continued and the longer we walked, the more comfortable it became.

The woods began to change, the trees spreading farther apart. There were more pines and evergreens than oaks. Moss dotted the floor in a few places, untouched by the frosty winter.

I folded my arms, tucking my hands into my sides to keep them warm. Now that I wasn't running, the chill seeped in. I glanced up at the sun wandering toward the center of the sky and sighed. We needed to start for home before they sent a search party. Alex knew it too from the way his eyes tracked my line of sight.

Stubbornly, I kept walking.

My stomach growled and I licked my dry lips on a heavy sigh. "We can head back now," I said finally.

"Okay."

I scowled. "Don't be sarcastic."

Alex's lips twitched but he said nothing.

"Olivia's dead," I said a few minutes later as the pines faded back into oaks.

"I know."

"It wasn't an ambush, it was a rescue," I added.

"I know," he said again.

"She escaped to attack. She hurt Steppe because she knew it would hurt me," I said.

"She was a sick person. Reminds me of her son."

I glanced over and found him watching me. The concern in his slanted brows reminded me of memories I hadn't thought of in a long time. Alex had been there for me when Miles had been stalking me.

He'd saved me more than once. And he'd first kissed me right smack in the middle of a freak out I'd had over seeing Miles on school grounds.

My eyes fell from his knitted brows to the shape of his lips before I could stop myself. I looked away quickly and stared at my feet as they navigated the path. The air between our arms suddenly felt more like a magnet or a gravitational field of attraction. *He doesn't love you. He loves the idea of you.*

Alex stopped walking and I felt my cheeks heat at whatever he was about to say. I braced myself for some teasing come-on or cheesy pick-up line, but he didn't do either. Instead, he spread his arms wide and looked right and left. "Recognize it?" he asked quietly.

"Recognize what?" I asked.

"We're not far from Wood Point. We used to run through here."

The moment he said it, I realized where we were. This was one of our favorite places—okay, favorite was a strong word for me when it came to working out—to run together back when Alex had been my trainer.

"Everything's so much different now than it was then," I said wistfully.

"Would you go back if you could?" he asked.

"Would you?"

He stared at me like he could see directly inside me. I shivered and he blinked, the spell broken. "Living in the past isn't healthy," he said.

"Well, the present isn't very healthy either. In fact, it's kind of a threat to my health—or life in general," I said.

"Which is why I prefer to keep moving forward."

"You think we have a future?" I asked. The second the words were out, my cheeks flamed. "I mean, that came out wrong. Do you think we could … all of us, you know, win or live or whatever?" I mumbled.

Alex smiled. "I think your future is bright, Tara Godfrey," he said. "I'm just happy to be in your orbit."

I wasn't sure what that meant but I was too afraid to ask. I started walking again. Alex joined me. "Kane wants Cambria, Logan, and Victoria to return to school," I said for lack of something better.

"Do you think that's wise?" he asked.

"I … it's not up to me," I grumbled.

"Sure it is."

"No, it's not. Kane made that clear. So did Cambria, Cord, and my mother. I don't run their lives. I can't force anyone to do anything."

"No one said anything about forcing. But you get to weigh in on—"

"Why?" I demanded. "Why should my opinion carry any weight, even a single ounce? Cord was right. Who died and left me in charge? No one, that's who. And besides, I'd only screw it up. Screw them all up. I don't have experience. I don't know the right thing."

"Being a leader isn't about knowing the right thing," he shot back. His voice rose until it was a perfect match for my own angry words. His eyes blazed with conviction and, just like Cord had, he poked my shoulder with his finger as he talked. "You don't need to know everything or be everything to everyone. Being a leader means you care. You care more about who you're leading than you do about yourself sometimes. You'd lay down your life for your friends. Regardless of whether they want your help, they're getting it, because you care. And nothing's going to keep you from protecting those you love. And in the middle of all that, because you care, you do the whole thing with integrity and love and compassion. All of that makes you a leader. All of that makes you a badass. The kind of badass that kicks her trainer in the crotch in order to show him they're equal. In order to make him love her."

I opened my mouth—though I had no idea what I should say—but he cut me off and kept talking. "Cord was wrong. She was angry so she was being a bitch and she was wrong. When do you listen to her, anyway?"

"I—"

"Victoria had it right. You've always been a leader. We've always been waiting for you to see it. But it's time now. No more waiting."

"I can't—"

"You can," he interrupted. "Remember Vera's visions of you? You can do this."

I eyed him, frowning. "You didn't let me finish."

"I don't need to. Whatever it is, you can. I've known that about you since the day we rolled down that hill together. If you want to lead, you can. If you want to save everyone, you can. If you want to kiss me again, you can."

"Alex," I warned.

His mouth quirked. "It's a hard choice, I know."

"It's not a hard choice," I said.

"Right. I forgot. You said you've always known."

I gave him an apologetic look, but he shook his head. "That wasn't meant to be a dig or anything. I mean it. As far as choosing a path to lead from, you've always known that too. You're just afraid."

"How do you know?"

"Please. I've never needed to get inside your head to know what you're thinking. I knew it that first day I ever kissed you. And the second." He grinned but it fell away quickly. "And in the hotel, I knew then," he said quietly.

"But you kissed me anyway. You tried, anyway," I said.

"What would we be without our convictions and our efforts?"

It sounded like something Professor Kane would say. Or Vera. I scowled because, once again, we were talking about two things at once.

"Not as hopeless," I muttered.

"I'm not hopeless," he said. He reached up and smoothed my hair away from my face, his fingertips brushing a cold trail down my cheek. "Sometimes love is temporary, for a purpose. Doesn't make it an ounce less worth it."

My head snapped up and I stared at him. The wind pricked at the edges of my eyes, drawing moisture to the corners. Or that's what I told myself. His expression was so calm, so serene. I stumbled over my words, feeling awkward but unable to keep from asking.

"You don't love me anymore?" I whispered and the old panic from earlier threatened to climb up my chest and into my mouth. I stepped closer, willing him to argue. To swear things. For some reason, this felt scarier than that. This felt new, like turning a corner. I didn't want to see what lay around it.

But he shook his head and whispered, "You don't need me to."

When his hand dropped away, my skin went cold. Was he right? Did I not need that from him? If that were true, why had I ever needed it in the first place?

I swallowed. "I'm sorry, Alex."

"Don't be, Godfrey. Don't ever be sorry."

"I don't know what to do," I whispered, thick tears leaking into my eyes as I admitted the thing I'd been terrified to say. This was the reason for my guilt and my shame. And my temper.

With Olivia gone and Cord stubbornly resolved, I had no idea what to do next.

Alex took my hand, squeezed, and led the way back onto the path that would take us home. "My advice," he said casually as we walked, "is to get that weasel out of your head."

"Right, because that's easy enough." I snorted. But it worked. I no longer felt ready to cry.

Alex glanced sideways at me. "Have you talked to your boyfriend lately?"

Something about his voice told me he already knew the answer. "Why?" I asked.

"The only person on this planet more determined than you is him." Alex shook his head and I watched in a sort of awe at the lack of animosity in him as he spoke of Wes. When the heck had that happened?

"What does that mean?" I asked.

"It means he's been sweet talking crazy Uncle Astor to pretty please up his genius and figure out a way separate you from your basement-squatting brain buddy."

"That's not possible," I began, but Alex squeezed my hand.

"I've learned nothing is impossible," he said, his words an exact replay of the ones Wes had spoken. "Especially for you."

Hearing them from Alex made me smile, but it was nothing compared to the feeling I had when Wes had said them. Alex had always believed in me. From day one. Sort of an innocent until proven guilty. With Wes, I'd had to earn it.

And it looked like I finally had.

Maybe Alex was right about my being a leader, but he was wrong about one thing. And so was Cord and Victoria and all of them. I hadn't always been this dormant badass leader just waiting to realize it. I'd been a normal teenager, clueless, unworthy, and fumbling. But, somewhere along the way, I'd been molded.

Shaped and sculpted through trials and fires and loss. And now I was something capable. If Alex was right about my caring, if love and commitment to the safety of my friends and family qualified me, I could lead whomever and whatever.

And maybe I couldn't save us a single individual. But that's not what leaders did. Leaders stood at the head of the line and marched everyone through the battle to the safety on the other side. We'd do this thing as a team.

One army. One family. One race.

I smiled, squeezed Alex's hand, and let him lead me home.

Chapter Nineteen

From the hill at the edge of the woods, Professor Flaherty's house was a deceiving Stepford. The view from the back looked quiet and serene—if you pretended not to notice the two broken windows and the patches of bloody fur matted to the grass in places. But from a distance, it was utterly uniform. A carbon copy of the rest of the street: unassuming suburbia at its best. I still had no idea why Flaherty would choose a place like this when she was so completely unlike the picture she was creating for herself. Or maybe that was my answer.

Alex and I got as far as the woods' edge before we ran into company. I sensed him before I saw him and judging from the way the hair on Alex's arms stood up, he did too. But, unlike Alex, I recognized the flash of fur as it darted among the holly bushes bordering the ravine below.

"It's just us, Derek," I called.

Alex's hand, which had been inching toward the stake I knew he kept in his boot, relaxed and hung back at his side again.

A second later, Derek appeared as a brown wolf, his paws silently falling as he came to meet us. "Hey." He frowned at my appearance and I remembered the cabin, the borrowed clothes. "That's why we lost your trail," he muttered.

I didn't feel like getting into it. "Have you seen Wes?" I asked.

Derek cast a long look into the woods. "He's not back yet. Still out looking for you."

Guilt worked its way in, but I didn't feel like getting into that either. Derek glanced to Alex. "How'd you find her?" he asked suspiciously.

"I don't rely on scent," Alex said with more than a little smugness coating his words. Derek's eyes narrowed and Alex sighed like he knew better than to keep goading him. "I'm a tracker. I followed her trail."

"Huh," Derek grunted, and his gaze cut back to me. "Glad you're safe. Your mom was looking for you."

"Thanks." I started to go, but then remembered the other concern. It wasn't one I felt like asking the others. "Did Olivia's body…? I mean, someone should—"

"Jack and Cord took care of it," he said. Cord. Of course she did.

"And Steppe?" Alex asked.

"They moved him into a room upstairs with a bed. He's bruised and has a nice hole in his stomach, but he'll mend."

"I'll be out later to relieve you," I said.

He grunted again and moved on, breaking into a swift stride as he continued his patrol of the woods. Alex and I slipped through the back gate and made our way to the house.

The back door clicked closed behind us just as the front door opened and slammed shut again. Across the space, I spotted Wes. He saw me and halted in his hurry, his eyes cutting from me to Alex and back. He wore a pair of ragged sweats that, even from here, smelled like someone else and an oversized sweatshirt. A leaf was stuck to his hair and I wondered how long he'd been on two legs.

"I'm going to check on Steppe," Alex said.

"No, stay," Wes said in a tight voice. He came over and pulled me into a quick hug. I picked the leaf out of his hair and hugged him back. "I was worried," he said quietly. And before I could offer an explanation, he stepped back and gestured for us to follow. "Come on."

"What's going on?" I asked, trailing behind him. His expression was harried—and it looked like more than just worry over my personal time.

"We need to find Edie and the others," he said without stopping.

"For what?" I asked.

But he didn't answer. He crossed the empty kitchen and circled back around to the living room and down the back hall. In one hand, he held a large rock. With the other, he pushed open doors and, when he found the room empty, ducked out again, intent on his search. I caught Alex's eye and he shrugged.

"There you are," Wes said, poking his head into the last room. Alex and I followed him inside. I caught a few words of broken conversation before it abruptly halted at the sight of us.

"This is not good news. It will only complicate—" Grandma said.

Grandma, Professor Flaherty, Professor Kane, and my mother all looked up with matching startled expressions. What the heck had we interrupted? And why were they meeting without us?

"Wes? Alex, Tara? What's going on?" Professor Flaherty asked.

Grandma and Professor Kane both gave us curious looks. Or, they gave the boys curious looks. By the time their expressions landed on me, it was more irritated concern.

I hung back near the door, the room way too crowded between all the people and their opinions.

Wes held out the rock he'd been carrying. "I found this in the yard," he said.

"What is it?" Professor Kane took it and turned it over in his weathered hand. "There's a letter attached."

"Read it," Edie said.

"Who would leave a note with a rock?" Professor Flaherty said.

"I think it was meant to come in the window," Wes explained. "I guess they gave up and ran off when Olivia…" A few eyes shifted to me and Wes changed directions. "When they realized they'd lost."

"No, I think this was only meant for us because they lost," Kane said, his scar pulling tight as he frowned.

"What do you mean?" my mother asked.

Kane held up the rock. "See there. It says *Give us Steppe or go to war*. I think this was a contingency. If Olivia had been successful, Steppe wouldn't be alive to give them."

Grandma sighed. "The man has a point."

None of them seemed the least bit surprised Olivia had turned on Steppe to begin with. Then again, neither was I. And, if I poked around enough, neither was Steppe.

"Well, obviously, we can't give them what they want," my mother said.

"Which means they'll be back," Grandma added. She and Kane shared a look and she slowly nodded.

"What's going on?" Wes asked.

Broken Blood

"Professor Kane suggested we split up and I think it's the best way. We're a bunch of sitting ducks holed up in this house," Grandma said. Her eyes met Alex's and something passed between them. "Professor Flaherty is going to return to Wood Point with Kane. As will Cambria, Logan, and Victoria."

"What? No," I said, stepping forward at last.

"It'll keep them safe," Grandma said gently.

"I'll go with them," Alex said and Grandma nodded like that had been the plan all along. I tried not to take that as another betrayal.

"That doesn't—We can't split up," I said. "It's what they want. They're just waiting for us to leave—"

"We can't stay here forever," my mother said.

I looked at their faces, one by one, and my shoulders sagged. Clearly, they'd made up their minds. Telling me was just a formality. Which also meant my friends already knew. "What do Cambria and Logan say?" I asked.

"They agree it's the best course," Professor Kane said, but I caught the way my mother's eyes slid away.

"Do they?" I pressed.

"Tara, don't start this," Grandma warned.

"Start what?" I asked. "I'm just saying, it's interesting my friends all know the plan; in fact, everyone in the house seems to know the plan except for me."

"It's not like that. It was their choice. They needed to be consulted before we could reach a decision," my mother said in a hard voice.

Heat crept up into my neck and face and I took a step closer to her, the rest of them fading away. This was so typical. My mother always inserting herself, shutting me out in some twisted version of protectiveness. "Right. We," I echoed sarcastically. I folded my arms over my chest. "Well, if it's *we* then tell me, what were you four discussing when *we* came in?"

Professor Flaherty, Kane, and Grandma all shared a look and then aimed it at my mother, but she ignored them in favor of our stare down.

"Well?" I prompted.

"Is there something you're not telling us?" Wes asked and I smiled. If I hadn't been committed to this alpha-stare game my mom was playing, I could've kissed him for it.

"Maybe we shouldn't—"

"Shut up, Alex," I snapped. "Mom?"

She sighed and Edie scowled. "They've formed an inquiry board to look into Steppe's ... dealings," Mom said slowly.

"Who formed a board?" I asked. "Hunters?"

"Yes." She nodded. "Ex-CHAS board members and other prominent community members. They'll conduct an investigation and offer a verdict when it's complete."

"Isn't that a good thing?" I asked.

My mom hesitated. The others looked grim. "What?" I pressed. "Someone freaking tell me already."

"If he's guilty, they'll give Steppe to the Werewolves themselves," Alex said finally.

All of their hesitations clicked into place.

"There is one advantage," Grandma said. "I've managed to secure Alex a place on the board."

I whirled on him. "You knew about this?" I demanded. "This whole time? During our walk, spilling your story, repairing this," I said, gesturing between us. "You knew about this inquiry board and didn't tell me."

"I didn't know I'd made it," he protested, but I was unmoved. "Sorry," he mumbled with a furtive glance at Grandma.

I shook my head. "Of course," I muttered.

"Of course what?" he asked.

"Nothing." I turned back to my mom and the others. "If Steppe's guilty, he'll die. Fine. It's what he deserves. It's justice," I said. "But here we are repeating history. Keeping things from each other. I thought we were past that. I specifically remember that night on the gazebo," I said, my eyes burning into my mother's. "When you gave me the third degree and I thought we fixed things. We promised not to do this anymore."

"I knew you'd say that," my mother said. "This is why I didn't want to tell you. Your hunger for justice is going to hurt you. How do you think it will affect you if Gordon is executed? Do you see your uncle? Do you see the damage caused by losing someone he was bonded with? It could kill you or permanently damage you. I can't let that happen," she said, her voice rising to nearly a yell.

The others shifted uncomfortably, but I couldn't see them through the hot tears burning as I struggled to blink them back and finish this fight. "You have no idea what will happen to me. I can handle it," I said.

"But how do you know that?" she asked.

"Because it's already happened!" I roared.

"What?" She blinked, the anger immediately leaking away into worry.

"Tara, when? Are you all right?" Grandma asked, concern dripping from her words.

Professor Kane and Flaherty stayed silent, but everyone's attention was riveted on me. Wes stepped back so we were shoulder to shoulder and slipped his hand into mine. I squeezed, grateful for once for his mind-reading capabilities. He understood.

"More than once," I admitted. "When I was with the hybrids in the woods and … several times when I was with Steppe."

Like a moth to a flame, I felt him slip into the front row of my mind. *Sorry I'm late,* was his greeting and he dove into the vault I'd tried locking away of the conversation preceding this moment. I sighed as he cracked it open and let himself in to explore.

"Why didn't you tell me?" my mom asked.

"Because you don't react well to the dangerous parts," I said. She opened her mouth as if to argue and I said, "Specimen A, this conversation." She shut her mouth again.

"Tara, Steppe is different," Grandma warned. "You said it yourself."

To Fee. Not to her. But apparently, that was the same thing. "I know that," I snapped.

"No, you don't," she said, her voice suddenly firm in that no-nonsense tone she used just before entering a fight. It made me shut up. It made everyone shut up. "I don't mean he's different. He is, but what I mean is, the Werewolves or Hunters in charge of his execution, depending on the parties involved, will draw it out. They will want to hurt him. Retribution, justice, whatever you want to call it. They won't make it painless for him, which makes it different than the other times. You need to consider all of the possible outcomes here. Make sure you can handle the worst-case scenario."

"And what's the worst-case scenario?" Wes asked.

Grandma faced him, her expression grim. "Honestly," she said. "That the Inquiry Board will find him innocent. And the verdict will start a war."

"Best case is that he's guilty and executed," I said, finally realizing their real concern.

"Yes," Grandma confirmed sadly.

Inside my mind, Steppe was thoughtful. I could practically feel my brain buzzing with all of his calculations, strategies, and discarded plans. There were flashes of his surrender, his imminent death, what would happen if he gave in. All of them were quickly cast aside in favor of some devious diversion or another. Mentally, I shoved him out of my way, and refocused as Wes broke the silence.

"The best way to solve all of these problems would be for us to sever her bond with Steppe before the verdict is delivered," Wes said.

"Obviously," Grandma began. "But that's just not possible without—"

"I'm not severing the bond," I said.

Wes frowned at me. "Tara, after what happened with Olivia, I think you should consider the hold he has—"

"No. We need this connection," I said, falling silent as Steppe's mental musings continued to shove their way to the forefront.

"It hasn't done us any good so far," Wes pointed out. We shared a look and I knew he read my thoughts easily enough. *Cord,* I thought and Steppe mentally scowled. But Wes was undeterred.

Around me, the conversation swirled with speculations that included a hypothesis as to the possibility of redirecting or severing without harming me. I ignored all of them and concentrated on Steppe. There was something there and in the chaos of this room, I couldn't connect the entire thought train. I couldn't see if it was authentic or if he was playing me.

I squeezed my eyes shut and tried blocking them all out.

"Tara?" Professor Flaherty asked and they all fell silent.

I felt their eyes on my face, but I kept my lids shut. Steppe was working something up. I could feel his web weaving its way around his central idea. Flashes of a speech, of words like "my successor" and "well-deserved retirement" floated in and out. A podium, a roomful of people—no, a video feed like all the others. But he was imagining all of the shock and mayhem that would follow. It slipped away in the midst of a roaring crowd of Hunters and I couldn't quite reach whatever back room of his mind he'd locked it inside.

I growled at how well he could retract and produce his own thoughts for me when all of mine seemed on display for him.

"What is it?" Wes asked.

I opened my eyes, heading for the door. "I need to talk to Steppe," I said.

"Why, what's going on?" Wes pressed.

"I don't know, but if I'm right, this proves the effectiveness of the bond, and we need to keep it," I said. "I'll find you later. Don't do anything."

I left them all standing in silence and hurried down the hall and up the stairs. I didn't bother to ask anyone what room he was in. I already knew.

At the door, I paused. The voices coming from the other side confirmed what I'd gleaned through the bond. I turned the knob and stepped inside.

"Logan," I said.

He looked up from where he stood over Steppe, a half-filled glass of water in his hand. His eyes widened when he saw me. "You're back. I was worried," he said.

"I'm fine," I assured him,

"They told me about Olivia," he said quietly. With concern—as if it were my loss to mourn. Maybe it was.

"Inconvenient," I said, brushing his words aside. I pushed the door shut behind me. Logan narrowed his eyes, unconvinced, but he let it go.

"How's the patient?" I asked.

"Difficult," he said and then, without warning, flipped the cup on its side and poured the contents on Steppe's face.

Steppe sputtered and strained against the restraints that held his wrists and ankles to the bedframe. Logan grinned.

"Why is he wearing his suit?" I asked amid Steppe's colorful curses.

Logan shrugged. "I think whatever he was wearing before was dirty. This was all we had left."

I started to say something about Jack probably having something wearable, although admittedly a little big, but thought better of it. "I need to talk to the patient," I said. "You can take a break if you want. Check on Victoria."

"Nice try. She's resting. I'll stay."

"Logan, I'm not going to let him go or anything," I said.

"I'm not worried about that."

"What are you worried about?" I asked.

"Edie made me swear on a venomous Werewolf tooth that I wouldn't leave him alone with two specific people. You're at the top of the list. I'm staying."

"Who else is on the list?" I asked.

"Cord." Logan shuddered as he stepped back and leaned against the far wall. "Your grandma is one scary lady."

I rolled my eyes but I couldn't argue. "Fine, you can stay."

I pulled up the single chair beside the bed and sat. Steppe had recovered from his dousing but eyed me with a curled lip. I glanced back at Logan, who pulled his ball cap low over his eyes and leaned back, unconcerned. I turned to face Steppe again. "Don't look at me like that. If Logan did this, you definitely deserved it," I said.

Steppe scowled.

"He was talking crap about my hat," Logan said, adjusting the worn blue baseball cap he never took off. "I love this hat."

"He does love that hat," I said.

"What do you want?" Steppe asked. "And whatever it is, couldn't we communicate remotely? I'm not in the mood for visitors." He stared pointedly at the popcorn ceiling.

"Not in the mood or too busy strategizing your great escape?" I asked. "I know what you're up to," I said when he didn't answer. "Are you really that incapable of real human emotion that you would betray your own daughter—again?"

"I don't have a daughter," he hissed.

"And now the cock can crow," Logan said.

Both Steppe and I turned to look at him with drawn brows. "What?" I said.

"You know the story in the Bible where Peter denies Jesus three times before the rooster crows? No? Huh. Tough crowd."

I shook my head and turned back to Steppe. "Don't worry. You're not in danger of having to actually be parental," I said. "I've never met someone less willing to admit their parentage. You must've done something truly evil."

Steppe didn't meet my eyes or offer up an answer. In the far corners of his mind, images sprang up. I could feel the effort it took to shove them back, but a few slipped out and what I saw was a repeat of that first moment the knowledge of their connected had seeped in. I sat back, unable to bring it up out loud.

This was still Cord's story to tell. And maybe she was right, I couldn't expect her to put it all aside, not even for all of us.

"I can't force you to step down, to name a successor, any easier than I can force her to accept it," I said. "But I know what you're up to and it won't work. Don't bother volunteering yourself for your little plan. I'm officially vetoing it. Just like I vetoed severing the bond. I'm on to you."

"I have no idea what you're talking about."

"I saw your idea," I said. "And you're not getting anywhere near Cord. Besides, even if you did, she'll never agree. She doesn't want the job and even if she did, she would never take it from you and secretly give it back once the danger passed. She's not you. Not even a little."

I rose, knocking the chair out of my way. Steppe didn't offer an argument. I hadn't expected him to. Mentally, he shrank back to his side of things and I stalked out.

Behind me, the door opened again and I heard, "Wait."

I turned and found Logan with his head sticking out of the bedroom door. I folded my arms, half-expecting some "let's keep this little chat between us" pep talk.

"You could actually force him, you know," he said.

"What? How?" I asked.

He slipped all the way out and shut the door behind him. "Cambria could compel him," he said.

"No way," I said immediately. "She was weird the last time, remember? The drinking, the compelling all the time. She hates to use it ever since Miles."

"She'd do it. For you," he said. Something about his expression suggested more than just friendship and loyalty.

"Me?"

"You should talk to her. She could use an assignment to distract her," he added.

I frowned. "Do you know something I don't?"

"Just talk to Cambria. I've gotta get back." He started for the door.

"Hey, Logan," I said and waited for him to turn back. "Speaking of distractions, I know there's a lot going on but I just wanted you to know I'm sorry ... about your dad."

Logan's features hardened into some practiced expression. "Thanks," he said flatly, but his pupils dilated and I knew he wasn't as okay as he pretended.

"He really loved you," I said.

His eyes flashed. "Is that why he betrayed me and all of my friends? For love?"

"He thought he was on the side of right," I said quietly.

"He was wrong."

I nodded and awkward silence fell between us. I was struck by how much Logan had always taken care of me and this was the first moment I'd ever felt our roles reversed. Without a word, I reached out and put my arms around him in a hug.

Logan stiffened and then his arms came around me and he squeezed me back. We stood that way for a long moment, the gesture conveying all of the words our tongues couldn't. I stepped back just in time to see him swipe the back of his hand over his cheek.

He cleared his throat as he turned to go. "Oh, and if you see Fee, tell her the patient could use some of that tea that tastes like feet."

"He isn't in pain," I said, feeling for anything I might've missed.

"I know." Logan smiled. "I just want to see his face when he's forced to drink it."

"I worry about you," I said, but mostly I was relieved.

"Cambria's influence is finally rubbing off," he replied before disappearing back inside with the prisoner. I laughed and went in search of horrible tea.

Chapter Twenty

Wes gave up his spot in bed that night for extra patrols. I replaced him with Cambria. On the other side of the closed door, footsteps passed back and forth in regular intervals.

Heels, boots, and house slippers all came and went until all hours. My mother checked on us twice until she realized Wes really was outside watching the house instead of hiding under the bed. Cambria kept calling me back, fussing at me when the bond or a passing set of footsteps distracted me from the two of us practicing for her new assignment.

"Go get me a pet unicorn. Now," Cambria said.

"What? No," I protested.

"Really, you're not even tempted?" she asked, more suspicious than disappointed.

"Not even a little," I assured her.

"Good, so the compulsion isn't bleeding over." Another pair of heavy footsteps passed our room. The door at the end of the hall clicked open. Voices drifted out before the door clicked shut again.

"Do you think it'll work?" she asked me.

"I think we could always find another way," I said.

Cambria looked at me through the mirror, where she sat braiding thin pieces of her currently magenta-streaked hair. "I told you, I want to do this before I go. It was my choice."

"I know that, I just…" I picked up a hot-pink tee strategically ripped in places and set it back down on the pile of clothes on the bed. Apparently, Cambria's version of packing was a massive laundry dump. "I just hate when you put yourself out there for me."

"It beats putting yourself out there for someone else," she muttered.

I tried to catch her eye again but she was furiously concentrating on her braiding.

"What did your mom say?" I asked.

"Nothing."

"Cam."

"No, really. Nothing. I tried calling her back after I talked to you and she didn't answer. Still hasn't." She frowned. "But that's my mom for you. It's hit or miss. She'll resurface. Always does. Anyway, this isn't about her."

"What's it about?" I asked, remembering Logan's words from before about Cambria needing a distraction. Cambria continued braiding and avoiding my eyes. "Cam, whatever it is, you can talk to me."

"It's Derek," she said finally.

"What do you mean?" I sat up straighter. Problems in paradise for those two were a first. Cambria had definitely played the field before him, but from the moment they'd met, it had been true love. Or lust that became love. Either way, Cambria had never mentioned problems before.

"What happened?" I asked when she didn't answer.

"This new law happened," she said. "Angry Werewolves happened. Steppe happened." She dropped the half-done braid and turned on her stool to face me. "Last night's attack and the one before in the parking lot … these aren't the first we've encountered. After you were taken … The Cause was on some sort of hit list. Derek and Jack and Fee. Wes— all of them had to run. It wasn't just Steppe. Everyone hated us."

She stared at a picture hanging on the wall behind me, but I had a feeling she wasn't really seeing it. Her mouth tightened as she went on, "I'm a good fighter. I would've stayed. And I'm not mad at him for making me go back to school. He was only trying to make me safe, but…"

"But what?"

"Derek was on his way to drop me off at Wood Point when we got the call you'd escaped," she said. "That's why we were so close by and together."

"And that's why Logan was with you," I guessed. "He was taking you both back."

"Kane only showed up here because Flaherty called him to let him know we wouldn't be coming after all."

"Were you guys going to break up?" I asked quietly.

"Chances of survival for a Hunter and Werewolf relationship aren't exactly ideal under the current circumstances." Her hands sat limp in her lap. I hated the defeated way she talked, but I understood it. My heart broke for what she was losing because of the state of relations between the races. It was everything we'd been fighting against for so long.

"How does Derek feel about it all?" I asked.

"Frustrated. Angry, like me. He gets messages about us. About how he's betraying his kind … He's just trying to protect me."

"Is that why you agreed to go back to Wood Point?" I asked. "I mean, it wasn't because you thought it was best, since my mom suggested it?"

"Your mom didn't suggest it but she didn't talk me out of it," she said. "It was my idea. Derek and I just need to be apart for now. For everyone's sake." Her expression turned to pleading. "You know I want to stay and fight with you, but … I couldn't forgive myself if something happened to him as a result of our being together. And it's really painful to be close to him if we're not …"

"I know, Cam. It's okay," I assured her. "I actually thought this was … never mind, it's dumb."

"Let me guess. You thought I was taking your mom's side or something, right?"

"Am I that obvious?"

Cambria shook her head. "I'm on your side. Why would you think otherwise?"

"I don't know." I picked up another shirt and then threw it back on the pile in front of me. "It's my mom. She's been so weird, lately. Trying to take over or something."

"She's worried about you," Cambria said—and something about the certainty in her words gave me pause.

"You sound really sure," I said.

"Well, duh. She's your mom."

"Hmm."

"Stop reading into things and just talk to her," she added.

"Fine, I'll talk to my mom if you promise to do something for me," I said.

"Anything."

I smiled. "Fix Victoria."

"Hell to the no. Anything but that."

"Cam, she's broken. You've seen her. Steppe did a number on her and no one deserves that mess. She needs fixing and she's headed back to school with you. You're great at pulling people out of their shells. Please."

"Tay, it's Vic the Sick," Cambria pouted. "Do you remember how she was last year with the bullying? It sucked like a Dyson in steroids. Please don't make me do this."

"People change," I reminded her. She scowled. "Logan will appreciate you more."

She gave me a dubious look. "And that's supposed to motivate me how?"

"Good karma," I tried.

"I'm an atheist," she said.

"That's not..." I shook my head. "I promise to make sure Derek doesn't cozy up to anyone else while you're gone."

Cambria was quiet for a moment. Underneath our banter I could see her hurting at the thought of leaving Derek behind. But this was Cambria. Tough—and in her weakest vulnerability, there was always a joke. I let her have this one. "Deal," she said. "And if he does get cozy, you'll bite his Werewolf legs off at the kneecaps and give them to Astor for prosthetic experimentation?"

"Absolutely. What are friends for?" I said.

She grinned. "Indeed."

Chapter Twenty-One

Arctic Monkeys were the perfect blend of listening but not letting it soak in. Cambria would've yelled at me to turn it up if she knew I'd even allowed the bits of conversation to flow in around the ear buds she'd forced on me at dawn.

Cambria awake at dawn—now that was the real headline.

"…heard anything from Headmaster Whitfield," Professor Flaherty said from the front seat of the van on Friday morning. She sat shotgun, Kane's navigator. Beside me, Wes had one arm wrapped tightly around my shoulders, as if cuddling would somehow create world peace. But I didn't pull away—just in case he was right.

On my other side, my mom was a stiff wall of listening in and "insert opinion here." Behind me, Grandma called out her two cents to Professor Flaherty's update on the Inquiry Board investigating Steppe. "Should've had Elizabeth do the honors," she said snarkily. "I suspect he'd have answered on the first ring."

I pretended not to hear.

My mother broke her stillness to twist around, a glare perfectly aimed. But Grandma snorted and I knew the look she wore would be one of carelessness. The one person in the world these two women weren't scared of was each other.

Steppe could learn a thing or two.

As quickly as I thought it, I zipped my mental lips shut. But it didn't matter. He was secured three cars behind us, tucked in with Derek and George, probably shoulder to shoulder with his new bestie Cambria herself. More importantly, he was under the heaviest dosing of compulsion Cambria knew how to give. And I was currently operating under a mental gag order: think quiet thoughts.

I wondered who'd been voluntold with the job of informing Cord of Steppe's impending announcement to name his successor. I tried convincing myself she couldn't be mad. I'd respected her wishes, she couldn't be mad. It wasn't her.

Thank God it wasn't me, either.

"The others have been notified," Kane said. "They've agreed to bear witness. And to spread the word to their contacts."

"And you think they'll come through?" Professor Flaherty asked. "That it'll be enough to enforce the changes, including his successor being outside his family line?"

"Two days wasn't very long to organize this thing, but I think they'll come through," Kane said. I sat behind him, and through the far edge of the rearview mirror, I saw him glance at her with a stoic expression. "If nothing else, they'll want to see the show."

Professor Flaherty snorted. "Wouldn't Steppe love to know he's been demoted to nothing more than a sideshow," she said.

"He's never been the main event," Grandma said from behind me. "And that's always been his problem. It's why he wouldn't leave The Cause alone. The unworthy always feel threatened by the true leaders. The world changers. This car's full of them. He's always hated that."

"In the meantime," Fee said, "I would feel better if we could count on the audience we need. The new law, even if it's only to rescind an old one, can only be recognized if there are ample witnesses, yes?"

"It's more than rescinding if Lexington's being named successor," Jack said.

"I still can't believe we're letting him take the reins," Wes said.

"We'll have the witnesses we need," Grandma said. "Alex has gone ahead to make sure of it. Don't you worry. And Lexington isn't a concern. He'll do the right thing for his daughter. I think he's more than proven that."

"The important thing is the legal recording," Professor Flaherty explained. She glanced at me and then back to Fee. I kept my head down, pretending to be wrapped up in my music. I shouldn't have been listening—but I couldn't help it.

"With The Draven," Fee said, "Right?"

"Not just any Draven. The official Draven for CHAS, the one that has been passed from generation to generation of leaders," Professor Flaherty explained.

"Don't forget Steppe's blood," Jack said from the far end of the bench seat behind me. He sounded almost gleeful and I couldn't blame him an inch for it. But his anxiety showed through and I hated how they all spoke with the same hint of worry.

"We won't forget," Fee said wryly.

"Damn right," Grandma muttered. I almost sat up at that. Grandma cussing meant she was seriously worried.

"This is only going to work if the new law is written into the official Draven of the CHAS leadership while those in charge bear witness," my mother said. In her lap, her folded hands twisted the edge of her jacket in a tight wad.

I reached over and covered my hands with hers. Our eyes met and I tried for a reassuring smile, but I only made it halfway before the images bombarded me. I gasped, rocking at the intensity of them.

These were not the foggy layered dreams I'd had when Steppe had held me prisoner. These were not the nightmares I'd woken from in the bedroom at Professor Flaherty's. These were real; living, breathing—memories. Only they couldn't possibly have happened yet. And they weren't coming through the bond; these stemmed directly from my own subconscious.

One by one, they bombarded me until they'd sucked me right in and I became a part of them. Not just a guest, a participant. A roomful of Werewolves, hot with the heavy breath of a growling force. The room itself glowed with the fierceness of the yellowed eyes glinting back at me, at each other. One pack, sinewy and rugged with a sly look in their angry eyes as they faced off with another pack. The second pack broader, bigger, stronger than the first. Steppe standing at the front of the first, his glittering smile so full of victory it made my chest hurt. And the other—Who was the alpha for this one?

In the center of the room I spun in a panicky circle trying—and failing—to spot the alpha. Like the note had predicted, war was in this room. I could taste it.

I heard the gasp from far away and the vision was sucked sideways while I somehow managed to stay behind. The feeling was like a river rushing away from the edge of the falls—dropping into thin air before it vanished. I came aware, still gasping, and realized a moment later, the noise had been my own breath all along.

"Tara," my mom was saying, shaking my wrists. "Tara, wake up," she pleaded.

Wes still had his arm wound protectively around my shoulders. He peered down at me anxiously with knitted brows and shallow breaths. As the vision cleared away, I caught and held his gaze. "What's wrong? What happened?" he asked.

"Don't give in to the panic," my mom said. "It's not real."

I cut away from Wes long enough to study my mother. "How do you know?" I asked.

She hesitated and something foreign clicked inside my gut. Some strange puzzle piece I hadn't known I was missing. I filed it away for later and turned back to Wes, who was still demanding answers. No one else spoke. Every spare eye was trained on me. "I'm fine," I told him and then again to the rest of the van. "I'm fine. I fell asleep and had a bad dream," I said. My mother relaxed.

Slowly, the tension in the air dissipated.

Someone's phone rang.

"Hello?" Jack said from behind me.

A pause and then, "We understand. No, this is not an attempt to realign—"

"Tara, headphones," my mom whispered.

I sighed and reinserted the ear buds that had come out when I'd begun flailing. Over the sound of Vance Joy singing about whose mess this was anyway, Jack's deep baritone bled through. And I let it.

"Yes, that's fine. All we're asking is that you bear witness," Jack said. And after a pause, "It's not about their laws. We need you to bear witness for the purpose of goodwill. The law will be rescinded. He will step down."

Werewolves, I realized, trying my best to keep my thoughts muted just in case. They were going to ask Werewolves to bear witness to this. Would that put them in the same room as where we were headed? Like my dream just now?

Of all the times to be kept in the dark…

Broken Blood

I resisted the urge to sit up and listen harder or demand answers I'd already agreed not to be told. This would only work if Cambria's compulsion held, if I muted my end of the bond, and filled any connection or influence that might be left with white noise.

Determined to hold up my end, I resettled myself into my earlier position, tucked into the crook of Wes's shoulder, and focused on the music. It lulled me.

I dozed and woke with no sense of time or place.

The sky was streaked with slanted sunlight and the traffic was thick. The clock on the dashboard put it at the early side of rush hour. We were nearing the city.

At the sight of the familiar skyscrapers in the distance, the sea of brake lights and never-ending construction zones, my stomach cramped. I remembered the conversation I'd overheard earlier. About The Draven, the official book for recording our laws. Steppe would've kept it close to him. Almost as close as he'd kept me for those weeks…

I realized where we were going. We were returning to the site of my prison. We were going to CHAS headquarters. The drive in had been far less eventful than my journey out—or maybe that was the benefit of my checking out in favor of the music. Had this really been the way I'd operated for months once? Back when all those voices had risen to a crescendo, before I'd learned how to control the mental demands of my pack in order to be the alpha.

It felt like a lifetime ago.

Leo. Miles. Liliana—that accidental meeting in the alley one night. The first night. The encounter that had changed everything.

Except that, according to Steppe, it had been no accident. Neither was the choice Vera had insisted I make.

None of this was.

It was coming for me no matter what I did. Liliana had been a catalyst, but she wasn't the cause. I sat up enough to glance at my mom. Her head pressed against the glass of the window beside her as she dozed.

For once, the worry lines in her face were relaxed.

I leaned closer and caught the scent of oven cleaner and smiled. Some things never changed. Maybe that was a good thing. Maybe that was life. Nothing was permanent, not really. Not the past, not that fear and uncertainty I'd felt that night in the alley, not the worry I'd felt over Wes that night I'd driven off in his car and left him to fight Leo's Werewolf minion by himself or the countless other times we'd faced danger together or apart.

I snuggled closer to Wes and felt his hand wrap tighter around my shoulder, squeezing lightly in that protective way he had. I turned my face toward his shirt and inhaled the musky scent that was his animal and human intertwined. Nope, that hadn't changed either. I still remembered it like it was that first night. Muscle memory.

So many things felt like ancient history and yet simultaneously like they'd just happened yesterday. I thought about that as we exited the highway and drove over a bridge with a lion's head statue on either side of the gateway ahead. When our tires crossed onto pavement, we were here.

DC.

I was back.

And rooted, for better or worse, in the here and now.

I wound my fingers around a handful of shirt and Wes looked down at me. "You're awake," he said. I hesitated, unsure if I should turn up my music or admit I'd paused it.

"You can take a break from the tunes," he said.

I sat up and slipped the ear buds out.

"Feeling better?" he asked.

"I think so. Surprised I was able to sleep," I said. I glanced behind me and found Grandma, Jack, and Fee typing on their phones. In the front seat, Professor Flaherty did the same. All of them wore matching frowns of concentration.

"What did I miss?" I asked lightly—we both knew he wouldn't tell me.

"A bathroom break," he said. "Candy bar?" He held up two choices.

"Caramel," I said.

"Figured." He smiled and handed it over. "The other one was for me."

We ate a few bites in silence as Kane took us farther into downtown and then, slowly, out the other side again. We crossed New York Avenue and kept going, the route quickly becoming familiar.

I lowered the candy bar. "We're going back there, aren't we?" I asked quietly.

Behind me, the telltale sounds of buttons being pressed went silent.

"Yes," Wes said finally.

"Are there ... How many others are meeting us?" I asked, trying to figure out a way to ask my question that would solicit a real answer. "Werewolves, I mean. How many of them?"

"None," Wes said.

"What?" I looked up at him and back at Grandma. "Why not? I thought you—"

"We're going to broadcast Steppe's speech via a live internet link. That way, everyone who needs to see it will, and we'll all be safe." He leaned in close. "You'll be safe," he added.

I stared at him. "We're going to rescind the law, save the world, via a webinar?" I deadpanned.

Wes sat back and fought a smile. "I knew you'd be excited. See, Edie?"

"It's the safest route," Grandma said and went back to her typing.

I shook my head and twisted to glance at Fee. She shrugged. Jack blinked back at me. "This is not about you," he said sternly. "I don't feel like getting shot again."

I smiled. "Of course."

"If you're going to argue, you can just put your ear thingies back in," Grandma said.

"No," I protested. "I've listened to my entire play list twice."

"Ornery. Just like your mother," she grumbled but I caught her smile.

Kane circled left and we pulled into a deserted lot and stopped. Outside, a gray building loomed up, unassuming, nondescript—basically, terrifying.

My breath caught as I read the sign that advertised CHAS headquarters to the outside world: Council for Himalayan Affairs and Security. C.H.A.S. It would've been amusing if I'd been able to see it as anything other than my prison.

My pulse sped.

"It's okay. No one in there can hurt you," Wes said as the other filed out.

"I'm not worried," I lied.

Outside, the rest of our caravan joined us in the otherwise deserted lot. From the middle car—Grandma's Hummer—Mr. Lexington, Victoria, Astor, and Logan climbed out. The last car was crammed tight with Derek, George, Emma, and Cambria—with Steppe bound and sandwiched between the girls in the back. Cambria had insisted, despite her better judgment, the compulsion would work best if they were in direct contact.

I felt for her.

The group assembled slowly, most eyes trained on Grandma. Hers, however, were trained on Mr. Lexington. "Can you still get in?" she asked.

"I would think so. It's not like Gordon's been around to change the codes," he said, making his way to the double doors that led inside.

A block letter sign read "Staff Only" and below it in small lettering, "No Admittance. Secured Building. Government Officials Only."

"Pretty much any variation of *Don't Feel Welcome Here*," Wes commented.

Up ahead, the door clicked and Mr. Lexington held it open. One by one, we filed inside.

The lobby was sparsely furnished with gleaming tile floors, tasteful but forgettable artwork, and not a single reception desk in sight. The only next step was another set of doors directly across from where we'd entered. This was, apparently, nothing more than a landing pad. And without a receptionist in sight, I could only assume there had once been security of some sort and now—

"The security force—what was left of them—we found downstairs a few days ago when we came to retrieve Olivia," Mr. Lexington explained.

"Can you check to make sure the building hasn't been accessed since you were here?" Grandma asked.

"Security booth is this way," Mr. Lexington said.

"Jack," Grandma began.

"On it," Jack said, already falling into step with Mr. Lexington.

Grandma turned to Kane and Professor Flaherty. "We'll need to search and secure the perimeter before we go live."

"We're on it," Kane said.

"We can help," Derek said, stepping forward with George beside him.

"No, I need you two on Steppe. Don't let him leave your sight," Grandma said.

Derek nodded, but George hesitated and glanced at me. "Do what she says," I told him, biting back a smile at his confusion. No matter who tried giving orders, I was his leader and a part of me—the alpha part—loved knowing that. They filed back outside to get Steppe from the car.

"Everyone else, let's get inside and set up," Grandma said. She gestured to a set of doors in the center of the row facing set we'd come in.

Steppe's glare looked frozen in place as he was led inside and the sunlight abruptly cut away as the door shut behind him. His sweater was crooked and his pants wrinkled but mostly, the brooding grimace he aimed at everyone except Cambria told me all I needed to know about his opinion of the plan. He would do it, but he didn't like it.

"You doing okay?" Wes whispered in my ear as the group dispersed and got to work.

"I'm fine, I told you," I said, but my shoulder blades were firmly pressed against the wall just inside the door. Just the thought of moving deeper into the building set me on edge. I tried to take a deep breath, but it got stuck in my chest.

Wes grabbed my hand and led me along the wall into the corner. "Tara," he said, brushing his thumb across my cheek as he cupped my face. "You don't have to be fine. You don't have to always be the one taking care of everyone else. It's okay to let us take care of you once in a while."

He was right, of course. I'd agreed to step aside and stay out of the plans for today, knowing that was the best way for Cambria's compulsion to work. But it was one thing to stand by and another to actively relinquish the reins.

I stayed quiet and when I didn't readily supply whatever answer Wes was looking for, his gaze dropped to my cheeks, my mouth, my neck, before returning to my eyes again. And just like that, I forgot what we were discussing. All I could see was his mouth forming an unspoken question.

I was so caught.

After all this time, the mere sight of Wesley St. John, up close and personal, was enough to send my knees buckling. My muscles went liquidy and it was like an organic truth serum had leaked into my heart and escaped through my open mouth. "I'm scared," I admitted.

Instead of judgment or pity, Wes looked back at me with relief.

"Don't look so happy about it," I grumbled.

He smiled. "I'm just a little shocked you actually admitted it. I thought it would be much harder than this."

"I'm getting better at admitting my faults," I said.

"We're both improving," he said. "Thank you for telling me."

"I don't know how it's supposed to help," I grumbled.

Wes leaned in and pressed a kiss to my lips. "It allows me to be here for you," he whispered, his lips brushing mine as he spoke. "It allows me to rescue you. Something I never get to do."

I smiled ruefully. "Sorry about that."

"Don't be. I love your strength. I always have. It's what attracted me to you in the first place. But that just means I love it even more when you show vulnerability and let me take care of you. I have an idea," he said.

"What?" I asked, wary at the way his eyes lit up when he said the word "vulnerability."

"You and I can watch Steppe's speech via the video feed from the parking lot. We'll act as lookout for the perimeter so we'll be doing something helpful but we won't have to spend another minute inside this building."

"Wes, I don't know," I said.

He leaned in and pressed his nose to my cheek. "Come on. Edie's got this one. Let her have it. By tomorrow, you'll be back in charge. With any luck, we both will, and after that, we won't have this luxury. And besides, if I play my cards right, I'm hoping I can multi-task and use the time to make out with you."

My lips twitched. "You seriously think they've got this covered? That we won't be missed if we wait outside?"

"More than covered. Besides, it's no secret where we're filming from. Or it won't be once the feed goes live. Another body or two watching the exits would be a big help. What do you say?"

How did he expect me to say anything other than yes when he looked at me with those doe eyes? I sighed. "Let's do it," I said.

Wes grinned and planted a lingering kiss before wandering off to inform Grandma. I swayed where I stood, happily buzzed from the after-effects of Wes and his mouth. If this was what it felt like to admit my fears, I'd spill my guts every day of forever.

Chapter Twenty-Two

Wes and I ended up in the backseat of the Hummer. Leather seats made warm by a layer of blankets Wes found in the back and enough room to stretch out but hidden behind the window tinting. I hadn't been able to bring myself to cuddle up in the back of Mr. Lexington's creeper van and Derek's car was way too small.

We'd spent the last hour cuddling, kissing, and reassuring each other every acorn that fell on the hood wasn't a pack of Werewolves here to kill us. I was jumpy, though. Even parked safely outside CHAS and with everyone I knew already settled inside to protect me, I couldn't stop seeing memories of my confinement every time I looked up at the plain gray walls.

I'd dialed back from Gordon's awareness as much as I could, opting instead to let Cambria have control of his thoughts—and his willpower. So far, everything I allowed myself to read from him was wrapped up in what he would say when the cameras went live. I sensed a deeper part of him that was aware of his coercion and the controlled fury he felt over what he was being made to say, but Cambria's abilities were strong. Stronger than I'd realized until now.

I was proud of her, but not without also feeling a twinge of sympathy for him. Mind control, no matter the reason, wasn't something I readily condoned. I knew it was necessary, our only option, but I didn't love what we were stooping to. I didn't mention it to Wes, who seemed more concerned with linking up to the right web address in time while still holding hands. I reached over and adjusted his shirt, fastening a button he'd missed earlier.

He caught my gesture and smiled just as the screen on his phone went from black to moving color. I recognized the office I'd passed through on my way out a few days ago, the memory more of a blur of tables and chairs that appeared in sharp focus now. Grandma stood with her profile in full view, her mouth moving soundlessly as she gave instructions to someone off-camera. There was a flurry of movement and then a hum over the speakers as someone turned the sound on.

"Here we go," Wes said, shifting in the seat to offer us both a better view of the small screen. My hand tightened in his.

The moment Steppe realized the feed was streaming, he came to life. The wrinkles around his mouth relaxed, his frown disappeared, and his shoulders lowered. He was the epitome of cool confidence—unless you knew his mind.

The bond had been a muted static for almost twenty-four hours. Even now, with curiosity pricking at me, I caught only bits and pieces. Shadows of images and lines of text he'd burrowed into his psyche while he'd studied his assigned speech during the drive over.

Grandma stepped in front of the camera again, so close her softly lined face filled the entire screen and blotted out Steppe and the rest of the room. "Hello, friends. Edie Godfrey here. If you're watching this live stream it's because you've been exclusively invited to witness the changing of Hunter policy and formal leadership under the direction and authority of CHAS and its officers."

Grandma stepped back to gesture to the room and continued. "We're broadcasting from the inner offices of CHAS headquarters in Washington, DC and we ask you, the viewers, to bear peaceful witness in these troubled times to a ceremony that our kind has recognized as necessary and required in order to uphold our traditions in accordance with Hunter law. Today, we bear witness."

Grandma stepped aside and the camera followed her outstretched hand to Gordon Steppe. He stood at a small podium at the center of the room, his hands draped over the edges. He met the camera with an even stare and then smiled, full of teeth.

For a harrowing second, I wondered if he'd somehow shucked the compulsion and was operating on his own agenda. But then the camera shifted as Mr. Lexington cleared his throat to deliver the opening minutes and call the meeting to order. When he'd finished the introductions and explained the items to be brought to the council, including Olivia's death, the camera shifted again, zooming in on Steppe as he returned to the center of the podium.

"And so we mark these changes to the law today with blood and bear witness to the spilling of the sacrifice necessary to proceed," Mr. Lexington finished.

At the corner of the shot, blood dripped from a newly opened wound along his left palm, and then Lexington concluded his speech with a shot of The Draven sitting to Steppe's left. Fresh blood marked the place where he'd recorded Cambria's scripted law reversals and policy changes.

Steppe's voice was clear and carried easily over the room. His expression was lit with that spark only really available for the truly gifted, the charming. Politicians. But better than any of that, he was convincing in the way he spoke. "Good afternoon and thank you all for tuning in to this special broadcast from CHAS headquarters," he began.

Another acorn hit the Hummer's roof and I jumped.

Beside me, Wes cursed and automatically scanned the empty lot, but I was glued to the performance.

"Before I go into the details of the decision that brought me to your screen today, I'd like to talk to you about some of the things that brought us all here. Humans in general, but Hunters, especially, have been influenced by and certainly even led the way in creating the kind of world-changing, life-altering, culture-infusing technology and changes that can only come from the passionate and committed search to progress."

In the background, someone muttered something about "narcissistic much...?" It sounded like my mother.

"In my time as board chair, progress was king. Hunters, CHAS, our esteemed scientists, we were royalty. And together, as a united front, we affected such changes as metals modified to better protect against superhuman threats, alliances made, and, best of all, a cure was found. Hybrids, turned against their will, had the option to return to their God-given form. So much progress."

Steppe shifted and the light in his eyes took a dark turn. Something vicious sliced through the bond but I couldn't quite reach it before he went on. I was wrapped up in his words, in their delivery, in his ability to paint himself the hero even after all he'd done. Even under compulsion.

"Cambria's certainly making it believable, isn't she?" Wes muttered.

I didn't answer.

"And then, in the wake of progress, it became necessary to slow down, to realize the tension and conflict our progress had created," Steppe said, his gaze burning into the camera. "There was strife and our united front was destroyed. We became individuals fighting singular wars. And in the wake of such destruction to our progress, we are now forced to learn forgiveness."

The room was deadly quiet. I knew, without asking, this was the crucial moment. It wasn't hard to guess what came next. Law reversals and successors. I held my breath.

Steppe opened his hands, palm up, exposing his bandaged wound. "I stand before you today to accept the consequences of my push for progress. To announce my resignation, name my successor, and to rescind the law that allowed for open extermination of Werewolves, hybrids or otherwise. This law has been recorded as rescinded and is, effective immediately, null and void. Werewolves will be…" His voice dropped and the last words were delivered through closed teeth and a struggle to push them out, "Tried for their crimes and a fair verdict will be awarded."

But then his demeanor shifted again and the vicious satisfaction returned, both through his expression and through my own mental poking.

Someone moved into the edge of the shot—Cambria—and the look on her face was fierce. She whispered something to Steppe, but he ignored her. Her lips moved faster, clearly barking out some demand or order, but again, he ignored her and kept going, talking faster now. "But I'm also here today to offer something else: forgiveness of my own. It has to start somewhere, doesn't it?"

He leaned in, his gaze and psyche all trained on one thought. His knuckles were white with strain as he gripped the edges of the podium. "Tara Godfrey, I forgive you. For your crimes against Werewolves, Hunters, and peace itself. For your crimes against me. Even now, as you coerce my hand in naming you my successor, I forgive you."

The room erupted in shouts, all muted by Steppe's mic and his speech, now delivered in bursts of shouting. He blinked and his arrow-tipped gaze widened to include the world itself, it seemed. "She is the dictator behind it all. She dissolved The Cause to take over CHAS herself, to make war! She has killed the other members of the board, leaving only myself at least until the end of today's broadcast. And even in the face of her crimes, I forgive her—"

The camera jerked violently, angling away from Steppe and his microphone died. In the right corner of the screen, Steppe continued to rant from his place at the podium but none of his words could be heard over the din.

A door banged open somewhere off camera and a pair of arms darted in to snatch up The Draven.

"We have to get in there," I said, but Wes was already out of the car and running for the doors. I kept one eye on the parking lot—still empty as far as I could see—and one on the video stream as I ran to catch up.

On screen, a table was violently upturned by a pair of hands belonging to someone I couldn't see, chairs flew from left to right, and someone screamed. I watched, helpless, as Werewolves poured into the room from the two backdoors. Their eyes gleamed and their jaws hung open in ready. Someone ran by, momentarily obscuring the view, and then the camera shook and fell.

I looked up to see Wes standing in front of the door. I blinked, trying to understand why he hadn't rushed inside ahead of me. Slowly, I realized he wasn't trying to get in because he was keeping me out.

"We have to get in there," I said, leaning around him and feeling for the handle, but Wes grabbed my arm and held me back.

"No. They're here for you," he said. "Look." He pointed at the screen, where a roomful of Werewolves now surrounded my friends and family. "They're leaving Steppe alone. He called you out and now they want—"

Even as he said it, a gray wolf leaped into the picture, paws out, claws extended, and landed on Steppe. They tumbled backward with Steppe on bottom. Limbs struggled helplessly against paws as they fought.

Cambria grunted as a book case fell in front of her. She jerked backward and stared at where Steppe lay, grappling. I felt the moment the compulsion was broken. So did Steppe. The bond sprang up between us, a rushing current of panic and terror and pain. I felt Steppe reaching to crawl out from under the Werewolf ... and I felt the moment he knew it wouldn't do a bit of good.

"You ... win," I heard him whisper and the words were like a sledgehammer to my mental defenses.

I dropped to my knees on the cracked asphalt, the echo of his pain just as great as the pain itself. I could feel the slice of claws down his torso. Its teeth as they sank into his throat and ripped his flesh free.

"Tara," Wes said, dropping beside me and cradling me against him. I watched in helpless horror as the video continued to play out the gruesome scene. My throat pulsed, my heart sped along with his, struggling with the added effort of pumping blood onto the floor rather than through his jugular.

I cried out as he sucked in a sharp breath and then the bond ripped free as he died and I crumpled against Wes, automatically curling in on myself for protection. Wes scooped me up and carried us both to the overhang next to the building's entrance. He tucked us in against the wall and lowered us both to the ground.

I felt the phone being slipped free of my fingers and a moment later, I heard Wes speaking. "She's fine," he said. "No, we don't see anything out front but we're sitting ducks."

There was a pause where I gritted my teeth through the aftershocks of the bond as it ripped away from me. "We'll wait outside," Wes said and disconnected.

The pain receded and the familiar nothingness was left in its wake. The empty void that meant my mind was once again my own. No trespassers, no voices, no comfort in company, however unwelcome they might have been. Silence in the wake of noise always hurt.

I stayed where I was, crumpled into a tight ball, and watched the video still streaming from the phone. Wes held it up so we could both see and pulled me onto his lap without a word.

On the screen, bodies rushed by, some human, some not— causing the view to go in and out. The buzzing in the background became a collective growling. In various corners of the room, I saw my friends— battling with beasts.

I whirled at the low droning noise of an engine, spinning in a panicked circle to spot the intruder. From the narrow side street that ran alongside us, a loud engine approached, chugging and working as it slugged forward, but I couldn't see around the building and there was no other noise, no other evidence of a threat.

They were all inside.

How had we missed them?

On the other side of the wall, footsteps pounded closer. Wes pulled us both up and we jumped clear just as the door was shoved open. Cambria was first, her cheeks whiter than I'd ever seen. A thin sheen of sweat coated her forehead and collarbone and she gripped a single wooden chair leg in her hand. She raised it and then lowered it again as recognition dawned.

"Holy Breadsticks," she said. "Are you guys okay?"

"We're fine," Wes assured her.

She shot a quick look around the lot. "None of them are out here?"

"They're all inside," I said and shot Wes a pleading look.

"Good. You stay," she said, stealing my argument before I could offer it.

"What? No, you need my help," I protested.

"No, we don't. There's only six or seven of them. We can take them without you, no problem," she said. My relief was minimal; I still wanted in.

Behind Cambria, the door banged open again and Logan appeared, his blue ball cap slid backward and slung low on his forehead. He dragged a shocked Victoria alongside him, her eyes glassy and wide. "She's having a panic attack," he said.

"Vic, you okay?" I asked.

She didn't answer.

Logan's forehead creased and his mouth quirked into a sorrowful frown. "Her dad's dead," he managed, his words halted and clearly painful as they each left his lips.

"Lexington?" I said, shaking my head. "No, he can't. He's the next—"

From inside, someone yelled. Behind me, on the street, the approaching engine chugged louder. Closer. "Watch her for me. Put her in the car or something," Logan said, the words rushed. He turned to dash back inside and called over his shoulder, "Don't let anything happen to her, you hear me?"

And then he was gone.

Behind me, an axle creaked as tires jostled and the engine puffed and groaned. "What the heck is that noise?" I demanded.

"A tour bus?" Wes asked, staring with knitted brows as the bus rumbled into the parking lot and parallel parked across four spaces. Cambria, one foot inside the building, one hand on the door, stopped and stared.

It was a tour bus, I realized—or it had been in a former life. The dull black paint job was badly streaked in what looked like a do-it-yourself crafting day gone wrong. The windows had all been blacked out to match, the thick stripes still dripping in a few places.

"What the heck..." Wes muttered.

The driver's side window slid open and a face craned out to greet us. Even from here I could see his five o'clock shadow quickly becoming more like six-thirty and his scruff was blotchy, like it was incapable of filling in no matter how long he let it grow. But even from here, I recognized him. Still, I sniffed the air to be sure, my wolf senses hyper-alert.

"You kids need a ride?" he called.

I sniffed again. "Benny?" I said.

"Benny!" Wes called and broke into a run. His tone was stuck somewhere between relieved and suspicious. "What are you doing here?"

A face appeared over Benny's right shoulder. A woman I recognized from the single photo Cambria still kept in the Kaboodle organizer box she got when she was six. They had the same pitch-black hair that shone under the light and the thick lashes that framed wide eyes that always saw more than they let on. She was tanner than Cambria and her smile was bigger. Cambria never smiled that wide—she rarely had a reason to these days. But I knew who she was.

"Cambria, Cambria, it's me. I got your messages. We're here to rescue you!"

"Mom?" Cambria said under her breath and then to me, deadly serious, "Is this really happening or am I hallucinating? I swear, I didn't have anything to drink today."

"It's really happening," I told her.

"Pinch me," she said.

I did.

"Ow!"

"Sorry."

She sighed. "Fracking A. It's really happening."

Broken Blood

She started walking over to the tune of her mother's way-too-cheerful greetings, but I hung back. Now was my chance at getting back inside. My heart pounded and I took a step closer to the door.

I kept one eye on Wes, still locked in conversation with Benny, and one on the handle. Slowly, I reached out and wrapped my hand around the cold metal. Then, all at once, I pulled and rushed forward through the opening—and collided with my mother.

"Tara, dear God, there you are," she said, shoving my shoulders until I was right back outside. Wes looked over and our eyes met. He frowned, said something to Benny, and headed for where I was being detained. "Are you all right? Are you hurt?" my mother demanded, looking me over.

"I'm fine," I snapped at her. "They're all inside."

"Well you don't have to be rude—"

The door slammed open again and almost knocked my mom off her feet. I caught and steadied her as we jumped clear. Astor stumbled and almost fell before Wes caught and righted him.

"Good man," Astor said, panting.

His eyes focused on me, clouded, and darted to my mother. "Edie … was looking for you," he said to her.

"I'm going," she said.

"Mom, no. You can't go back in there," I said.

"I have to. And you're staying out here," she said. Her tone left no room for argument. Didn't mean I wasn't committed to trying.

"You need me—" I began.

"To stay out here," she finished. "Wes," she said. He nodded and I groaned.

"Now is not the time to finally start getting along," I said.

"Benny and Cambria's mom are here," Wes said, ignoring me. He pointed to the blacked-out tour bus idling in the lot. "They brought transport. I think we should ditch the vehicles we came in. Better not to leave a trail for these guys."

My mother nodded, her chin dipping once and her lips pressed tight. "Good. Get everyone on board you can. In fact, I'll go send the others out. Be ready to hustle. Wait. Who is Benny?"

Wes hesitated and I said, "A friend."

My mother nodded and we both knew it was just one more thing I'd never told her. Story of my life. Literally.

My mother leaned over and pressed a quick kiss to my temple. "I'll be back when I can," she said and slipped inside.

Grunts and growls leaked out from the open doorway. It clicked shut behind her and everything went quiet except for the bus. "Let's get on board," Wes said.

"I can't believe you're leaving your friends to fight without you," I said.

Wes stopped and stared at me, his face hard. It was a low blow and we both knew it, but my guilt was overshadowed by desperation. With Steppe gone, my head and my hands were too empty for this. I needed to help. Cambria threw a glance between us and then said, "Vicky, Astor, let's go. Hopefully, there's a minibar or something."

She led them away and I stepped closer to Wes. "I mean it. How can you do this?" I asked. "What if something happens to one of them? How will you live with yourself? How will I?"

His expression clouded. "What if something happened to you?" he demanded. "I can't …" He swiped a hand through his hair. "I promised Edie I'd keep you out of it."

"Wait. That's where your 'let's make out in the parking lot' idea came from?"

He winced. "When you say it like that, it sounds bad."

I stepped closer and poked a pointed finger in his chest, my temper flaring. "You are not Edie's boyfriend," I said and he made a face. I ignored it. "You are mine. Which means you are loyal to me." With every statement, Wes took a step back and I took a step forward. His retreat stirred my wolf and my limbs ached to shift. My wolf wanted to let him know exactly what she thought of all this.

I snarled, barely managing to hold my form. "Tara," Wes warned, still backing away. "Don't do this. Not now. I'm sorry."

"Don't ever lie to me again, Wesley St. John."

"I won't," he said. "I shouldn't have before, but, I didn't think anything like this would happen." His expression softened. "I thought by keeping you out here, I was protecting you from yourself. I know how much you didn't want to go back in there."

I felt the anger draining out of me. He was right, and I was only taking out my worries and fears on him. "I understand," I said quietly.

Behind us, the main door slammed open again, but this time it was a line of Werewolves and Hunters that poured out. They appeared in a steady stream of stumbling retreats that turned quickly to leaping attacks. Wes and I flattened ourselves against the building to avoid being taken out by their momentum.

"You could shift," I said. "Might be safer."

"You go ahead. I'm staying human."

We dodged a set of teeth and Wes snuck in a hard punch to the Werewolf's jaw before it ducked away. "Any particular reason?" I asked.

His brow crinkled and he shot me an amused smile despite the violence around us. "What did Alex say? Opposable thumbs?"

A wiry brown wolf sailed past us, landed silently on his paws, and spun. But he wasn't fast enough. Grandma was already there, crossbow raised. The metal-tipped arrow sank into the wolf's shoulder in a downward arc that perfectly pierced its heart. He dropped to the pavement in a heap, dead before he hit the ground.

"Your grandma is such a badass," George said as he ran past on all fours, chasing down his own prey.

"They can't bring the fight out here," I said. "It's broad daylight. In downtown DC. They can't—"

"Tara, get to the bus!" my mother yelled. She was dodging a creamy white wolf that already had two blood-stained patches on its left flank. The determination in its eyes was no match for her gracefully quick dance and seconds later, she had driven a small sharp object through its chest.

"Is that a pen?" Wes asked.

I shrugged, pretending the sight of my mom killing a Werewolf wasn't the weirdest part of my day. "I get my creativity from her."

He snorted. "It beats a plunger."

I elbowed him in the ribs and then we both jumped clear just as Derek and another wolf rolled over the spot where we'd just been standing.

"I heard Benny brought a party bus," Derek said from somewhere inside the tangle of fur and claws. Only Derek could have a conversation around a mouthful of enemy fur.

"And a new girlfriend. Painted it himself," Wes said.

"The bus or the girlfriend?" Derek asked.

"Come and find out," Wes said.

"Be there in two shakes," he said and then bit down on the other wolf's leg and shook it wildly.

"Show off," Wes yelled to Derek as we ran.

Around us, Werewolves littered the lot. And there were more than half a dozen like Cambria had first counted. Some still on their feet, fighting, but most were on the ground, unmoving. I scanned for my friends and family as I let Wes lead me toward the bus.

Derek and George were each wrestling, end over end, with another wolf. Jack and Fee were doing the same without nearly as much scuffling as the boys.

"Where's Emma?" I called.

"She's here," Cambria called from the bus. I found her watching through an open window halfway back, still on two legs. "And Astor and Victoria," she added.

"Has anyone seen Cord?" I asked.

Wes stopped running and we scanned the lot together. "I don't think I've seen her since they started filming," I said.

"She was supposed to be guarding the back. Come on," Wes said and we sprinted off toward the far end of the lot.

Wes got there first and disappeared around the corner. "Tara, here," he yelled almost immediately.

I rounded the corner and found him crouched over Cord. She was lying on her back, her eyes closed, a spray of blood staining her cheek and her shirt. In her hand lay a metal stake coated in blood up to her fist.

My heart stuttered and my breath caught. I dropped to my knees beside her.

"Cord," Wes said, leaning over her and wiping her hair out of her face. "Wake up." He hit her cheek lightly with his palm.

I picked up her free hand and wrapped it in mine. "Cord, please," I whispered. "We need you."

Cord's eyes fluttered. "When have you not?" she said, the words punctuated by a moan. She dropped the stake and pressed her hand to her forehead. "My head is killing me," she said, squinting up at us. She froze when she saw her other hand in mine. I dropped it abruptly and sat back on my heels.

"What happened?" she asked warily.

"An ambush. They must've knocked you out and gone in the back," Wes said.

"Why didn't they just kill me?" she muttered, still rubbing at the knot on her temple.

"I don't know. Maybe they weren't sure whose side you were on,"

Wes said. "They weren't here for us."

Cord struggled to push herself up. She wavered where she sat but I could see the understanding dawning at Wes's words. "We have to get to Steppe," she said.

"Steppe is dead," I told her as gently as I could.

"What?" She blinked at me and for a split second, I caught a glimpse of the cracked wall she'd constructed to keep him out, the father who had thrown her out. But then, the crack shored up and Cord's expression turned to concrete. "What a bastard."

"For dying?" Wes asked.

"Yes, for dying," she snapped. "Help me up."

Wes propped his hand underneath her elbow, but I hung back. I knew Cord way too well to try and help her now. She grunted and heaved but managed to get on her feet. Her blonde hair hung in knots around her shoulders. The blood stains on her cheeks combined with the vacant expression made her look a little zombie-ish.

"What's happening?" she asked, breathless and still leaning on Wes. Not a good sign.

"They're fighting in the front. Benny showed up with a bus. We're leaving the cars here and riding with him."

"Casualties?" she asked.

From the front, someone yelled but I couldn't make out the words. My skin twitched from the inside.

"Steppe and Lexington so far," Wes said.

"Lexington?" Cord said and mouthed something else that looked like a curse. "What about Kane and Flaherty?"

"Tara! Wes! Let's go!" Cambria's voice echoed off the walls and around the corner to the alleyway before bouncing back. It was loud and serious. I exchanged a look with Wes and ran to the corner.

The bus was moving, slowly at first, but then Cambria yelled, "There! In the back, I see them. Go!"

The engine roared and the bus creaked forward, faster now. "They're coming to pick us up," I said. "Everyone else must already be on board. Come on."

Wes helped Cord and we made our way to meet the bus. I climbed the steps first, greeting Cambria's mom and Benny with a simple hello. There would be time for more later, but for now—

"Where is everyone?" I asked, stopping short just past the driver's seat. Only half the seats were filled. "Where's my mom? And Grandma? Jack and Fee? Where's—"

"Hang on," Benny called from the front. The bus lurched and I grabbed the seat to keep from being thrown sideways. "Hang on," he added.

Cambria rolled her eyes. Behind me, Wes lowered Cord into an empty seat and made his way to the window. "They're still fighting," Wes said. "It looks like more of them. How are there more? Where the hell are they coming from?"

"Coming around," Benny announced.

The bus swung wildly and somehow, Benny managed a U-turn. He pulled alongside the group, now fending off the newest wave of Werewolves.

Grandma looked up and her expression clouded. "You guys need to go," she called. "Steppe and Lexington are—"

She broke off and twisted sideways to avoid the sharp teeth at her back.

"Holy ... How did she even see that coming?" Cambria muttered.

"George, Derek, get the hell out of here!" Grandma called, swinging her arm up and around to grab another arrow and load her gun.

The boys, both with blood on their jaws, looked up. First at Grandma, then at the enemy assembled. I could see the argument forming, but then so could Grandma. By now, several of the Werewolves had spotted the bus and half a dozen broke off from the fight and ran toward us.

"We have to go, people," Benny sang nervously.

Across the lot, the door banged open and Professor Flaherty and Kane stumbled out, a trio of wolves at their heels. Both looked exhausted but otherwise intact. They glanced at the busy lot and paused when they spotted the bus.

"Derek, don't sass me," Grandma called out. "You boys need to stay with Tara. Protect her. We'll stay and hold the fort."

"Um, Tara," Emma said quietly.

"Yeah. What's up?" I asked quickly, still watching Grandma trying to convince the boys to get on board.

"You should look at this," she said. She handed me her phone and I glanced down, barely registering what I was seeing. I started to hand it back but then the picture clicked and made sense through my panic.

"This is the live feed from inside. It's still streaming," I said.

Broken Blood

"And that's Mr. Lexington," she said, pointing. Sure enough, at the edge of the screen lay a body. There was a large, bloody gash in his throat but I recognized his profile easily enough where he stared, unseeing, at the ceiling.

"What the..." As I watched, Mr. Lexington's form shivered. First his arms and then his feet and legs. They shivered and almost vanished before reappearing, stretching, shrinking, and morphing. It was the slowest shift I'd ever seen. "He's shifting," I said.

Wes peered over my shoulder and, one by one, the others crowded in to watch. Victoria was the only one who didn't look. I caught a tear streaking down her pale cheek. She brushed it away when she saw me watching.

"We can't leave him," I said.

"What?" Wes, Cambria, and Benny all said in unison.

"I mean it," I said. "We need to bring him. If it were one of us lying there, we'd do it. And, in the end, he is."

No one argued, but no one agreed either.

Outside, Grandma was screaming at George and Derek. They broke off and ran toward the wolves now circling our bus. "Guys..." Benny said.

"Tara, we can't—"

"I'll go with you," Cord said, struggling to her feet.

"No," Wes said quickly. "No one on this bus is getting off." He leaned over and called out the window to the others, the words so rushed and muffled around the growls and yells beyond that I barely caught it.

Near the door, Professor Flaherty and Kane nodded and darted back inside. "Pull to the back, Benny," Wes said.

"Uh, dude, we're surrounded," Benny said.

Even as he spoke, Derek and George took out the two wolves blocking our way. Benny hit the gas and we lurched toward the back of the lot for a second time. When we turned the corner, tires squealing, Professor Flaherty was already at the back door, dragging Lexington along behind her.

George rushed into help, using his teeth to get hold of Lexington's scruff and the two of them dragged Lexington, now a wolf, to the bus door.

Victoria nodded at me, brushing tears from her cheeks. "Thanks," she said.

"He's one of us," I told her. And, without overthinking, I hugged her. I felt her shoulder wrack with silent sobs. "So are you," I whispered.

When I let her go, Logan was there to collect her and lead her to the back where Mr. Lexington's wolf form now rested. I watched Victoria walking slowly toward her father, my heart aching.

He'd been so sure Steppe had cured him. So sure his wolf was gone. In death, it had returned. "Your body takes your true form," Alex had once told me when I'd asked what determined the shift after death.

I wondered what mine would be. And I hoped I wouldn't have to find out anytime soon. One dead Werewolf in the back of the party bus was enough.

Chapter Twenty-Three

Mr. Lexington stared back at me from the corner of the bus floor. Well, his eyes were open and he faced me. But I knew he wasn't seeing anything. I looked away but couldn't help darting back to the sight of him as Benny bobbed around traffic and attempted to navigate us out of the city. Victoria's father, the man who'd spent his whole life as a Hunter, had shifted into a wolf after death. I knew what that meant. Alex had told me once that the dominant creature always took over after your heart stopped beating and your brain stopped shoving one side of your soul to the back.

According to Steppe, Mr. Lexington should've been cured of his wolf. But clearly, that theory had just been proven wrong. Strange, how a man who'd spent his whole life as human became an animal in death. Maybe there'd been a version of animal in him before the change.

"Are you thinking about Liliana?" Wes asked, sitting beside me and blocking my view. I looked up in surprise but then shook my head. He knew me so well.

"Sort of," I said. "Mostly, thinking about what form I'll take when I die."

"Maybe you'll go Dutch, half and half like your uncle."

I smiled at his joke and saw the relief color his expression. "I'm fine," I said in response to his unanswered question.

"I know." He pressed a kiss to my cheek. "But just in case," he whispered and kissed me again.

His phone beeped and I leaned in close as he checked the incoming text. "It's from Fee," he said and his mouth quirked deeper and deeper into a frown as he read.

"What does it say?" I asked. "Are they all right?"

"They're fine. Cleaning up and disposing of ... everything," he said. "Alex says the inquiry board saw the whole thing. They know Steppe was blowing smoke about you. But ... that's not why she texted."

"What's going on?" Derek asked, rising from where he'd huddled close to Cambria two seats ahead. She rose beside him and they leaned over the back of the seat with matching looks of concern.

"She said they're getting messages from the packs. Allies are interested in what happened to Lexington."

"I bet they are," I muttered.

"No, they're not angry about it. They're curious but they also saw Professor Flaherty carry him off. They want to know what we're going to do with him," Wes said.

"We're going to bury him," I said.

Wes typed something back to Fee and a second later, his phone beeped again. We waited while Wes read the message. He looked up and his eyes landed on Victoria. She'd risen as well, with Logan beside her, and her cheeks were dry. "Fee says we should broadcast the burial. She says the packs seem open to the possibility that Steppe was playing them."

"Showing them we're sympathetic to Werewolves," I said slowly, "could help diffuse things."

"Steppe outing us, outing you, is my fault. I'm sorry," Cambria said.

"None of this is your fault," I assured her.

"They'd have to be idiots to believe him anyway," Derek put in. "I mean, Tara's half Werewolf herself."

"Yeah, but at some point, my list of crimes overshadowed my similarities to them," I said. "Steppe was all Hunter but he committed plenty of hate crimes against them in order to get what he wanted."

"And don't forget the videos he released portraying Tara as the criminal instead," George added. He'd shifted back and now sat as close to Emma as humanly possible on their shared seat.

"I'd say he got what he wanted," Derek said, giving me a pointed look.

My throat closed as I remembered Steppe's last whispered words. "Vic, would it be okay if we streamed his service?" I asked.

She blinked and the expression she wore was such a blank slate, it made my chest hurt. This was not, nor would it ever be, the Victoria I'd met at Wood Point.

"Yes, that will be fine," she said quietly. Logan leaned in beside her and spoke quietly, rubbing her arm.

When I turned back to the others, I found every one of them waiting, watching me expectantly. And I realized this was it. I wasn't being sidelined for strategic reasons or overshadowed by a worrywart mother. Nor was I out of my depth of experience compared to a badass warrior Grandma. It was up to me. Always had been.

I channeled Vera and squared my shoulders. "Okay, so, here's the deal. No more compulsion or running. We stream the funeral and then we face them. Once and for all. And we do it together, no more sitting out while the adults do the fighting."

"Tara, we have to think this through," Wes began, but I stopped him and climbed over him to stand in the aisle.

"I am thinking it through," I insisted. "Remember once you told me the difference between chess and whack-a-mole?"

"Strategy," he said.

"Right. And I've thought this through. In fact, I've had plenty of time to fine-tune it while everyone made me rest and heal and stay behind to protect me. The bond is gone. I'm ready and I know what we have to do," I said.

I looked from face to face and found all of them leaning in. Even Victoria had stood up again and her face shone with a thin layer of determination. Cambria opened her mouth but Derek nudged her and she closed it again.

Everyone waited, watching Wes.

He looked from them to me and back. Finally, he exhaled and nodded at me. "All right," he said. "How do you want to play it?"

Derek and George grinned and offered Wes a high five. Cambria rubbed her hands together and I couldn't help but laugh at the surging of emotion I felt in this moment. We were a team, a great one. Always had been, and now, when it counted, we got to act like it.

"Tell us what to do, Tara," Emma said.

"We need a way to unite everyone. Hunters, Werewolves—and to recreate The Cause," I said. "Before it escalates into something out of control."

"They're pretty united in hating you," Cord said. Cambria shot her a glare. "Well they are," she muttered.

"Something else," I said.

"They were united in the cure, until that happened," Derek said.

I winced at his insensitive reference to Mr. Lexington slumped in a heap behind us, but Victoria held it together.

"But there is no cure, not really. And even if there was, they'd never believe it or go for it at this point," Logan pointed out.

"No, they wouldn't. They aren't united in a cure, just in the option to choose," I said.

"Are you saying you want to give them that?" Derek asked.

"I'm saying we don't need a cure. Astor," I prompted.

He threw his hands up just as the bus hit a bump and he almost tumbled. Cord caught him and righted him again and he scowled. "Oh, now everyone wants to hear the truth. Fine, I'll tell you all about how the wolf's nervous system—"

"Astor. English," I said.

"Right." He crossed his arms in a huff. "The cure was a lie."

"You couldn't have told us that before?" George asked.

Astor snapped back with something that sounded like a scientifically-inspired insult. George's face went red and he called Astor a "periodic table," which made Astor guffaw. Logan smiled and attempted to explain how that made no sense but I tuned them all out as the phone Wes still held beeped again.

He didn't notice so I reached over and turned his hand so that I could see the incoming message. "What are you—?" He looked down and we read the screen together before locking eyes in disbelief.

"Do you think it's for real?" I whispered, not daring to hope.

Before he could answer, the phone beeped again and the text was followed up by a picture of The Draven page in question.

"It's real," Wes said quietly.

Just like that, the holes in my plan—or the really sketchy ones anyway—sealed up and I finally felt like it had a shot at working.

Around us, the argument stalled.

"Why do you look like you're holding a pair of Aces?" Cambria asked.

"Because I am," I said, trying to contain my excitement until I knew everyone was on board. "We all are. I have an idea, but it's dangerous."

"When is it not?" Cord muttered.

I looked at her sharply but let it go. For now.

Instead, I told them my plan. "I think we're looking at it backward by pursuing the cure angle," I said. "The packs, the allies, even the Hunters and what's left out there of the hybrids—there's only one way to prove to them Steppe lied. That I'm not out for destruction. I have to embrace both sides and, more than that, I need to embrace anyone else straddling both sides."

"Are you trying to tell Wes you want to see other people?" Cambria joked. "I mean, isn't one Dirty Blood enough for you?"

"Funny," I said. "No. I'm saying instead of curing people we should turn them. Willing people, of course. And we should do it in full view of Hunters, hybrids, and Werewolves everywhere. Maybe we do our own live stream."

"You want to infect people?" George asked, skepticism lacing his words.

"I want to allow people a choice. A true choice. Not like Steppe's 'be a Hunter or die' ultimatum but a real option. No judgment."

"God, Tay," Cambria said.

"What you're proposing is pretty crazy," George said. I could only nod in silent understanding. He knew better than anyone what a change like that could do. But I'd already thought it over. This was the only way to get their attention. To repair the damage Steppe had done.

"And when the change doesn't take? When they can't battle the darkness alone?" Logan asked quietly. "What then? Another blood bond? You and the whole world in each other's head?"

"Astor and I have talked about it," I said. "He would use a small amount of my DNA structure in order to solidify the change and help make it easier for them. And he would give me an injection of someone else's blood immediately after, redirecting any bond that might form."

"Whose blood will he inject you with?" Wes asked, concern already knitting his forehead into tight lines.

I reached up and smoothed them away and managed a timid smile. "Yours," I said.

He hesitated. "Are you sure?" he asked, leaning in.

"I'm sure."

The collective pause felt like a defining moment—and I was thrown back into a memory of another gathering, another planning session that felt so much like this one it made my heart hurt. We'd stood in Astor's living room in Nevada and I'd finally glimpsed what it felt like to be a leader. The love and loyalty and commitment were beautiful—then and now. A tear slid down my cheek and Wes wiped it away.

Derek cleared his throat pointedly and my lips curved in a rueful smile.

"With Steppe and Lexington dead and no CHAS leadership in place, this is a long shot," Derek said.

"I know. For this to work, we need leadership. Someone to step up." I looked at Cord. There was something knowing in her eyes as she stared back. "We need you, Cord. We can't do this without you," I said.

"You've never been able to do it without me," she pointed out and I realized she was right. For better or worse, she'd always been there when I needed her. Albeit, grouchy and unwilling, but still.

"You wouldn't be doing it alone," I said and the fragility in her expression said she knew exactly what I was talking about. "We'd do it together."

The pause felt like a lifetime before she finally said, "I'm in. But I'm not taking his last name."

"She's in for what?" Benny called from the front, but we ignored him. I hadn't doubted for a second that his silence equated to eavesdropping. Benny had a particular talent for finding things out. Or lurking. Or both. But, rescuer or not, now was not the time to bring him up to speed.

"What is your last name, anyway?" George asked Cord.

"Probably Diablo," Cambria muttered and Cord glared at her. "What? I went with something exotic. It's a compliment."

"It's Hunter, of course," Cord said. "I paid good money for that name. And I'm keeping it."

"Hold your horses," Logan said, holding up his hand. "How is Cord taking over going to help us?"

"Because she's Steppe's daughter, sweetie," Victoria said and there was a hint of bitchy impatience there that almost made me smile. "Keep up."

"I know that. But Steppe wrote Lexington's name in The Draven before he ... you know."

"No, he didn't actually," Wes said. "Look."

He held up his phone and everyone leaned in close. "Is that—?" Derek began.

There was a beat of silence and then exhales.

"My name," Cord said flatly.

"Edie says she's delivering it to Alex now," Wes said.

"He was legitimately crazy," Cambria said. "He actually wrote her name even though he said Lexington."

"I told you he was a bastard," Cord said.

"But that means she can actually do this. CHAS will have to recognize it," Cambria said.

I nodded. "Exactly. We need that inquiry board to examine it and deem it authentic and then Cord can be officially selected."

"How long will it take?" Derek asked.

"A couple of days," Wes guessed.

"We need to buy time," Logan said. He cast a worried glance to Victoria, but she already looked better than before. Color had returned to her cheeks and I knew having a plan of action was helping.

"Derek, call Jack and Fee. Ask them to send word we're having an official service for Mr. Lexington and everyone can tune in," I said.

"I'll set it up," he said.

"Logan, can you and Astor get us a list of everything you'll need to perform the change?"

"Sure, but…" Logan hesitated and his glance slid to Mr. Lexington's furry form. "Who's willing to be changed?"

Everyone halted, phones halfway out, and looked back and forth at each other. This was the part I hadn't exactly worked out beforehand. Because I couldn't. Whoever volunteered, it would have to be one hundred percent their choice. And it's not like Wes or I could do it.

"I'll mention it to Jack and Fee, put the word out we're asking for someone to step up," Derek said.

"Make it clear it's a volunteer-only situation. We can't look like we're forcing anyone," Wes said.

"Got it, man." He slid out of the seat and paced up the aisle, hitting buttons on his phone.

"Victoria and I can do the same with some of our contacts from school," Logan said half-heartedly.

"That's a long shot," I said. "Wood Point isn't exactly open to the idea of Dirty Bloods." Victoria's face fell and I knew she was remembering everything she'd put me through when I'd first arrived.

I reached out and laid my hand over hers where it rested on the seat. "Vic, I didn't mean—"

"I'll do it."

My words fell away, as did the phone against Derek's ear, and every other activity, including Benny's navigation. The bus pulled to a stop in the middle of the back road we'd just turned on.

"Cambria?"

Cambria's mother shuffled her seat belt off and stood at the far end of the bus, staring uncertainly at her daughter. But Cambria didn't turn. Her only reaction was the tightening at the edges of her mouth as she stared at me.

"Cam?" I asked softly.

"I'll do it," she repeated, her chin high and her back stiff as she faced me. "I'll take the injection. I'll become half-Werewolf."

"Cam, are you sure?" I asked. "This is huge. There's no going back. We can find someone else—"

"But I won't." She looked at Derek. "Is it okay?"

"Is it what you want?" he asked her.

"I want you," she said.

"You have me even without this," he told her.

"Well, I want it anyway." She looked at me, still ignoring her mother, who had wandered much closer and was silently taking it all in with nervously twisting fingers. "Shoot me up, Scotty."

I laughed. "You mean beam me up."

"Whatever." She shrugged. "Make me a wolf."

I started to ask her one more time if she was sure, but Derek grabbed her and kissed her. And everyone clapped and cheered.

Wes took my hand and squeezed. "She looks sure to me," he whispered.

And I knew, as I watched Cambria and Derek, that he was right. She was sure. They both were. In that moment, we all were. Sure of each other, sure of our future, our commitment to overcoming the conflicts of two races pitted against one another. And I knew, looking around at them all, I'd do whatever necessary to make this plan work.

Chapter Twenty-Four

The drippings of the dream were like ice cream on a hot day. One image melted into another faster than I could keep up. My empty brain, devoid of voices and interruption, felt like a circus tent at show time. I couldn't control it much less make sense of anything I saw. Vaguely, I knew I was asleep—that I could stop this anytime—but the images were torturously specific. No fog or smokescreen obscuring.

I blinked into the crystal-clear image of the cabin. The one Astor and Grandma had somehow spelled to include a wall that made the whole thing invisible and impenetrable to both Werewolves and Hunters. I'd stayed there up until I'd been taken by Steppe. It had been the only place I'd felt truly safe in … as long as I could remember.

But now, it was dark and the air felt heavy, like a weight pressing down around the group assembled. Wes, Logan, George, Derek—all of my friends stood in a gathering in the yard, every pair of eyes aimed into the woods beyond the front steps. Breathing was shallow, hands were fisted, shoulders rigid. I watched them—us, a spectator in my own dreaming, trying to understand.

My eyes tracked the line of theirs and, finally, a blurred outline took shape. A girl, lying face down on the ground at their feet. She was convulsing and sobbing, her nails digging into her own skin as she hugged her arms to her chest, clearly in agony.

I reached out a tentative hand and yanked it back again when her convulsion suddenly sent her flailing. Her scream rent the air and, from within the shadows of the trees, wolves howled. Lots of them.

I didn't need to understand their particular pack's call to battle to understand that's what would come next. I leaned into the girl again as she bucked and finally rolled to face me.

I gasped, stumbled backward on all fours—and came abruptly awake.

"No!" I said aloud.

Wes caught me, bracing my shoulders with steady hands. "It's just a dream," he said, but it wasn't just a dream. It was more than that. I just couldn't figure out how much more. Over the sound of his soothing words, his phone rang. "Answer it," I said, struggling to catch my breath.

"You sure?" he asked.

"It could be important."

"Hello?" he said. There was a pause as he listened and inserted a few uh-huhs before he handed the phone to me. "It's your mom."

I took the phone and smoothed my shirt and hair, willing my breath to return to normal. My heart still pounded, but I was not about to give in to the fear and doubts the dream had left me with. At least not while my mom was on the line.

"Mom," I said, aiming for normal—considering the abnormality of my life in general.

"Tara, don't be scared," she said.

"Mom?" I held the phone away from my face to double check I wasn't on video chat or something. "What are you talking about?"

"The visions, Tara. I know about them. I was … Apparently, we were on the same frequency or something for that one."

"Are you talking about my nightmare?" I asked, thoroughly confused. "It was just a bad dream."

"No, it's not," she said gently. "It was a vision, Tara. And judging by your lack of surprise, I suspect this wasn't the first one you've had."

"I've had … a few," I said warily. "How do you know? And why are you calling them visions?"

"Because I have them too," she said. "They're in your blood. Remember Vera?"

I couldn't find my voice. Of course I remembered Vera. Her visions were what had sparked this entire business of my leading some group or another or choosing between some alliance or another. It had led to Steppe's interest in me. Leo's attempted murder of my whole family, starting with my dad all those years ago. Miles. Olivia. Those damn visions were responsible for everything.

"Tara?" my mother prompted.

"Of course I remember Vera," I snapped, my temper flaring at what she was proposing. And why had she waited so long? "When were you planning on telling me her gift fell on our side of the family tree?"

"Don't be angry. God, don't be—you have no idea everything I've done for these stupid visions." Her own anger eclipsed mine and made me think twice about whatever accusation I was about to throw.

"What do you mean?" I asked.

"I saw what Vera saw," she said. "Long before you ever appeared to her, I saw it. The pack, The Cause, the choice you'd have to make for us all to survive. It terrified me, so I ran away with you. Hid you. From this world and from the visions ever manifesting into truth. Obviously, that worked out well for me," she said wryly.

I shook my head, trying to make sense out of what I'd known five minutes ago and what she was saying now. "But I thought you ran because of Leo. To keep us safe."

"That was part of it. This was the rest. Visions are liquid, Tara. The future isn't concrete because people are constantly making choices that change the big picture. Which is why I didn't see, I guess…"

"See what?"

"That by hiding you, I was delivering you to the exact place you would need to be in order to fulfill what I'd tried to prevent. And now, here we are."

"But why am I only now seeing these visions?" I asked, frustration replacing my confusion in streaks of hot temper.

"Your father's cocktail prevented it for most of your life, along with your ability to shift. After that … I think the Unbinilium was suppressing it before now."

"But I've been able to shift for months before these visions started."

"Tara, you have a fair amount of Unbinilium in you. How do you think you were made to be immune in the first place?"

I had no idea what to say to that. Frankly, I'd never delved too deeply into the mechanics of my immunity. I looked over and found Astor watching me from three seats away with a knowing look. He probably would've told me if I'd asked. But, of course, I hadn't. Instead, I'd been riding the superhero high and becoming more and more reckless with danger.

"I tried to tell you," she added, "but we've had a lot going on."

I remembered our abandoned conversation in my bedroom at Professor Flaherty's house and couldn't help but agree with her there.

"Does Grandma have visions?" I asked finally.

"She showed an affinity for wards when she was young, but she was much more interested in combat and weapons training. Her skills are a little rusty."

In the background, I heard Grandma yell, "I resemble that remark."

My mom chuckled but I was too preoccupied with this new truth. And the vision itself. Especially this last one.

"I saw Cambria," I said, careful to keep my voice low. I spotted her near the front, talking to her mother, but I wasn't taking any chances. "The change wasn't working. She was dying, Mom." My voice broke a little and I squeezed my eyes shut, pulling my knees to my chest and curling against the seat.

"I know that scared you. But that's why I called and why I'm explaining everything. Visions are liquid, Tara. You have to remember that."

I sniffled. "So, there's a choice I can make that will keep that from happening?" I asked.

"Yes."

"What then?" I asked desperately.

"I don't know," she said quietly. I huffed and let my feet fall back to the floor. "You will, though," she added. "I have full confidence in you."

"Yeah, right," I muttered.

"It's true," she said, her tone firmer than I'd ever heard outside of being in trouble. "I have always believed in you. I know it doesn't always seem that way, but I do. The visions have kept me from giving you freedom, but it doesn't make it right." She took a deep breath, exhaled. "The adults have made a decision. We're sitting this one out. We're letting you guys handle it."

"What?" I pushed to my feet, screeching loud enough that everyone else turned to look. Benny eyed me through the mirror and the bus swerved lightly before he righted it again.

"You're ready," my mom said and my knees gave. I sank back down again in shock. "And, more importantly, I'm ready to let you do this. I'm sorry if I held you back. I was just ... Maybe someday you'll have a daughter of your own and you'll understand." This was the last thing I'd expected her to say. Even more unbelievable than visions, she was giving up control? This was not the version of my mother I knew.

"Mom, you're talking crazy. How are you just sitting out? And Grandma? And Jack and Fee? I don't believe you."

"Believe it. We trust you. Now you have to trust yourself."

"But…"

"Alex is already gathering the inquiry board and bringing them to witness. If you need us, we'll be close by. But you're going to lead them. They need you, Tara. It's time for you to make your choice."

My heart hammered in my chest. "Mom," I whispered. A hot tear streaked down my cheek and I sat back down with a heavy thump.

"Take them to the cabin. You know what to do," she said. "I love you, Tara."

"I love you too," I managed and she disconnected.

Wes looked up from where he and Logan were going over the supply list, but I waved him off.

"You going to let us know what just happened or are you going to be one of those 'don't ask don't tell' type of leaders?" Cord dropped down beside me, her long blonde hair spilling over onto my shoulder. I resisted the urge to pick it up and toss it away. Better to make nice with the girl who was going to save our ass.

"The adults have given us their blessing. They're going to sit this one out," I said, staring out the blacked-out window. There was a small chip in the paint and when I looked just right, I could see the lines on the pavement whirring by us as we wound around the back roads Benny was intent on taking.

We still had no destination. "Go west," Astor had said and no one had argued.

"Did she say why?" Cord asked with a decided lack of surprise coloring her words.

"She said they believe in me. In us."

"Huh."

"What?" I demanded.

"I don't know. I guess I'm coming up empty on what about that scenario could have your panties in a knot."

I shot a glance up at Cambria. She was still seated up front talking quietly with Benny and her mother. She laughed—it was short and cut off abruptly but it was there. And it made me feel a little better about everything.

Quietly, I told Cord about the visions and everything my mom had said. When I finished, she whistled low.

"Wait, you're not going to back out, are you?" I asked. "Cord, you already promised—"

"Relax, I keep my word."

I exhaled and forced myself to stay calm. My eyes sought the crack in the paint and I went back to staring at the yellow lines on the road.

Silence fell and I knew Cord was wrapped up in her own thoughts. I didn't rush her.

"Steppe was—" she broke off and stared down at her hands.

"Not a good dad," I said when she didn't finish. "I figured it out."

"Well that's something. I always wondered if his version of events would be different. Less his fault or something." She leaned forward, her elbows propped on her knees, until her hair created a curtain between us. I looked over, waiting it out this time. Cord was talking. To me. I didn't want to ruin it.

"You saw it so I might as well tell you," she said finally. She raised her head slowly and I was stunned to see tears brimming. "He was abusive. God, not that way. He never hit me," she added quickly. "Abuse comes in so many forms, though. Words and lack of attention can be just as bad." She shook her head.

"What happened?" I asked even though a huge part of me suddenly didn't want to hear the story at all. Or watch her have to tell it. Maybe she just needed to say it. Maybe she knew I'd seen it already and that made it easier. Either way, I had to let her talk.

"My mother died when I was young. Three or four. I don't remember much about her except that her death marked the before and after. Gordon—Dad—changed after she died. Not that he gets to use it as an excuse because obviously he wasn't a saint beforehand, but after we lost her, he, I don't know, gave himself permission to be an asshole. He would pick at you. Nag and wiggle his way in with words and insinuations and guilt trips that made you feel like you couldn't do anything right. He was, essentially, a world leader and I lived in that shadow.

"When I hit middle school, it escalated. He was on me all the time about securing my future by making right choices. Academically, socially."

She rolled her eyes. "I was destined to take his place but before that, I had to measure up. In sixth grade, the physical combat training started."

She sat back and leaned her head against the seat; her eyes were on nothing inside this bus. "He never had to hit me. My trainer did it for him. But he never let up on the verbal assault. He would stay just to yell at me while I was getting my ass kicked. 'You have to be tougher, better, smarter. You're a girl and girls are weak. I should've had a son. You'll have to work twice as hard to get their respect. To get mine.' He had an answer for everything and all of it was designed to make me feel less; no matter how much better I was, it was never good enough."

I tried to picture a Cord who stood by in silence while someone insulted or berated her. It was a difficult picture to put together. If I didn't still have the brief snatches of memory from Steppe's mind, I wouldn't have been able to believe her.

This Cord sitting in front of me now was nothing like that girl.

"So you ran away," I said softly.

"Eventually. Took me a long time to get there. I was fifteen and my weapons training was in full swing. I was on a camping trip with my trainer. It was summertime, hot as hell, so we went swimming in a creek. I didn't think anything of it. I'd trained with him since I was ten. He was like an uncle or something. But that night ... while I was in my tent getting changed... he came in. I didn't see him until it was too late."

She fell silent, swallowed hard. I stared at her strong jaw, her muscled shoulders. Everywhere but her face. My chest ached for her. My throat burned—but I couldn't allow myself to cry. That felt wrong somehow when she was sitting here dry-eyed.

"I didn't see that," I said finally.

"No, you wouldn't have. Nothing happened. Well, nothing he had planned, anyway." Justice and violence clashed in her eyes. "I killed him," she said simply.

"You did what you had to do," I said.

"Oh, don't worry. I don't lose any sleep over what I did. I knew the alternative and I don't regret it. Anyway, I got out of there and called my—called Gordon. His response after I told him what happened was that I'd turned an unfortunate situation into a mess. He'd clean it up this once but next time, I should plan to handle it better."

"Next time?" I repeated.

"I was a decently attractive young woman. Things like this were bound to happen. The sooner I understood that, the better. Those were his words."

My jaw hung open wider and wider the more she talked. I'd known Steppe was a bad guy, but this? Telling your own daughter to expect rape and accept it?

"I never went home after that," she said. "I cleaned out the little bit of savings I had, used it to pay some documents hacker to lose my paper trail and change my last name. I've been on my own ever since."

"Cord, I'm so sorry," I said.

"Don't. I don't want your pity. You of all people should get that."

"I don't pity you. Not a single bit," I said honestly. "You're the strongest person I've ever met. If you had to go through that to make you who you are ... It sucks, but I don't feel sorry for you. I'm proud of you. And I get you. Wow, never thought I'd say that."

Her lips twitched, and I knew we'd reached a milestone.

"I get why this is so hard for you," I said. "That part, at least, was something your—Steppe understood too. He knew the pressure he'd put on you and that it would be extremely hard to live underneath that if you took his place."

"Was he sorry?" she asked, staring down at the calluses on her hands.

"He regretted the conversation that night," I said, choosing my words carefully, but it didn't fool Cord.

"But he didn't disagree with what he'd said. I brought it on myself just having boobs." She sighed.

I didn't answer—I didn't need to. "You can't measure yourself against his truth," I said instead.

"Can't I?" she demanded. "Even if it's only to make sure I don't become like him, it'll always be there. I can't escape it so I might as well embrace it."

"I never meant to force you."

"You didn't," she said. "I think I always knew, no matter how far I ran, it'd always come down to this. And, if I'm honest, there's a part of me that wants it. I want a chance to do some good for the people who deserve it. The ones he stepped on. There's been so much collateral damage. It's time to end that."

"You're talking about Bailey, aren't you?"

"Yes," she admitted. "He didn't have anyone until he found us, The Cause. We need to get that back for everyone still alone out there. And anyone else who has ever been caught in the crossfire of my dad's prejudice and persecution."

"You're going to make a great leader," I said.

"You think? I mean, you can still have it if you want. I know you're supposed to make some big choice and all that."

I smiled. "I just did, Cord. I chose you."

Chapter Twenty-Five

Astor's nose twitched and he rubbed his hands together like warming tinder.

"What the heck is he doing?" George whispered—loud enough to earn a glare from behind Astor's thick goggles.

"I'm *doing* science," Astor said crisply and turned back to the tree he stood hunched beside. Logan snorted but Astor ignored it.

George's jaw opened and he shot a scowl at Logan. "Teacher's pet," George muttered and earned a dirty look from Logan—and the rest of us.

"Sshh. Let him work," Cambria hissed.

I rubbed my hands over my arms, the evening air biting its way through my hoodie. October in Virginia and October in Colorado were two completely different things. I looked around for someone to share body heat—an instinct I'd gained from my wolf—but Wes was still back at the bus with Derek, doing his best to hide it underneath a ginormous pile of pine branches and dead leaves.

I shivered and watched as Astor poured a milky liquid into a smaller, already half-full container. His tongue stuck out, caught between his teeth as he concentrated on measuring the chemicals exactly right.

"I'm starving. I hope that cabin has a stocked fridge," George said.

In unison, half the group turned and said, "Shut up!"

Broken Blood

George scowled and Emma huddled closer to him, wrapping her arm tightly around his. I suspected it was more an effort in saving George than borrowing warmth.

My stomach growled too, but I ignored it. It had been a long three days on that bus and everyone was ready to get some separation that included walls and some peace and quiet. After two drugstores, one grocery store, and six fast food stops, we'd made it. Without a single attack or interception from an angry webinar viewer. So far. Now we just needed Astor's chemical cocktail to get us inside.

Apparently, it wasn't something you could rush.

Behind me, Benny stepped forward, craning his neck until he invaded my personal space.

"Back up," I said, grouchy from lack of sleep. I'd napped on and off but mostly, I'd bought bad gas station coffee and played hangman with Cambria. I couldn't afford any more visions that might make me doubt our plan.

"Sorry, but I don't see anything," Benny said. "Do you see anything?" he asked Cambria's mother. Piper, according to her one brief conversation with me two days ago when she'd introduced herself only to ask me what I wanted from the drive-thru. Other than that, she'd stayed far away from me while somehow managing to stay close to Cambria. And Benny, which was kind of gross.

She'd asked me to call her Piper instead of Ms. Hebert. Normally, manners would've made that impossible, but one look at her skinny jeans and heeled boots and it wasn't hard to tell Ms. Hebert was determined to get younger with every birthday.

I wasn't thrilled with their being here, but we didn't have much choice. It was either allow them to tag along or be dropped off at the base of a mountain and climb up it in the dark. I'd chosen the first, but now, listening to their whispers, giggles, and kisses behind me, I was swiftly regretting it.

A loud pop broke through the whisperings of the group and I looked over just in time to see an electric spark flash. The liquid Astor poured from the cup sizzled and evaporated into a thick pillar of steam before it ever hit the ground. A stray spark shot up and zapped Astor's hand and he dropped the empty cup. "Ow." Astor wrung his hands, mumbling, and shoved his thumb into his mouth.

"Astor, what can we do to help?" I asked.

"Just be quiet," he said with a pointed look at George. "I need quiet."

We all fell silent and Astor began again, muttering words in a language I couldn't understand and rubbing his palms together. He leaned in and caught his lip between his teeth in concentration, staring as if something in the empty air had caught his attention.

Slowly, a thin line of electric blue light formed at Astor's fingertips and lengthened in the air. It shot left and right, growing quickly into a wide opening. In the center, the air popped and crackled but otherwise, the view of the ground on the other side was unchanged.

Astor looked up and beamed. "Got it."

"It looks the same," Benny said.

"Think so?" I asked. And, without waiting for an invitation, I stepped through. The second my foot landed on the grass inside the growing electric window, the cabin appeared to me in the center of the clearing.

It looked untouched, exactly the same as when we'd left. My chest tightened when I thought of all that had happened since then. On the other side, Benny still had brows raised in skepticism. "Come on, Benny," I called, impatient. "Don't make me come and get you."

Timidly, he approached the hole and put one scuffed combat boot through to the grass on the other side. Instantly, his face lit up and he wobbled, finally losing his balance and toppling through. He landed at my feet with a look of awe. "This is awesome," he said, struggling to his feet and staring at the house.

His T-shirt, sporting a picture of open-mouthed Pac-Man chasing ghosts with the words "Eat me" printed on it, was streaked with dirt. I rolled my eyes.

One by one, the rest of them stepped through. By now, the hole had widened to become almost as large as a doorway. Astor came through it last, looking smug and satisfied with himself. "How long will it last?" I asked.

"The electric charge won't be visible after another hour or two," he said. "But the hole will remain. I cannot close it without reconstructing the entire perimeter of wards, which would take time we don't have."

"He's right. Time's wasting. Let's get inside." Piper, Cambria's mom brushed past us and climbed the porch steps. Her heeled boots were loud and heavy against the wooden stairs. "Come on, Cambria," she called.

Cambria exchanged a look with me. "Duty calls," she muttered and followed her mom inside.

I trailed behind, doing a full lap around the house before I joined the others. I met George in the front yard. He was coming from the woods and gave me a knowing look as we climbed the steps together where Emma waited. The lights were on inside, casting an orange gleam over his features.

"Everything good around back?" George asked.

"I don't see any signs of visitors," I said. "You?"

He climbed the steps and slipped his hand into Emma's and squeezed. Something passed between them and when he answered again; his voice was gentle and included Emma. "I checked Janie. It didn't look disturbed." He leaned down to press his lips to Emma's hair and added, "We'll go see her tomorrow."

"Thanks," she said quietly, her eyes shining.

"I'd like to go too," I said. "If that's okay with you, Emma?"

Emma blinked. "Of course, Tara. You knew her as well as I did. Maybe better," she added. There was no trace of accusation or grudge and I smiled back at her, grateful. Janie had been Emma's sister, but she'd been my responsibility. When the darkness had taken her, I'd done what I had to in order to protect myself and the others. But that didn't make killing any easier. For me or for Emma.

"It's a date," George said, forcing his voice lighter. He opened the door, held it wide for us. "Let's get inside. It's freezing out here and I don't have my fur coat."

We slipped inside and soaked in the warmth and light. Despite what we were going to do tomorrow there was plenty of both, I realized as I stood in the tiny foyer. My friends, the people I loved most, were here. And that was enough to strengthen me, to strengthen us all.

I found Cambria and Piper, arguing in front of the kitchen sink while water ran from the faucet. Neither one paid it any mind as it escaped down the drain. "I'm not doing it. I like it the way it is," Cambria said.

Piper pressed her lips together and pinched the bridge of her nose. Cambria only seemed to dig in. I suspected this was a body language they each knew well and had often repeated. "Cambria, you need to look presentable. There will be a large audience and—"

"No," Cambria shot back. "I need to look like myself. That's the only way this will work. Tell her, Tara," Cambria said and my feet stalled.

"Tell her what?" I asked, wary of inserting myself.

"My mom thinks I should dye my hair back to the original color. Get rid of the blue streaks. She says it'll look more presentable," Cambria said, mimicking the last word in a nasty voice.

Her mother glared for a second longer and then turned to me, her expression melting into a sugary smile. She extended her hand toward me, a ring on every finger, and waved me closer. "Yes, Tara, come and tell us what you think."

"Okay," I said uncertainly.

Up close, I could see she wasn't as young as she'd looked when I'd spoke to her on the darkened bus. Lines creased the corners of her eyes and mouth and her trendy top and fitted jeans reeked of stale cigarettes and alcohol. But the look she gave me was surprisingly direct.

"I was just trying to explain to Cambria that it's best if she make a good impression tomorrow." She leaned in to me and lowered her voice to a stage whisper that was almost as loud as her speaking voice. "And she's not very good at making those types of decisions for herself. As you can see." She gestured to Cambria, who wore, along with her neon-blue hair streaks, faded black jeans and a white blouse with tiny skull-and-crossbones designs printed on it. For Cambria, it was conservative.

Piper either didn't know that or didn't care.

I hesitated, hating to get into the middle of a spat, especially so soon after their reuniting. But one look at Cambria's expression and I made up my mind. This girl had always had my back—against any enemy. And I would always, no questions asked, have hers.

Piper propped her hand on her curved hip and watched me expectantly.

"Actually, I think it's more important that Cambria look like she usually does," I said. "If the viewers see a difference between her appearance tomorrow and what she looked like in the live streaming, for example, it could make them suspicious that she's been forced into this. We need her to be herself now more than ever."

"I see," Piper said quietly. Her face fell and she licked her lips. Then, her head snapped up and her dark eyes bored into mine. "Are you sure about that, Tara? I mean, really sure? I know Cambria's your best friend, but I think you should listen to the voice of authority here. I've had a little more experience with this sort of thing." Her voice mellowed, its sharp edge rounding out into a cozy crooning, and I felt my lids droop.

Heavy. All my limbs felt heavy. My muscles, my mind, even my mouth as I tried answering her. I swayed in place. "Now that you mention it," I said slowly, the words think on my tongue.

A beat of silence passed and I became aware I'd stopped talking. "What was I saying?" I asked.

"Mom!" Cambria's hands fisted and she shoved herself in between us. "You're compelling her?"

Piper waved Cambria away. "I was just—"

"Knock it off. Now," Cambria said, her tone shooting from indignant straight to scary.

I blinked and shook my head, the fog clearing. But it didn't matter. Cambria was livid and she only leaned in closer, her nose inches from her mother's. "How dare you?" Cambria yelled.

Footsteps approached behind us and stopped in the doorway as the others crowded in. I stayed alert, my attention on Cambria. This might be her mom she was facing off with, but I wasn't sure if that made it better or worse.

"You have no right," Cambria went on. Her mother backed up a step but Cambria followed. "Coming here after all this time and thinking you have any say or that I give a single crap about what you think of me."

"I was only trying to suggest—"

"Not suggest, Mom. Compel. And you reek of vodka. She was probably half-drunk with agreement. God, you could've hurt her. Or yourself. You don't get to come back into my life and still be this version of you."

"I thought you'd be happy I came back," Piper said. Her bottom lip quivered but something about it felt too dramatic. Too contrived. "A daughter should be happy to see her mother."

"I'd be happy if you were sober. And not trying to mind control my friend," Cambria said. "Besides, you have no idea what a daughter should be. You don't know me anymore. They do. You're a stranger. And a drunk, threatening one at that. We don't take kindly to compulsion without permission. In fact, usually we kick the offender out."

She folded her arms and the tears brimming in Piper's eyes suddenly dried up. Her expression hardened. "I sent you away to that school to learn some manners, some self-control for this temper of yours. Apparently, it didn't do what I'd hoped."

Piper slid by an unmoving Cambria—whose face had gone white as a sheet. "I'm going to bed. We'll discuss this in the morning when you've calmed down." She rounded the corner of the counter and I stepped in front of her to stop her. She pulled up short, her eyes widening. Behind me, someone snickered; it sounded a lot like Cord. Piper's eyes flickered to the offender and I watched a slight flush rise to her cheeks.

"You won't talk to her about this again in the morning," I said quietly.

"What?" she stuttered. "Excuse you, but I will talk to my daughter about whatever—"

"No, you won't. All due respect, *Ms. Hebert*, she's right. You are a stranger. You don't know what's best for her. And you were wrong earlier when you called yourself the authority here."

"Oh, really?" she said, her darkly lined eyes narrowing. "And who is? That crazy old scientist?"

"Me," I said quietly. "And I'm not going to kick you out. Not yet. But when tomorrow's show begins, you will stay inside. And if you try to interfere, I will do more than just kick you out of this house. Respectfully," I added through closed teeth.

Ms. Hebert's mouth opened, and the flush in her cheeks deepened to a bright red. "Well." She gave a pointed look over my shoulder. "Benny, let's go," she said.

"She better not take the room with the claw-footed tub," Victoria muttered behind me.

I waited while Ms. Hebert stepped around me and then I turned. "Benny," I said.

"Hmm. Yeah?" he asked quickly.

"That goes for you too. Inside tomorrow or you'll be asked to leave."

"Got it," he said and then hurried to follow Ms. Hebert up the stairs. At least he didn't need to be told twice. He'd already seen me in action. I almost smiled in spite of myself at the memory. George, Emma, Logan, and Victoria blinked back at me from the doorway. None of them spoke. Slowly, we all turned to Cambria. Her chest rose and fell with heavy breaths, but she didn't say a word.

The front door opened and closed. Booted steps approached, along with the voices of Derek and Wes. They stopped abruptly when they rounded the corner and caught sight of us. Derek's gaze sharpened into something like understanding as he took in the sight of Cambria by the sink looking murderous, but Wes looked completely confused.

"What's going on?" Wes asked.

"My mom happened," Cambria said.

I told him about the compulsion attempt and he wrapped an arm around me. "Are you okay?" he asked.

"I'm fine, just a little shocked," I admitted.

"My mom's capable of more than she looks," Cambria said with a sad shake of her head.

"What about you?" Derek asked her. "You okay? Because if you're having second thoughts about tomorrow—"

"No second thoughts," Cambria interrupted. "God, all she had to say about it was that I still hadn't learned manners. Nothing about how tomorrow I'll be a new species."

"Cam, your mom doesn't know you anymore. Not like us. We're here for you," Logan said and even Victoria offered a murmured agreement.

"She knew one thing," Cambria said, her words twisting into sarcasm. "My mom's prediction for my future is going to come true. After tomorrow, I'll really be a bitch."

Chapter Twenty-Six

The bedroom still smelled of mothballs and lavender soap. And if I sniffed in just the right place—near the bench at the foot of the bed—I could still detect the lingering scent of a familiar aftershave.

"It's just like we left it," I said.

Wes closed the door behind us and looked around. Inevitably, his eyes darted to the rug. Along the outer edge of the braided fabric was a small red stain. Janie.

"It is," he agreed quietly.

He came forward, arms out, and pulled me in. He lifted me slightly and buried his face in my hair, breathing deeply. I grabbed handfuls of his jacket collar and held on just as tight. His breath was warm on my neck and grounded me in a way that made everything feel so much more manageable than it had down in the kitchen. One moment stretched into another and, when I didn't move, Wes sat down on the bench and pulled me down into his lap.

"Did you speak to Alex?" he asked.

"He says they'll miss the service but they'll be here in time for … Headmaster Whitfield doesn't fly so they had to drive."

He huffed. "This inquiry board—"

"Is necessary," I said.

He sighed. "And Cambria? How is she?"

"She's okay, I guess. I think mostly she's nervous about tomorrow."

"Her mom certainly didn't help things." I watched while he slid his toe against his heel and slid his boots off.

"I don't know," I said. "I think in the long run, maybe she did."

"What do you mean?" he asked, shrugging his jacket off while still managing to keep me firmly planted in his arms.

"Cambria needed to say those things. Her mom needed to hear them. Even if things between them don't change as a result, it was necessary for Cambria to move forward," I said.

I turned and let Wes help me out of my own jacket. He set it aside and pulled my feet up, unlacing my boots and pulling them off one by one. "Thanks," I said.

The lamp light flickered, casting shadows. His expression was soft, full of shadows as he pulled me closer.

"It's okay to be worried," I said and he smiled, leaning in until our foreheads touched.

"That's good. Because I can't seem to turn it off." I reached up, running my hand over his face and weaving my fingers into his hair.

A thousand different reassurances were on the tip of my tongue but I couldn't bring myself to offer a single one. No matter what happened tomorrow, everything was going to change. One way or another.

"I feel stronger with you beside me," I said instead.

"I've always …" He trailed off and there was more in his expression than there'd been a moment ago.

"Always what?" I asked, smoothing his hair away.

He hesitated, searching for words, and when he spoke again, his voice was hoarse with emotion. "Falling in love with you has been the single happiest experience in my entire life. I can't imagine a world where you aren't beside me in it."

"Even when being together has made things harder?" I asked. Not because I wasn't sure but because the lump in my throat was preventing me from agreeing and letting the moment be simple.

"Especially then," he assured me. "I know it hasn't been easy, but after everything I've been through, everyone I've lost, I do know one thing." His eyes shone with moisture and I couldn't move or look away from the beauty of the way he stared back at me. There was no sadness when he mentioned having lost people, only gratitude and affection as he spoke about what he had gained. It was the first time I'd ever seen him smiling when he talked about his parents.

"And what is that?" I whispered.

"This is what love is. Suffering together rather than alone."

Tears fell before I could blink them back. I hadn't even realized they were brimming until I felt them casting wet tracks down my cheeks. I sniffled and shoved the words out before crying made them impossible. "Love is you, Wes. Love is sitting in your lap and listening to you tell me that we're stronger together—"

Whatever else I might've added was cut short as Wes slid in, pressing my parted lips to his. His mouth was hot and fierce on mine, no gentility, no holding back. His hands slid down my torso and gripped my hips, pulling me off the bench and onto his lap.

I wound my arms around his neck and pulled him as close as we could get through the fabric of our shirts. My skin heated at every contact point, my nerves all bunching and coiling—and having nothing to do with tomorrow's risk.

Every nightmare, every stress point, every nightmarish memory and anxiety-ridden possibility looming in our uncertain future all dropped away. Wes kissed me like there was no tomorrow—and maybe there wouldn't be.

Maybe we would only ever have tonight.

My fingers loosened their grip and I explored with my hands, my mouth hot and busy on his. My fingertips felt for the edge of fabric and when I found it, I slid his shirt up and over his hardened abs and broad chest.

Instead of leaning in and assisting my advances, Wes went still. His mouth stopped moving, his hands stopped caressing. The only movement left was his labored breaths against my face where he sat staring at me with wide eyes.

"What is it?" I asked.

"Nothing, I ..." He looked away and when he faced me again, his eyes were shuttered against whatever it was that had gotten to him. He grabbed my hips and lifted me, setting me down beside him. The air around me thickened, like a wall between us.

"What's going on?" I asked, my cheeks heating. I shoved past the embarrassment. This wasn't the first time he'd called a halt and I couldn't figure out the reason behind his rejections.

"Nothing," he repeated. He scratched his head, tousling his hair. "I'm tired. Tomorrow's a big day. We should get some sleep." He stood and went to work turning down the bed covers and arranging the pillows. I watched him with narrowed eyes while I tried—and failed—to suppress the angry outburst building inside me.

"You want to sleep," I said, my voice flat.

He flinched but kept moving, taking care to fluff the pillows and not look at me.

"What is going on with you?" I stood up and, when he didn't answer, slid between him and the bed. I snatched the pillow and tossed it behind me. "Talk to me. Why do you keep pulling away?"

"I can't do this. I just can't … do it."

I blinked extra hard at the emphasis he put on the last word. We both knew what he meant by it. He'd obviously read my willingness—a willingness that had been there on and off for a while now. He'd always been the one to slow things down, but this felt different.

"IS this still about my virtue and not wanting to piss off my mom?" I demanded. "Because I think we're a little past that. We're both adults now," I pointed out.

"I know. It's not that."

"Then what?"

"I can't do it letting you think it's your first time." The words fell out so quickly I almost missed them.

"What?" I asked, shaking my head in order to better organize each letter in my mind. "That doesn't make any sense. Of course it's my first time. I think I would know if—"

"No, you wouldn't," he said quietly. He sank to the mattress but I hung back, suddenly apprehensive. The only other time he'd spoken like this was that first day … when he'd erased—

"Wes, what did you do?" I asked.

"Only what you asked. No, demanded," he said quickly, jumping to his feet again. He threw his hands up in a defensive motion and I hardly blamed him, but I was far past humor. "I swear. I didn't want to but you made me. And it wasn't safe before now to even mention it but with Steppe gone and … after tomorrow, you'll be in my head. Anyway, I thought you should hear it from me this way before you discovered it in my thoughts somewhere."

I stared at him, studying his expression. "You're serious," I said.

"Deadly."

"What happened?" I asked warily. "Tell me everything."

"Will you at least sit down? You're making me nervous."

"Fine," I said and threw myself onto the mattress. "Happy?"

He muttered something, but I let it go. I was too desperate for an explanation to summon the energy to argue with him.

"You'd been missing for weeks already. I was convinced you were still in DC somewhere so I'd rented out that apartment I told you about near the train station so I could spend my days chasing down leads." He turned away to pace and I watched the way his mouth somehow managed to look pinched even while he talked. Nerves rolled off him, his steps clipped and stiff. This boy was crazy nervous.

"It was the middle of the night. I don't know what time, two or three I guess. I was in bed. One minute I was sleeping in my empty apartment and the next I was waking up and you were standing over me."

"I was in your apartment?" I asked, momentarily forgetting all about where this was headed. "How is that possible?"

"I had no idea. Still don't. But you were there. You were sad, scared, but you didn't look hurt. You said you didn't have much time, seemed just as surprised as I was to be standing in my room. We kissed and … I pulled you into bed."

He fell silent but I was enthralled, my brain on a fast-track of possibilities. "And then what?" I asked. His cheeks flushed and I waved an impatient hand. "I mean after that. How did I get back? Why would I want to forget it?"

"You got called back or pulled or something. Neither of us really understood it. You were scared of Steppe. You said he would find out what had happened and use it against you or me. Or both. You made me promise to take the memory away so that he couldn't get in your head."

"What was I so worried about him finding?" I asked quietly, finally focusing on the event itself. "What happened?" My pulse sped, but I needed him to say it.

His gaze was piercingly sharp on mine, his dark eyes swimming with a mental image I couldn't conjure. "We made love, Tara."

My mouth went dry. I nodded, numb all over. Wasn't a girl supposed to feel differently after something like that? Shouldn't I have noticed it when I woke?

Before I could think of what to say next, Wes was there. He knelt in front of me on the floor, his hands grazing the outer edges of my thighs.

"Please don't be mad," he whispered.

"I'm not mad," I said honestly when the shock began to clear.

"You're not?" he asked, one brow arched in skepticism. "Because if you are, I understand."

"You did the right thing. I wouldn't have wanted Steppe seeing that. He already saw enough and he definitely used it all against me at some point or another." I shuddered.

Wes exhaled, clearly relieved.

"I'm not mad," I said again. "But I am disappointed I can't remember. Can you give it back to me?"

"Yes. I can do that, but…"

"What now?" I asked. "Dear God, how many times have we done it?"

"Just one," he assured me quickly.

"Then what?"

"I just want you to be prepared. It's … a lot."

"Okay. I'm prepared," I said, settling in.

He shook his head but didn't press it. Probably a good thing. I didn't want to explain that a girl could only be so prepared to experience her first time—for the second time. But I didn't have to. The look on his face said he knew exactly what I was thinking. This was going to be really interesting when we could hear each other's every thought.

"Close your eyes," he said.

I did, and shivered when I felt his fingertips run down my arms before his hands settled over mine. "Ready?" he asked.

"Ready," I murmured.

It was a rushing of emotions, images, and remembered heat. The memory was a slow love song in front of a roaring fire. The experience was the light, the heat, comfort. But underneath it all, I'd been terrified. Lonely, and scared, and terrified.

I shuddered as it all settled, embedding itself once and for all into my consciousness. It had been beautiful, but it had also been desperate. I could see now, as all the old fears came crashing back in, why I'd forced him to erase it.

All in all, I was glad to have it back. It had happened, forgetting wouldn't change it, but it didn't diminish the utter fear and desperation I'd carried back to that cell with me that night.

I would never admit it to Wes, but giving myself to him in that way had made me happier than I'd ever been in my whole life—followed by the most profound sadness I'd ever experienced.

"Are you okay? Did it work?" he asked quietly.

"It worked," I whispered.

I shoved back against the onslaught of tears that threatened and forced my eyes to his. "Thank you," I said. I leaned over and threw my arms around him, clinging tight. "That was..."

"A lot," he said again and I relaxed into him.

"Exactly."

He drew back, his fingertips smoothing my cheeks. He spoke with lowered lashes, uncharacteristically shy. "Tomorrow, when we're connected, I can let you see it from my side. Let you feel how I felt. I think it'll help you let go of all that stuff you were feeling after. See it as nothing but a happy moment."

I tiled my head in surprise. "You knew I was upset?"

"Of course. I don't need your blood in my veins to read your moods, Tara Godfrey. I've always understood you, always been connected to you, no shared DNA required."

Without warning, the tears sprang up again, this time escaping into tiny wet tracked down my cheeks. "An entire pack with ESP, a dictator determined to destroy my brain, and you know what I'm feeling, what I'm thinking, with a single look," I said.

He caught a tear with his thumb and brushed it away. "I'm glad you're okay with it. After tomorrow, you won't be able to escape me."

"I've never wanted to," I said.

"Well ... except for that one time. But that was definitely me being stupid."

I laughed. "Please tell me you're not talking about that night I went to the dance," I said.

"That could be the one."

"That was actually one of the best nights we had together," I pointed out. "Well, after you made me angry and I ran away and almost got killed."

"Right, after that," he agreed.

"I stayed the night at your apartment," I said.

"And if I remember correctly, the high point of the evening looked a lot like this. You and I in bed together. Tears of joy." I rolled my eyes and he laughed. "Your mother conveniently in the dark that we were sharing mattress space."

"Good point," I said. My smile faded as I said, "And just like before, we're going to end the night with a kiss and go to sleep."

His smile disappeared too, but there was no disappointment. "Is that so?" he asked, and I could hear the attempt at a joke, but I shook my head.

"Wes, I can't ... I can't do this from a place of fear a second time. The memory you gave me, the experience with you, it was beautiful and I don't regret it for a single second, no matter what. But I don't want to bring all that fear and desperation into it again. The next time we're together, I want only us. Only love and joy and gratitude."

His grin spread slowly, his mouth tipping higher on one side in a mischievous quirk. "So, what you're saying is tomorrow night works better for you?"

I laughed and threw my arms around him. "Every night forever works for me."

"So, all I have to do is make you happy every second of every day?" He whistled. "No pressure."

"Easy," I agreed and I leaned in with my mouth at his ear. "You already do."

Chapter Twenty-Seven

We went over the plan four times before breakfast. Everyone knew their part and every contingency we could think of on top of it. Astor was armed with his medical supplies. Ms. Hebert was allowed out of her room and onto the main level to hover near the front window. Dishes were cleared. Whispered reassurances were offered. By the time we assembled on the lawn, I was covered in goose bumps.

"Nerves," I muttered when Derek asked me if it meant anything.

"And Jack and Fee are close," Cord said, sliding her phone into the pocket of her dress before taking her place at the head of the gathering.

I stood stiffly between Logan and Cambria, waiting for the clock to strike the hour signaling the beginning of our broadcast. The hairs on the back of my neck tingled. I felt the wrath of Ms. Hebert's glare through the window and halfway across the front yard.

"Is she still staring at me?" I asked.

Beside me, Logan glanced back. "Yes." He pulled his cap lower on his forehead and took Victoria's hand again. "You really made an enemy last night."

"Me? She's the one who compelled—"

"Relax, killer. I know," he said, chuckling.

Victoria leaned across him and said, "He's only trying to start something with you because he's hoping I'll jump on the bandwagon

Broken Blood

and use social torture as a way to distract myself from the fact that we're about to bury my father."

"Vic, I..." Logan trailed off, clearly busted. Clearly lost for a defense. "I'm sorry," he said finally.

She patted his chest affectionately and I caught sight of her bright-red, freshly manicured nails. "I'm not mad, honey. Any time you want to insult Tara to cheer me up, feel free. It can't hurt."

I narrowed my eyes, debating whether it would be okay to rag on her right back. "Didn't you just stick up for me during the last round of 'let's gang up on Tara'?" I asked instead.

Victoria straightened, shoving her shoulders back and chin up. "Yes, and I totally stand by it. You're our leader, no question. Doesn't mean I'm going to stop giving you crap. It's my duty."

"Your duty for what?" I demanded, feigning anger. But the relief at hearing her give someone a hard time, sounding like her old self, overshadowed any irritation I might've felt.

She rolled her eyes. "Everyone has that friend. The one who dishes it out, makes witty comebacks, but is sweet deep down with this other side of her that only the cute, quiet guy gets and they live happily ever after." I stared at her and she sighed as if forced to over-explain to a slow child. "I'm *that* friend," she added.

On my other side, Cambria snorted. I opened my mouth but she grabbed my hand and squeezed. Hard.

On the far side of the circle, Wes cleared his throat. He gave me a pointed look, smoothed his suit jacket one final time, and then nodded to Benny.

Benny, the group's elected cameraman, pushed a button on the video camera and held up three fingers to signal. He didn't look nearly as happy to have his house arrest lifted as I'd expected. I wondered if he thought he'd chosen the wrong side or was just being jumpy toward danger, in general. With Benny, you never could tell. "And three ... two..."

"Here we go," Cambria said under her breath.

"One," Benny finished. "You're on."

"Hello, friends, and welcome," Wes began. "We're gathered here today to pay tribute to one of our fallen: Douglas Phillip Lexington. Mr. Lexington was singularly neither Hunter nor Werewolf. He was both. He was a hybrid. A Hunter by birth and turned against his will before finally choosing the cure. But Werewolves know that in death, we return to our truest form. The form our soul calls out for. And as some of you witnessed on our last broadcast, in death, Mr. Lexington took the form of his wolf.

"You've been invited to join us for this memorial ceremony as the first act in a two-part effort of goodwill. First, we gather today to honor the life of a man who belongs to both races. I commend his acts of bravery, loyalty, and honor at the end as he defended his friends and the efforts of peace against lies and manipulations."

Wes leaned forward and placed a single rose on the casket and stepped back.

Cord stepped forward, her black dress a sharp contrast to her pale skin. Her icy blue eyes swiveled and locked onto Benny's camera and there wasn't a trace of the fear in them that I knew she felt. "Wesley St. John has spoken for the Werewolf community and now I do the same for the Hunters. Mr. Lexington was a hybrid and for too long, that term has meant something derogatory among us. Something undesired. But today, as we honor him, I challenge you to change your impression of the word. Hybrid is one who lives in both worlds. Who has a connection to or an emotional investment in both Hunters and Werewolves. And that's exactly the kind of community we need to be."

Cord paused. For anyone watching, it would probably have seemed natural, but I could see the tension in her shoulders. The winded way she gulped for air. Cambria squeezed my hand.

Farther out, somewhere in the trees behind her, branches cracked. Derek and Wes jerked toward the sound. Benny twitched in the same direction, but Logan whispered to keep filming. I crossed my fingers, hoping the noise belonged to my mom or Grandma or even Alex, but I knew better. None of them would be so loud.

"Gordon Steppe lied to you," Cord said to the camera and the branches broke closer now. Leaves crunched and voices drew near as faces emerged from the within the cover of the trees.

"We have company," Cambria whispered.

"George," I began.

"I'm on it," he said as he and Emma retreated toward the far corner of the yard to guard the hole in the wards.

The faces continued to drift closer—a dozen or so Hunters all staring unseeing right through the place we all stood. I breathed a sigh of relief.

Broken Blood

Despite what I'd told myself, what I'd witnessed every time I'd stood there and saw what looked like an empty clearing, I'd still been half-convinced something would go wrong.

But the uninvited group of Hunters only stared through us as they consulted their GPS and sent confused glances back and forth.

"We're good. They can't see us," Derek whispered to no one in particular. And to Cord, "The wards are soundproof. Keep talking."

"Steppe wanted us to fight and be at odds. He wanted the power that came with violence and war. And he wanted to make us hate each other, to divide us so he could control us," Cord said.

The Hunters wandered closer to the edge of the clearing, staring intently at what no doubt appeared to be an empty patch of frozen grass. Probably right where their GPS claimed the video was streaming from.

I held my breath as one of them—a boy close to my age with a buzzed military cut that reminded me of Alex—seemed to look right at me. Around him, the group of Hunters—looking more and more like one of Kane's famous strike teams—crept closer to the edge of the yard.

"Stupid technology. They're going to walk right over us," Cambria whispered. She stared at a woman dressed in camouflage pants and combat boots. The woman had broken off from the rest of the group and was exploring the exact same trail we'd arrived on. The one that led straight to the hole we'd all come through. Her sharp eyes took in the broken leaves and I silently berated myself for not covering our tracks better.

Across the fresh grave, Cord went on about peace and a new government. I could feel the tension building in my friends as Cord took us closer and closer to the point of her announcement. This was it. Even the Hunters paused to concentrate on Cord's words as she echoed out of their various mobile devices.

With every eye trained and ear cocked, Cord delivered her punch line in a clear voice: "Which is why I'm standing before you today. My name is Cordelia Steppe and I am the new Director of the Council for Hunter Affairs and Security."

Silence washed over the clearing. The Hunters all stared at the screen and then exchanged looks of disbelief and confusion with one another. Cambria squeezed my hand again but it was difficult to know if she was nervous about whether they'd accept her claim or about what would happen if they did.

Cord moved away from her place at the end of the coffin Derek and George had built and went to Victoria, embracing her. The camera panned left to offer viewers the chance to witness their alliance. Victoria pulled away and faced the camera, her hand wrapped around Cord's. "My father died protecting Tara Godfrey from Gordon Steppe's lies. He died a hybrid, like her. Like many of you. I will honor him by supporting our new leader and her efforts to unite Hunters and Werewolves in discussions instead of violence. I am a supporter of the new CHAS because I am a supporter of peace."

Wes stepped up beside them and gave his own version of Victoria's endorsement: "My name is Wesley St. John. I am a hybrid. I am a supporter of the new CHAS because I am a supporter of peace."

On Victoria's other side, Logan joined them in the shot and gave his own identical statement for the camera.

"Ready?" Cambria whispered, her boot tapping the grass lightly.

I opened my mouth to answer, but a snarl from behind cut me off. I turned, half-expecting to find George warning off a visitor that had gotten too close—not that they would hear him—but George was nowhere in sight.

Instead, I caught a glimpse of a large gray wolf sliding among the trees on the other side of the wards. Its bushy tail was tucked low, along with its nose. It moved quietly until it caught a scent and then it raised its head up and snarled again.

I followed its line of sight—directly to the Hunter woman who'd wandered away from her group. She spotted the Werewolf at the same moment and her expression shuttered into an expression I'd always seen on Alex just before a fight. No emotion. Utter determination. With careful movements, she extracted a stake from her boot and straightened.

The wolf's eyes narrowed to slits and it crouched. I knew that body language all too well. It was about to spring.

"No!" I yelled and Cambria stumbled in her rehearsed speech for the camera.

Benny panned over to me and I stared wide-eyed into the camera. My mouth was open but I couldn't remember the words I was supposed to say. The sounds of snarling and grunting and footsteps replaced the frozen silence. Everyone looked over just as the Hunter woman and the wolf slammed into each other. I watched, helpless, as the scuffle turned into a brutal match.

Broken Blood

The rest of the Hunters let out a cry and rushed to help the woman, but the gray wolf wasn't alone either. I knew he wouldn't be. Another five wolves emerged from the cover of trees from the same direction as the first. They spotted the enemy and sprang toward them, jaws open and teeth aimed.

"We have to do something," I yelled.

Benny spun back and forth, clearly confused about what to aim for. "Don't film that," Cord told him and he immediately swung back to her.

"We can't fight amongst ourselves anymore," Cord said into the camera. But the group beyond the wards didn't hear or didn't agree.

From around the corner of the house, George and Emma appeared. Emma was close at his side and both had already shifted to their wolf forms. "There's another couple dozen wolves coming in from the north side as well," he said. He shook his coat out—a sign he was jittery. "What do we do?"

"Astor, get the injection ready," I said.

"It'll take a couple of minutes," he said with a frown.

"Logan, Victoria, can you help him?" I asked.

They both nodded and hurried to the porch to bring down the supplies we'd set out earlier this morning. I turned to Cambria. "Are you ready?" I asked.

"They're not paying attention," Cambria said. "We need them to see this or it won't work."

"There are people watching that video. They'll see," I said.

"Are you sure this is going to work?" she asked.

I wasn't, but I couldn't say it. Not with so much to lose and Cambria's fear rolling off her in fumes. "Yes," I said, my tone way more certain than I felt.

"Where is Alex?" Derek muttered. He stood behind Cambria, a protective shield, as he scanned the woods. "He should've been here by now."

"I'll call him," Wes said.

"We should go out there," Derek said, still staring into the trees where a wolf and a hunter were circling each other.

"No," Cord said. "As hard as it is to stand by, we can't engage or we'll undo everything we just said."

"Cambria, come help me," Logan called from the porch.

"Go," I told her. "I'll be right there."

At the far end of the yard, the gray wolf and the woman Hunter rolled in a tangled heap as each fought for the upper hand. I was amazed at the woman's strength as she managed to fight off the Werewolf's massive paws. It had more force behind its weight than she did, though, and it shoved against her, sending them both tumbling end over end.

I saw it coming about three seconds before it happened and sprinted for the opening, but it was too late. The woman tumbled and rolled away from the wolf—right through the hole in the wards.

Wes, Derek, and Cord came up behind me. There was a ripping sound and by the time I looked back, both boys were wolves. They crowded in around Cord and me, positioning themselves between us and the woman.

The woman lifted herself on an elbow and shook her head to clear it. Leaves and dirt clung to her clothes. She looked up at us, brows wrinkled in confusion. "What…?"

Behind her, the gray wolf prowled near the opening, back and forth in short, pacing bursts, nose stuck to the ground. It growled incessantly and pawed at the deadened leaves.

"It's a wall of protection," Cord explained. "You're safe." She extended a hand, knocking Derek out of the way as she did it.

The woman took Cord's hand and allowed herself to be pulled to her feet. "Thanks," she said uncertainly, eyeing the wolves.

"We would be honored if you would bear witness," Cord said.

"To what?" the woman asked. Her confusion and disbelief was fast turning to wary suspicion. She was doing her best to pay attention to Cord, but her gaze kept flickering to Wes and Derek. I eyed the stake she still held.

"Tara! We're ready," Cambria called from behind me.

I hesitated only a second longer and then raced back to where Cambria stood with Astor. "Wes," I called, "Let's do this."

He didn't move and I huffed, grabbing Logan by his sleeve. "Go to him. Take the syringe," I said.

"But—" Logan took one look at my face and his argument died on his lips. "Going."

I waved Benny closer with the camera and Cambria smoothed her hair with a nervous gesture. Benny signaled and Cambria offered the lens a tight smile before beginning.

"My name is Cambria Hebert. I was born a Hunter and I'm a senior…

sort of," she mumbled and then louder, "at Wood Point Academy. I am entering into this change willingly and by my own volition. No one as forced me. I am a supporter of peace between Hunters and Werewolves."

With shaking hands, she turned away—to face Astor. Benny stepped back to pan out and include them both in the shot. I offered Cambria an encouraging smile but she wasn't looking at me. She wasn't looking at anyone.

Astor hovered over Cambria's arm with a syringe full of my blood and the necessary cocktail to usher in the changes to her DNA that would make her a Werewolf.

"Ready?" he asked Cambria.

She nodded and bit her lip. Astor swabbed her inner elbow and then adjusted the syringe's tip near her skin. He'd assured me the accelerant was safe and would ensure the process happened over the course of a few minutes instead of a few days. Of course there'd been no way to test it.

"Here's to hoping," Astor muttered, which only made me more nervous. Then he shoved the syringe expertly into the crook of Cambria's arm.

She winced and he depressed the contents into her vein and pulled the needle free. Immediately, Cambria wavered. "Whoa," she said, blinking furiously. "Head rush."

"Sit down," I said, guiding her to the grass. She sat heavily, her eyes already wide and glassy.

"Now mine," I continued, yanking my jacket sleeve out of the way and offering him my arm.

Along the tree line, the fights had turned more to scuffles as more and more of the Hunters turned their attention to the member of their team who'd suddenly vanished. Three Hunters had joined the gray wolf in his search near the wards' hole. I watched them drift closer to the opening as the needle pierced my skin.

George looked back at me and caught me watching. "At least they aren't fighting," he called.

The moment the words left his mouth, the gray wolf stuck its head through the hole.

Everyone on our side froze. Including Astor and Logan, both with syringes containing the next round of injections held in their limp hands. Wes stepped forward, including the Hunter woman in his layer of protection. Derek joined him.

The gray wolf's eyes narrowed and he stepped all the way through. Behind him, the three Hunters spilled into the yard and the rest of their group, including the remaining Werewolves, all sprinted for the hole.

The gray wolf's eyes widened as it took in the sight of the crowded yard. Behind him, as the rest of them crossed the ward line, two groups formed. Hunters huddled together on one side and the packs of Werewolves merged into one group on the right.

They faced off, emitting growls and snarls amid raised weapons.

Wes and Derek rushed between the two.

"Stop!" Cord strode into the center of them all, head high. I motioned for Benny to stay on her with the camera. He inched forward, looking terrified of getting too close. "This is a gathering for peace," Cord said. "No violence is permitted."

"How can you claim to want peace when your friends are the reason our kinds are at war," said the woman. Her gaze flicked to Wes and then back to me. I raised my chin, my mouth a hard line.

"Gordon Steppe was the reason. He lied to you," Cord said.

"And how do we know you're not lying to us now. You claim to be his daughter," the woman said. "But Steppe has no family."

"Because he disowned me when I left," Cord said.

"Prove it," the woman said.

The wolves whispered among themselves, heads bent close together.

"Do you have something to say?" Cord asked.

"Steppe had a daughter once," the gray wolf—clearly the leader—said.

An angry murmur went through the assembled group of Hunters. The boy I'd seen earlier stepped forward. "How do you know that and we don't?" he demanded.

Several of the wolves growled in response but another voice called out, "Because Steppe erased the proof from the world by living his own lies so believably, he had everyone fooled." A second later, Alex appeared. He stepped through the hole as if he'd seen it all along, a large bound volume in his hands.

I sighed in silent relief and caught his eye for a brief second as he made his way into the throng. He stopped next to Wes, which made my pulse race all over again.

"Who are you?" one of the wolves demanded.

Broken Blood

"Alex Channing," said the Hunter boy, awestruck. "You're the guy who single-handedly killed all those—"

"Let's not live in the past, all right?" Alex interrupted.

The boy fell silent and the wolves up front pawed the ground. One of them, its fur the color of dark brown, lunged and caught one of the Hunter's ankles in its jaw. The Hunter screamed and brought his fist down on the wolf's head. The wolf abruptly released the man's foot and slunk away. All around, the two groups inched closer, violence written on their faces.

Out in the woods, the sound of footsteps approached, and I scanned until I spotted the movement. Everyone fell silent, waiting to identify the newcomers. I sucked in a breath when I spotted them all.

My mother, along with Jack and Fee, appeared just left of a stand of trees several yards out. Nearby, Grandma, Kane, and Professor Flaherty flanked right. None of them were looking at the clearing. Instead, they had weapons trained on something I couldn't see, something behind them. They stopped and waited.

A second later, their target emerged. In their crosshairs was a pack of lanky, mangy Werewolves, every one with gleaming yellow eyes.

Steppe's failed hybrids. They were here. And they'd never been great at listening or saying no to a fight.

At my feet, Cambria tugged on my pants. "Tay," she said in a wobbly voice. I looked down and my breath caught in my throat as I saw what she'd become in the space of a few minutes. "I can't be sure I'm not drunk, but I think my skin has hair," she said.

She made a noise like a grunt and then her eyes rolled back in her head and she slumped sideways, unconscious.

Chapter Twenty-Eight

"**Alex,** show them The Draven. Now," I called.

Without waiting for an answer, I snatched the syringe from Astor. "You have to stay with her," I told him, pointing at a still-unconscious Cambria on the ground between us. "Don't let anyone near her. Do whatever you have to."

"What am I going to do? I have no weapon," he said, barely avoiding a stutter. I felt horrible at putting this all on him, but there was no choice. The hybrid pack angled closer to the hole—as if they'd been watching. As if they knew exactly where it was.

My mom and the others tracked along with them in a parallel line, but the hybrids were ignoring them. Intent on their destination. And I knew Grandma would only resort to violence if they attacked first. We were here for peace. Cord had made that clear. We couldn't go back on it now.

I turned back to Astor, laid my hand on his arm. "Shift if you have to," I told him. "Be scary. Like you showed us before. You can do this," I said.

"But..." he sputtered but I was already running.

I caught sight of Ms. Hebert watching me from the window. Her eyes were wide, her arms wrapped around her middle in a tight hug. Worry lines creased her forehead. I turned away and ran for the others.

Broken Blood

I was hyper-aware of the metal stake I'd hidden in my boot, but I didn't take it out. My syringe was the only weapon I'd need—I hoped.

Up ahead, Alex had The Draven open and was showing it off to anyone who'd look at it—along with the parchment he was waving in the air out of reach. Benny was bent close, zooming the camera to offer a clear view of Steppe's last act as leader. When I got close, I saw drops of blood littered the bottom half of the page. Steppe's markings made the words above absolute law. I spotted Cord's name and the words "rightful heir and leader" before Alex shifted away again.

"Today's new treaty, the shifting of our leadership, will only work if both sides will sign it and take the message back to your families and friends," Alex said.

"Dude," said the Hunter kid with the wannabe-Alex haircut. "*You want peace with Werewolves?*"

The gray wolf snarled and I couldn't blame him. The way the kid said the last word made me want to snarl.

"Yes," Alex said firmly. He met my eyes as I wedged myself in between him and Wes. "I've made my choice," he said, his eyes glinting with the meaning of something so much deeper than the words he used. "But only because I've seen what conflict will do. And I believe in Tara Godfrey, in Cordelia Steppe, and in their commitment to peace. They really do see us all as equals and if they can do it, I can too."

There was a collective pause as everyone considered Alex's words. I itched to point out Cambria and the change already happening, but I knew better than to rush any of it. Or any of them.

"How'd I do?" Alex whispered.

I smiled at him, ready to assure him he'd done perfectly. Outside the circle, a wolf howled, shattering the thoughtful silence.

A battle cry from the hybrid wolves.

As a single unit, they rushed at the hole in the wards. At the noise, Cambria stirred and a connective line sprang up between us, invisible and weak but there. It was happening. We were already beginning to connect.

"What's—" the Hunter woman began.

But her question abruptly ended as we watched Grandma's crossbow fire an arrow that sank quickly into the shoulder of the leader. His soldiers poured around him, some even stepping over him as they rushed for the entrance.

"Everyone get back," Cord warned.

"Who are they?" one of the wolves asked. "I've never seen them."

"They were Steppe's army," I said, casting a desperate look at Logan. He still hovered near Wes, the syringe ready, but I couldn't. Not yet.

I could feel Cambria's struggle in my mind as she alternated between fighting and embracing the change. She still wasn't conscious, but the bond was getting stronger. I knew without turning she was still lying in the grass at Astor's feet near the porch. And she was in pain. So much pain. She needed me, I could feel it.

The longer she suffered through the transition, the stronger our connection became. I wasn't ready to take it away. Not yet. Not when my own mind gave her strength while hers was broken down and reconstructed again as a new creature.

"Tara, what's the plan?" Logan asked nervously. He inched backward, still within reach of Wes, but his torso was twisted to protect Victoria, who huddled behind him.

"Back up," I said. "If they make it inside, we need room to fight them."

"We can't fight—" Cord began.

"These we can," I insisted. The Hunters and Werewolves assembled around us stared as Kane and Professor Flaherty took down a set of wolves in tandem.

"These are hybrids who have embraced the darkness that comes with the change. Steppe used them to incite conflict, to kill innocents and sow discord between us. These are the reason we are at odds. Steppe and his army. Not me, not my friends," I said.

I stepped away from Alex and the book and brushed shoulders with the Hunters, including Alex's biggest fan. He looked over at me with wide eyes, as if my touching him made the whole thing more confusing, and then glanced at his comrades in uncertainty.

"She's telling the truth," Alex said, "I can vouch for her."

After a moment's consideration, the boy planted his feet beside me with a firm nod. "I'll fight with you," he said.

The first of Steppe's hybrids crossed the line and ducked through the hole. Behind him, his friends fell with sharp cries and muted yelps as Grandma and my mom unleashed arrows. Jack and Fee darted among the pines, their jaws coated in blood.

"What about us?" the lead hybrid growled. Jasper, the one I'd seen in Steppe's lab, working with Olivia. His yellow eyes glowed through the slits of its narrowed lids. His fur was patchy; matted in some places and missing in others. It reminded me of Rafe after he'd been burned—only, these wounds stemmed more from their bodies rejecting parts of the change than anything else. Somehow, it made them look more dangerous.

I shifted, putting myself between Jasper and the closest Hunter. "What about you?" I asked.

In my mind, Cambria stirred. She was waking slowly, but I couldn't allow myself the relief. Not when we were evenly matched by an enemy that had never been one to show mercy.

"Who will we trust? All I ever see from you is violence," Jasper said in a gravelly voice. It stalked closer, unconcerned with the Hunters who crept in at its back, slowly surrounding it.

"You can trust our promise for peace," Cord said, appearing beside me. She offered her hands, palms up, both empty of any weapon. "We won't fight you unless you give us no choice," she told it.

"Just like your father gave us no choice," Jasper growled.

And then he leaped.

I jumped clear, dragging the Hunter kid with me. We fell in a heap and I scrambled to my feet, stumbling and barely breathing in my panic. Jasper hadn't jumped at us but around us. He was aimed for someone—something—else entirely.

"Cambria!"

Derek's voice was raw and panicked and would've matched mine had I been able to find and use it.

I heard the others' footsteps pounding behind me, but we were never going to reach her in time. Jasper's jaw fell open, his grimy teeth wet with drool over its anticipation. My stomach lurched and I screamed through whatever connection there was for Cambria to move.

But she could barely blink her eyes. Everything about her movements felt heavy. She lifted an arm but it fell again and she squinted up at the approaching wolf.

Behind her, the porch door tore open and Ms. Hebert launched herself off the landing. She fell with a thud over her daughter's body and both of them grunted. I felt, rather than saw, the air whoosh out of Cambria's burning lungs at the exact moment the hybrid's teeth sank into flesh.

An exaggerated moment of silence hung and then Ms. Hebert screamed, her body arching into a rigid line. Jasper released her, hesitating and clearly confused over the last-minute redirect of his attack. In his mind, he'd missed.

Derek was on him then, knocking him clear of both Cambria and her mother. Astor, struggling on his stocky legs, half-man, half-wolf, lumbered after them. Logan handed me the syringe meant for Wes.

"Here," he said, already hurrying past, headed for Astor. "Someone needs to save him from himself."

Along with Logan, the gray wolf and the Hunter woman sprinted by me, headed for the fight with the hybrid. I turned, wondering why more hadn't joined them, but the space behind me was empty.

The rest of them had poured back through the hole in the wards and joined in the takedown of the rest of the hybrid pack. As I watched, Alex and his new protégé tag-teamed a lean black wolf with patchy scabs. The rest of them had also teamed up, some even working with a member of the opposite race as they fought the hybrids back from the entrance.

Victoria and Emma rushed forward and bent over Ms. Hebert. "She's alive," Victoria said, "but she's losing blood. We need Fee."

"I'll get her," Emma said, racing off.

Victoria hooked her arms around Ms. Hebert and swung the woman up into her arms. Ms. Hebert moaned, her lids fluttering as she hung limp in Victoria's grasp. "I'm taking her inside," Victoria said.

"I'll come with," Benny said. He handed the camera off to Cord and followed Victoria inside.

"Keep filming," I said, hating that we were doing this to Cambria. But there was no choice. We were all beginning to work together and none of that had been filmed. This was our last shot.

Cord scowled but repositioned the camera and pointed it down at Cambria.

"What's happening to her?" a voice beside me asked.

I looked up and found a Hunter girl with almond-shaped eyes and a scar along her collarbone. She looked vaguely familiar and I blinked, trying to place her.

"Kristin Walters," she said. "I graduated with Alex."

"Right," I said, remembering her in the closing ceremonies we'd attended. "She's changing," I said, glancing back down at Cambria.

Kristin crouched and looked up at me. "Cambria, right?" she asked.

"I remember her. We had study hall together."

Wes appeared on my other side, bumping me with his furry shoulder. "Not yet," I told him, already fully aware of what he was after. "She needs me."

Kristin gave me a quizzical look.

"In order to keep her body from rejecting the change, we injected her with my blood. It's the missing ingredient Steppe didn't include for them," I said with a nod at the forest.

"So, your blood helps make her strong enough?" Kristin asked.

"Yes. But it also psychically bonds us. I promised her I'd remove that part once she was strong enough to handle it on her own," I said.

"Why are you doing this to her?" Kristin asked.

A few other Hunters crowded around, some panting, just returned from the fight. Several Werewolves trailed behind. The gray wolf, the leader, joined us and I spotted a jagged wound opened on his left shoulder. A thin trail of blood leaked from it and pooled on the ground at his feet.

"She chose this," I said, raising my voice and facing them all. "She wanted to be the first to show you that Hunters and Werewolves—even someone who is both—will be treated equal with Cord in charge."

A dark-skinned Hunter with freckles covering every inch of his exposed skin stepped forward and peered down at Cambria. "She volunteered to go through that?"

I winced as the pain crawled around inside Cambria's veins, seeping into her organs, stretching and pulling against the confines of her skin.

"Are you all right?" the man asked, peering at me.

"I'm…" I doubled over, the pain rushing up and out into the reaches of my mind. It wasn't even a fully formed bond and already the pain was overwhelming. I hoped, for her sake, Cambria didn't fully wake up.

My knees buckled and the freckled man caught me inches before I hit the ground. "She's in pain," he said and I looked up at him, startled.

"How do you know?" I asked.

"I'm Koby," he said quietly, cradling me in his arms. It was strangely comforting and I had to remind myself this man was a stranger, not someone to lean on and cuddle. "I'm an empath and a healer. I can take some of the pain from you but you have to keep your arms around me. Can you do that?"

I didn't bother to speak; I figured my compliance was answer enough.

Growls were everywhere and I wondered if Derek had managed to take that hybrid down yet or if there were any more trying to sneak through, but the crowd pressed around me and Koby and I couldn't see beyond all of their legs.

"Her pain," I managed through clenched teeth. I wondered how Koby would understand but he simply nodded and pulled Cambria closer, tucking her sleeping form underneath his opposite shoulder.

The pain dialed back a little, but I could see her arms and legs stretching and lengthening into something new. There was a loud pop and I watched her knee jerk forward. Her bones were breaking.

Tears streamed down my cheeks as I stared down at my friend. A wolf appeared beside me, nudging my hand until he'd slipped in underneath where I'd braced my palm against the ground. I looked over at the russet coat of fur and a narrow face containing a pair of caramel eyes.

"She's strong enough," Logan said from where he stood over us.

My gaze flicked from him to Cambria and back to Wes. The pain had receded but I knew it was thanks to Koby. It was evident in the strained expression he wore as he smoothed Cambria's hair from her sweaty brow.

I dug down into the depths, reaching and straining to read the bond that hovered like a shadow between us. I couldn't tell if Logan was right. And I wasn't going to abandon her.

"Look," said a growly voice. The gray wolf.

My head snapped up and, as I watched, fur sprouted from Cambria's bare arms. Her jeans, already ripped at the knees from her bones lengthening and snapping, tightened until the seams burst. Derek arrived, panting and wincing at a rip along his left flank. He planted himself over Cambria just as the rest of her clothes filled with her expanding torso and her pants and shirt ripped free.

He growled up at us, his eyes intent on Koby. "It's okay," I assured him. "Koby was helping take her pain away."

Still, Derek didn't move. I knew the only thing he cared about now was protecting Cambria, including her dignity. Koby and I scooted away.

Cambria's lids fluttered and then sprang open. She screamed, her back arching off the ground as her body gave another loud pop.

"What's happening?" someone asked. I recognized the boy Alex had left with earlier. He was panting but unharmed. I strained around the others, my panic spiking all over again.

"He's right there," Wes said in a low voice and I followed the direction of his nod. My shoulders sagged in relief as Alex returned, sliding through the crowd until he reached me.

"She's shifting," Logan answered the boy in a strained voice.

Alex reached out and squeezed my hand. "You okay?" I whispered. He nodded. "You?"

Before I could answer, Cambria's awareness rushed in and the mental whiplash knocked the wind out of me. I gasped for air. Wes jumped up, hovering nervously beside where I'd doubled over. Alex lowered me to the ground.

Wes whimpered and Logan shouldered his way in until he was crouched between us. "Give me your syringe," Logan said.

"No, I have to make sure she's okay," I said.

"She's shifting, Tay. If you don't redirect the bond now to clear things, this won't work," he explained. "You both agreed."

"What about the darkness?" I demanded. "What if she's not strong enough?"

He leaned down so we were nose to nose and said, "This is Cambria we're talking about. There's no one stronger."

Cambria coughed and sputtered and her skin disappeared. Derek was forced aside as she rolled and convulsed. Fur sprouted along her torso and her human parts were replaced with a heavy black coat. The crowd behind us backed away.

Cambria sat up, her face a strange and disturbing collage of human and wolf parts. She looked right at me, her mouth pinched in pain. "Do it," she said. "Get out … of my head."

Logan raised the syringe and jammed it into my arm.

"Wait!" I tried to pull away but Logan held my arm until he'd emptied the entire contents of the syringe.

I whimpered and tried to escape, but Wes crowded in, licking at my face until I couldn't see enough to get free. "I'm sorry," he repeated over and over again. "I'm sorry. So, so sorry. Don't be angry."

"Did you do it yet?" My mother's anxious voice penetrated the dull fog that coated over my connection to Cambria. There was something else in her voice, something besides the expected note of worry. But I couldn't break through to ask what.

The chemical cocktail Logan had dosed me with ate through slowly, erasing as it went. No more flashes of memory. No more magnetic pull.

Only blank space. My mind was once again empty and alone in its thoughts.

Despite the weak connection we'd shared, this one hurt much worse than losing Steppe.

"Logan just gave it to her," Cord said. I kept my eyes shut so no one would ask me to talk. It hurt too much to admit out loud. "What about the hybrids?" Cord asked and I knew she wasn't speaking to me.

"They're dealt with," Grandma said.

"How's Tara?" Professor Flaherty sounded breathless and antsy. I couldn't look but I knew there were all there, watching me. The air felt expectant. Like it was about more than just waiting for the bond to redirect.

"Why haven't you injected Wes?" I asked.

No one answered. Logan drifted back and disappeared. I caught sight of him hurrying into the house before the door slammed behind him.

"Where is he going?" I demanded, but the words sounded weak. Everything felt weak. I caught whispers—some belonging to the audience gathered and some containing orders, instructions for the others.

A few were aimed at Koby and Derek, who were still attending to Cambria. A few were given to Fee to help the wounded fighters returning from the forest. But mostly, everyone was centered on me.

The numbness in my head dialed back and in its place was something else. I forced my eyes open wider, searching their faces for what was really happening to me. Cord refused to meet my eyes. Wes stopped apologizing—which only heightened my panic.

"Why aren't you injecting Wes?" I repeated, my voice high-pitched in panic.

"Because we aren't bonding you two," Grandma said.

"What? Then who ...?" I trailed off, thoroughly confused and struggling to name what was happening to me.

I waited for Grandma to say more but she just watched me, tight lines pulling at the corners of her mouth. No one else offered anything more either and I held back a scream of frustration.

I shook my hands and feet, testing them. When I was certain they were working again, I scrambled to my feet and ran, putting distance between me and all of them. When I turned, I found all of the faces of those I loved staring back at me—and I felt no connection to a single one of them.

"We weren't sure you'd go for it," my mom said slowly.

"So we decided to let it be a surprise," Grandma added.

"And we knew you'd be disappointed if it didn't work," Cord put in.

"It was Cambria's idea," Derek said.

"What are you all talking about?" I yelled. "What is going on?"

No one answered. They watched me, waiting expectantly, and I knew they weren't going to tell me a thing until I figured it out. Or until they knew if it'd worked. Whatever *it* was.

Inside my mind, far back in the depths of memories cast off and forgotten, a fissure cracked and opened. It felt like the moment you remember something long lost, like a light going on in a dark room. It was something you wanted to grab for before it skittered off again, something on the tip of your tongue.

I looked into the trees without seeing a bit of it, concentrating on the images forming.

Vera, in the conference room at Wood Point. So beautiful and regal … and already frail with the sickness. "I've seen you in my visions. An older you. A different you. You're amazing, breathtaking," she had said then.

And sitting by her beside at Jack's, wishing it wasn't the end. "I'd hoped for more time…" she'd said. I'd wished it too.

Every vision, every prophecy, every prediction Vera had ever made came rushing back. But this time, so did the affection and the certainty. She'd believed in me so completely. She'd seen this very moment. She'd known all along the choices I would make.

I looked back at my mother, my mouth open

"Fee took countless blood samples before she—" My mother halted and started again; she still couldn't bear to say the words. "Anyway, we preserved a few for research in case her debilitation becomes hereditary," my mother explained.

"So? Did it work?" Jack asked, leaning forward in excitement.

"Do you have her memories inside you?" Grandma demanded.

"Yeah," I said, still in shock that it was even possible. "I do." I looked back at Cambria—now fully a wolf with ebony black fur that was, impossibly, streaked with neon blue—and smiled. "It worked," I told her. "Vera is … her essence or something … is in my head."

Cambria tried responding, but it came out a growl and I laughed, the sudden surge of joy inside me too big to contain. I found Wes, my russet wolf, and started to go to him, but he danced away.

"I will be right back, I swear. But I need clothes because I'm definitely making out with you in front of all these people." He dashed off to the sound of several whistles.

Our audience drifted back in, asking questions and listening to my friends as they attempted to explain everything that had happened. With Cambria, with The Draven, with me, and finally, with the peace treaty Alex was passing around the group.

"We're going to sign a new treaty," Cord explained. "One that recognizes The Cause and its members for providing amnesty but also one that outlines a plan where amnesty isn't a privilege, it's a right. There will be rules and punishments for those who break them but there will be fair trials."

"How do we know that?" asked one of the wolves.

"Because you and I both will serve on that jury," she told him, and instead of scoffing like they'd done earlier in the day, the wolves tilted their heads, considering her idea.

At the back of the crowd, I watched the large gray wolf—the Werewolf pack leader—dart away and disappear around the corner of the cabin. I started to follow but Cambria stopped me.

"You okay?" she asked. Her voice came out somewhere between concise language and a growl. "You're not mad, are you?"

"I'm not mad," I assured her. "I was worried for you."

"I'm okay," she said, clearly still just as surprised as everyone else at her new appearance. She tilted her head, her eyes deep pools of curiosity. "I'm still me inside," she said. "But I'm ... more. It's so weird."

She shifted her weight, stepping sideways as if off balance. "Can we run? For some reason, I seriously need to move."

I laughed. "Logan was right. I don't know why I was ever worried. You're clearly the strongest of us all."

"Clearly," Derek agreed, rubbing up beside her. My heart warmed watching them.

"Is my mom okay?" Cambria asked, her wolfish face clouding with worry.

"She will be," Derek assured her. "Victoria updated me a little bit ago. Fee's in with her now. She'll pull through."

"Maybe we can send Koby to help," Cambria said. "He's pretty great at pain management."

"I'd be happy to," he said.

"I don't think it was management so much as a time share thing," I said.

"Tara, can you come here?" Alex called. I joined him at the head of the assembled group, next to Cord, and he handed me a pen.

"Tara's going to join Wes as leader of The Cause," Cord said.

"I am?" I stared at her and she continued, ignoring me. All I could do was listen along with everyone else.

I caught Jack's eye and he grinned—the equivalent of his blessing. "There will be a training period, of course," he said. "I'll get to teach you again."

"Great," I said sarcastically but I was smiling too.

"They'll act as ambassadors to spread the word of our treaty and all that's happened today," Cord explained. "They will still act as a safe haven for Werewolves and Hunters alike. One day soon, we hope you'll come to trust that you don't need sanctuary. You're safe already no matter who or what you are."

"You want us to sign that thing?" Kristin asked.

"We aren't going to force you but we hope you will. You did stand with us today against my father's army." Cord flashed a smile and a few of the men in the crowd—including wolves—blinked at the sight she made. Blonde hair glowing in the sunlight, teeth flashing as she offered an encouraging smile, shoulders squared with confident power. "We're already a team," she added. "Don't you think?"

There was a heavy silence and then Koby appeared. "Where do we sign?"

I faltered—too overcome with relief and surging hope to even answer—but Alex stepped up and held out the Draven where the parchment with the treaty lay over the page naming Cord as successor. "Here."

Koby shrank away. "I can't sign that. It's the same paper from the book." His eyes flickered up to Alex and away. "We don't write in each other's books."

"You do now," Cord assured him. She held out a pen and pointed. "Here, next to my name."

Slowly, Koby pressed the pen to page and scrawled his name. When he'd finished, he stepped back and flashed me a small smile. One by one, the others leaned over and clapped his shoulder or patted his back. The Hunter woman I'd met first stepped up and took the pen.

"Thank you … Gail," Cord said, reading the signature as Gail handed her pen back.

"Thank *you*," Gail said. "It's an honor." She handed the pen back amid applause and shouts.

"I'd like to sign," said a deep voice.

From the back of the crowd, a man with a long gray beard shouldered his way to the front. He wore a pair of ratty sweats that had thinned to holes in several places. "What's your name?" Cord asked.

"Abraham," Jack said, clapping the man on the back and walking beside him to stand in front of Cord.

"You know each other?" Cord asked, looking between them.

"You know me too," the gray-haired man said. "After today, I should think we can call each other friends."

"The gray wolf," I realized.

"My friends call me Abraham. Nice to meet you, Tara," he said. "I've heard a lot about you." He looked at Cord. "And you. I'd like to sign your treaty if you'll have me."

"We would be honored," Cord said, handing him the pen.

He scrawled his name and handed the pen to Cord with a broad smile. "My pack will sign but we'll need some clothes first. Otherwise, your first official gathering as leader might lead to unnecessary frowns in the community."

"Sir," Cord said, her eyes sparkling, "We've been causing frowns our whole life."

Abraham laughed at that and Jack joined him, their deep voices filling the clearing with the last noise I expected to hear today. Everyone began talking and moving at once.

Everyone with two hands and working thumbs pressed in to add their names to the treaty. A few at a time, wolves ducked behind the house to shift and share clothes in order to add their names. Somewhere during the commotion, Cambria and Derek slipped away. I started to go after them, still worried for how Cambria was adjusting to her new body.

"Whoa, there." Wes grabbed my hand, spinning me around to face him. "Don't run off just yet." His arm snaked around my waist and he pulled me against him, torso to torso. His hair was disheveled, his jeans slung low on his hips, offering a peek of abs from underneath the hem of what was obviously a borrowed shirt.

"I hurried back just for you," he said, his voice seductively low.

"I was checking on Cambria. She and Derek—"

"Will be fine," he assured me, leaning close. He brushed a hand over my cheek, catching strands of my hair between his fingers as he inhaled deeply. "You smell amazing, whether I'm human or wolf, you know that?"

I smiled and leaned in, my mouth upturned to meet his.

From somewhere behind him, George yelled, "Is that my shirt? Are you wearing my clothes again?"

Wes pulled back just far enough to wink at me and I laughed.

"Wes, I'm talking to you," George said.

"We did it," Wes whispered. "Me, you, all of us, we did it."

"We did," I agreed.

The kiss was magic—pure joy, love, and hope. All light, no darkness or fear, and I pressed harder into it, breathless with the ecstasy of the moment. Wes was right. We did it. And tonight, we'd do the only thing left for us. The one act we'd yet to perform out of such love and light.

Wes pulled back, his mouth hovering hotly over mine, and whispered, "Make love, not war."

And I wondered how I'd never realized, blood and injections and science aside, we'd been bonded this whole time.

Chapter Twenty-Nine

Jack's backyard bonfire had never looked so huge. More wood than I'd ever seen at once was piled high on the pyre that stood halfway between the farmhouse and the tree line out back. The flames danced and crackled, warming against whatever chill managed to creep inside my fur coat.

It was a first for me. Not a first for attending a Cause meeting, I'd done that before. I'd never attended as a Werewolf though. Apparently, it was a requirement for the ceremony and selection happening today. Beside me, Wes rubbed his forehead against my ear in animal affection. I leaned into him, snuggling right back. In the month or so since we'd returned home, we'd spent lots of afternoons on four legs, making up for lost time.

Energy was high today.

At the head of the flames, Jack and Fee spoke animatedly with two of the newer guests. Professor Kane and Professor Flaherty both listened intently to whatever instruction they were being given. They were being inducted today and I, for one, was still floored about Kane joining up. But as Grandma said, bigger miracles had happened.

Recently, too.

As proof, Cambria yelped and sidestepped Derek, her wide jawline pulled back to reveal shining sets of sharp teeth. Her coat was black as night, still streaked with neon blue. I always smiled at the sight of her as a wolf. And if watching her was any indication, she enjoyed it just as much. She and Derek had been inseparable since we'd left the cabin in Colorado behind four weeks ago.

The only time I had her to myself was our mandatory schooling overseen by Fee. Online lessons three hours daily. "To get caught up on all you've missed," she'd said. And with a matching stern look from my mother had added, "Especially you, Tara."

Like it was my fault I'd been kidnapped for the fall semester.

You'll be at your public school soon enough, I could practically hear Vera's memory whispering at me.

That was happening lot lately, but not in that chaos-as-noise kind of way I'd had to listen to from my pack or George or even Steppe. This was calm, peaceful, and certain of the future in a way that always seemed to make me jumpy. I was grateful for it; not just her insight but her wisdom and ability to remain calm amid the storm. It was a trait I was working on.

At last, the final member of today's cast arrived and took his place in the circle assembled around the fire. There was a beat of hesitation beside me and then, across the fire, Jack stepped forward. He cleared his throat and looked out over the faces gathered before beginning.

"Thank you all for coming," Jack said, his normal deep voice even more of a growl as he spoke though the mouth of a wolf. "This meeting marks the official reconvening of The Cause."

Jack paused while a chorus of cheers and howls went up among the group. I couldn't help joining in.

When we'd quieted again, Jack continued. "Originally, we were a small group. The only safe haven for Hunters and Werewolves caught in the crossfire of a world that knew only guilty until proven innocent. But today, we've become a part of something much bigger. The very thing we've fought and bled for. As of today, we are the official ambassador of peace for CHAS under the new leadership and authority of Cordelia Steppe."

"Cord," she said, correcting him quickly. "No last name. Just Cord."

"Like Cher or Madonna," Derek snorted.

"Or Bieber," Cambria added.

Cord glared at her but Cambria was unruffled. Nothing much got to her these days. She was in a permanent romance-induced fog, which was fun to watch on a girl who thought candy hearts should come with candy weapons to pierce them.

"Cord, we're honored to have you here," Jack said.

"Thank you, but today is my last meeting," Cord said. "Tomorrow, I head to DC and will begin rebuilding the CHAS headquarters and repairing the damage done under my father's leadership. Both structurally and psychologically," she added.

"My first priority will be overseeing the repairs of the building and establishing a permanent residence. In the meantime, I need you all to get the word out. When the work is complete, I will be personally inviting every leader of every pack or community, Hunters and Werewolves, to visit me there for a summit."

She looked from face to face as she spoke. Her gaze was direct and her shoulders squared and confident. I knew, without a doubt, I'd made the right choice in giving CHAS to Cord.

The choice was always yours, whispered Vera's memory. *But the position was always meant for her.*

I felt my eyes go wide at that. "Really?" I muttered, earning a quizzical stare from Wes.

I shook my head and kept my voice internal. After all this time, the anguish and uncertainty about what I would do when the time came, and Vera had always known how it should go. I stared into the flames, trying to resist the flare of temper that came with the realization. I felt like Dorothy at the end of the movie, being told she'd always had the power to go home, she just needed to realize it.

I glanced over at my mother, who stood next to Jack across the flames, and glared suspiciously. She watched Cord, her expression more peaceful and relaxed than I'd seen her in months—maybe years. I wondered if she knew what Vera had known. Maybe. Probably. She'd admitted she'd had the same visions for years before Vera even found me.

She and I would chat later, that was for sure.

I tuned back in as Cord wrapped up her outline for how The Cause would get the word out about her new plan for laws and leadership. "...a democracy," she was saying. "And you all are the voices. I'm counting on you to make sure the people are heard."

"Thanks, Cord," Jack said, taking over again. "We look forward to it." And then to the group, "We're officially forming a new coalition of members today. I will announce the nominations and you will confirm your memberships with a group vote. Belonging to The Cause and committed to extending and upholding the burden of peace among conflict are: Fiona Chapman—Fee," he corrected as she flashed him a look, "myself, Jonah Kane, Anna Flaherty, George Landry, Emma Stacey, Elizabeth Godfrey." He turned to my mom and said, "Welcome back."

She smiled.

"Tara Godfrey, Wesley St. John, Derek Carpenter, Cambria Hebert, Koby Elias, Gail Dresser, and our newest—and most unexpected—addition, Alex Channing. All in favor of these faithful members, say aye."

Around the fire, there was a loud chorus of, "Aye."

I looked over and found Alex watching me. He winked and said his own, "Aye."

A strange feeling rippled through me at his gesture. It was so foreign for me to feel it for Alex that it took me a moment to pin it down—pleasure without the confusion of attraction, I realized in relief.

Finally, Vera's memory whispered. And before I could blast a sarcastic comeback, the voice added, *You've made your choice. And he's made his. Finally.*

I faltered as Vera's predictions and visions came rushing back. There'd been an entry in her journal. *He'll do as much to save them as she will ... but the alpha has to make her choice before he can choose a side.* Alex—I had to choose before he could choose. Of course. I stared at him, my chest pounding with the rush of my realization. He caught my eye and raised a brow, but it would have to wait.

Jack was talking again and I focused on what came next. This was it.

Beside me, Wes shifted in nerves and impatience. I wanted to reassure him but held it back. I'd smother him in kisses later, when I had human lips again.

"And finally," Jack said, "there is the business of our leadership. Fee and I, we've had a great run, but we both agree, the future belongs to the next generation. It belongs to the ones who made this all possible to be standing here today, reformed and ready to usher in a new era. An era of peace. That credit, that leadership, belongs to another couple."

Jack smiled at Wes, from one end of the bonfire to the other. "Wesley St. John, Tara Godfrey, you've each been nominated and chosen for the role of leader. Do you accept the role as it is offered and promise to execute your duties to the best ability of your conviction and commitment to peace and democracy and protecting the weak?"

Wes straightened, the fur along his chest puffing out. "I do," he said in a clear voice.

I tried to do the same, putting off an air of confidence, but I made the mistake of catching Cambria's eye and I could see the laughter in them. I fought a grin, which, as a wolf, felt like a snarl. A few in the crowd looked back at me with crinkled brows. Cord rolled her eyes.

"I do," I managed.

And everyone cheered.

I turned to face Wes and the happiness in his yellow orbs was evident, overflowing into the very air around us. "You just wait until I have thumbs again," Wes said.

I laughed. "What are you going to do with those thumbs?"

He leaned in, his voice gravelly and low. "Nothing compared to what I'll do with my—"

"Congratulations, you two!"

We jumped apart. Alex looked back and forth between us in mock innocence. "Sorry, did I ruin a moment?"

I scowled and Wes cast his face to the sky. "I must be crazy to have taken this on," he muttered.

"You talking about working with me or Tara?" Alex said and I snapped my teeth at him.

Around us, the meeting was breaking up and groups were forming. Jack and Fee huddled with Kane while Professor Flaherty and my mom made their way slowly back to the house where Grandma was laying out a Thanksgiving Day buffet.

Everyone looked happy and content and, aside from Alex's barb—or maybe even because of it—the moment felt full.

"Is there something you wanted?" Wes demanded, but the words lacked any real bite.

"Just checking in with my new boss before I go out on my first assignment," Alex said.

"I'm not your boss," Wes said. And then his head tilted. "Unless that means I get to order you around. Let's try it. Get lost."

"Okay, maybe boss is a strong word," Alex said. "How about point of contact?"

Wes remained stubbornly silent.

"Where are you going?" I asked.

"I head for DC tomorrow with Cord. I'm going to make sure she gets settled in and then I'm headed to Wood Point for a bit. I wanted to leave you both my new cell number so we can keep each other updated on the situation there," he said.

"Sounds good," Wes said.

"Wait, what situation?" I asked.

Alex raised his brows at Wes. "You didn't tell her?"

"We've had a lot going on," he said. "I haven't had a chance."

"Uh, now works for me," I said.

Alex looked at Wes who just nodded. "Someone's been leaving messages in the form of graffiti and unauthorized flyer distributions. A new group has formed that is against CHAS and its new democratic approach to leadership. Their numbers are small but they're starting to get attention from the parents and alumni, a few of which seem to be buying into their accusations and conspiracy theories. Headmaster Whitfield has asked me to investigate."

Headmaster Whitfield had proven to be an ally after all, even though he'd stayed hidden in a copse of trees that day at the cabin. He'd claimed he'd single-handedly fought three hybrids, but whenever my mom was around, his story get bigger and different. I suspected he just wanted to impress. Either way, he'd signed the treaty and gone back to his desk job without much fight.

"Do we have any suspects?" I asked.

Alex sighed and shared another look with Wes—a new habit I was quickly tiring of. "We think it's Demi," Alex said.

I frowned. "She's a Queen Bee but is she capable of all that? Sounds pretty high-level for someone like her."

"She's a master manipulator. You know that firsthand," Alex said and I remembered how Demi had known all along that Miles was no good and helped him anyway—even when she'd known he was after me. Especially then.

Alex was right. That girl was smarter than she acted.

"Be careful," I said.

"Don't worry about me, babe. If I get into trouble, you'll be the first one I call."

Wes huffed. "Excuse me—"

"Relax, I meant the two of you. You're a matching pair, no question."

Wes bristled but he didn't argue it further. "Just text me your cell number and give us an update when there is one. We'll be doing some traveling of our own." He shot me a look and then said, "Well, I will. Tara will be here until graduation."

Now it was my turn to give the silent treatment.

I was going back to public school next week and I wasn't happy about it.

"Wes," Jack called from across the yard.

"Excuse me," Wes muttered before leaving us alone. He moved way too quickly and I suspected he was happy for the escape.

I glared up at Alex. "You don't have to bait him like that."

"But he makes it so easy," he said.

I shook my head and looked up as my mother called my name from the house. "Go," Alex said. "I'll find you before I leave."

I hesitated, unsaid words piling up in my mouth, but when my mother called again, I went. I was given instructions to "shift and put this on" as a dress was shoved at me and I was propelled up the stairs. By the time I returned, Wes was being given the same instructions along with a pair of dress slacks and tie. We managed only a fleeting smile as we were herded past one another from one dutiful leader task to the next.

Thanksgiving afternoon passed in a blur of celebration and congratulations. Fee and Jack danced around the fire—still in wolf form. Hot chocolate was passed around, although for some reason, I opted for the green tea Vera had always been fond of.

Back in human form, Derek and George managed to heft Wes up onto their shoulders and parade him around. They sang something that sounded like a garbled version of, "For he's a Jolly Good Werewolf," that hurt my ears.

"Boys are so ridiculous," Cambria said, coming up beside me with a steaming mug.

"Nice to see you back on two legs," I said over the boys' off-key tune.

"Yeah, my mom's coming over later, so I figured, two are better than four. For now." She sighed. "Normally, I wouldn't make allowances but…"

"Fee says she's healing," I said. "Is she still recovering at Benny's?"

Cambria gave me a sideways look. "Is that what they call it?"

Broken Blood

I didn't love the idea of Cambria using her pseudo-relationship with her mom to gather intel, but she was our best shot at cracking the gambling ring Benny was rumored to be running. And I was a leader now—a weird feeling, but I was determined to act like it.

I snickered, but Cambria's good humor was short-lived. "How can he promote violence among Werewolves, even for sport, after being there with us last weekend?" she asked, her tone clearly disgusted.

"Word is he's running the books on the fights he's putting together. I guess money talks," I said, my lips pursing as I stared at the boys.

Wes had fallen and was now wrestling on the ground with Derek and George. They were laughing and I caught Alex watching them from the other side of the yard with a strangely wistful expression where he stood talking with Cord.

"I spoke to Logan earlier," I said, changing the subject. "He and Victoria are settling into their place in DC. He says Astor likes it there."

"That's good. I never thought Victoria would end up working for a living," Cambria said.

"Serving on the board for CHAS isn't exactly blue collar," I said. "And it keeps her close to Logan since he's staying on to study with Astor. Headmaster Whitfield even said he'll issue a diploma for it. He's deeming it a work-study thing and calling it good."

Cambria huffed. "Only because it's Logan and he's a genius. If it were me—"

"Are you complaining?" I cut in. "Because you've got a pretty good deal yourself, if you ask me."

"A GED online is a good deal?"

"If it means you can stay here with me and Derek and the rest of us, especially since CHAS is officially paying you a salary," I reminded her. "Yeah, that's a pretty sweet deal. At least you don't have to go back to public school."

Cambria smirked. "I will if you want me to. Can you imagine me and you together in that school?"

I pretended to shudder. "I couldn't stay out of trouble without you," I pointed out. "I don't want to think about what would happen if we were together."

She laughed. "Exactly. Besides, we always have college."

"True."

We watched the boys another minute, jumping aside when their tumbling veered too close. The back door opened and closed. Emma joined us, a quiet smile spreading over her pink cheeks as she watched George with the others.

"Hey, Em. I hear you're on your way to a family," Cambria said and Emma's smile widened.

"We go to court on Monday to make it official," Emma said and I put my arm around her and pulled her in for a hug. Steppe's attempt to get to me had backfired. When the smoke had cleared and I'd learned my mom had started the process to adopt Emma, I'd been ridiculously excited over it.

"Replace you?" my mother had said in horror when I'd admitted what Steppe had tried to make me think with his half-truths. "Tara, I can't handle one of you much less two. I'm happy to adopt Emma because she's the exact opposite of you."

I had laughed at that.

"Tara, you and your mom have been so kind," Emma said now. "Thank you for letting me stay with you until I graduate next year."

"Emma, you're not temporary," I said. "That's what the adoption is for. And Cambria's right. You're already family. We're a pack, remember?"

"Thank you," she said again, this time with tears brimming.

"Don't get too excited," I told her. "You might not be thanking me when people at school find out who your new sister is."

"Why? Do people not like you?" she asked.

I shared a look with Cambria and then shook my head, thinking of Cindy Adams and the bloody nose that got me expelled last spring. "Let's just save that story for another day, shall we?"

Someone tugged on my hand and I turned to find Alex. He nodded at me to follow him and lead the way around the corner of the house. The noise died off as the crowd disappeared behind us. The afternoon light slanted across the roof, sending this part of the yard into chilled shadow.

I rubbed my hands over my arms, half-tempted to shift just to get warm. "What's up?" I asked.

"I'm headed out," Alex said. "Just wanted to say goodbye."

"When will you be back?" I asked, suddenly very aware of the shift I felt happening between us. This was it, the next chapter. We'd won, and now life would go on in decidedly different directions.

"A few days. I'll pass back through on my way to Wood Point." He grinned crookedly and flicked my shoulder. "You won't be getting rid of me that easily and never for very long," he added.

"I'm glad," I admitted. "Alex, you and I…"

"We took a little longer than most to figure out how we fit," he said, his words full of quiet understanding.

I nodded and bit my lip, suddenly too close to tears to talk.

"I'm sorry, for what it's worth," he said.

"For what?" I asked, looking up at him with crinkled brows.

"For making it difficult. I love you, and I think I always will, but mostly it's a love borne from that strange place of connection when one person helps transform another."

"Are you saying I'm like your therapist or something?"

"No," he said, laughing. "Hardly. I just mean…" and the humor faded as he struggled to find words. "I'm who I am because of you. Open-minded, hopeful, accepting of people's differences … I'm helping enact a peace treaty, for goodness sake. I couldn't have done this on my own. I will always be grateful to you for challenging me to see the world differently. Angela says—"

"Angela?" I raised a brow.

"We keep in touch," he said with a shrug, but I caught the flicker behind his chocolaty irises and my eyes narrowed. "She was there in the hospital when I woke up and … I promised her I'd keep her safe and out of it all. I've looked in on her from time to time."

"Looked in on her," I repeated knowingly. "Alex Channing, are you catching feelings for my very human best friend?" I demanded.

"Don't make it weird," he muttered, suddenly staring at some speck of dirt on the siding.

I grinned as I thought back over it all and something inside me released. Alex glared but not even a dirty look could dampen my surprise. Him and Angela? But that was crazy talk. We might've come a long way in a short while but humans and Hunters? That was still a no-no. Then again, if anyone could change the world's mind, it was Alex.

"Sorry, no weirdness here," I assured him. I cleared my throat. "Angela? You were saying?"

"Nothing," he muttered. I decided not to point out that his cheeks were flaming red. "You should call her. She misses you."

"Oh, I plan on it, trust me," I said.

His mouth tightened and he exhaled sharply. I'd gotten to him. It was kind of ridiculous how much fun I was having just knowing I could tease him about something like this.

Alex was fast, but I was faster. I danced out of the way just as his hand shoved at empty air where my shoulder had been. He dropped his bag to the ground behind him and crouched low. "I can still take you, Godfrey," he said.

"You think so?" I challenged, matching his stance. "I fight dirty."

His lips quirked. "I'm counting on it," he said.

He leaped just as I turned and ran screaming for Wes and the others, Alex laughing and yelling behind me.

Wes saw me coming, struggled out from under Derek, and climbed to his feet just in time. He caught me in his arms as I barreled into him. I watched his eyes widen as he caught sight of Alex.

"Help!" I yelled desperately but there wasn't time.

Alex caught the edge of my shoulder as he ploughed into Wes. Derek and George were caught in the crossfire and we all went down in a tangled heap.

"Dog pile!" I heard Jack yell and a real ripple of alarm pulsed through me at the thought of his massive bulk jumping on to the writhing pile of bodies.

From my place between one person's arm and another one's knee, I watched as Fee tried grabbing Jack and holding him back—but he dragged her along her foot tangled with his. They tumbled toward us.

Thankfully, George's hand shot out from the bottom of the pile at the last second and hooked around Jack's ankle. He went down on the outer edges instead of on top of my already-buried torso.

"Seriously?" my mother said, but everyone ignored her.

Cambria gave a battle cry and leaped and then I couldn't see past the twisting of hands and legs around me. Laughter mixed with squeals and squirms as everyone tried for the upper hand.

Breathless and utterly exhausted, I crawled away on my stomach, only to be grabbed and hauled back again. The cry—halfway out of my mouth—died on my tongue as I spotted my attacker.

"My face hurts from laughing," I pleaded. "Five minutes."

"Two," Wes retorted, smiling down at me with twinkling eyes the color of warm caramel. He leaned down and brushed the tip of his nose against mine. His breath was warm and full on my mouth and my lips tingled simply at the sensation of being so close to his.

Broken Blood

I looked up at him, pure joy and love overflowing from my heart. It had all begun with a Werewolf showing up, offering his help to a frightened girl. After all this time, here it was, beginning again. Same Werewolf. Same girl—but so completely different than they had been before.

In that moment, I couldn't bring myself to regret a single moment of fear or uncertainty or misery. It had all made me who I was. It had all led me here. To the choices I'd made. And the life I was ready to begin living.

Wes regarded me with a knowing expression, as if he'd read the thoughts as they'd come. Blood bond or no, an alpha and its mate were bonded by more than any science could ever explain. "Looks like you made all your choices. Are you happy with them?" he whispered.

Somewhere behind us, the wrestling continued and over the sound of it all, I heard my mother fussing at me. Probably for publicly displaying … ourselves.

But I ignored her and gave him a private smile. "I've never been happier," I told him honestly.

His expression melted into soft and sweet. His lips lowered, hovering over mine. "You will be," he promised, stroking my hair with gentle fingers. Fingers capable of making love and war. "Just wait."

In my mind, Vera's spirit sat back in contentment, and I knew this was the moment she'd been waiting to show me all along.

Chapter Thirty

The final bell rang and I gathered my things, headed for my locker and then the closest exit. A familiar set of faces waited at the corner and I hurried to join them.

"Where's the fire?" Angela joked as I bypassed her and Sam with little more than a grunted hello.

I concentrated on my lock combination and, when the door popped free, dumped my stuff and turned to face my two childhood friends. Angela had gotten new frames since the last time I'd seen her. These were dark and slimmer and, according to Sam, librarian-sexy; a compliment that always made Angela blush furiously. Sam hadn't changed much. Her hair was still a shiny rich chestnut color that matched her eyes and her skirts were still just this side of the dress code. She'd gotten a job at a tanning salon over the summer so her skin was tinted a shade of brown that looked out of place in Virginia in December.

But her smile was still just as mischievous as I remembered. It had taken Angela much longer to forgive me for my desertion than it had Sam. Even now, after owning up and telling Angela everything—she was the only one of the two who knew what I really was—Angela still eyed me with a hint of suspicion.

I knew their trust was something I'd have to earn back. I'd left without so much as a phone call to Sam but for Angela, I'd done worse.

I'd put her in danger. I still felt terrible no matter how many times she assured me she didn't blame me for it. I'd yet to ask her about Alex. We just weren't there yet.

"Emma and I have plans today," I said, shoving my books into the narrow space.

"Is this that ridiculous running club thing you guys do?" Sam asked, rolling her eyes. She was typing on her phone and missed the look Angela shot me and the secret smile I offered her back.

"Yes, ridiculous running. We're getting T-shirts made and everything," I said.

Sam snorted.

"Are we still on for tomorrow?" Angela asked.

"Girls night. Pool championship," I said, nodding. "You're all going down."

"Tell Cambria she agreed to supply the booze," Sam said.

"Just because we're doing it at her apartment does not automatically mean she can get alcohol," I said. "She's barely eighteen."

Sam gave me a blank look and then her attention went back to her phone. "Fine, I'll have my brother pick us up something," she said, her fingers already flying over the keyboard once again.

Angela and I shared another look.

"What about you, Ang?" I asked. "Any big plans tonight?"

"Um."

I didn't miss the way her cheeks flamed a dark pink color before she looked away. "Maybe," she said. That got Sam's attention—finally.

"No way," Sam said. "If you have another date with that GI Joe you better own it. He is positively—"

"Watch it," Angela cut in and I shut my mouth—she'd taken the words right off my tongue. I was glad I hadn't spoken up, though. This was Angela's man to defend now. And I was okay with that.

Sam gawked at her and almost dropped her phone. "Ohmygod. You really like him. Is he your boyfriend?"

Angela pushed her glasses up and sighed, sending me a pleading look. I knew that look well. Rescue time. "What about you, Sam? You've been awfully cozy with your phone lately. What lucky guy has proven himself capable of stringing sentences together? Anyone we know?"

Sam opened her mouth but Emma walked up, smiling brightly and bouncing with energy. "Ready?" she asked me.

Mason Harding trailed behind her. He slowed when he reached Sam and stopped long enough to bend near her ear and whisper something. Sam giggled. "Okay," she whispered.

Mason grinned, hitched his bag higher on his shoulder, and hurried off.

I stared after him and then leveled my gaze on Sam. Her dark hair was a sharp contrast to the cherry tint in her cheeks. "Mason?" I asked in disbelief.

Partly because Sam had once said his chin reminded her of a newborn baby's "little bits" but mostly because Mason was a Werewolf.

A fact I knew. Sam did not.

She tossed her hair, her jaw high and hard, as if daring us to challenge her. "Maybe," she said haughtily. "Maybe not. See you tomorrow," she added.

Emma caught my eye as Sam disappeared through the same door Mason had used. "What?" she asked, her blue eyes wide.

"Yeah, what?" Angela echoed.

I debated for a split second and then made a decision. "Nothing," I said. Neither girl looked convinced. "Really. I'm surprised that's all. I'm just glad we live in a world where Sam's love life is our biggest problem."

The other two agreed and we headed out.

On the front steps of the school, a group of girls had gathered into a huddle. Giggles and high-pitched voices rose from the center. A voice I knew well spoke over the others and I pretended not to notice, hurrying in the other direction. But it was too late.

"Tara," a female voice called in a whiny sing-song.

I cringed and turned around. "Hi, Cindy," I said.

Her gaze was sharp as she took in the sight of me, then Angela, and finally Emma beside me. Despite the halo of golden hair, she reminded me of a vulture just sitting around and waiting for the next carcass to pounce on. "I heard you were in court last week," she said. "Your mother switched you out for a new version. Someone more malleable, easier to control?"

My hands tightened into fists and I clenched my teeth. "Tara," Angela warned.

Emma was still as stone beside me. "I'm Tara's new sister, Emma," she said quietly. She stuck her hand out and I held my breath.

Broken Blood

Cindy looked down at it and then up again like she couldn't decide. She reached slowly for Emma's outstretched hand but the glint in her eye gave away her true feelings. "Emma, nice to meet you. If you want someone to show you the ropes around here, someone who can connect you with the right crowd, you just let me know," Cindy said with special emphasis on the word "right."

I opened my mouth, hot temper overriding my better judgment despite all of my best intentions. "Tara," Angela hissed and I shut my mouth again. But Cindy smiled. She knew she'd gotten to me.

"Babe," a male's voice called from behind us and cut off whatever Cindy had been about to say next. "I've been looking for you."

Cindy spotted someone over my shoulder and her acidic smile froze on her face. "George?" she said as he walked up.

"I'm right here," Emma told him. She angled her face toward George and he dropped a kiss onto her cheek.

He slipped his arm around Emma's shoulders and looked at Cindy. "Hey, Cindy," he said.

"Hey," she echoed, completely at a loss. Behind her, the groupies looked on in surprised silence.

"We better go," Emma said. "Cindy, was it? Nice meeting you. I'll be sure to look out real carefully for the right crowd." Emma winked and Cindy's jaw fell open.

The four of us spun and left Cindy and her minions behind. I resisted the urge to hug my little sister right then and there. "Emma, ten. Cindy Adams, zero," I said instead.

"Wait, what did I miss?" George asked and we all laughed.

"I'll call you tomorrow," Angela said to me when we reached the steps.

"Later," I called. I watched her make her way to the used sedan she drove. When she'd gone, I grabbed Emma's hand and pulled her and George along.

"Let's go," I said, barely holding back my smile as the anticipation built.

"Let's hurry," she agreed.

We took the path across the lot to the track behind the school. We kept walking, cutting across the center lawn still set up for yesterday's track meet, until we'd climbed the hill on the far side.

"Do you seem them?" Emma asked, breathless and jittery. I knew it was excitement, not fear, because it matched mine.

"No, but Cambria texted me during last period," I said. "Everyone made it back. They'll be here."

Behind us, a branch broke, and I whirled with Emma beside me. I peered into the shadowed woods and blinked as several shapes loomed. They became larger and more solid as they approached. When I could make out faces, I grinned and took off in a sprint toward them.

Halfway there, I pushed off and leaped—shifting into my wolf in midair. I landed noiselessly on four paws and Wes was already there, shaking his russet fur in disapproval.

"Your mom's going to kill you for ruining another outfit," Cambria said. Her black fur shone even in the dull light. George was always bugging her about what conditioner she used.

I snickered and rubbed my face against Wes's shoulder. "I'll just borrow something from you. She won't notice the difference," I told her.

"Yeah, right. Because our styles are sooo the same," she said.

"Are we going to do this or stand here and talk about your fashion sense all day?" Derek demanded.

"We're doing this," Jack said. Fee stood next to him and I pulled my lips over my teeth in a wolfish smile. They'd been out of town with Wes for the past few days on Cause business. It felt good to have everyone back in one place again. Well, almost everyone. But if today's mission went well, by day's end, I'd have all of my loved ones with me.

Cambria shifted impatiently.

Jack looked up from the head of the pack and then hesitated. "Wes, do you want to lead?"

"Nope. I'm hanging back to goof off with my girlfriend," he said.

Derek chuckled but Fee pinned him with a look. "This is an official Cause mission, sanctioned by CHAS. You should take it seriously."

"When I know for sure that Logan and Victoria have Astor in position, I'll take point," Wes said. "For now, it's a run through the woods."

"You think they'll convince the old coot to do this?" George asked.

I glared. "Don't call him an old coot," I said.

"I hope so," Cambria said. "The look on Benny's face when he finds out his next fighter is ... what does Astor call himself? Wolfman?" She shook her head. "His expression is going to be priceless."

"Logan said he flew Jeeves in to act as his coach," Derek said.

Broken Blood

"His name is Mathias," I corrected but no one was listening.

"He does realize the match is a cover, right?" Wes asked. "He isn't actually planning on fighting, right?"

No one answered. "Let's get going," Jack said and started down the narrow trail that snaked through the woods toward the highway.

"If we weren't busting him for illegal gambling, I'd bet on Astor," Derek said.

"Me too," Jack muttered and earned a sharp look from Fee.

I suppressed a laugh and was shoved sideways by George. "What the heck?" I demanded.

His eyes were wild and full of an old challenge I recognized. "Race you," he said.

I glanced at Wes, who nodded, and Emma, Derek, and Cambria, who were already crouched, waiting for my signal. I looked back at George, my muscles bunched, my tendons already pulled taut at the ready.

"You're on," I said amid a rush of happiness and utter love for my pack. "Go."

Together, we ran.

The End

To my readers,

I don't know how to express the rush of emotion it gives me to share this series with you, the reader. Thank you for being a part of Tara's journey. For sticking in there until the end and then some. You've been patient with me and so invested in Tara and her friends. Your encouragement and, frankly, nagging, is one of my favorite things in the whole world. Seriously. I don't ever get tired of reading messages from you asking when the next book is coming. You guys have rocked my world for so long with your excitement and love for this series. Thank you all from the bottom of my heart.

~Heather

Not ready to say goodbye to the world of Hunters and Werewolves?

A new series featuring Sam's story is coming in 2016 and follows your favorite Dirty Blood characters! Follow their journey as they navigate this new world order of peace and politics as humans thrown into a world hidden in front of their very eyes.

For more information, sign up for Heather's Newsletter and get all the updates first!

www.heatherhildenbrand.com

Made in the USA
Middletown, DE
20 May 2017